BLOODLUST

Novels by Sandra Brown

Blood Moon
Out of Nowhere
Overkill
Blind Tiger
Thick as Thieves
Outfox
Tailspin
Seeing Red
Sting
Friction
Mean Streak
Deadline
Low Pressure
Lethal
The Crush
Envy
The Switch
Standoff
The Alibi
Unspeakable
Fat Tuesday
Exclusive
The Witness
Charade
Where There's Smoke
French Silk
Breath of Scandal
Mirror Image
Best Kept Secrets
Slow Heat in Heaven

BLOODLUST

SANDRA BROWN

GRAND CENTRAL

NEW YORK BOSTON

This book is a work of fiction. Names, characters, places, and incidents are the product of the author's imagination or are used fictitiously. Any resemblance to actual events, locales, or persons, living or dead, is coincidental.

Copyright © 2026 by Sandra Brown Management, Ltd.
Cover art and design by Eric Fuentecilla.
Cover copyright © 2026 by Hachette Book Group, Inc.

Hachette Book Group supports the right to free expression and the value of copyright. The purpose of copyright is to encourage writers and artists to produce the creative works that enrich our culture.

The scanning, uploading, and distribution of this book without permission is a theft of the author's intellectual property. If you would like permission to use material from the book (other than for review purposes), please contact permissions@hbgusa.com. Thank you for your support of the author's rights.

Grand Central Publishing
Hachette Book Group
1290 Avenue of the Americas, New York, NY 10104
grandcentralpublishing.com
@grandcentralpub

First Edition: March 2026

Grand Central Publishing is a division of Hachette Book Group, Inc. The Grand Central Publishing name and logo is a registered trademark of Hachette Book Group, Inc.

The publisher is not responsible for websites (or their content) that are not owned by the publisher.

The Hachette Speakers Bureau provides a wide range of authors for speaking events. To find out more, go to hachettespeakersbureau.com or email HachetteSpeakers@hbgusa.com.

Grand Central Publishing books may be purchased in bulk for business, educational, or promotional use. For information, please contact your local bookseller or the Hachette Book Group Special Markets Department at special.markets@hbgusa.com.

Library of Congress Cataloging-in-Publication Data has been applied for.

ISBNs: 9781-5387-43027 (hardcover), 9781-53877917-0 (large print), 9781-5387-4305-8 (ebook)

Printed in the United States of America

LSC-H

Printing 1, 2026

BLOODLUST

Prologue

"The choice is yours."

His voice was deep, and he'd spoken the sentence with such chilling detachment, it petrified her.

He had thick, wavy black hair only partially tamed by liberally applied wax. Dense eyebrows formed a ridge above his deep eye sockets, which appeared to have been smudged with charcoal. The irises were as black as ripe olives and void of animation. His nose was broad and flat, his lips fleshy. His stolid appearance bore the stamp of inborn brutality.

He was going to kill her.

She'd known that the moment she'd turned away from the kitchen sink, where she had just washed her last dish of the day. She'd been looking forward to putting her feet up, maybe watching a TV show, or simply sitting and relishing the quiet since Andrew was down for the night and sleeping peacefully in his crib.

The two of them had had a busy day that had included a

Gymboree class with children who, like Andrew, had just begun to walk. That was followed by a trip to the supermarket, which was always an adventure.

She hadn't planned on ending the day with having to barter for his life.

"Please," she said, her voice hoarse with terror, "don't hurt my son."

"The choice is yours."

"But...but..." She stopped there. No matter how desperately she pleaded, this man wouldn't be swayed. It was clear to her that he had a purpose, and he would see it accomplished. She knew that instinctually, like a rabbit that offers up his throat to a hungry wolf. The die was cast.

He'd been as still and silent as a statue when she'd turned around and discovered him standing within ten feet of her, his imposing presence seeming to shrink the kitchen.

He was expressionless. He wasn't wielding a weapon. He was nicely dressed in a black suit, white shirt, black tie. His arms were held relaxed at his sides. He didn't move. Nor did he need to. Without doing a thing, he radiated menace.

Already knowing the answer, she had asked anyway, "What are you doing here? What do you want?"

Speaking calmly and with complete confidence that she would comply, he had told her what she must do if she wanted to spare her son's life: She must sacrifice hers.

Now, having accepted that he was committed to his mission, she said, "How do I know that after I'm dead, you won't kill my baby anyway?"

"You don't. The only guarantee you get is that if you *don't* do as I say, he will die." Reaching into the front pocket of his suit jacket, he withdrew a length of thin wire with black handholds attached to each end. When he slipped his hands into them, she noticed that he wore a ring on his right pinkie. It was a signet ring with a red stone.

He yanked on the handholds with a sudden, snapping motion that pulled the wire taut between his hands. "You'll watch me kill your baby with this, and then I'll kill you the same way. I can make it slow and painful. Or," he said, "you can make it easy on yourself, do as I tell you, and I'll leave the baby alone."

He made it sound as though she should thank him for giving her an option, but his mild tone of voice didn't mitigate the cruelty of the choice he'd offered her. His features remained immutable, without a trace of emotion or humanity.

Unable to form words with her trembling lips, she blurted a sob. "Please don't do this."

"The choice is yours."

"I want to see my baby one last time."

He shook his head.

"Please." She clasped her hands beneath her chin. "Let me kiss him goodbye."

"You kissed him good night, didn't you? That's gonna have to do. Now, go into the garage."

As she turned, she noticed the knife block on the counter, every slot holding a sharpened stainless steel blade. She could try. She could put up a fight. But then he probably would put that wire around Andrew's neck and...

"No, no," she cried out and covered her face with her hands to blot out the horrific image. Andrew's life depended on her compliance. She wouldn't struggle.

He'd moved up close behind her. "Open the door. Go into the garage."

She did as told, although tears were almost blinding her. She took the two steps down. "Who are you? *Why* are you making me do this?"

"I'm not. The choice is yours."

Although he'd repeated it three times, he said it now with no more inflection than he had the first time.

Under her breath, she began reciting Hail Marys.

She thought of her parents and the anguish this was going to cause them.

She choked on sobs at the thought of Andrew growing up without her. "I love you I love you. Mommy loves you. I didn't do this. Please, God, let him know that I did not do this.

"Mitch, my love, tell Andrew," she whispered. "Impress on our son how much I loved him. Make certain he understands that I didn't abandon him. Oh, Mitch. *I love you.* I wouldn't do this." She sobbed and whispered his name again. "You'll know that I didn't. I know that you'll know. I know that you'll know. I know that you'll know."

Chapter 1

The jangle of his cell phone jarred John from a deep sleep and caused Beth to flinch. "Sorry, sweetheart." He slid his arm from around her and reached for the phone on the nightstand. "This is Bowie."

"Sir, it's Officer Brad Clarence. I'm sorry to disturb you at this time of night."

John checked the time. Actually it wasn't that long until dawn. He paired a face with the name Clarence. The patrolman was young and green, but earnest and strived to do well. "What's up?"

Clarence hesitated as though bracing to impart bad news. "It's, uh, it's Mitch Haskell, sir."

Muttering an obscenity, John sat up and swung his legs over the side of the bed. "What about him?"

"I got a disturbance call from a bar on Madison Street. Haskell was smashing up the place. One of the customers tried to calm him down, but Haskell was having none of it. When the bartender attempted to escort him out, it turned into an altercation. Haskell threw some punches, but none landed. Then he broke a liquor bottle against the bar and threatened the guy with what was left of the neck of it.

"It was gettin' hairy, so one of the least drunk patrons called it in. By the time I got there, Haskell had passed out. He went down face first. Landed on the jagged glass he was holding. Cut his own self."

"Bad?"

"Didn't appear to be, but another inch and he could've slit his own throat."

"So where is he now?"

"I brought him to the station. Took three of us to wrestle him into the drunk tank. When we tried to get some first aid on the cut on his neck, he put up a fight."

"John?" By now Beth was fully awake and propped on her elbows, looking at him with concern.

He covered the phone with his hand. "It's Mitch."

"Oh, no."

"Oh, yeah." Her tone had been sorrowful. His, pissed.

He shared a lot of history with Mitch, who was a detective in the Crimes Against Persons unit, which John headed. Mitch was a decorated Marine special ops veteran, a former DEA undercover agent, and also John's most trusted confidant, his go-to backup guy, and longtime best friend.

Clarence was asking John what he wanted to be done with him. "For now, leave him in the tank."

"He's being real... vocal."

"Ignore him. Whatever he says, no matter how offensive, don't respond, or he'll just keep doing it. I'll deal with him when I come in."

"All right, sir." The young cop hesitated, then said, "I'm awful sorry about this. I know y'all go way back. He didn't give me a choice, sir."

"Don't worry about it."

After disconnecting, John stayed as he was, tapping his phone against his chin, staring thoughtfully at the floor, until he felt Beth's cool hand on his back.

For a moment, he let himself enjoy her comforting touch, then turned and took her hand, lifted it to his mouth, and kissed her palm. She asked what had happened, and he gave her a recap.

"Is he all right?"

"Unruly and rowdy, as only Mitch can be." Then, temporarily shaking off thoughts of his next face-to-face with his friend, he placed his hand on Beth's distended abdomen. "How's the little fellow treating you tonight?"

"He kicked in protest when you left us to answer the phone. He knows your touch."

"Give me a break. My hand is bigger and heavier than yours, that's all."

"He knows you."

"You think? Really?"

"Um-huh."

Pleased, he said, "I wouldn't mind him coming out asking, 'Where's Dad?'"

Beth smiled and drew him down to her. Against his lips, she whispered, "And you've actually got people believing you're a badass."

The following kiss was deep, long, loving. When he broke it, he nuzzled her neck and snarled, "I am a badass, woman, and don't you forget it." Laughing softly, she pushed him away.

But John's playful mood didn't last. As he got up, he said, "I definitely need to be one this morning."

The midsummer humidity of Louisiana could drain an individual of all vitality within minutes. In Auclair, which was virtually surrounded by bayous and swampland, the heaviness of the atmosphere also lent an aura of somnolence to the streets of the small city.

Along John's route to work, few homes gave any indication that the residents were up and about yet. Even the breeze was desultory, barely disturbing the stringy gray moss that draped the far-reaching branches of stately live oak trees.

But this seemingly lazy Sunday morning was a deceptive harbinger of what the day would bring. John knew that all hell was about to break loose.

When he arrived at police headquarters, personnel who'd worked the graveyard shift were drifting out; the day force was coming in. He bid greetings to those he passed on his way up to the CAP unit, but didn't stop to talk with anyone except for Patrolman Clarence, who answered a few terse questions John put to him.

There really wasn't much more for the young cop to report except that Mitch's invectives had turned increasingly abusive before he'd finally settled down.

John thanked the officer for the update, went into his office, and called the police superintendent. He caught him sleeping in, but he had wanted to inform him of Mitch's misbehavior before the grapevine could beat him to it.

"It's your department, John. I trust you to deal with him as you see fit."

"Thanks for the vote of confidence."

After signing off, John took the stairs down to the basement and briefly consulted the three officers on duty in the jail. He was told that only one cell was occupied and was pointed toward the last one in the row.

John left them and approached the barred cubical enclosure.

Mitch was half reclined on the bunk, propped up in the corner formed by pitted concrete walls. His feet were planted on the stained mattress, his head bent over his knees, which he was hugging to his chest.

Whether he had heard John's arrival or merely sensed his glowering presence, he raised his head and said sourly, "About time."

Upon hearing that, the cops on duty stopped whatever they were doing. Mitch seemed either not to notice or not to care that the two of them had an audience, although John was keenly aware of it.

Mitch lowered his stockinged feet to the floor, stood up, and gave a shudder like a dog coming awake. Placing his hands in the small of his back, he arched it and stretched. He popped his neck, rolled his shoulders, then ambled over to the bars separating him from John.

A trail of dried, crusty blood extended down from his earlobe onto his neck and the collar of his rumpled shirt. His eyebrows were drawn into a frown that hooded his eyes. Piercing blue and sniper sharp, they managed to project hostility and insolence despite being bloodshot.

He said, "Took you long enough. Didn't they call you?"

"Yeah, they called me. Told me they had a drunk and disorderly asshole in the tank. A repeat troublemaker who might have gone too far this time."

Mitch snorted. "Oh, like you've never been shit-faced. Many a time when you and Jose Cuervo were like this," he said, crossing his fingers, "I had to come along behind and scrape you off the floor. Remember?" When John didn't respond, he huffed and said, "Whatever, bro. Just get me out of here."

John held Mitch's surly stare for so long, the officers watching became uneasy. There was a shuffling of feet, an exchange of wary glances, a quiet cough. Finally, John motioned the officer at the desk to remotely open the cell door.

The mechanism squeaked, and steel clanked against steel as the door slid open. "That needs some WD-40," Mitch said as he walked out of the cell. Sidestepping John, he yawned and said, "Man, do I look forward to grabbing some z's in my own bed. See you tomorrow."

John let him get a few feet past him, then grabbed him by the shoulder, turned him around, and slammed him back against the bars of the cell.

"What the fu—"

"Shut up," John said, getting right in his face. "Just shut up."

Mitch retaliated by ramming his shoulder into John's chest. But John shoved him back, hard, and held him against the bars with a hand on each of his shoulders. "Only because, *only because* you did have to scrape me off the floor a few times, I'm going to do you a favor and give you a choice.

"Option one. You can choose to be booked right now, stay in here until you're arraigned or until you can persuade somebody to bail your sorry ass out. Or, option two, you can go home, wash off your awful stink, and, within one hour, report to the unit, where you'll call the owner of the place you busted up. You'll plead with him not to press charges in exchange for covering the cost of repairs. Then, I expect you to be ready to perform your assigned duties. And I had better not smell any gin on your breath or discover it's not water in your YETI."

"It's Sunday."

"I don't care if it's the second coming," John fired back. He released one of Mitch's shoulders and pointed an index finger directly at his nose. "Within *one hour*, Mitch. If you don't show up, I'll issue a warrant. Public intoxication. Assault. Destruction of property. Any damn malfeasance I can think of. And I am *not* bullshitting you." John released him and took a step back. "What's it gonna be?"

Mitch's chest rose and fell with outrage. His eyes glittered with fury. Between clenched teeth, he said, "Take a wild guess."

"Option two? Good."

"My truck's at the bar. Unless it's been stolen."

John looked over at the speechless officers who'd witnessed the scene. "Return him his belongings, then somebody drive him over to get his truck." He came back around to Mitch. "See you in an hour."

Mitch's heavy-duty SUV was where he'd left it parked behind the bar, and it appeared not to have been messed with. As he pulled onto the road, he lowered the driver's window because John had been right. He stunk.

He wore the stench of the cleaning agent used in the drunk tank. While strong enough to make your eyes water, it failed to eradicate the rank odors of unwashed bodies, vomit, piss, misery, and despair, all of which seemed to have seeped into his pores.

It was a cloudy morning and all the window shades in his apartment were down, so the rooms were gloomy, but he didn't bother to turn on a light until he went into his bathroom. The fixture above the sink was bright, its glare unforgiving as it shone down on him. If a casting agent was looking for someone to play the skid row bum, he'd get the part, hands down.

He brushed his teeth ruthlessly, but shaved with care, gingerly guiding the razor around the cut on his neck. The neck of that broken bottle had come perilously close to his carotid.

In the shower, he lathered twice and scrubbed his hair and scalp. Clean and dressed, he checked his watch and figured he had time for at least one cup of coffee, which he was in desperate need of.

He made quick work of brewing one, then, holding the steaming mug in one hand, he used the other to call a number he had on speed dial. His mother-in-law answered.

"Good morning, Mitch."

"Morning, Mary. I called to apologize for not making it last night."

She waited for a count of five before responding. Her frequent pauses like that were intended to underscore his shortcomings. "I had told Andrew you were coming. He kept his nose pressed to the window watching for you, asking when you would get here, and whining as it got later. He wound up crying himself to sleep."

Mitch set his coffee mug on the dining table and pressed against his temples with his thumb and middle finger. "I got held up at work. By the time I got free, there was no sense in driving to Lafayette. Andrew would have already been in bed."

"You could have called."

"It got late. I didn't want to disturb you and Hank. I'm sorry. Now please put Andrew on the phone."

"Hank is getting him dressed. We're about to leave for Mass."

"I know what time Mass starts, Mary. You've got plenty of time."

"Yes, just time enough for a quick hello/goodbye from you that will get Andrew upset again. As happens every time you call."

"An indication of how much he loves me, don't you think?"

"I've never disputed that he loves you."

The following five-count pause was to remind him that he'd brought this separation from Andrew on himself.

Then she said, "It sounds like he's putting up a fuss about having to wear shoes. Hank needs help. Thank you for the apology."

And just like that, the phone went dead.

Mitch cursed, dropped his phone onto the kitchen table, and covered his face with both hands. He inhaled and exhaled heavily several times, trying to get a grip on himself and suppress a riot of emotions.

But they were irrepressible. He swiped at tears that filled his eyes as the ever-simmering anger boiled up inside of him seeking an outlet, a target on which to direct his wrath with the impetus of a wrecking ball.

His mother-in-law? The exchanges like they'd just had, where more was left unsaid than spoken, didn't change or improve anything, so what purpose would be served by a full-out go-round with her? It would only create additional tension, which Andrew would sense, and that would be detrimental to a child not yet three years old. He didn't want to alienate Mary, anyway. She'd suffered just as he had. For the time being, Andrew needed her, and so did he.

To direct his anger at God would be a validation of his existence, which he, once a faithful believer, had soundly denounced.

But this seething rage that he'd lived with for two years was all-consuming and combustible. The only way he was ever going to be free of it was to rain down hell on the persons responsible for it.

He lowered his hands from his face and looked at the framed photo on his dresser, which he'd taken on the day of Andrew's christening. Angela, holding the baby in the cradle of her arms, was beaming into the camera, radiating joy.

"Angela," he whispered hoarsely, "I swear by the devil himself, we'll have our vengeance."

Chapter 2

Mitch made it to the CAP unit with minutes to spare. As he pulled out his desk chair, he looked toward John's office. Through the window in the door, he saw John check his wristwatch.

"Sanctimonious son of a bitch," Mitch muttered, then looked around to see if anyone in the unit had been observing or eavesdropping, and saw that most, if not all, currently pretending not to, had been. Sure as hell, by now the antagonistic scene in the drunk tank had been recounted dozens of times throughout the entire PD.

He tried to appear nonchalant as he booted up his computer in order to find the phone number of the bar where he'd wreaked havoc last night. It was owned by a guy he knew only by his first name. When he got him on the phone, he said, "Gus, Mitch Haskell. Please don't hang up on me."

He humbly offered to foot the bill for repairs in exchange for Gus not pressing charges. Gus was querulous and slow to forgive until Mitch turned on the charm—which once upon a time he'd been reputed to ooze. "Look, I admit that I was a jerk. You have every right to be pissed over the damage I did."

"It's not just that, Mitch. I thought you'd given up the booze."

"I had. What can I say? I backslid."

"To the max. You were out of your head. Violent. You threatened to cut my bartender's throat."

"I've got no excuse, Gus."

"No excuse, maybe," the man said around a heavy sigh, "but you've got a damn good reason." When Mitch said nothing in response to that, Gus continued. "Everybody knows about… well, your wife and all. And it sucks. Big time. In light of that, I'm willing to cut you some slack. I'm not going to press charges."

"Thank you." To lighten the mood, he said, "Tell you what. Cost of damages plus a bottle of Beefeater to replace the one I broke."

"Two bottles."

"Deal."

"Not quite. There are a few chairs I've got to replace. And that mirror was all I had left to remember my wife by."

"I didn't know she'd died."

"She didn't. She split. But still."

Mitch chuckled. "To all of the above, okay."

"Now we have a deal," Gus said. "You know, Mitch, for a cop, you're okay. I like you. I appreciate your patronage. But you gotta go easy on those double straight-ups."

"As my pal John Bowie keeps reminding me."

"Which brings me to something else. I don't want Bowie on my case for overserving you, so I've instructed the bartenders to cut you off after two. Got it?"

"Yeah. Got it." Mitch asked him to figure up what he owed. "And thanks again, Gus."

As Mitch was disconnecting, John came out of his office and walked over. Before John could say anything, Mitch held up his hands in surrender. "Gus is a decent guy. After some initial grumbling, we came to terms, and he agreed not to press charges. He accepted my apology and even told me he likes me."

"Glad to hear it. Also glad you came in."

"In under an hour, too."

"You look better. Smell a hell of a lot better."

"I had only one way to go."

"You hungry? Beth offered to cook breakfast for us."

Mitch patted his middle. "Thank her, but the tummy isn't quite settled yet. Even coffee didn't sit well."

John nodded but did so absently. He kept his eyes lowered as he contemplated the toes of his boots, then he lifted his head and said quietly, "Before I left the house this morning, Beth brought it to my attention that yesterday was the second anniversary of—"

"I don't want to talk about it."

"Did the date have anything to do with your bender last night?"

"I *said*, I don't want to talk about it."

"Well, that's too bad, Mitch. You've got to talk about it."

"Wrong, bro. I don't gotta."

"You do gotta. I'm making it mandatory."

Mitch recoiled as though he'd been clipped on the chin. "Excuse me?"

John repeated the simple statement, adding, "I consulted the superintendent this morning and got his backing. His full backing."

Mitch took a swift look around the large room. The detectives and uniformed officers scattered throughout it had made themselves appear busy, but he knew that they were attuned to what was taking place at his desk. Everyone in the department knew that his relationship with John was an unshakable, long-lasting friendship.

It had begun when they were partnered as detectives. Working together like a well-oiled machine, the partnership continued until Mitch was recruited by the DEA, based on his covert mission experience in Afghanistan.

Then, a few years later, and coinciding with Mitch's decision to quit the undercover work, John had cracked a cold case, the famous Crissy Mellin case, which his now-wife Beth had documented on the true crime TV series *Crisis Point*.

The fallout from John's investigative work, and Beth's compelling documentation of it, had culminated with the exposure of rank corruption within the CAP unit. The head of it was indicted, tried, and convicted of numerous felonies, including the murder of one of his own henchmen. He was presently serving what amounted to a life sentence.

John had subsequently been appointed to take over the leadership position of the unit, and one of his first moves had been to bring Mitch back into the PD. They'd picked up where they'd left off years earlier, working in tandem. Although it wasn't official, it was universally understood that Mitch was John's second-in-command.

Everyone in the department knew the strength of their bond. They had few, if any, secrets from each other. They'd seen each other at their ideal best and at their most miserable worst. For years, they'd served as each other's sounding board. Even if they disagreed, nothing had ever created a fissure in their friendship. No one had ever seen John pull rank on Mitch. He never had.

Until this moment.

"Let's go into the office," John said. "We'll talk there."

"I'm not going to talk about it in there, or out here, or anywhere. You ordered me to resume my duties. That's what I'm going to do." He swiveled his chair around and brought his computer to life.

John swore under his breath, then reached over Mitch's shoulder and laid a sheet of paper on his keyboard. Mitch picked up the sheet, read what was on it, and turned his chair back around to face John. "What's this?"

"Exactly what it looks like. A list of names with their contact info."

"Huh." Mitch raised the sheet closer to his face and scrutinized it. "I can't help but notice that all these people are designated as doctors."

"Of psychology."

"Shrinks?"

"Therapists."

"Huh," Mitch said again. "Why are we investigating them? What are they suspected of? Overcharging the unbalanced among us?"

John's eyes took on a familiar, quelling glint, but his tone of voice remained even. "These psychologists have ranging experience counseling law enforcement officers specifically, but all have excellent credentials and reputations."

"Says who?"

"I've vetted them myself."

"No one would ever accuse you of being a slacker, John."

John gave him a stern, "cut the crap" look. "Pick one."

"Pick one?"

"Doesn't matter to me which one you choose. All have agreed in advance to see you no less than twice a week for the next six weeks. If you stay sober till then, and the chip on your shoulder has shrunk to the size of a pimple, I'll consider cutting the sessions to one a week."

Mitch took another survey of the room as though to ask those eavesdropping if he'd heard right. Coming back to John, he huffed a laugh. "Are you fucking kidding?"

"No. You won't seek help on your own, so I am making it compulsory. You'll continue your duties and draw full pay. That is unless you fall off the wagon like you did last night. If you do that, I'll have no choice but to suspend you."

"You can't be serious."

"Dead serious. Because you've got a serious problem, Mitch, and, before you react, please hear me out." His expression changed to one less stern. "You've got to unload to somebody about Angela. You can't keep it bottled up, or it's going to destroy you. Will you ever get over losing her? No. But you've got to learn some coping skills. You need professional guidance on how to deal with it."

"I'll deal with it how I choose to."

"You're not dealing with it at all."

"Well, I don't need *guidance*. Coping skills? What the eff? That's all bunk."

"Says the guy who last night got drunk on his ass, brandished a broken bottle at a man, and then passed out and fell down face first."

"That was an isolated—"

"Not that isolated. You think I don't know that you fell off the wagon weeks ago, and that since then you've been half drunk half the time? You need help. You won't talk to me or Beth, and both of us have tried to get you to open up. You won't talk about it with your in-laws. They tell me—"

"You've taken this up with my in-laws? Behind my back?" he shouted. "Damn you, John. Where do you get off—"

"Your mother-in-law told me you're reluctant even to speak Angela's name."

Mitch shot up out of his chair, his hands forming fists at his sides.

John didn't even flinch. "What? Are you going to hit me?" he asked with maddening composure. "Threaten me with a broken bottle? Give me no choice but to fire you?" He waited, and when Mitch only stood there steaming, he said, "I'm begging you to listen to reason."

He leaned down and picked up the sheet of paper, which Mitch had dropped when he came out of his chair. John pushed it toward him and pressed it against his chest, holding it there.

"Call one of these doctors today and make an appointment for tomorrow. If I don't hear from one of them telling me that you've had your first session, don't bother coming in on Tuesday. Are we clear?"

"You son of a bitch. You're supposed to be my *friend*."

"I'm being your friend. I *am* your friend. I'd be no friend at all if I turned a blind eye and let you continue as you are." He applied pressure to the sheet he still held against Mitch's chest, then removed his hand.

Mitch caught the piece of paper as it fluttered toward the floor. He ripped it in half, then in half again and tossed the pieces into the air.

Unfazed, John said, "I'll text the list to you. Think hard on this, Mitch. If you don't care about what you're doing to yourself, think about what you're doing to Andrew."

"Don't...don't..." He pointed his index finger at John's face, but realized his hand was shaking. "Fuck you." He shoved his chair under the desk and stormed out, glaring at anyone who dared to make eye contact.

Chapter 3

"It turned ugly there at the end," Roland Malone said into his phone. He'd been relating to the man on the other end of the call what he'd been told by his plant in the Auclair police department about the drama that had played out there that morning.

While giving the account, Roland turned the signet ring on his right pinkie 'round and 'round his finger, as was his habit. Since he was never without the heavy gold ring with the ruby stone, one would assume it was a family heirloom with sentimental significance. In a way, it was.

Roland had taken it as a trophy off the first man he had killed: his father. He'd been fifteen. He'd fled the Bronx that day, wound up in New Orleans, and had never looked back. He considered the ring his good luck charm.

He continued his account of the standoff between John Bowie and Mitch Haskell. "My mole said their body language toward each other spoke louder than words. They looked close to coming to blows. Shocked the hell out of everybody within earshot. Nobody in the room said anything or barely breathed for a full five minutes after Haskell left, like he'd sucked all the oxygen from the place, created a vacuum."

"And Bowie?"

"Went into his office and closed the door. He made a couple of phone calls, then left, looking like a thundercloud."

"Hmm."

Roland knew that sound. It was his cue to stop talking. The man he did special jobs for often lapsed into contemplative silences. He never missed anything, not a beat, not a single minute detail, but he liked to mull over new information before proceeding with either further discussion or swift and decisive action.

On the street, Roland's partner in crime was called Oz. Like in the story, nobody knew the god-figure's identity, but he seemed omnipotent. His nickname, even spoken in a whisper, evoked terror.

Roland, who didn't suffer fools, held Oz in high regard. He was damn smart and ten times as careful. He had to be in order to maintain such a high public profile while simultaneously running the largest illegal drug trafficking operation in the southeastern United States. It was a dicey juggling act, but not only did Oz manage to pull it off, he'd mastered the art of deception.

While waiting out Oz's ruminating, Roland patiently played with his signet ring. Oz finally broke his silence. "New topic. What about the skimmer?"

"Adler? Still skimming. You told me to hold off till I had indisputable proof."

"Well?"

"Now I do. I had a nanny cam installed in his base of

operation, a ratty apartment out near the airport. This past week alone, he dealt himself ten K off the bottom of the deck. Camera shows him stowing the cash in a hole in the floor covered up by a leopard print rug."

"Indicating that he's too stupid to work for me," Oz said. "Stupid people are high risk."

"I agree."

"What kind of ripple effect would it have to take this Adler out?"

"None to the business," Roland assured him, and went on to recommend a young man from El Paso who was eager to relocate out of a zone that had become hot for him.

"He's been in the business since he could wipe his own butt. Knows it inside and out. Tough, savvy, has an attitude, and is as mean as hell."

"Then why is he eager to relocate?"

"Outrunning a girl he knocked up. Plus her brothers. Anyhow, he's qualified. He can slip right in and take over for Adler, who won't be missed except maybe by his current squeeze, who's also his best customer. Cokehead."

"Dispense with her, too. Make their departure from this life one for the record books. Grisly enough to change the mind of anyone with an idea to cheat me."

"Consider it done. Anything else?"

"Mitch Haskell."

Roland made a sound of dismissal. "Not a worry. He's history."

"I wouldn't be so sure. He's like a lit fuse. You know, like in the movies. It burns slow, then kaboom."

"He's a drunk. No kaboom left in him."

"I don't know."

"He's hit rock bottom and proved it last night. Even his bosom buddy John Bowie has written him off. Good as, anyway."

After a moment of thought, Oz said, "Well, I'm not ready to write him off. Bowie issued an edict. Haskell may cave to it."

"And start seeing a shrink?" Roland scoffed. "Doubtful."

"But possible."

"Okay, possible. But so what if he does?"

"I don't want him out there stirring up chatter about what happened to his wife."

Oz had a point, but Roland wouldn't exactly classify going to therapy as "stirring up chatter." Therapists abided by the same rules as lawyers and medical doctors. They were sworn to confidentiality, so whatever a patient said to one would never be repeated.

Nor could he envision the cagey ex-fed spilling his guts to anybody. According to Roland's source inside the PD, Haskell hadn't opened up to anybody about his late wife's death, not even Bowie. If he hadn't poured out his heart to his best friend, he wasn't going to confide in a stranger.

But Oz disliked being contradicted, so Roland kept those thoughts to himself.

"Bowie put his foot down," Oz said. "Let's see how Haskell reacts. Have your mole keep an eye on him."

Roland replied, "Will do."

He barely got the words out before Oz disconnected. Roland didn't take offense. That was standard operating procedure. Out of necessity, Oz kept to a tight schedule. When he wanted you, he meant ASAP, and when he was done, it was over and out.

Now Roland reclined in his high-backed leather desk chair

and absently rotated his signet ring while considering options for how to go about the follow-up on Haskell.

After giving it several minutes' thought, he placed a call to his mole, who answered immediately. Without preamble, Roland asked, "What's your take on this morning's showdown? Gut feeling? Will Haskell do as Bowie ordered or not?"

"Odds in the unit are heavy on the nays. When Haskell blew out of here, he looked ready to murder Bowie with his bare hands, friendship or no friendship."

As Roland digested that, he thought back on the events of two years ago. It had taken a while for him to learn the identity of the undercover agent who'd engineered several successful busts that were costing Oz's organization dear. It had lost product and valuable personnel to the individual who had won the confidence of unsuspecting dealers and mules—unscrupulous, volatile, violent cutthroats, seasoned felons all.

Yet this agent had hoodwinked them into believing that he was one of them. When in his congenial company, they had talked freely, unwittingly disclosing information he had then used to snare them, get them indicted, convicted, and put away for a long time.

This crafty spy had turned out to be Mitch Haskell. The name had been the last two words Haskell's partner, a fellow named Randy Nelson, had uttered before Roland nearly decapitated him with a wire garrote, his weapon of choice.

However, this hadn't taken place until months after Haskell had left the federal agency and returned to the Auclair PD to work as a detective with his friend John Bowie.

Even though Haskell had no longer posed a direct threat to Oz's operation, Oz had a long memory and an unforgiving nature. He'd vowed vengeance for the damage Haskell had left in his wake, and had called on Roland to bring it about. His only instruction had been for him to "make it hurt."

"I have an idea," Roland remembered saying to Oz. When he'd told him what that idea was, Oz had chuckled. "I like it. He'll hurt for a long time."

However, Oz, a wizard of secrecy, was too careful and cunning to trumpet that he'd been responsible for the "suicide" of Haskell's wife. What's more, the cocky ex-fed remained none the wiser as to who had been behind her death. And, as was evidenced by Haskell's drunken rampage last night, and this morning's meltdown at the very mention of his beloved's name, her death was still eating at him in a manner that exceeded your garden-variety bereavement.

Who knew? Maybe Haskell would surprise them all and consent to the mandated therapy. Roland didn't want to look back and regret that he'd been hasty to dismiss the likelihood of that. God forbid he would ever have to admit to Oz that he'd made a wrong call.

Haskell's memory might be just as long as Oz's, and his nature equally unforgiving, unmerciful, and vengeful. Despite the great quantities of booze he was reputed to consume these days, had he really lost his edge? Or was he as sly and deceptive as he'd ever been?

If Haskell was harboring deep-seated suspicions about his wife's passing, Roland didn't like thinking of him airing them. Not to anybody. Even to someone sworn to silence.

His plant had been waiting patiently for further instructions. Brusquely Roland asked, "What happened to the list of shrinks Haskell ripped up?"

"I guess the pieces are still there on the floor near his desk, unless someone picked them up and put them in his trash can."

"Get me that list," he ordered, then abruptly disconnected.

He sat for a moment in contemplation, then pushed away from his desk, went over to the door of his office, and flipped the lock. He didn't want any of his employees coming in and catching him engaged in his secret daily ritual.

He returned to his desk, opened the bottom drawer on the left, took out his rosary, and began to pray. He rushed through the first prayers, reciting them by rote, but he fervently mouthed the Fatima prayer, the one that appealed for forgiveness.

Roland Malone feared nothing on earth.

But he was terrified of spending eternity in the fires of hell, about which his mother had warned him so frequently and with such conviction that he believed in them.

Straight from his confrontation with John, Mitch set out for Lafayette. He didn't call ahead so as not to give his mother-in-law an opportunity to tell him that now wasn't a good time for a visit. He wanted to see his son, dammit.

The Duvalls lived in a middle-class neighborhood in the same house they'd occupied their entire married life. Angela had grown up in it. Her girlhood bedroom was still preserved. For the first year after she died, he'd spent time alone in that room on each and every visit to see Andrew. He no longer paid that maudlin homage to her.

His method of mourning had become much more proactive.

His in-laws' car was in the driveway; they were home from Mass. Mitch opened the front door and called out, "Knock, knock."

From the back of the house, he heard a commotion, then, "Daddy!" Andrew came chugging into the living room and launched himself into Mitch's arms. He lifted the boy against his chest and hugged him tightly, loving the feel of his solid body, his milky smell, the wet smear of his kiss on his cheek. "Miss me?"

After giving an affirmative nod, the boy said, "I wanna play cars."

"Absolutely. We will."

"Not until after lunch." Mary entered the room with a dish towel over her shoulder and a perturbed expression on her face. "We were just sitting down to eat."

Mitch had broken the rule of not calling ahead, but he didn't apologize, nor did he let her irritation provoke him. He sniffed the air. "Stewed chicken and dirty rice if I'm not mistaken. Is there enough for one more?"

"Always," said his father-in-law, Hank, who greeted him with a handshake and a slap on the back.

During the meal, they stuck to neutral subjects, and snarky comments were kept to a minimum. When Hank asked how work was going, he said, "Busy. The bad guys always seem to outnumber us." He quickly changed the subject before they could inquire after John and Beth.

Mary declined his offer to help clean up the kitchen. "Go play with Andrew's cars. He's about to bust."

"Thanks, Mary."

She gave him a rare smile. "I'm glad you came, although you could have let me know."

Ah. A dig. But a small one.

Hank excused himself to watch a baseball game on television, allowing Mitch cherished time alone with his son. They got down on the floor of Andrew's bedroom and played with the fleet of Matchbox cars and trucks Mitch had brought him on his last visit.

They then went out to the backyard to play on the elaborate playground set that Santa had brought him the previous Christmas. That was followed by a game of catch with a plastic ball and miniature glove.

When it came time for Mitch to leave, the tired little boy became cranky and whiny. He clung to Mitch when he hugged him goodbye. Mitch rubbed his back soothingly. "We had fun today, didn't we, buddy?"

Andrew gave a sullen nod and pressed his face deeper into Mitch's neck.

"If you play your cards right, I'll bet Grandpa will watch a video with you. And then you'll go to sleep, and before you know it, it'll be tomorrow, and I'll call you. Okay? Sound like a plan?"

Andrew whimpered and clutched him tighter. Mitch held him close and whispered, "Next time you come spend the night with me, we'll sleep together in my big bed. And guess what we're gonna have for breakfast."

"Fwoot roops," came the muffled reply.

Mitch smiled and nuzzled the crown of Andrew's head. "You got it. Froot Loops are our favorite, right?"

Mary disallowed sugary cereals, but she didn't comment as she reached for Andrew. "Time for Daddy to go."

Speaking as an obstinate two-going-on-three-year-old, Andrew said, "*No.*"

"Come on now, Andrew. Say goodbye."

Against his neck, Mitch could feel Andrew's inhalations escalating, signaling that a squall was brewing. To head it off, he said softly, "Hey there, who's my rock star?"

"Me."

"Who's your biggest fan?"

"You."

"You bet I am." He squeezed his eyes shut and whispered, "I love you, son."

"Daddy," he blubbered.

Hank appeared at Mitch's side and eased the inevitable severance by inviting Andrew to watch a video with him.

Mitch tried to put some cheer into his tone. "See, told ya. Go with Grandpa, and I'll call you tomorrow. Okay?" He forced a smile. "Where's my fist bump?" He and Andrew bumped fists, then Mitch handed him over to Hank, who carried him from the room.

About to lose his shit, Mitch thanked Mary for the meal and headed for the front door. She followed. "What happened to your neck?"

He'd almost forgotten about the self-inflicted injury. "I cut myself shaving."

The see-through, cheeky lie earned him an eye roll. "Always with the wisecrack." Then, her forehead furrowed. "Are you taking care of yourself out there, Mitch?"

"Always."

She looked as though she wanted to say more, but changed her mind. Setting her hand on his arm and giving it a gentle squeeze, she said, "Be careful driving back."

He let himself into his apartment and went about his nightly routine of securing it. Feeling low and lonely, he went into the bedroom, sat down on the side of the bed, and checked his phone. John had indeed texted him the list of psychologists.

It was almost too late to call to make an appointment. It *could* wait till morning.

But, no. To postpone for one more day wasn't in his best interest, and dwelling on it further only made him more anxious about this path on which he was about to embark.

He scanned the list of names and quickly punched in one of the phone numbers. He got a recorded menu and tapped in the required digit to schedule an appointment. Another recording instructed him to leave a message.

"Yeah, this is Mitch Haskell. I don't think an explanation is necessary since John Bowie has already *vetted* you. Call or text me with a time for tomorrow."

He clicked off, dropped his phone on the bed, and began undressing. But he'd only tugged off his boots before a ping notified him of an incoming text. It instructed that if he wanted to confirm an appointment with Dr. Dylan Reede for ten a.m. tomorrow, he was to reply with a capital letter C.

Chapter 4

Mitch was the only person in the waiting room except for the receptionist, who'd introduced herself as Ellie. She had a kindhearted, maternal aspect and was almost apologetic when she'd asked him to fill out the required forms, which were numerous and, to his way of thinking, irrelevant.

Ellie had informed him that Dr. Reede was still with another patient. She'd invited him to take a seat and told him that the doctor would be with him shortly.

But "shortly" wasn't short enough. He'd arrived fifteen minutes early, but wished he'd breezed in at the last minute, indicating that they were lucky he'd managed to work Dr. Reede into his schedule because he had better and more important things to do.

From behind Ellie's sliding glass partition, she smiled pleasantly at him, but he tried to avoid making eye contact, because, in the otherwise empty waiting area, he felt conspicuous, as though he were the one behind safety glass, a specimen so erratic that it required close and constant monitoring.

He'd been checking his wristwatch at brief intervals and saw now that he had several more crawling minutes to kill. Ten o'clock couldn't get here fast enough. On the other hand, he dreaded it like hell.

He sat with his hands on his thighs, his fingers tapping out the rhythm of a classic country song that was playing inside his head. But when Ellie caught him at the mindless drumming, he stopped. She might report it to the shrink, who would attribute his restlessness to a psychic anomaly rather than to plain ol' impatience.

So now he had nothing to do with his hands except to concentrate on keeping them still.

And why was it so freakin' hot in here?

The magazines stacked neatly in a vertical rack attached to the wall didn't interest him. A dish of individually wrapped hard candies was within reach, but what would he do with a piece of it if he were called up the moment he popped it into his mouth? Spit it out or swallow it whole?

Did this old office building even have AC?

Inside his shirt, his torso had turned clammy. He was thinking of removing his sport jacket when Ellie slid open the window. "The doctor is ready to see you now, Mr. Haskell. Right through there." She indicated a closed door on the opposite side of the waiting room. "She's waiting for you."

He was arrested in the motion of standing up. *"She?"*

Just then the door was pushed open, and a woman emerged. She smiled and came toward him, right hand extended. "Mr. Haskell? Dylan Reede."

Holy shit. He croaked, "Are you kidding?"

Maintaining her smile and keeping her hand outstretched, she replied, "Not about my name."

He stared down at her hand as though uncertain what it was and what function it served, then gave it a quick shake and immediately let go.

"Come on back." She turned away and started for the door she'd left standing open.

As though Ellie had used her sweet demeanor to deliberately deceive him, he shot her a dirty look over his shoulder. Her expression turned wary, although he couldn't tell if her concern was for him or the psychologist...the one with the beguiling smoky gray eyes and prima ballerina legs.

Swearing inaudibly, he followed her into a room he wished were a lot bigger and a lot cooler. She shut the door and motioned him toward a sofa while she sat down on a matching one facing it.

He remained standing and took in his surroundings. The room was furnished like a parlor in one of the French Quarter's antiquated townhouses. "No desk?" he asked. "Computer? File cabinet? Not even a telephone?"

She pointed out a closed door that fit into the paneling so well it was barely detectable. "All in there."

"Huh."

He continued his survey. The window blinds were half closed so there was little daylight to compromise the serenity of the setting. In front of the window was a round table where a potted ivy thrived, and a fragrant candle flickered in an amber glass votive. On the table at the end of the sofa was a low-wattage lamp with a linen shade, a box of tissues, and several unopened bottles of water. The sofa itself was crowded with throw pillows of various sizes and shapes.

This wasn't her workstation. This was a lair, made intentionally cozy and confidence-inspiring. This was where she listened to people weeping over dashed dreams, where they exposed their heartaches, and whispered confessions of darkest sins. Within these walls, Dr. Dylan Reede exorcised demons. Or endeavored to.

She'd find out soon enough that his demons stubbornly held their ground.

He looked down at her where she sat, seemingly calm, cool, and collected. He supposed that giving a new patient time to acclimate to the environment was part of the drill. "Is being made to wait the first step of the wear-him-down process?"

"I beg your pardon?"

"What happened to the patient before me? Or *was* there even a patient before me?"

Understanding his point, she indicated another door he had assumed was a closet. "The exit. It opens into a hallway where there's a back elevator to the ground floor."

"Ah. An escape hatch so patients won't be bumping into each other in the waiting room."

"In order to protect the privacy of both."

"Huh," he said again. Let her make of that non-word what she would.

One thing he had already deduced: Ruffling this lady wasn't going to be easy. She didn't appear to mind that he had remained standing and had the advantage of staring down at her where she sat. She stared back without flinching as she calmly waited him out.

But she had no idea of who she was up against. He hadn't

been an undercover narc for nothing, you know. He had a truckload of gambits he used to get people to crack. He wondered what it would take to heat her up, get under her skin, ignite a spark in those smoky eyes. In that moment, it became his life's mission to do so.

"I figured Dylan for a man's name."

She gave a small smile. "My paternal grandfather's name. It's sometimes mistaken."

"Did *he* know that you're a woman?"

"He?"

"Bowie."

"Yes. He *vetted* me," she replied, using the same inflection he'd used on his voice mail message.

So: eyes, legs, and a backbone. "I looked you up on the internet. Thought it was strange that your website didn't have a picture of you like most do. Now I know why yours doesn't."

"Why would that be?"

"You get people in here before they find out you're not what they were expecting."

"What were you expecting?"

He pretended to conjure an image. "Older guy in baggy pants. Food stain on his tweed vest. Bald and paunchy. Maybe with a fuzzy beard and wild eyebrows."

"And smelling of pipe tobacco?"

"For sure."

She swallowed a small laugh. "The stereotype."

"Yeah, but stereotypes become stereotypes for a reason. So you can imagine why I was taken aback when you walked through the door. You're far off the mark of stereotypical, Dr. Reede. You should post a warning sign on Ellie's desk."

He had hoped to nettle her. She remained unruffled. She even tried to conceal a smile. "In essence, I do give fair warning. The last thing I want is to take a potential patient unaware. So, whenever I get an inquiry about my practice, I set up a preliminary virtual meeting. Following it, if he or she doesn't wish to proceed with me for whatever reason, I wish them well and, more often than not, recommend a colleague that I think would be a better fit."

"What happened to my preliminary virtual meeting?"

"I had it with Lieutenant Bowie."

"Huh." Again.

"He explained the circumstances and made—"

"Circumstances?" he said. "Those should have been interesting."

She ignored his interruption. "He made clear that I wasn't the only therapist he was interviewing. My understanding was that he was going to provide you with a list of qualified candidates and leave the decision up to you."

"He did. But he could've given me a heads-up. Put an asterisk by your name or something."

"To indicate what? My gender?"

"No, that doesn't matter to me."

"Then what?"

That you're such a gorgeous representative of your gender, that's what. Swearing softly, he lowered his head to rub the back of his neck while staring down at the patterned rug.

Not at her legs. At the rug. The *rug*.

She was waiting for him to say something. After a sigh, he said, "Look, Dr. Reede, my reluctance has nothing to do with you. I wouldn't want to be here if you were the stereotypical fusty guy with the pipe and wild eyebrows."

She tilted her head and observed him with new interest and a slight frown. He would have given a million bucks to know what she was thinking. She said, "Then it's psychotherapy in general that you take exception to?"

He didn't respond, but she must've read his disgruntlement. "You aren't trapped in here, Mitch. If you choose to leave now, you can use the exit door. There'll be no hard feelings, and I won't charge for the session."

He looked over at the exit, then chuffed. "And have Bowie on my ass for not seeing this through? Un-huh. No way. But not telling me that Dr. Dylan Reede happens to be..." He stopped himself from saying "hot," and said instead, "...younger than expected is the kind of practical joke he and I used to pull on each other."

"I'd like to hear about some of those practical jokes." She picked up a notebook that was lying on the sofa beside her, set it on her crossed knees, and uncapped a pen. She motioned again toward the sofa across from hers. "Please sit."

He looked back at the sofa, looked again at her, then shrugged. "Sure. Okay." He removed his sport coat and tossed it over the arm of the sofa, pushed three of the blasted throw pillows out of the way, then shoved his hands into his pants pockets and dropped down onto the seat. He worked his butt deeper into the cushion, stretched out his legs as far as they would go, and crossed his ankles, settling into a slouch.

"I can't go back to work until I've undergone this session, so I'll stay for the full fifty minutes. No telling how many bad actors are getting away with heinous crimes while I'm in here, but my former friend, now boss, John Bowie thinks my time is better spent talking to you."

He took another look around the room. "And to be honest,

this beats trying to chase down bad guys. You've got a real cushy spot here for relaxing, and it's not my money the PD is wasting."

"You think this is a waste of time and money?"

"What gave me away?"

She tapped the end of the pen against the notepad. "If a patient doesn't seek help through therapy, it rarely yields the desired result."

"Then we're SOL already. That stands for shit out of luck."

"Yes, I know."

"I wonder why it's not SOOL." He waited. She didn't react. "Tough room," he said under his breath. Then, "I didn't seek anything, Dr. Reede. This was forced on me, so don't expect to yield a fucking thing. Oops, sorry. My bad. Slip of the tongue."

She didn't bat an eye. "In here, you're free to say whatever you like."

"Truly? And you won't tell anybody?"

"I'm bound by law not to."

He gave her another grin. "See, that was a test. Because I already knew that you're bound by confidentiality. Law enforcement officers despise it. I can't count the number of times your rules have been a pain in the ass when we're trying to nail somebody, and you psychology folks refuse to give over incriminating confessions confided to you."

"To turn over information requires a court order."

"Tell me," he said, grimacing. "And it's like pulling teeth to get a judge to issue one, and usually his or her honor outright refuses."

"Unless the patient poses an imminent threat to someone."

"Right. Imminent, i.e., before the fact. After the fact, a killer can relate to you in gory detail how he's murdered somebody, and enjoyed the hell out of it, and you don't tell."

She pointed to the wall behind her. Hanging on it was a framed doctorate diploma.

"I get it, I get it," he said. "Sacred oath and all. But…" He sat up straighter, leaned toward her, and lowered his voice. "Don't you ever break the rules? Or bend them? Just a little bit? Hmm? I mean, how do I know that as soon as I walk out of here, you're not going to get John Bowie on the horn and repeat everything I've said to you?"

Despite his taunting, which she ignored, she made a notation on her notepad. "Tell me about yourself."

Damn, she was a cool customer. If he stuck with this, her reserve would be an obstacle he would have to work around. He was accustomed to winning people over by joking. A smart-aleck remark could defuse a dicey situation almost as effectively as producing a lethal weapon. A well-placed wisecrack could disarm, or at least distract, even the toughest of toughies.

She appeared about as tough as a marshmallow, yet, so far, his jests had bounced right off her. But he wasn't done yet.

He flopped back and resumed his slouch. "Something about myself? Let's see." He snapped his fingers. "Just the smell of Brussels sprouts makes me want to hurl."

She set her pen on the notepad and moved it aside. Placing her elbows on her knees—which he had to admit were a distraction—and looking at him earnestly, she said, "I want to help you, Mitch."

His insolent smile vanished along with his levity. He narrowed his eyes. "Help me do what, exactly? Learn to cope with my 'circumstances'? What all did John tell you? Or are you bound by professional privilege to keep the lid on that, too?"

"My confidentiality applies to you, not him."

"Then tell me what he told you about me."

"That you have a sharp and sardonic wit, which, in the last few minutes, I've experienced for myself."

"It hasn't thawed you any," he mumbled.

"You definitely use it to your benefit. To charm, absolutely. But also to hide behind."

"Hide behind?" He frowned. "How's that?"

She gave him a look that said she knew he understood her perfectly, but she expanded anyway. "Lieutenant Bowie said he can gauge how troubled you are by the frequency of your wisecracks."

"He said that? Huh. Maybe he should go for one of those." He raised his chin toward the diploma on the wall. "I'll tell you one thing, my joke-cracking beats his brooding. He can sulk like nobody's business. For days sometimes. You wouldn't believe that a guy as mean-looking as he is could be so pouty. Drives Beth—that's his wife—drives her crazy when he's in one of his funks. She's finally learned, as I did years ago, to leave him be. Eventually he'll shake it off."

She heard him out, but then picked up where she'd left off. "He told me that you don't panic in a crisis situation. When things go wrong—"

"We use terms like 'fubar' or 'tits up.'"

"—you're the person he wants at his back. He trusts you to come through for him. You and he have a close personal friendship and working relationship."

"Both of which have gone tits up."

"Why? What happened between you? When did you stop playing practical jokes on each other?"

"Come on, Dylan. Can I call you Dylan? I wouldn't be here if things were rosy between John and me. He told you that I was screwing up, didn't he?"

"He told me he suspects that you're suffering from post-traumatic stress."

He looked away from her, stretched his neck, readjusted his shoulders, drew his legs in, and rubbed his hands up and down his thighs. "Did he tell you the nature of that trauma?"

When he looked at her again, she gave him a small nod. He noticed a tiny twitch at the corner of her lips and a sorrowful blink of her eyes, which held steady on his. Those subtle indications of sympathy were more effective than an outpouring of platitudes would have been. He couldn't have stomached that. He'd heard enough banalities to last him a lifetime. For all the goddamn good they'd done.

He didn't say anything for some time, his eyes roving around the room, his jaw working in spite of his trying to keep it from clenching. He was aware of her watching him closely.

Eventually, he came back to her. "Did John tell you that after…" He cleared his throat. "That after, I developed a fondness for the grape? Actually, that's a figure of speech. My drink of choice was gin, and it's not usually made from grapes."

"Tell me about that."

"About gin? Well, it's made from various grains with lots of botanicals added, but always juniper berries. In mid-nineteenth-century England, so many people got hooked on it, they nicknamed it blue ruin. Do you know why they called it that? Do you know that bit of trivia? Do you like trivia?"

She ignored his bullshit. "I was told you went on and off the wagon."

He gave a definitive nod. "Yesssss. Several times. Bowie, who was still my friend then, covered for me."

"Until he'd had enough, he said."

"Yeah. One morning when I failed to come to work, he

showed up at my house and found me..." He shuddered. "I'll spare you the details, but it was a messy scene. John wasn't touched by my, uh...illness. Rather than show some compassion, the son of a bitch drew a line in the sand. It was either AA or unemployment.

"So, I signed up for AA. Secretly, of course. Out of town. He and I kept it hush-hush. Beth knew. No one else outside our tight little circle. Wanna hear the twelve steps? I thought the ten commandments were rigid, but whew."

Unfazed, she said, "Lieutenant Bowie told me that you got sober and stayed sober for six months."

"Um-huh."

"Until last Saturday night, when you suffered a relapse."

"Relapse? That's a nice way of putting it."

"Bowie believes it was prompted by the date."

He chewed the inside of his cheek, saying nothing. Immediately after realizing that he was jiggling his knee, he forced it to be still.

Softly she asked if he would like some water and motioned toward the bottles on the end table. "No thanks." Then, "There's not a clock in here. Is that on purpose? How much time is left?"

"Don't worry about the time," she said. "Is Bowie wrong about the anniversary date contributing to the episode last week?"

"I can say anything I want to, right?"

"Yes."

"I can also sit here like a stump and say nothing at all, right?"

"Yes. But sitting here in hostile silence wouldn't be very helpful."

"Not helpful to *you*. But my hostile silence could be just the therapy I need." He stood, picked up his jacket, and pulled it on.

"I don't think you and I would ever be a good fit." He came this close—*this close*—to adding a sexual context to that, but thought better of it. "It's been nice knowing you, but I'm outta here, and I ain't coming back."

She had stood up along with him. "I wish you would reconsider."

"I'll bet you do. You'll miss out on a paying gig. The mandated sessions with me could really add up. Let's see, two a week for six weeks." He started counting on his fingers. "That's—"

"Mitch," she said in a chastening tone. "Insulting me is no more effective than wisecracking. Please think about—"

"I'll tell you what *you* should think about, doc. If you're getting men in this cozy little nook of yours with all the throw pillows, you really should consider wearing sensible shoes, a longer skirt, an ill-fitting cardigan, and a different face."

She gave him another look of reproof. "Sorry, that tactic doesn't work on me, either." She waited for a beat, then said, "Let's sit back down and talk calmly and reasonably. Because if you refuse these sessions, Lieutenant Bowie—"

"Bowie can go— Read my mind."

"We don't have to address the hard subjects until you're ready to. We can start with—"

"My birth? Childhood? The loss of my virginity? Work up from there to last Saturday night and my fall from Saint John's grace?"

"I have this same time on Thursday morning reserved for you. Please be here."

"Sorry. Can't make it."

"Then we'll work around your schedule. I'll see you any time you say."

The quip he had planned to say died on his lips. Instead, he jerked his head back and gave her a long, measuring look. "No," he drawled, "I don't think you will. See me as a patient, that is. In fact, I can guarantee that you won't."

He reached out and curved his hand around the back of her neck. Pulling her forward and up to him, he kissed her. Swiftly but with impact. Then he released her just as suddenly.

Holding her wide, disbelieving gaze, he smiled and dabbed at a damp spot on his lower lip with the back of his hand. "As rules of doctor–patient conduct go, that's a real no-no, isn't it, Dr. Reede? Ergo, we're done."

Then he went over and opened the door into the waiting room. "Screw the escape hatch. I'll go out the way I came in."

Chapter 5

After Mitch slammed out, Dylan stood rooted to the floor, too stunned to move. A full minute later when her silenced phone vibrated, she was still in the same spot, trying to think past what had just happened. Better yet, to convince herself that it hadn't happened at all.

She took the phone from the pocket of her blazer and clicked it on, hoping that her voice wasn't as tremulous as she felt. "Yes, Ellie?"

"Mrs. Trent has arrived for her appointment."

"Oh, thank you. I'm running a bit behind."

"Everything all right?"

"Yes, of course. I was just making some notes. Mr. Haskell declined to use the private exit. Did he manage to duck out before Mrs. Trent got here?"

"No. In fact, he very politely held the door open for her as she was coming in. He humbly apologized to both of us for coming through the waiting room."

Dylan envisioned him turning on the charm, capping off the apology with a self-deprecating remark, and leaving the two ladies all aflutter with his devilish smile. It made her want to throw something. "Give me a few minutes for a bathroom break, then I'll come out and escort Mrs. Trent in."

She went into her inner office, where she had converted a closet into a powder room. She wet a hand towel with cold water and applied the makeshift compress to her neck and cheeks. They felt aflame, and the mirror above the sink confirmed they were abnormally rosy. The blush extended down into the open collar of her shirt.

Which, by the way, was tailored, as was her blazer. There was nothing flashy or flirtatious about either. Her skirt was knee length, and the heels of her pumps were moderate. Not a single article of her clothing was provocative. How dare he suggest...

What was the matter with her? Why was she defending her wardrobe? His sexist remarks had been classically manipulative, intended to make her uncomfortable, to seize control of a situation he did not want to be in, and establish a power shift from her to him. She knew better than to let such transparent manipulation from a patient affect her. She had even told him the tactic wouldn't work.

But it had. It *had*, and she was shaky all over because that had never happened before. In all her years of practice, not even her most truculent, snide, and uncooperative patients had ever gotten to her the way he had.

Because the session had been mandated, she had expected him to go on the offensive, precisely as he'd done. From the start, he'd tried to devalue her opinion and certify his immunity to it.

But obvious to her was that his charm, rudeness, and joking

were all defense mechanisms used to detract from the pain behind his eyes. It had been apparent to her immediately. Mitch Haskell was in pain, and John Bowie had told her that this unrelenting emotional anguish had overtaken his life.

But it doesn't have to, Mitch.

That's what she'd wanted to impress upon him, but it would have been way too premature to approach that today. He would have denied having any pain, or would have deflected her by making a joke of it.

During her interview with Bowie, he had cautioned her not to be taken in by Mitch's wily avoidance tactics. "He's got a smart mouth and a naughty-boy grin, but don't let them fool you. Mitch is a serious guy. I've seen him cry over lost comrades, lost causes, and the rejected trees on the Christmas tree lots. He takes everything to heart, Dr. Reede, and his heart was put through a shredder when he lost his wife.

"I can relate. But he can't go on like this, or I'm afraid that one of these times he falls down, he won't get back up. If you take him on, he'll be a wiseass and probably offensive. Knowing that, are you still interested in counseling him?"

She had been very interested. Furthermore, she was qualified. She hadn't merely detected the degree of pain that had a stranglehold on Mitch Haskell, she had recognized it from a personal perspective. She had suffered similarly.

In the years since her life had been turned inside out by tragedy, she had fervently wished for enlightenment on the *why* of it. *Why?* Had there been a sanctified reason for it that was beyond her comprehension? Had she simply not grasped the higher purpose that had been served by her calamity?

Perhaps saving Mitch Haskell from himself could be that purpose.

But he'd robbed her of that opportunity, hadn't he? Damn him! That kiss, a violation of the code of ethics, hadn't been a minor setback. It had been a death knell... as he had known it would be.

From the medical office building, Mitch walked across the street to EATS, a landmark diner in downtown Auclair. It was especially popular with cops because they got a 10 percent discount.

The bell above the door announced his arrival. The floor was sticky, the red vinyl seats in the booths had tears from which padding sprouted, and the wall-mounted TV behind the counter was constantly on during operating hours.

Presently, a flamboyant personal injury lawyer, who called himself the King of Cash, was selling his services with evangelical zeal, promising thousands of dollars in reparation to anyone who turned their lawsuit over to him.

It was a little early for the lunch crowd, so there were plenty of unoccupied stools at the counter. Mitch claimed one and was greeted by Dodi, the waitress who'd been there almost as long as the building's cornerstone.

"Hey, Mitch. Don't you ever get tired of being so good-looking?"

He placed his hand over his heart. "Yes, but it's a cross I must bear."

She laughed. "How's your day goin'?"

"Just swell."

"That bad? How 'bout a muffuletta?"

"With everything."

"Cold beer to wash it down?"

"Iced tea."

"Sweetened?"

"Till it makes my teeth ache."

She grinned, revealing a gap where one of her own teeth had been. "Comin' up."

While she was filling his order, Mitch swiveled on his stool. Through the café's front windows he studied the building he'd just left. It had seven floors and few aesthetic attributes. It was at least a century old, but many notable doctors in the community had their offices in it, including Andrew's pediatrician. He didn't have a private exit door that Mitch knew of.

He counted up six floors and picked out the window with the half-closed blinds. He wondered how her session was going with the patient who'd followed him.

He wondered who in her gene pool had gifted her with those legs, and a long ponytail that was straight and sleek and the color of polished mahogany, and eyes that had a damn near inescapable magnetic field.

"Here you go." Dodi slid a plate onto the counter, then used a treacherously long butcher knife to quarter the generous sandwich for him. Glancing up at the TV, she reached for the remote and turned down the volume, muttering, "I wouldn't let that loudmouth handle a citation for not picking up dog poop." She reached for a plastic jug and poured strong tea into a glass of ice. As she thumped it down in front of him, she asked, "Where's your buddy?"

"Bowie?" He shrugged. "Haven't seen him today." Dodi eyed him knowingly. He took a sip of tea, then said, "You've heard."

"Heard? Every cop who's darkened that door in the last two days has related a version of y'all's falling out."

"Well, all the versions you've heard probably have at least one grain of truth."

"Hate to hear that, Mitch. Is he gonna fire you?"

"Not if I keep my nose clean."

"Do your best."

"I'm playing it by the book." With the notable exception of kissing the therapist. On the mouth.

"How's your boy?"

"He's great. Actually, I need to call him. Mind if I take this to a booth?"

She motioned him toward the row of them along the windows.

He carried his meal over and made the call. Andrew was having a "gwilled cheese samish" for lunch. They ate together. Mitch kept the dialogue upbeat, but, as always after talking to his son, he felt despondent when they said goodbye. He stared vacantly out the window, calculating when he would be able to work in his next visit to Lafayette.

He was distracted from his thoughts when he saw a woman emerge from an unmarked side door of the medical building. He recognized her as the lady he'd held the door for as she'd entered Dylan Reede's reception room. She must have used the private exit.

"All done?" Dodi was standing at the end of the booth. "Want a refill on tea?"

"No thanks." As he scooted out of the booth, he pressed a twenty-dollar bill into her hand.

"I'm free if you want to run away together," she said.

He grinned. "You know I love you, but I can't today. I'm due at a meeting."

After seeing Mrs. Trent out, Dylan went into the waiting room where Ellie was preparing to leave for lunch. "Lock the door behind you, please. I'm going to stay in and snack out of the mini fridge."

"I could bring you something."

"No thanks. Any messages?"

"Lieutenant Bowie called."

Her heart bumped. "About Mr. Haskell?"

"He didn't say. Just asked that you call him back at your earliest convenience."

"I'll get right to it." Forcing a smile, she said, "Enjoy your lunch."

Once Ellie had left, she returned to her private office and sat down behind her desk. As she picked up her phone, she noticed that her palms had turned damp in anticipation of what she would tell Bowie. Before she could overthink it, she punched in the number she had saved in her contacts.

He answered with, "This is Bowie."

"Dr. Reede."

"Yes, I saw your name. Thanks for returning my call."

"Of course. Are you checking with everyone on the list of potentials, or did you know Mitch had been to see me?" She had a horrifying visualization of him bragging to Bowie about the manner with which he'd sabotaged future sessions.

"Mitch texted me at nine forty-two this morning saying that he was on his way up to your office. He included a selfie where he was pointing to your name on the roster in the lobby."

"A subtle way of giving you the finger, I think."

"Undoubtedly. Did he say why he chose you?"

"I believe he picked me at random."

"Luck of the draw."

She wondered if Bowie meant good luck or bad luck, but she didn't ask. There was a lengthy pause before he spoke again. "I'm sure you can guess why I wanted to speak with you."

"You know that I can't disclose anything confidential."

"I'm not asking you to. But I need to confirm if Mitch is taking this seriously. On a scale of one to ten, how would you rate the session, and when is his next appointment?"

She sighed. "Well, Lieutenant Bowie..."

Chapter 6

Mitch returned to police headquarters in record time, but when the elevator doors opened for him, two detectives almost ran him over as they emerged, obviously in a hurry. He dodged out of their way and then, with the impulse of a lemming, fell into step with them as they headed for the employee exit. "Where's the fire?"

"No fire, but two bodies found in Bayou Coeur."

Barbara Nix was a tall, slender thirty-something, a workout fanatic, and an energetic detective. Soon after John took over the CAP unit, she had applied for a job. Her experience had been limited to smaller police departments, but she'd impressed John, he'd hired her, and she had proven herself to be a valuable asset.

"One male, one female," she continued as they wove their way through the corridors. "Discovered by a trio of fishermen. Obvious foul play."

Mitch knew that bayou well. Years back, he and John had

dragged out of its sluggish waters the body of an undercover DEA agent named Randy Nelson with whom Mitch had worked. "What about the fishermen?"

"Old geezers," Nix said. "They're not suspects."

"That bayou is outside the city's jurisdiction."

"Right," Nix's partner said, speaking for the first time. Ed Lear was a veteran investigator who was methodical to the point of being plodding. Nix had spontaneous tendencies; Lear kept a rein on them. Their approaches to solving crimes complemented each other. "Sheriff's office is handling the investigation, but they asked us to take a look."

"Who's the lead?"

"Glenn Darcy."

Mitch knew the detective well. Their investigations often overlapped. Mitch got to the exit door ahead of the other two and pressed the bar to open it for them. "How come Darcy asked for help?"

Nix answered, "No ID found on either body. Thought we might recognize them."

"Manner of death?"

Maintaining her ground-eating stride, Nix called back to him over her shoulder. "All we've been told so far is that it's nasty."

As Mitch watched them go, he had to tamp down the rush of adrenaline he experienced whenever action was called for. His heart rate kicked up. His gut drew taut.

Even as a kid, he'd been attracted to danger. His mother used to say of him, "It's like he's got a fire bell inside his head."

After Angela's death, danger's allure had lessened, but every once in a while, like now, he felt its tug and envied the two detectives who were off to investigate a nasty crime scene.

He wondered what Dylan Reede would make of that aspect of his psyche.

He returned to the elevator, then, to expend some adrenaline, opted to jog up the three flights of stairs. As he entered the CAP unit, he saw that the meeting he was supposed to attend had already commenced in John's office. He removed his sport jacket and tossed it onto his desk chair, never breaking stride until he reached the closed office door.

He pushed it open and went in, interrupting John as he was saying, "...then once we've completed this initial training, the superintendent proposed that we conduct periodic refresher courses. The goal here is to keep those guards in a continual state of preparedness."

John had formed a task force of four patrol officers with Mitch serving as their overseer. They were charged with training school security guards how to respond to an active shooter situation. For several weeks they had been conducting workshops. John had called this meeting to get a progress report.

Before continuing, he looked over at Mitch, who'd propped himself against the wall because all the chairs had already been taken. Of course everyone in the crowded office knew about their rift, which made for palpable tension.

"Sorry I'm late," Mitch said. "I ran into Nix and Lear on their way out. They told me about the bodies found in Bayou Coeur."

"Darcy's on it."

That's all John said about that topic before asking each of the officers in the group for a status report on their particular workshop. Mitch was saved for last.

Since all the officers' input had been positive, he didn't want to dilute their optimism for the success of the project. He said,

"Without question these guards are dedicated to keeping their campuses, the kids, and faculty safe. Based on what you've said here, it sounds like they're quick studies." He smiled and gave a thumbs-up. "We're making headway."

"Pleased to hear it," John said. "I can go back to the super with a positive report." He adjourned the meeting. When they began to file out, he asked Mitch to stay. "Close the door." Mitch did, but remained standing.

"What's on your mind?" John asked.

"About this training program?"

"Your feedback sounded rehearsed."

"It was."

"And I sensed a silent *but* at the end of it."

Mitch folded his arms and looked down at the floor. "It's a noble endeavor. The superintendent doesn't want Auclair put on the map with a school shooting. Nobody wants that. But there are obstacles to this training program."

"Let's hear them."

Mitch absently pulled on his earlobe, trying to think of a way to explain his reservations. "Manners. Trust. Naivety. Those are obstacles." He brought his gaze back up. "Please don't get me wrong here, John. I'm not putting these school guards down, but they're not looking for... They're... too..."

He grimaced, thought about it, then started over. "Maybe this'll illustrate what I'm talking about. In one of the workshops I conducted myself, I mixed up photos of actual school shooters with some of the worst of the worst criminals serving time in Angola, and asked the class to pick out the shooters."

John must have gathered what was coming. He dragged his hand down his face. "How bad was it?"

"Eighty percent in favor of the badasses. The guards would

have missed anyone in the twenty percent bracket, whether he had walked in off the street or was a student at the school.

"So what I see as a problem is that, as passionate as these people are about protecting school kids, we're asking them to act instinctually on an instinct they don't have. You and I were born with it. That's why we do what we do and why we're good at it." He spread his arms at his sides in a helpless gesture. "I don't think you can teach or instill the instinct to look past what's obvious and detect what *isn't*."

Roland Malone tore a chunk of garlic bread off the loaf and dipped it into the buttery shrimp scampi, one of his restaurant's specialties and a personal favorite of his.

Ristorante Italiano remained dark and atmospheric even in daytime. He had designed it to be conducive to clandestine business meetings and illicit romantic trysts, and he'd engaged in both over the years. But he preferred to eat alone, and he usually took his main meal during the lull between lunch and dinner when there were few other diners.

Blocks away, the noisy streets of the French Quarter teemed with sweaty tourists. Neon signs flashed enticements to wickedness. Saxophone-heavy jazz blared from the open doorways of murky bars.

But in Ristorante Italiano, the tables were occupied mostly by regulars, candlelight flickered on snow white tablecloths, and the playlist that was softly piped through speakers in the ceiling was exclusively Frank Sinatra and Tony Bennett.

Almost forty years ago, when he'd escaped the Bronx with fresh blood on his hands, his Irish father was lying dead on the kitchen floor, and his Italian mother was weeping and wailing in her native tongue over the catastrophic turn her son's fate had taken.

His uncles on his mother's side, who'd considered the murder of the abusive drunk a blessing, had impressed upon Roland that this was farewell, that he could never return to New York.

He never had. He'd never seen his mother again.

But when he fled, he'd brought with him not only her rosary beads and fear of hellfire, but also her recipes. After making a name for himself in New Orleans's underworld by doing "favors" for the criminal elite, he'd asked one grateful client to bankroll a restaurant.

"A nice place where people with taste and discretion can meet, eat, drink wine, talk business. You know." The concept that the "you know" implied had appealed to the investor, who was a lecherous and corrupt city councilman.

There was only one succulent shrimp remaining in his dish when Roland's cell phone vibrated near his glass of excellent Brunello. Knowing it was the awaited return call from Oz, he picked up immediately.

Oz said, "I couldn't talk when you called. I was in a heated meeting."

"Is there a problem?"

"Not really. A nuisance, a gnat. Now tell me some good news."

"The skimmer and his bitch are done and done," Roland said. "I did the girl first and made him watch."

"Did he beg for her life?"

"Hell, no. He begged for his."

Oz laughed and asked for gory details, which Roland provided. Oz wanted to know if the bodies had been discovered.

"Yes, but the cops are scrambling to identify them. Watch the news tonight. It's sure to be the lead story." Roland waggled his right-hand fingers near the flame of the candle, admiring how it turned the red stone in his ring the same color as the Tuscan vintage he was drinking.

"What about the stockpile he stole from me?" Oz asked.

"Recovered by the new guy I told you about."

"The one from El Paso?"

"You can call him that. He's using it as a nickname. Anyway, he hand-counted all ten grand out to me. I put it in the slush fund."

"Fine," Oz said. Then, "Listen, I don't want anything to go wrong this week."

Roland had been lifting his wineglass to take a sip, but at the abrupt change of topic, he set it back down. "I don't want anything to go wrong at any time. What's special about this week?"

"Just make certain that you're on standby."

"I'm always on standby."

But, as though he hadn't spoken, Oz said, "In case something comes up and we have to move fast."

"Sure. But you want to tell me what—"

"No. It's tentative. I'll tell you on an as-needed basis."

Roland didn't like it, but he trusted Oz to inform him of whatever the sensitive matter was when he was good and ready. "Okay."

"Any update on Haskell?"

Roland had been expecting Oz to ask about the bad-penny detective, and he'd dreaded it. He covered his uneasiness with a soft belch. "The Adler issue took precedence. But Haskell is on my radar."

Oz grunted approval, then lapsed into one of his thoughtful stretches. Roland picked up the last shrimp, ate it, and was licking his fingers when Oz said, "The heated meeting I mentioned was with my ad man. He's trying to talk me into changing my slogan."

"What the fuck?"

"Right? He said it's 'tired.'"

"Fire the stupid jerk," Roland said. "He's lousy. You don't want to mess with your slogan. You are the King of Cash."

Chapter 7

After his brief conversation with John, Mitch went to his desk and made himself look busy catching up on paperwork. Obviously John and Dylan Reede hadn't conferred yet because John hadn't confronted him about it. But it was only a matter of time. Something to look forward to.

Meanwhile, he was interested in learning more about the crime scene where two unidentified bodies had been discovered in the bayou. Like an itch he couldn't scratch, it had been bugging him since Nix and Lear had told him about it.

It was almost four o'clock before the two of them returned, and by then that unreachable itch was driving him mad. They were making their way toward John's office when Mitch rolled his chair from beneath his desk right into their path and stood up to face them. "What happened out there?"

The instant John saw them, he came out of his office and started toward them. Lear cast him a cautious glance, but Nix showed no such restraint as she replied to Mitch. "It was grim, and that's an understatement."

John, who'd reached them, asked, "How'd they die?"

"Strangulation," Lear said.

Nix added, "With what the coroner guesses was a sharp garrote, possibly a wire. The young woman was almost decapitated."

Hearing that, a sizzling reaction like a lightning strike shot through Mitch from the top of his head to the soles of his feet. He cut a glance at John, who either didn't see it or pretended not to.

John asked the detectives if the time of death had been estimated. Nix said, "Coroner broadly guesses within the last twelve to eighteen hours. There wasn't enough blood at the scene for them to have been killed there. The bodies were dumped, but they hadn't been in the water all that long."

"Have they been identified?"

Nix shook her head. "And until they are, it's hard to determine a motive."

"Retribution." Mitch had mumbled the word, but it got the attention of the other three, who turned to him for elaboration. "This doesn't sound like a crime of passion, swiftly carried out in a fit of rage. Not like shooting two people. Bam, bam, and it's done." He shook his head. "Whoever did this was making a point, sending a message, wouldn't you say?"

Nobody said anything until Lear spoke up. "We weren't much help. Darcy thanked us and sent us back. He and the SO's crime scene unit are on it."

Mitch looked at John and asked hopefully, "Want me to check in with him, offer to go out there, take a look around?"

John shook his head and addressed the other two detectives.

"Follow the progress of the investigation, but from a respectful distance. If Darcy wants more help from us, he's not too proud to ask for it."

Lear nodded, then turned and headed for his desk. Barbara Nix looked reluctant to leave the conversation on that awkward note, but she said, "Yes, sir," then walked away.

Mitch's temples were pulsing. He rolled his chair back to his desk, sat down in front of his computer, and stared at his screen saver—a picture of Andrew with a slobbery smile that showed off two rows of perfect baby teeth. Angela hadn't lived to see that smile.

After a few moments, sensing that John was hovering, he tilted his head back and looked up at him. "What?"

"You all right?" John asked, speaking in an undertone.

"Don't I look all right?"

John didn't answer, which probably meant that, no, he didn't look all right. This man who knew him all too well had sensed his reaction when those killings were described. John would know that he was desperate to be in the thick of the investigation.

"So you're good?" John asked.

Through clenched teeth, he said, "I'm good."

Still, John lingered.

"Something else?" Mitch asked.

"I spoke with Dr. Reede."

"Ah." Mitch planted his booted foot on the corner of his desk and swiveled his chair back and forth. "Good one, John. You get extra points for pulling a fast one."

"Fast one?"

Mitch snuffled. "Don't play dumb."

John raised his hands at his sides, palms up. "You've got me."

"I understand that you had a virtual meeting with Dr. Reede."

"I had a virtual meeting with all of them."

"Um-huh. But wasn't she a standout, different from the others? Distinctively, overwhelmingly, obviously different?"

He saw the instant it dawned on John what he was leading to. "You chose her, Mitch, not me."

"Yeah, sight unseen." He wagged his index finger. "Admit it. You winked to yourself when I texted to let you know she was my random choice. You could have given me some warning, or at least a hint of what I was walking into."

"You make it sound like the lion's den. She came across very well in our interview, or I would have struck her from consideration. What didn't you like about her?"

"Are you kidding? What's not to like?" he said expansively. "She's a treasure. So earnest. 'I want to help you, Mitch.'"

At his mocking tone, John gave a look around. "This isn't the place," he said under his breath. "Let's go get a cup of coffee."

Mitch swiveled around to take in all the eyes and ears homed in on them. "It's okay, John. It's hardly a secret that you forced this therapy on me. Just like my parents did when I was eight years old and my puppy got run over by a car. I didn't want to bawl my eyes out in front of a stranger, so I suppressed my emotions. The therapy was more traumatic than watching Rascal bleed out in the middle of the street."

John, knowing damn well there had been no such incident, looked ready to throttle him. As it was, he only glared through slitted eyes. "What happened with Dr. Reede?"

Mitch kept his expression blankly innocent. "Pardon?"

"What did you do, Mitch?"

Unable to hold back any longer, he grinned.

John's jaw turned to granite, as it was wont to do when he was furious. "What did you do?"

"You talked to her. What did she say about our session?"

"As befits her profession, she didn't offer much. She was very reserved."

Mitch laughed out loud. "I'll bet she was."

"Really, all she said was that she'll see you again on Thursday."

Mitch abruptly stopped laughing. His boot slid off the desk and hit the floor as he bounded out of the chair. "She said *what*?"

"Ten a.m." John then turned his back and went into his office.

Mitch watched him go, but when John shut the door decisively, Mitch spun around, kicked his chair, and shouted, "Fucking hell!"

Then, realizing that all eyes were still on him, he collected himself, squared up the chair beneath his desk, shut down his computer, and said, "Coffee sounds good after all," and strode out.

He avoided the coffee shop around the corner, where most PD personnel took their breaks. Instead, he walked the several blocks to Gus's bar. Too early for happy hour to get into full swing, the place was occupied mostly by vacant-eyed souls day-drinking alone. He'd been there.

Mitch was relieved to see that Gus himself was tending bar and not the guy he'd threatened with the broken bottle. He gave Gus a sheepish smile. "I came to ask how much I owe you."

"I'm still getting estimates."

"Estimates? For a mirror and a few busted chairs?"

"Simmer down. I'll take the lowest bid. Bowie given you the boot yet?"

"No, but the day ain't over."

Gus frowned. "Mitch, he won't like knowing you're drinking."

"Coffee, please. Iced, but black and strong."

"Then it's on the house."

"You're all heart."

Mitch carried the coffee to a corner booth, took out his phone, and scrolled through his contacts until he found the number of a DEA buddy. Amid a lot of background noise, his call was answered by a man who sounded short on time, breath, and patience. "Tucker."

"Jim, Mitch Haskell."

Tucker expelled a profanity. "You didn't waste any time."

"You expected to hear from me?"

"As soon as you got wind of that double murder."

"So y'all *are* on it?"

"Yeah."

"What brought you in?"

"Two of our undercovers separately identified the male vic."

"No shit," Mitch murmured. "Talk to me."

"Mitch, I—"

"Please."

Tucker was an office agent, but from his desk he moved field agents around like a master chess player. He was well liked, highly respected, and known for his liberal use of blue language, which he utilized now before sighing with resignation. "Hold on."

Mitch heard him tell someone that he needed to take the call but that he would be right back. The background noise receded. On the phone again, he cut to the chase. "How much do you already know?"

"Table scraps. Only that the discovery wasn't pretty."

"Pretty fucking gruesome," Tucker said.

"It's the SO's jurisdiction, but Darcy called our department seeking help to identify the bodies. Bowie dispatched two detectives. They came back and gave us the skinny as they knew it, which was precious little."

"Well, the male vic was one Paul Adler. Our agents recognized him by photos from the scene."

"Your guys recognized him by a photo alone?"

"Wasn't a challenge. He was well known to them. Sneaky as a sewer rat and twice as filthy."

"What about the female?"

"No name yet. Young. Sixteen, seventeen. Probably a runaway. Their landlady said she'd been shacking with Adler for a couple of months."

Mitch glanced around. Gus was at the tap drawing beers for a pair of tired-looking construction-worker types who'd come in. The day-drinkers were nursing their neat drinks, seemingly oblivious to Mitch, to everything.

Even so, he spoke in an undertone. "Jim, was this Paul Adler one of Oz's?"

"You know I can't divulge—"

"Of course you can. It's me."

After a brief pause, Tucker said under his breath, "Likely one of Oz's. But a no-class street hustler like Adler would've been near to or at the bottom of Oz's chain."

Mitch said, "But he ranked high enough to warrant Roland Malone taking care of him." Tucker was too smart to take the bait. He didn't respond; Mitch had to goose him. "A garrote?

Probably wire? Come on, Jim. Remember you're the one who first tipped me to this asshole Malone."

That conversation had taken place six months ago on a slow day at police headquarters. Finding himself sitting idle and trying to stir up business, Mitch had called Tucker to see if there had been any leads on the investigation into the murder of his colleague, Randy Nelson. At that point in time, the case had been cold for over two years.

The consensus was that Nelson's murder had been payback for a successful drug bust that had yielded a huge harvest of cocaine, fentanyl, and Oxy. You name it, the DEA and affiliated agencies had scored big, largely due to the undercover work of Randy Nelson and, in conjunction with him, Mitch Haskell.

Somehow—probably no one would ever know how—Nelson had been found out. The agency was certain that his murder had been a contract hit intended to make an impression that would discourage anyone else from interfering with Oz's lucrative enterprise.

On that slow day when Mitch had asked about a new lead, Tucker had hedged, but eventually agreed to meet Mitch for coffee. After ten minutes of more hem-hawing, he'd relented and told him about Roland Malone.

"He owns and operates an Italian restaurant on Esplanade. I checked it out. Delicious food. Classy place. But it's a front. He's high up in the trade, hand in glove with Oz."

"How'd you get on to him?"

"From a traitor who shall remain nameless."

"Jim."

"Nameless, Mitch. We have the snitch on about twelve felony counts, including conspiracy on a hit. We applied enormous pressure, he became cooperative, and then completely turned.

He's tucked away, in the protective custody of US marshals, and will be an important witness in court. *If* we ever get Malone indicted."

"How close are you?"

"How far's the moon? We can't build a case on this felon's word alone, and if we tried to get an indictment without something substantive in our back pocket—"

"You'd be tipping your hand to Malone."

"Who's as slick as owl shit. Also, real bad news. There's been another hit since Nelson."

"Another agent?"

"No, one of Oz's dealers. Flashy guy. Flamboyant, loudmouthed, big spender, and therefore dangerous to the operation."

"Killed the same way as Nelson?"

"Yes. And now Paul Adler and that girl. Choked with what the ME guessed was a razor-sharp garrote. We believe Roland Malone not only has fingers in Oz's business, but that he's Oz's executioner of choice."

"What does the snitch say about it?"

"Not a goddamn thing. He stonewalls on anything regarding Malone, which, of course, makes us believe Malone does Oz's wet work. But he does it so cleanly, we can't nail him."

In the six months since that conversation, neither the DEA nor any other agency had gathered evidence strong enough to get Roland Malone indicted. And they had to have Malone before they had a prayer of getting to the overlord he worked for: the faceless mastermind nicknamed Oz.

Mitch took another cautious look around the bar. Gus was schmoozing three young women who'd ventured in and were being ogled by the construction workers. No one appeared to be interested in Mitch, but paranoia was ingrained.

He asked, "Any significant evidence found at the crime scene on Bayou Coeur?"

"They're still looking."

"That means either no or you're not telling."

"That means they're still looking, Mitch."

"I was told the victims weren't killed at the scene. Bodies were dumped, just like Nelson's was."

"So was the talkative dealer's," Tucker said.

"In Bayou Coeur?"

"No. He was found in a lake across the river in Mississippi."

Mitch took a moment to process all this, then said, "The Adler hit has Malone's imprint all over it. You know that, Jim. Talk to me."

"Damn you, Mitch," he grumbled. "I shouldn't be talking to you at all. We're not advertising that we're involved in this investigation. Not yet. It would be like switching on the light in a room full of roaches. They'd scatter."

"But you're looking at Malone?"

"Discreetly."

"But closely."

"*Discreetly*, Mitch. And I mean it."

"I got it, I got it. Just keep me posted."

"If I can."

"You owe me, Jim."

"For what?"

"For setting you up with...what was her name? Teresa? Terry?"

"We had one date!"

"Not my fault you mucked it up."

Tucker swore again, then, "Look, I've gotta ask. What's up with you and Bowie?"

Shit. "You've got a double hit on your hands, but it's our tiff y'all are talking about over there?"

"So it's true? You two are on the outs?"

"It'll blow over."

"Will it?" He paused, then asked, "Are you sober?"

"I wasn't last Saturday night."

"So they're saying."

"John got his shorts in a wad over it."

"And then some, I heard."

Jesus, the grapevine was thorough. "And then some," Mitch admitted. "But we're chill now."

"You swear?"

"We're chill."

"All right then. I'll update you if something worth sharing turns up."

"Thanks, Jim." He was about to click off when the other man halted him.

"One more thing," the agent said.

"Still here."

Tucker took a breath, blew it out. "You didn't ask for advice or coaching. But I gotta say this. It's no secret that the past couple of years have been hell for you. Under the circumstances, understandable.

"So cut yourself some slack, all right? The last thing you need is to bring down more shit on yourself. After I told you about Roland Malone, you said Bowie was lukewarm on him. So don't get under Bowie's skin over this possible-but-not-proven Bayou Coeur tie-in. You're an outstanding cop. It would be a damn shame if you fucked up your future by going off on a wild hare. Okay?"

"Okay."

"Okay?"

"Okay."

Tucker sighed. "Yeah, right." He clicked off.

Jim Tucker wouldn't have told him everything he was privy to about the double murder or what the DEA had or didn't have on Roland Malone. Remaining tight-lipped was a rigid rule of federal agencies.

But Mitch hadn't told Tucker everything he was privy to, either.

Ellie had left at six o'clock after showing out Dylan's last patient.

Dylan had stayed to review the handwritten notes she'd taken on a legal pad during today's sessions, as well as those from yesterday, and had spent the last three hours transcribing them into each patient's computer file.

Because her mind had continued to drift, the work had taken longer than usual. She was ready for home, a glass of wine, and a soaking bath. But she had one more patient file to review. The one she'd intentionally saved for last. Mitch Haskell's.

She opened the leather portfolio and lifted out the yellow legal tablet. She wasn't surprised to see how very little there was on it to transcribe, so she pushed away from the desk in her inner office and, taking the notepad with her, went into the other room where she could contemplate more comfortably.

She hadn't taken many notes during her session with Mitch because most of what he'd said hadn't been noteworthy. She'd recognized his derisiveness as a shield against any serious subject she might broach, but it had left her with very little to work with. She hadn't jotted down any key words she could later use in an effort to unlock something important that he was withholding.

The only time he'd revealed anything significant was when he hadn't said anything at all. It had been when she'd asked him if last week's drinking binge had to do with the anniversary date of his wife's death. He'd divulged more by saying nothing than—

Suddenly the lock in the private exit door clicked, the knob turned, and the subject of her thoughts walked in. "This won't keep until Thursday," he said, and pushed the door shut with the heel of his boot.

Chapter 8

Dylan tossed the notepad aside and was across the room in three strides. "What do you think you're doing?"

"You didn't tell John about the kiss."

"You scared me half to death. How did you get in here?"

"I picked the locks."

"You picked... Both? The downstairs exit, too? How did you—"

"I'm multi-skilled. Why didn't you tell John?"

"You can't just break in here."

"Evidence to the contrary." He spread his arms and grinned.

Grinned! His audacity was astonishing. "You'll be caught on the security cameras."

"Tsk, tsk, Dr. Reede. That's a fib. There aren't any security cameras. Do you think I'd break into a building without scouting it out first?"

"Leave. Now."

"After killing so much time before getting in here? Un-huh. I saw Ellie leave. Hung around, planning to intercept you when you followed. Except you didn't come out, and I got tired of waiting."

She pointed to the door behind him. "Go."

"Why?"

"I can think of a dozen reasons, but mainly because it's a breach of protocol and ethics."

"Kissing you was against the rules, too. How come you didn't raise a ruckus over that?"

"Because you were clearly trying to manipulate me into dropping you as a patient. I planned to tell Lieutenant Bowie, but after thinking it over—"

"Every time you refer to him as Lieutenant Bowie it sets my teeth on edge. Make it John or Bowie, all right? It's easier. Now, about the kiss. You were saying?"

"I wasn't saying anything about the kiss per se."

"I've never been quite sure what per se means, but I'm positive that our subject was the kiss."

Although she was fuming, she kept her voice under strict control. "Tattling on you was exactly what you wanted me to do."

"Oh, so you spent time analyzing it."

Suddenly she realized that somehow the distance between them had shrunk, although she couldn't say who had taken the steps necessary to bring that about. "Move back, please. You're invading my space."

She had to look up several inches in order to hold his gaze, but she did. She also held her ground. Although it didn't feel like solid ground beneath her. More like the deck of a boat riding gentle swells.

He raised his hands shoulder high and took several steps back. "Invading your space wasn't my intention. I came over here so I could see if my break-in had been noticed."

He moved to the window and peered down at the street through the slits in the blinds. "Do you keep these half closed to create an intimate atmosphere?" he asked as he turned back to her.

Actually, yes. She kept them half shut to induce trust and confidentiality. But because of his terminology, she said, "The window has a southern exposure. Sunlight comes in at an uncomfortable angle for some patients."

"Especially when they're sharing the juicier aspects of their lives."

She didn't address that at all. "You should go before your break-in is discovered."

"What's gonna happen if it is? Every cop on the force knows me. I'd say that I'd seen your light on in an otherwise dark building without either security cameras or an alarm system. By the way, why is that?"

"The expense of installing them in a building this old was too much for some of the tenants."

"Huh. Then aren't you glad I'm the only one who broke in?"

"Not really. By the way, that amounted to a confession."

"All right. I broke in. I'd tell any investigating officer that I was here to check things out, see if you were all right, and that would be the end of it."

"No, because I would tell him differently."

"Yeah?" He cocked his head to one side. "What would you tell him?"

The challenging question was as good as a thrown gauntlet. The smug hike of his left eyebrow indicated that he knew she didn't have a comeback, because she'd made clear to him this morning that she would never betray a patient's confidence.

Completely out of context, he said, "Your hair looks better loose like that."

She had freed it from the tight ponytail she wore during office hours. Now, she reflexively hooked it behind her ears, and then cursed herself for that self-conscious response to his compliment, which she didn't acknowledge.

"In fact," he said, "you look looser all over. Blazer gone. Shirttail out." He looked down at her bare feet. "No high heels."

From the moment he'd appeared, she'd been well aware of her "looser" appearance and had tried not to let her embarrassment over it show. But she'd be damned before she simpered over his comments. "I wasn't expecting an intruder."

"Ain't life just full of surprises?"

"Some of them unpleasant."

That bounced right off him. With a frown of concentration, he was still assessing her. "You know, you might get more out of your patients if you let them see you like this. A little messy and undone instead of all buttoned up."

"That wouldn't be very professional."

His grin faded slowly and, like twin lasers, his blue eyes sharpened on hers. "That detached, professional demeanor is your security blanket, isn't it?"

Taken off guard again by both his sudden shift of mood and his disturbing insightfulness, she gave a slight shake of her head. It dislodged a hank of hair from one ear, but she didn't call attention to it by correcting it. Coolly, she said, "I'm not sure what you mean."

"Come on now, Dylan. Don't pretend. You know damn well what I'm talking about." He took a look around the room before coming back to her. "This morning, it struck me right off that your straitlaced appearance and poised manner were in direct contrast to the cozy atmosphere of this room.

"You came across as a role-playing actor who'd wandered onto the wrong set, but was still sure of her lines, and confident of her position. Don't get me wrong. You play it well. A little too well. It makes one wonder if you're a real person with a heartbeat."

Every word of his monologue had stung, but she wasn't about to let him know it. "If I were role-playing, my costume would have been baggy trousers and a food-stained vest."

He gave a huff of amusement. "Good one, doc. But back to what we were saying."

"What *you* were saying."

"Okay, what I was saying, or was about to say, is that I freely admit that my defense mechanism is cracking jokes. I deflect by wisecracking. Yours is to assume a cool, calm, controlled professionalism. It's like a... what do you call one of those things?"

"You called it a security blanket."

"Yeah, but that's too soft and cushy. Your composure is more like a..." He snapped his fingers several times. "A bell jar. That's it. It encases you. It's see-through, but impenetrable. What's it there to protect you from, I wonder."

Her arms went rigid at her sides. Her hands formed fists. And, of course, he noticed.

"Whoa. That observation struck a chord. Because I nailed it, didn't I?"

Realizing that she was playing right into his hands by reacting to his prodding, she relaxed her hands and took a steadying breath. "Mitch, what's see-through is your motivation for tonight's surprise attack. You're here because your attempted sabotage this morning failed."

"Is that how you see it?"

"You're trying to intimidate me into refusing to see you as a patient."

"And you're trying to keep that bell jar securely in place despite your..."

He made a gesture with both hands that seemed to indicate her dishevelment. She didn't respond.

Again, he tipped his head inquisitively. "Not going to refute that?" When she still didn't speak, he shrugged. "Doesn't matter. I think I know why you never let your guard down."

"You don't know anything about me."

"But see, I want to, Dylan." He took another look through the blinds, turning his head this way and that to take in the whole street below, then went over to the patient sofa, sat down, and stretched his arms across the back of it. "Pretend I've lifted off that bell jar. Tell me something about Dylan Reede."

"I don't discuss my personal life with patients."

"Well now, that's not fair. You want to poke around in my head, my heart, my psyche, but I don't get to know anything about you?"

She remained silent and impassive.

"Tell you what. I'll go first and reveal something about me." He lowered his arms from the back of the sofa and sat forward, elbows on his knees, hands clasped between them. He met her gaze directly.

"I love my son Andrew so much that when I watch him sleep, my heart hurts from the strain of loving him. Sometimes it's so overwhelming, I'm moved to tears. I lie there, looking at him, listening to him breathe, and cry over the...the marvel... of having made this awesome little person."

She searched his eyes, took in his body language and

expression, and didn't believe that this was another manipulation. Whether it was or not, she wanted to explore it. She sat down on the edge of the sofa behind her. "How old is Andrew?"

"Almost three. He lives with my in-laws. John probably told you that."

"He did. He also told me that it was your decision, not a court mandate."

"No, there was no legal hassle. Nothing official. I just thought it would be best for Andrew. He was only nine months old when Angela... when we lost her. I had to work, and, even if I could have afforded child care that met my standards, I didn't want his formative years to be guided and overseen by strangers. Angela would have hated that, too."

"Is it a good living arrangement?"

"No, it fucking sucks," he said shortly. Then with more introspection, he added, "It's just the best I can do right now." A look of torment crossed his features, but it was quickly gone. "Okay, doc. Your turn."

"I don't take a turn."

"Come on. Be a sport."

"These sessions are for you, Mitch. You exclusively."

"Hmm." He sat up straight. Stroking his lower lip with his index finger, he stared at her with acute intensity. Ponderous seconds ticked by. She reasoned that he was weighing either to disclose something that was difficult for him to address or to keep it to himself for now. She didn't nudge him in either direction.

Finally, he said, "Did you have any idea what you were getting into when you married a martyr?"

He'd posed the question quietly, but it rent the silence like crashing cymbals. Or breaking glass. Like a bell jar shattering.

Her breath leaked out slowly through her lips, taking all her strength with it. She sank against the back cushion of the sofa, staring at him with dismay and asking herself how he—?

But of course. He was a detective by trade. He had resources that were available only to law enforcement officers. He was multi-skilled. Canny and quick was how John Bowie had described him.

"I looked you up," he said, still speaking in a voice with the texture of velvet. "I had to do some digging because you don't go by your married name. Why not?"

She had to swallow before attempting to say something, and she was relieved to discover that she could speak at all. "Not in order to conceal it."

"No?"

"No. A lot of women use their maiden name for their profession."

"Where did you meet your husband?"

She swallowed again. "George. You can say his name. I won't fall apart."

Although she very well might, and soon, if she didn't regain her sense of balance and reestablish boundaries. *Now.* She smoothed her hands over her skirt several times and then stood up.

"But you won't be referring to him at all within my hearing, because I've made plain that we won't be talking about my life. Any aspect of it. I also told you this morning that I wanted to help you, and I meant that, Mitch. I believe I can help you." She paused before adding, "Besides, *Lieutenant Bowie* is paying me to try."

That was a cheap shot, but it felt good to sling something back at him after the blow he'd dealt her. She expected him to react to the snide remark, but he didn't, so she continued. "It really was outrageous of you to come here tonight, but your machinations are so transparent, I'm willing to disregard them. We'll resume on Thursday. For now, good night." She glanced toward the door. "I hope you didn't break my lock."

"No, just picked it. You can still lock it behind me."

He stood up, but, instead of making for the door, he walked slowly but purposefully toward her. He didn't stop until he took up her entire field of vision. She could feel his body heat, his breath warm on her face. Not for the first time, she sensed in him a coiled vitality ready to spring with dangerous unpredictability.

What stunned her now that they were standing so close—and, if she were being nakedly honest with herself, since he'd barged through the door—was her powerful reaction to his physicality, a response that hovered somewhere between anxiety and desire.

Yes, that. In spite of everything, and totally against her code of ethics and self-will, *that.*

Speaking low, he said, "I think I would enjoy watching you fall apart, Dylan. Because you're not nearly as cool as you let on. Know how I know?"

Before she knew what he was about to do and prevent it, he had encircled her wrist and placed his thumb on the inside of it where her blood vessel was pulsing. "You have a heartbeat, after all," he said. "Strong and fast, too. But that's not the giveaway." He leaned in and whispered, "The dead giveaway is the red toenail polish."

He gave her a second or two to think about that, then dropped her hand and grinned down into her face, which had been suffused with an ungoverned, unwanted, and unacceptable heat.

She pulled her wrist from his grasp. "Joke about something else."

"Wasn't joking." He gave her another smile, but not the naughty-boy one, or the one laced with sarcasm. This one was rueful.

He left her and went over to the door. When he looked back at her, his smile was gone and so was any trace of arrogance. "This isn't a joke, either, Dr. Reede. It's a true story without a 'once upon a time.' It begins on the night I found my wife dead in our garage."

His bluntness struck her; she caught her breath.

"Her death was ruled a suicide," he said. "It wasn't. She was murdered. People don't believe that, but I know it, and I'm going to avenge it. I'm going to find the men who conspired to kill Andrew's mother, and when I do, I'm going to kill them."

He spoke with clarity, candor, and conviction. No comedy. In fact, his monotonal seriousness was chilling.

"After they're dead," he continued, "if the authorities come to you and ask to see your records on me, or ask what you know about my psyche, you have my permission to tell them that I confessed my intentions to you without qualification or remorse. Tell them that I was an 'imminent threat' to those men." He motioned behind her to the sofa where her notepad lay. "Write that down so you'll be sure to remember."

He looked at her for several beats, then left through the door and gently pulled it closed behind him.

Chapter 9

Mitch thumped the back of his head against the elevator wall. *Damn! What the hell had just happened?*

Ambushing Dylan in her office had been intended to shock-and-awe, to completely disarm her so that she'd be more susceptible to his clever prying techniques. He'd wanted to come away from the encounter with more information about her and her practice.

His brilliant plan had backfired. Big time.

He'd wound up waxing poetic about his love for his son, and had recited to her the vengeful pledge he'd made after Angela's murder. To have wormed that out of him, she must be a better therapist than he'd given her credit for.

She should bill herself as "Dr. Reede, Analyst Extraordinaire."

Dylan, the female person, was something else entirely. A snake charmer, maybe. Hypnotist, enchantress, siren. Whatever, she had cast some kind of spell over him that had shut down his brain but had thrown another part of his anatomy into overdrive at warp speed.

Those moments when he'd had his thumb against her wrist, he'd been conjuring up fantasies as rapidly as her heart was beating. Her hair, loose and silky, sliding over his chest, his...

Christ! He couldn't be thinking about that now. He had to banish all thoughts of her. The eyes, the lips, those legs. Red toenails. He'd wait to indulge the erotic fantasies when he could do so leisurely and without distraction.

Now definitely was not that time.

The elevator reached the ground floor, and the door slid open. The lobby remained dark except for security lights at both ends of a long corridor that ran parallel to the building's facade.

He followed that corridor to a corner where it intersected with another long hallway lined with offices. Midway down that hall was the door to the outside through which he'd entered. It was unmarked, but he'd located it when he'd seen Dylan's patient using it to exit. The lock had been easy enough to pick, but the door was made of solid metal. There was no way to see what waited beyond it except to open it.

He pushed it open an inch and put his eye to the crack.

EATS's neon sign was dark. All the surrounding offices and businesses were also closed for the night. The city street was vacant except for the car he had spotted as he'd left Gus's bar. It had been parked halfway down the block on the other side of the street. He hadn't been at all surprised that he was being tailed, but he'd pretended not to notice.

Evidently, he'd been followed to the medical building. Through the window blinds in Dylan's office, he'd seen the same car on the street, and it was still there. Unfortunately it was parked facing this exit door. He couldn't go out this way without being seen, and he wanted to take the driver of that car by surprise.

He pulled the door closed and walked along the dim hallway until he reached the entrance to the fire stairs. He took the treads two at a time up to the third floor landing where there was a window that opened onto an exterior fire escape. He'd made note of it while studying the building from his booth in the diner.

The lock on the window had been painted over so many times that it wouldn't budge until he applied his pocketknife to it. It finally gave way, but also cracked the glass pane and splintered the wood frame. He didn't worry about the damage overmuch. It wouldn't be that noticeable.

He raised the window only high enough for him to climb through and then conscientiously closed it once he was out. The fire escape was rusty, creaky, and loosely attached to the building, but he reached the bottom without mishap and made the ten-foot drop to the sidewalk without difficulty. He then jogged to the corner of the building and peered around.

He was now behind the car.

He started toward it, walking stealthily but quickly in the shadow of the building. As he approached the car, he slowed, slid his pistol from its holster at the small of his back, and held it down at his side as he crept up to the car.

The driver's window was down. The driver was talking on a cell phone. Mitch heard him say, "No, not a sign of him since he went in."

Mitch lurched forward, simultaneously pounding on the driver's door with his left fist, raising the pistol with his right hand, and aiming it through the open window.

The driver nearly jumped out of his skin and whipped his head around.

"Clarence!" Mitch exclaimed. "Jesus!"

Staring bug-eyed into the bore of the pistol, the young patrol officer who'd arrested him on Saturday night was gasping. When able, he said, "Hi, Mitch."

"'*Hi, Mitch*'? Why the fuck are you following me? Who are you talking to?"

"B...Bowie."

"You gotta be shittin' me. Give me that." He reached through the open window with his left hand and snatched the phone from Clarence. He brought it up to his ear and said with exaggerated congeniality, "A pleasant evening to you, John. How's it hanging?"

"What were you doing in the medical building?"

"I've got this fungus on my scrotum."

"Oh, you're funny."

"Okay, I had a session with Dr. Reede. Isn't that what you dictated?"

"Your next appointment wasn't until Thursday."

"What, you're my personal assistant now? You keep my day planner?"

"Don't turn this around on me, Mitch. If you were in some kind of emergency situation and needed—"

"No emergency. Relax. I just needed to talk through some things with the doc."

"What things?"

"*Private* things."

"She agreed to see you after office hours even though it wasn't an emergency?"

"Well, she didn't kick me out." It didn't count that she had tried. "But we're getting off the subject here. I could've fired a bullet into Clarence's ear canal, and he never would have seen it coming. Why'd you send him to follow me?"

"I was worried about you."

"I'm touched. Truly, truly touched."

"That's great. Your sarcasm is always so helpful." John paused, sighed, then, "Mitch, you left here mad as hell. I was afraid you'd go on another bender, or do something even crazier."

"Like what?"

"Like take out your anger on Dylan Reede."

Mitch lowered the phone so he could glare at it. When he put it back to his ear, he said, "Did I hear you right? The possibility that I would harm her—any woman—actually crossed your mind?" He rolled his lips inward, mentally counted to ten, then said, "You know what? Fuck you."

"Look, I'm sorry. That was out of line."

Mitch didn't accept the apology. Speaking tightly, he said, "First of all, don't flatter yourself into thinking that I would ever become that unhinged over a squabble with *you*."

"I said I was sorry."

Clarence couldn't help but overhear this conversation through the telephone and wasn't even trying to conceal his avid interest. He was listening so hard, he was barely breathing.

Mitch decided it had gone far enough. "You wasted your worry on me, John. I'm stone cold sober. I'm sure Clarence reported to you that I went to Gus's. I did. For coffee, and Gus will vouch for that. When I left Dylan Reede, she was sound of body and mind." A little disheveled and flushed, but otherwise...

"What she and I talk about during our sessions, which you

insisted on, is private. From here, I plan to go straight home. If you don't trust me, you can have Clarence follow me and see that I'm tucked in. He can even read me a bedtime story."

"You're still pissed."

"Damn straight. I have every right to be."

John cursed under his breath. "See you tomorrow."

Mitch disconnected and handed the phone back to Clarence, who gave him a shaky smile. "I think y'all can patch things up in the morning."

Mitch huffed a dismissal of that prospect. "Clarence, a few tips on the art of tailing somebody? I spied you the second I came out of Gus's. An innocuous, unmarked vehicle without school decals, a soccer mom license plate, or tacky bumper stickers is always suspicious and as good as advertising that a cop is inside.

"Also, when on a stakeout, it's best not to park under a streetlight. And, most importantly, constantly check your side mirrors. You had no idea anyone was around. You could easily be on your way to the morgue."

The young cop swallowed noisily, nodded, and said, "Thanks, Mitch. I'll remember. And I'm sorry about my part in this. Bowie—"

"No need to apologize. You were only following orders. My car is parked around the corner. Drive safely."

With that, he replaced his pistol in its holster and struck off toward the corner he'd indicated. When he reached his truck, he climbed in and started it. For good measure, he gave Clarence a toodle-oo wave as the young cop drove past.

The first thing Dylan did when she got home was pour a glass of wine and take it with her into the bathroom. She sipped at it while she watched the tub fill.

Neither the Chardonnay nor soaking in a warm bath was going to help her think clearly, but that was the point of indulging in both. She didn't want to think clearly. She wanted thoughts of what had taken place in her office to fog until they were totally obscured.

She didn't want to think about Mitch, or how intimate it had felt when he'd pressed the pad of his thumb against her pulse. The whispered line about her red nail polish hadn't been explicitly sexual, but its suggestiveness had been alarmingly effective.

By the time the tub was full, her wineglass was empty. She considered returning to the kitchen for a refill but thought better of it and, instead, half reclined in the bath.

Whether she wanted to or not, she must review what had passed between her and Mitch Haskell, her *patient*, and determine what she was going to do about it.

Before arriving at a solution to this dilemma, she first must acknowledge its cause. Pure and simple, there was no getting around that she was attracted to him. He was cute, clever, funny, charismatic, charming, and flat-out sexy.

There was also no getting around that he was a deeply troubled man. He had admitted to being hell-bent on getting lethal vengeance for what he believed was the murder of his wife.

During her interview with Bowie, he'd told her there'd been no evidence that Angela's death was a homicide. But in the two years since, Mitch had refused to accept that she had chosen death over the life she shared with him and Andrew.

As a clinician, Dylan knew that he must come to terms with it, or the prospect of a happy future for him and his young son was improbable. Healing from a loved one's suicide was an arduous, complex struggle that, in addition to mourning, involved self-blame and even anger over the selfishness of the individual. That struggle would be doubly hard for Mitch because he didn't acknowledge either the suicide or that he was in need of healing.

But Dylan was confident she could help him. Which was why she must stay focused on his *struggle*, and resistant to his appeal. She wouldn't be struck by lightning for anything that had transpired tonight, but she had definitely entered a danger zone.

Before something absolutely prohibited happened, she would be wise to tell John Bowie that she wasn't the therapist Mitch needed after all and recommend a reliable colleague.

But on a personal level, she wanted to see Mitch through this. If she turned him away, he might refuse therapy, despite Bowie's mandate, and continue along his path of self-destruction. Could she live with the guilt of having failed a patient because of her sexual attraction to him? She didn't think so.

Giving up now wouldn't be unfair to Mitch solely, but to herself as well. In the wake of George's death, she'd had to work diligently to get her life back on an even keel and under control.

She liked her life just the way it was, without drama and chaos. Her highs were moderate, her lows not too deep. She couldn't allow Mitch Haskell, the man, to interrupt her carefully reconstructed life.

At their next session, she would lay down some guidelines that he could not cross. She would make clear to him that if he so much as tested the boundaries, he would face serious repercussions from both her and John Bowie. As for herself, she could resist a grin, for heaven's sake.

She would.

She must.

Roland Malone made one last circuit around the main dining room, bidding good night to the last of his customers as they straggled out into what had become a rainy night. For a Monday evening, Ristorante Italiano had catered to a satisfactory crowd.

But crowd size was irrelevant except for show. It was *who* came in on any given night, not *how many*. Tonight, deals had been made, plans laid, payoffs collected. The safe in his office contained more cash than it had earlier in the evening. Oz would be pleased.

As soon as all the customers were gone, work lights came on and staff began cleaning up and laying place settings for tomorrow's lunch crowd. Roland was headed for the kitchen to discuss tomorrow's seafood specials with the chef when he got a call.

He took his phone from his pocket and saw that it was the call he'd been anticipating all day. His mole in the Auclair PD had come through late last night by texting him the list of proposed therapists for Mitch Haskell. He hadn't heard anything since.

He answered with, "Talk to me."

"Mitch Haskell and John Bowie had another quarrel this afternoon over Haskell going to therapy."

"Did he go or not?"

"Did."

"Which therapist?"

"Her name is Dylan Reede."

Roland went very still, then began turning his ring around his finger. "If he went, what was the quarrel about?"

"I think Haskell thought it would be a one-and-done, but Bowie insisted he keep his next appointment, which is scheduled for Thursday. Haskell dropped an eff bomb and stalked out."

"Then it probably was a one-and-done."

"Just the opposite. He didn't wait till Thursday. He went tonight."

"*Tonight?*"

"They met alone in her office after hours."

Roland pulled a chair from beneath the nearest dining table and sat down to think over this unexpected development and its possible implications. He didn't like any of them.

He knew his informant at the other end of this call would be gauging his reaction, so he was careful to conceal it. He had instilled a fear of reprisal if ever there was a screwup in their delicate arrangement. He didn't want to reduce the potency of that fear factor by giving off any sign of weakness, indecision, or doubt.

He asked, "Any scuttlebutt as to why Haskell chose that particular therapist?"

"He told Bowie he had picked her at random, sight unseen."

Maybe, Roland thought. *But maybe not.* Maybe not would be worrisome. "Keep me updated."

"Yes, sir."

He disconnected but remained seated at the table, rotating his ring around his finger, lost in thought, until one of his custodial employees came near him with a vacuum cleaner.

He got up, went into the kitchen, and was listening to the chef's proposal to remove Dover sole from the menu because of its inflated price, when he noticed that several of his kitchen staff had collected at the rear door.

He held up a hand to halt the complaint about the cost of fish. "What's going on back there?"

The chef glanced over his shoulder. "They're giving leftovers to the homeless."

Roland just stared at him, expecting a punch line and a burst of laughter, because surely he was jesting. When he realized the man was serious, he stepped around him and walked the length of the kitchen until he reached the group of workers.

"Move." Immediately they parted, clearing the doorway for him. He stepped out into the alley behind the restaurant where a ragged pack of homeless were huddled under the eaves to get out of the rain.

Roland pulled a carry-out carton of food from the grubby clutch of the man nearest him, opened it, took an appreciative sniff, and then emptied the aromatic contents onto the grimy pavement of the alley.

"Get the hell away from my door. If you come near my place again, I'll exterminate you like the vermin you are."

He hadn't even raised his voice, but they had gotten the message. They scuttled away, moving off in both directions down the alley. Roland turned and reentered the kitchen, where his employees were standing stock still. Even a faucet continued to run because no one had had the courage to move in order to turn it off.

He walked over to it, stuck his hands into the stream, and washed them with disinfectant soap, then lifted a fresh towel from the shelf above the sink. He took special care to dry around his signet ring and polished the red stone with the towel before folding it and setting it aside.

He turned off the faucet, then faced those who depended on him for their livelihoods and, in many cases, for their lives.

"You know what happens when you feed a stray? It keeps coming back. You never get rid of the fuckin' thing. You think my clientele want to wade through human garbage to get to the entrance? You want to ruin my business by performing good deeds?"

He picked up a meat cleaver. "If I catch any one of you giving my food to those bums, you'll be fired... *after* I cut off your hand." He made a vicious chopping motion with the cleaver, then set it down on the metal countertop so gently it didn't make a sound.

"Do you understand me?" There was a unanimous nodding of heads. "Good. Now get back to work before I get mad."

Outside in the alley, one of the homeless shuffled along behind a few others as they made their way in the opposite direction of Esplanade Avenue. He'd blended in with the other "vermin" so well, Roland Malone never would have suspected that he'd taken the food carton from the hands of Mitch Haskell.

Chapter 10

Mitch and Roland Malone had stood eye to eye, nose to nose, toe to toe. Mitch in holey, filthy sneakers now freshly spattered with lasagna, and Malone wearing polished Italian leather loafers. Malone had had no idea he had been face-to-face with an enemy who was dead set on a reckoning.

When Mitch reached the end of the alley, he separated himself from the others and turned down a side street where the traffic was much lighter than on Esplanade. He avoided eye contact with what few pedestrians there were, and, fearing panhandling, all gave him a wide berth.

He walked the now familiar circuitous course that he'd mapped out for himself over the past six months. It wove through the darkest back streets and sinister-looking alleyways to the rear parking lot of a thrift store, which, according to the sign in the window, had gone out of business three years earlier.

Weeds sprouted up through cracks in the buckled asphalt, so his means of transportation for these nocturnal round trips to New Orleans looked right at home there. The pickup truck was a holdover from his days of undercover work for the DEA. It looked like a patched-up, rusted-out piece of shit with bullet holes in the bumper. But the engine and brakes were new, and the battery was kept charged. He used it exclusively for these excursions to the city.

He'd initiated them shortly after his meeting with Jim Tucker when he'd first told him about Roland Malone, seeming restaurateur, actually a drug dealer's right-hand man and executioner.

Sensing the interest he'd stimulated in Mitch, Tucker had admonished him not to go off on a "wild hare" that would cause more trouble for himself. But that had also been Tucker's way of telling Mitch not to do anything that would alert Malone to the DEA's interest in him and his extracurricular activities.

Mitch had made no promises and, within days of that conversation, had begun his self-commissioned undercover work. Since, he tried to go to the city two or three nights a week to surveil Malone's restaurant in the guise of one of the homeless population, which had its own societal hierarchy and rules of conduct.

In order to avoid any kind of altercation that would draw attention to him, he'd been careful not to breach anyone else's territory or even appear curious about their stuff. Nor did he buddy up to anyone. Giving mumbled, unintelligible answers to direct questions, he'd eventually been accepted as a loner and now was generally ignored.

He hadn't staked out a permanent spot for himself, but on each visit had taken up a different position along the street that had given him a vantage point from which to observe the goings-on at Roland Malone's establishment.

Few tourists happened upon Ristorante Italiano, but the place had a loyal following made up of locals, and it hadn't taken him long to mark the regulars. Some he'd recognized as people who held positions of power, while others were minor celebrities of one stripe or another, wannabes, or has-beens. Using the smallest camera possible, he'd surreptitiously taken photos and now had an extensive file.

He'd paid close attention to the customers Malone personally welcomed with demonstrative affection or deference, and then bade goodbye in a conspiratorial manner. He'd paid just as much attention to those Malone observed with a speculative scowl or overt disfavor as they left.

Each night toward closing time, Mitch had ventured into the alley behind the restaurant, where sometimes food from eateries along the avenue was given away on a first-come, first-served basis. The service door to Malone's restaurant had always remained closed except for employees going in and out, hauling garbage bags to a dumpster.

But tonight, as Mitch had entered the alley and seen a ragtag group already clustered at Malone's door, he had rushed to join them, elbowing his way to the front in the hope of catching a glimpse into Roland Malone's domain.

He'd no sooner grabbed the proffered carry-out box from a benevolent kitchen staffer than Roland Malone himself had appeared in all his greasy glory.

Mitch's heart had lurched. Until that moment, he'd seen Malone only from a distance. Suddenly, he was looking straight at the man from no more than a foot away. Only from having years of practice doing undercover work had he managed not to reveal his shock and near irresistible impulse to go for the man's throat and kill him on the spot.

Malone was built solidly and squarely. His dark suit had been tailored to perfectly fit the blocky frame. Running through his heavily waxed hair were parallel channels plowed by a comb. A diamond-studded Rolex twinkled on his left wrist.

His voice was monotonal and as weighty as an anchor, but oddly soft-spoken. It was the voice of someone devoid of emotion. If eyes emitted sound, Malone's would match his voice. They were flat, blank, emotionless, soulless. Looking into them, Mitch had been convinced they were the eyes that had passively watched as Angela died.

In the seconds they had stood facing each other, Mitch had registered and mentally catalogued as many of these details as he could.

But it wasn't until Malone had gestured when he'd ordered them to scatter that Mitch had seen the signet ring on his right pinkie finger. Its red stone had caught the bright beam of the overhead security light, flashing its fire directly into Mitch's eyes and searing his heart with savagery and exaltation.

The two emotions struck him simultaneously, one as powerful as the other. Miraculously, he managed to keep both harnessed.

But, as he'd turned away, he'd smiled into the zipped-up neck of his hoodie and whispered, "I'm on to you, cocksucker."

He had so much to think about, the ninety-minute drive home seemed to go quickly. At the storage unit, he swapped out the ratty pickup for his other with the efficiency acquired by routine.

As soon as he'd secured his apartment for the night, he rid himself of his disguise. First came off the knitted stocking cap. Sewn into it was what appeared to be straw-colored, unwashed, lice-ridden, stringy hair that draped his shoulders like an unraveling knitted shawl. It made his head itch, but it was essential.

Next, he unzipped the filthy hoodie and pulled it off inside out. Then, wincing, he peeled off the stick-on beard and mustache. If he'd actually been working undercover, he would have had to grow his own, but for a drizzly night in a dark alley, the artificial had been sufficient.

He scrubbed off the "dirt" makeup he'd learned to apply in special ops, took a hot shower, then got into bed, where, finally, he let himself relax—as much as he ever relaxed—and let his thoughts drift back to the time he'd spent in the company of his therapist.

It was time to ponder this dilemma also known as Dylan Reede.

After waving goodbye to Officer Clarence, he'd driven around the corner and pulled into one of the covered and shadowed drive-through bays of a bank across the street which had afforded him a view of the medical building's parking lot.

He hadn't had to wait long before Dylan emerged from a door with "Personnel Only" stenciled on it. She'd taken in her surroundings with a cautious look around. But not all that cautious, because she'd missed his truck. She'd then gotten into the only car left on the lot.

He'd been responsible for making her late to leave, so he'd figured the least he could do was make sure she got home safely. He'd followed her, at a distance, to one of the coveted townhomes that backed up to Auclair's only country club's golf course. He hadn't headed for New Orleans until she'd gotten inside and the lights were turned on.

When he'd first seen her this morning, he'd been struck by how attractive she was. That was a forgivable offense. He wasn't blind. But he'd kissed her only to rile her and test how she would react, not because of unbridled desire.

Tonight, however, in that small space, with no Ellie in the next room, with Dylan looking as rumpled as she had, he'd come close to kissing her again for another reason entirely: He'd wanted to.

He'd wanted to a *lot*. If his tongue had touched her lips again tonight, he would have slipped it between them, stayed a while, taken his time to taste her, and given vent to the pressure below his belt that had been increasing since he'd walked in and seen her all tousled.

Tousled was not an adjective he'd thought he would ever use in his lifetime. But here he was, using it.

Tousled Dylan, looking up at him with dazed eyes as he'd counted her heartbeats, was an altogether different animal from buttoned-up Dr. Reede tapping her pen against her notepad. Tousled Dylan had roused the animal inside him that had been sleeping since Angela's death.

He'd spent his first eighteen months as a widower in full-blown mourning. More often than not, drunken mourning. The past six months, since that fateful meeting with Jim Tucker, he'd spent plotting his vengeance against the men who'd robbed Angela of her life and Andrew of his mother.

First profound grief, then vengeful wrath, had been inhibitors to his sex drive. He'd had no interest in, nor inclination toward, romance on any level. He'd curtly rebuffed every tentative inquiry whether he was ready to start dating.

It wasn't as though he'd taken a vow of celibacy out of respect for Angela. He had loved her body and soul and would cherish the memory of her and their time together until he drew his last breath.

But she would be the first to encourage him not to live the rest of his life alone and lonely. She wouldn't want that for him or for Andrew. He wasn't against the prospect of having a future relationship. He just hadn't met a woman who'd sparked his interest.

Dylan hadn't sparked it; she'd ignited a bonfire. Even if his head and heart had rejected the very idea, his libido hadn't. But why, when his future was dependent on the success or failure of their doctor–patient relationship, had she been the one to elbow his dick awake?

If ever there was a DO NOT GO THERE, this was it.

If he still believed in the Almighty, he would take him to task over this cruel joke.

And if John could read the train of his thoughts right now, he would shit.

With all ten fingers, he raked his hair off his forehead, held it back, and asked the ceiling above his bed, *What am I going to do about this? What? What?*

But hold on. He hadn't crossed a line. Not yet. He hadn't acted on the urge to kiss her again, had he? Okay, he'd held her wrist and counted her heartbeats. Big deal. And maybe his thumb had made a few stroking passes against that super-soft skin. But it was her wrist, for crying out loud. Not her…something else.

Dylan, the buttoned-up rule-keeper, wasn't going to tell John or anybody else that he'd touched her in a way that was… *iffy*. And even iffy was a stretch. Nothing seismic had happened. This quandary was all inside his head without any actuality on which to base it. None. At all.

Bottom line? No harm, no foul. Everything would be all right if he stuck to the plan, stayed the course, and didn't think about his therapist in that light.

In soft light. Unbuttoned. Tousled. Falling apart. Under him.

Chapter 11

Dylan always arrived at her office using the door reserved for occupants only and the elevator that accessed her privacy exit. This morning, as she stepped off the elevator on the sixth floor, she was searching the bottom of her shoulder bag for her key ring, so she didn't see Mitch standing just to her left until she ran into him.

Hands raised and patting the air, he said, "Don't freak out."

Oh, God, no. Not yet. It was too soon to see him again after last night.

She would have had to face him tomorrow at his scheduled appointment, but by then she'd have had time to decompress. While in her bath, she had resolved to regard him only as a patient and reestablish the balanced, ordered life she led.

That resolution hadn't yet gained traction. She'd slept restlessly, and morning had brought its own round of upsets. She discovered she'd failed to charge her phone overnight. Each step of her two-mile jog had felt like she was slogging through quicksand. Her hair dryer had blown a fuse.

Now *him*. She was certain he had banked on catching her unexpectedly and alone in this rarely used hallway. Once again he had caught her unprepared to see him, and that made her furious, which she made no effort to hide.

"When someone tells you not to freak out, it's usually because they sense that you're on the verge of it."

"Are you?"

"Never," she snapped.

"Honestly? Never? Huh."

She ignored his feigned bafflement. "Mitch, you must stop just showing up like this. It's—"

"Against the rules. I know, I know."

"Then why are you here?"

"I didn't know how else to reach you."

"By phone?"

"I tried. I called the emergency number on your business card. Twice. Both times I got this infernal, *eternal* recording about your charges per quarter hour for unscheduled counseling by telephone." He quoted, "'If it's a life-threatening episode—'"

"*Is* this a life-threatening episode?"

"Can you be more specific?"

"Is it or not?"

"Well, depends, doesn't it? It's life-threatening to take the ramp onto the expressway. To pull your socks on while standing up. To eat sushi at a truck stop that sells live bait."

She gave him a droll look. "I won't play your straight man."

"You should at least give it a shot. You might be good at it."

When she didn't return his goading grin, he exhaled heavily.

"Okay, no more joking. I really did need to talk to you as soon as possible this morning, and intercepting you was the only way I knew to go about it."

Reminding herself to think of him only as a patient in need of psychological help, she dialed down her annoyance. "If you genuinely feel an urgency to talk to me today rather than wait until tomorrow, call the office number." She checked her wristwatch. "Ellie is due in ten minutes. I'll tell her to work you in. For now, you'll have to excuse me."

She sidestepped, but he did the same to block her. They kept up that dance until he said, "Bowie put a patrol officer on my tail last night."

She stopped her efforts to go around him. "Why did he do that?"

"Yesterday, when I learned that you hadn't told John about *the kiss*, essentially giving me no choice except to continue our sessions, he and I had words, and I left headquarters in a huff."

"I'm guessing it was more than a huff."

"Well, apparently John thought so."

"That's why he had you followed?"

He gave a curt nod. "My tail, this young cop named Clarence, reported to him that I'd broken into this building. John jumped to the conclusion that I'd come here to take my anger out on you."

"You mean physically?"

"That was the implication." Her genuine shock must've shown because he followed up quickly. "That's right," he said with bitterness. "Can you believe it? Made me livid, and I told him so."

He described how he'd exited the building unseen and surprised the officer who'd been dispatched to spy on him. "I took

Clarence's phone and lit into John. I assured him that when I left you, you were sound of body and mind."

The statement ended with the hint of a question mark, which she pretended not to notice. "I regret that this drove another wedge between you," she said, meaning it. "Where did you leave it with him?"

"He apologized. Still, it was an insult that I won't soon forget."

She stared at the V-shaped depression under his Adam's apple as she thought that through, then looked into his face again and gave him a small smile. "I think you care for John Bowie and his opinion of you more than you're willing to admit. You're on the outs. That happens between even the best of friends.

"But I understand why you're upset. A slight from a good friend hurts more than a slight from someone who doesn't matter so much."

He watched her for a moment, then hooked his thumbs into his belt and rested his hands on his hips. "That sounded like shrink talk. Are you going to charge me for this session? If so, I prefer your parlor sofa with all the pillows to standing out here in the hall."

This was only the third time she'd seen the man, yet she'd become familiar with his shrewd squint and the lines it caused to radiate from the corners of his eyes. He tilted his head to a certain angle whenever he was appraising her, as he was now.

Realizing just how familiar and attractive those characteristics had become to her, realizing how badly she wanted to smile, she pulled her gaze from his and looked at her watch again.

"My first patient is due in fifteen minutes. We'll begin your next session by addressing Bowie's hasty judgment and how it affected you. Ellie will be at her desk by now. Call her to reschedule for later today."

"No need. I only came to explain the situation and give you a heads-up. John will be calling you to ask about my visit here last night."

"If you made it clear to him that all was well, I doubt he'll contact me."

He shook his head. "I guarantee that he will. He's a thorough son of a bitch. He'll want your word for it. He'll want to hear from your own lips that I didn't lay a hand on you." He waited a beat, closed the distance between them by an inch, then, very low, asked, "What will you tell him, Dylan?"

They stared at each other long enough for her to know that she would soon be in violation of her own guidelines and boundaries as yet to be drawn. She had to move away from him.

This time, he didn't block her. She walked to the private exit door before turning and answering his question in the coolest voice she could muster. "I won't tell Bowie anything except to remind him that what we talk about in our sessions is confidential."

"Confidentiality. Your number one rule."

"Yes."

"Just checking to see if you had changed your mind about that."

"I'll never change my mind about that."

He gave a hitch of his chin. "Right."

He punched the down button on the elevator, and it opened immediately. After stepping in, he turned and gave her a look that originated not only from his eyes. His entire aspect was behind that look. It caused a purling sensation where she definitely should not be feeling one. He held that look until the door slid closed.

Almost frantically, she went digging into her shoulder bag in search of her key ring, that damn elusive key ring that refused to be found. Then, surrendering to her shakiness, she pressed her forehead against the cool metal surface of the door.

Dylan, what are you doing, what are you thinking? You cannot do this.

The keys, which she hadn't realized she'd located, were being squeezed so tightly they were digging into her palm. She fumbled with them until she isolated the right one. But when she went to insert it into the old-fashioned lock, the doorknob turned in her hand. She gave a slight push, and the door swung open.

She stared, frowning with puzzlement as she wondered how that could be when she distinctly remembered locking the door behind herself when she had left last night.

Then, with a soft gasp of realization, she looked back toward the elevator. It had already reached the ground floor.

Chapter 12

You suck. The slogan stands. I'm the King of Cash, and I'm staying the King of Cash. Don't bug me about it again or I'll switch advertising agencies. If I pull my account, your agency will fire you."

"No, I wouldn't want that, Mr. Busby. You're our most valued client. I just thought—"

"Didn't I just tell you what I thought about what you thought? Now get out of here. They're waiting for me on the set."

The humiliated young man left the makeup room with his laptop tucked under his arm and his tail between his legs.

Allen Busby sat at a dressing table in front of a lighted mirror. He smiled into it at the young woman who was applying under-eye concealer with a sponge. "Do you think I was too hard on him?"

She smiled back and asked him to look up, please. "I'd say he got what he had coming. Why would you fix something that ain't broke?"

He laughed. "Why indeed?" She finished with one last dab and stepped back so he could assess her handiwork. Turning his head this way and that, and liking what he saw, he said, "Thank you, sweetheart. Another excellent job."

He whipped the protective towel out from under his white shirt collar and walked into the studio, eagerly rubbing his hands together. "Ready to roll!" he called out to the production crew.

Over the course of the next two hours, Allen Busby recorded six new commercials for his namesake law firm, which handled personal injury cases exclusively and was dedicated to exposing and crushing the alleged rip-off schemes of insurance companies. With his hand over his heart, he pledged never to abandon a case until a client was awarded the money he or she was rightfully owed for the pain and suffering they'd endured. Phone lines were open twenty-four/seven to take calls.

"I'm the King of Cash. If you've been injured in an accident, call me first! Call me now!"

His sixty-second commercials were overblown productions of which he was the undisputed star. These high-octane recording sessions would have exhausted an ordinary individual, but they were energizing to Allen Busby. He was pumped as he strode off the set, hailing the production team as the best in the world, thanking them for making him look and sound good.

The King of Cash was known by millions of TV viewers whether they wanted to be exposed to him or not. His commercials ran around the clock on multiple networks. His face was on billboards and the sides of city buses. In his flagship office in New Orleans and in annexes in three states, hundreds of minions toiled like worker bees to keep up with the demand for the firm's services.

The irony was that Allen Busby had never handled a lawsuit, in court or out.

He'd earned a law degree, but the flamboyant, high-profile pitchman on TV was a caricature that he had conceived and perfected for another purpose: to protect his reclusive alter ego, Oz.

While the law firm was ridiculously lucrative, it earned only 10 percent of his wealth. The other 90 was generated not by the King of Cash, but by Oz, the kingpin.

Twelve-year-olds selling fentanyl-laced pills to their middle school classmates probably had never heard of Allen Busby, or the King of Cash, for that matter.

But they knew Oz's name. They were in awe of him, revering and fearing him in equal measure. Undoubtedly some harbored a secret aspiration to one day overthrow him and become head of the cartel themselves, but none would ever speak of such an audacious ambition. It would be like trying to unseat God from his throne in heaven.

Feeling exceptionally springy today, Busby exited the building where he'd recorded. His chauffeur, having been notified that he was on his way out, was standing by to open the car door for him. "There's ice in the cooler, Mr. Busby."

"Thank you."

Allen Busby didn't use any of the controlled substances he peddled. He didn't smoke tobacco. He didn't drink alcohol.

Once he was settled into the luxurious back seat of his Bentley, he filled a glass with ice from the cooler built into the door, poured a can of Mountain Dew over it, and drank it while en route to his sixteen-room mansion in the Garden District.

The property was enclosed by a wall ten feet high and shrouded in leafy ivy that concealed concertina wire and the components of a continually monitored security system that was more sophisticated than that of the White House.

He lived there alone. No wife. No kids. No thank you.

For appearance's sake, he occasionally squired an attractive woman to this or that social or charity event. He slept with a few of them. But the accumulation of wealth was what really turned him on. On the ecstasy chart, sex ranked much lower than maintaining the secret that he was amassing a fortune, illegally and directly under the nose of the entire world.

Throughout history, had there ever been a better inside joke?

Upon arriving home, he sequestered himself in a soundproofed room that he personally swept each day for listening devices. He got a fresh Mountain Dew from the mini fridge and set it on the table next to his favorite easy chair. He shrugged out of his suit jacket, loosened his tie, toed out of his shoes, and put his feet on the ottoman.

Allen Busby was done for the day.

Oz's workday was just beginning.

He called Roland Malone, who answered on the second ring. "You done recording?"

"I just got home."

"How'd it go?"

"Another day at the salt mine."

Malone made a grunting sound that passed for his laugh. "Did you fire the ad guy?"

"Didn't have to. I issued a threat. It took."

"Good."

Oz said, "As you predicted, the lead story on last night's news was about the two bodies found in Bayou Coeur. Any buzz about how the investigation is faring?"

"Last I heard, no identity on the girl yet. No leads on where the two were killed. No motive. My worry factor is at negative five."

Busby's worry factor was never that low. "I asked you to be on standby this week."

"I always am. But why particularly this week?"

"Because, as of last night, the Caballeros are short three truckloads of product, now headed east."

Roland went still. He even stopped turning his ring. "Holy shit, you really did it."

It smarted a bit that Oz had carried out a scheme that he'd proposed to Roland months earlier, and which Roland had advised against.

Oz had presented a large-scale heist as a way to profit by "brokering a deal," when what it amounted to was stealing product from a notoriously vicious Mexican cartel, then turning around and selling it to a customer in St. Louis who was eagerly standing by with suitcases of cash.

"Then," Oz had told Roland, "as an act of good will, I'll give a share to the Caballeros."

Roland thought the idea stunk. First off, you didn't mess with the Caballeros unless you were looking to die. Second, they weren't accustomed to being treated as a Johnny-come-lately cartel and having someone, even the mighty Oz, brokering their deals for them. Certainly without their prior knowledge. They would regard the theft of their product as *theft*, pure and simple, and weren't likely to favor settling for a good-will-gesture share when they could have trafficked it themselves and kept every peso.

But rather than squelch Oz's enthusiasm, apparently Roland's cautionary advice had done just the opposite. Roland figured the ballsy move had appealed to Oz's ego and tipped the scale in favor of his going through with it. It had been a challenge he'd been unable to resist.

He said now, "Our people got in, got out. I doubt the Caballeros even know it's missing yet."

"Congratulations."

"A little soon to be popping corks. Those trucks have a lot of ground to cover. ETA by the end of the week, but could be earlier or later. That's why I wanted you ready to act at a moment's notice. And why I didn't want anything going wrong this week."

"Understood, boss. So maybe I should hold off on this."

"What? A problem?"

"A nuisance. The homeless riffraff around here are getting bold. Last night a bunch of them showed up at my kitchen door. Staff were giving them handouts."

"Bad for your business, bad for mine."

"Exactly. I'm thinking of putting this kid, El Paso, on it."

"What's his real name?"

"I think we're better off not knowing."

"Put him on it how?"

"Have him dole out some *discouragement* to the derelicts. Send a message that they're not to come anywhere near my place again, or else."

"Hmm."

"But the kid is officially your employee, so I wanted to run it past you first. One or two unfortunate incidents ought to fix the problem."

"Fine. Use him. But nothing fancy that would draw attention. Have him keep it low-key."

"Absolutely."

Thoughtfully, Busby reached for his drink and took a sip straight from the can. "You haven't mentioned Mitch Haskell."

"Oh, yeah. Forgot. He went to see a shrink yesterday."

"So he gave in to Bowie?"

"Not entirely." Roland told him about another quarrel between the two. "I'm told it was more heated than the previous ones. Haskell kicked his desk chair before storming out."

"What set it off?"

"Haskell didn't want to continue therapy. Bowie stuck to his guns. At this point, how the feud unfolds is anybody's guess."

"Hmm," Busby said again. He wasn't a big fan of guesswork. "Who's the shrink?"

"A Dr. Dylan Reede."

"What do you know about him?"

"It's a her."

"Interesting choice."

"My plant says she was a random pick. And actually, the more I got to thinking about it, the more I believe a female is a good thing."

"How's that?"

"Maternal instinct. If Haskell talks to her about the death of his wife, she'll mother him. Sympathize, urge him to stop drinking, make amends with Bowie, find a new love. Like that. Now, whether or not Haskell takes her advice remains to be seen."

Busby said, "I don't favor waiting to see. Why don't we save ourselves the anticipation and simply eliminate the problem?"

"You want to hit Haskell? Now?" Roland's tone implied rejection of the idea.

"Why not?"

"He's got a spotlight on him because of his current battle with Bowie. As that drama unfolds, we're not the only ones watching to see what's gonna happen next between the two of them. With all the attention he's getting, we'd be risking exposure to make a move on him, especially during a week when you don't want anything to go wrong."

That was a reasonable point, but Malone's reluctance didn't sit well with him. For the time being, he tabled the subject and decided to give it more thought. "You think this El Paso can handle your problem with the homeless?"

"Oh, yeah. He's a mean little bastard."

"Tell him not to be too mean. Keep it simple."

"I'll impress that on him."

"Let me know how it works out." Saying nothing further, Busby clicked off. But for a long while, he ruminated on the bothersome matter of Mitch Haskell talking about the death of his wife with a therapist.

He made a mental note to find out more about Dr. Dylan Reede.

Roland was at the hostess stand looking over the dinner reservations for the evening when El Paso pushed through the swinging kitchen doorway and sauntered into the dining room like it was he who owned the place.

He topped out at around five feet five and was slight of build, but he had the aggressiveness and voracity of a wolverine. If Roland didn't know better, he would think the kid filed his teeth into sharp points.

As he came toward Roland, he took in his surroundings, a smirk of derision on his face, as though amused by all the finery. "You wanted to see me?"

Roland didn't deign to reply. Instead he turned to his maître d' and gave his approval of the seating chart for tonight's most important diners. He then headed for his office, assuming the kid would follow, which he did.

"Shut the door."

After doing so, El Paso, without invitation, flopped into the chair facing Roland, who had sat down behind his desk. "Niiiice," El Paso said after surveying the office.

Roland wanted to smack him on principle. "There's something I want you to do for me. I've cleared it with Oz, and he—"

"Who is he anyway? This Oz character."

Roland gave him several slow blinks, then continued as though the kid hadn't spoken. "Oz gave his approval."

El Paso shot him a sly grin. "The head honcho's identity is a big secret, huh?"

Roland leaned back in his chair and rotated his ring around his pinkie several times as he stared at the younger man. "Maybe you're not suitable to work in this organization, after all."

"Naw, naw. I was just—"

"You were being an arrogant dickhead, which you can't afford to be. Lots of people would like to know your current whereabouts. David." He kept his cold stare fixed on the kid, who'd suddenly become a lot less smug.

"David Rodriguez," Roland continued. "DOB October twenty-sixth, 2005. You think I believed that bullshit story about a girl you knocked up?" He rolled his ring around his finger. "Don't fuck with me again."

El Paso chewed the inside of his cheek through an uncomfortable silence, then, with more civility, asked, "What do you want me to do?"

He explained the problem and what he wanted done about it.

"Keep it low-key. Simple," he said, using Oz's word. "No

grand gestures, nothing that would draw the cops. Just get the message across that these lowlifes are to steer clear of Ristorante Italiano."

El Paso nodded. "Sure. I can do that. When do I start?"

"You know the neighborhood?"

"Not good. I just got here."

"Take tonight to scope it out, get a feel for the area. Strike tomorrow night."

El Paso shrugged. "Sure, okay. Is that it?"

"That's it. Now get the hell out of here."

He snuffled a laugh, said, "Yes, sir," rolled out of the chair, and saw himself to the door. He made an exaggerated effort to close it without making a sound.

Turd.

But as soon as the kid was gone, Roland focused his thoughts on the more complex matters raised during his conversation with Oz. Of all the people working for Oz in one capacity or another, Roland was the only one who knew his identity. And that had happened more or less by accident.

The first time Allen Busby had come into the restaurant for dinner, Roland had recognized him as the carnival barker on TV, but hadn't made out like he knew him. Busby had eaten alone and had spent a lot of time on his cell phone.

Then, Roland hadn't known that Busby was exchanging texts with a swarthy, elegantly dressed diner who was at another table. Also a first-timer at the restaurant.

The two hadn't acknowledged each other at all. As Busby left, he'd shaken Roland's hand, complimented him on the food and service, and promised to return soon.

After all the staff had left, Roland had gone around checking locks. Through the door into the alley, he'd heard raised voices and had opened the door just in time to see the South American type produce a pistol and aim it at Busby's forehead.

Never one to miss an opportunity to make friends with a celebrity, Roland had his garrote out and around the man's neck in under a second. He'd struggled, of course. But Busby had done nothing to dissuade Roland, had just stood there and watched, and, when the tension on the garrote was released, the man dropped to the alley pavement, dead.

Busby had taken a breath, patted down his hair, and straightened his necktie. "Much obliged."

"No problem."

"What do we do with him?"

"You? Nothing. I'll take care of his disappearance."

"He's got enemies and allies. They'll all come asking."

"I don't even know his name. First time he's been to my place. How would I know where he went or who he saw after? Do the enemies and allies know you?"

Busby shook his head.

"Then don't worry."

"What do I owe you?"

"You just watched me kill a man in cold blood, and I'm gonna ask you for money? No."

"I've never seen anything like that," he'd said of the garrote.

"You never will." A cousin in the Bronx custom made them for him. "Once used, it's disposed of."

Busby looked down at the body, then back up at Roland. "You do this often?"

Something in Roland's implacable gaze must've been answer enough. Busby held out his right hand. "Allen Busby."

"I know who you are."

He'd flashed a smile that was startlingly white even in the dark alley. "Not really. But you're going to."

That had been seven years ago. He'd started working for Oz that night by being given a list of other people Oz would like to have disappear. Over time, Oz had also come to rely on him as a sounding board. By now, Roland had earned his complete trust.

Tonight, for instance, Oz had confessed to stealing millions of dollars' worth of goods from the Caballeros, who weren't going to take the theft lightly. Then he'd turned right around and stressed that he didn't want anything to go wrong this week. That looked like tightrope-walking to Roland.

Oz also continued to harp on Haskell. God forbid that the boss get the impression he was going soft on the detective, especially in view of this week's happenings. He saw the need to seize the initiative, do something moderately chancy that he could report to Oz as a step toward Haskell's annihilation. But what? If he got anywhere near Haskell...

But maybe he didn't have to. Minutes ago, hadn't he advised El Paso to check things out, gauge the situation before striking?

Suddenly motivated, he swiveled his chair around to the console behind his desk. A lower drawer concealed a built-in safe with an old-fashioned dial lock. Inside it, amid bricks of banded currency, several pistols, boxes of bullets, and two new garrotes in standby readiness, was a seldom used burner phone. He checked the battery, saw it had enough of a charge, and tapped in a familiar number.

"This is Dr. Reede."

"Hi, Dylan. It's Roland Malone."

"Roland, hello," she said, sounding surprised and pleased. "I haven't heard from you in a while."

"I've been busy. You know, the restaurant and all. How are things in Auclair?"

"Hot and muggy."

"Here, too. Different summer, same swelter."

After covering the weather, there was a lag, then she said, "I'm glad you called. It's been weeks since you've come in. How are you doing?"

"I'm okay, but, you know, like you said, it's been a while. I could use an appointment."

"Of course. When were you thinking?"

"As soon as possible."

Chapter 13

Mitch's Wednesday morning began with a visit to Child Protective Services to talk to a caseworker about one of his ongoing investigations. Three young children, living with their mother and her boyfriend, had gone to neighbors asking for help after being beaten black and blue and bloody. One of them was still in the hospital recovering from a head injury.

Now at his desk in the CAP unit, Mitch finished writing his report on the status of the case for the assistant DA who would be prosecuting the two offenders. His own report left him depressed and feeling pessimistic about the redemption of humankind.

The only tonic for this particular type of despair was to talk to Andrew, whose laughter was like a reboot, a refresher. He called Mary, and she put Andrew on.

Mitch chatted with his son for about ten minutes before Mary came back on the line. He remarked on Andrew's crankiness. "Don't take it personally," she said. "He's had a busy morning and needs a nap."

"He told me something about a bunny rabbit, but the details escaped me."

"They had one at the preschool roundup. Andrew was fixated on it. We had trouble moving him along to other—"

"Hey, back up a minute. What preschool?"

"We can talk about it when you're not busy."

"I'm not busy now."

He could visualize her straightening her shoulders and taking a breath in preparation to tell him something she had procrastinated about. "We've enrolled him in the fall semester of the parish's preschool. Today was the first of three roundups. They're like orientations for first-timers to become familiar with the school environment and get to know their teacher before the start of the semester, which is the week after Labor Day."

Mitch had listened in stunned silence while, with every word, his fury had increased exponentially. By the time she'd finished what had sounded like a scripted explanation, he was seeing red. He also doubted that Hank had played any part in this. There was no *we*. *She* had enrolled Andrew.

"Let me get this straight," he said. "You—"

"Don't take that tone with me, Mitch."

"You enrolled my son in preschool before consulting me?"

"I had to grab a spot. They were filling up quickly."

"Too quickly for you to make a phone call?"

She didn't respond to that. "It'll be good for him, Mitch. He'll learn social skills, how to interact with other children. It's only two mornings a week. I know the teacher of his age group. She's a very nice lady and great with the kids. You have no reason to get angry over this."

"Too late. I'm already angry, Mary, and I have every reason to be."

"The school has a wonderful program."

"I'm sure it does. I'm not against the school, or the idea of it. I'm angry at *you* for taking it upon yourself to do this without one single mention of it to me. I'm his father, goddamn it!"

"An *absent* father." The harshness with which she'd fired back seemed to surprise even her. It was a moment before she continued. "Andrew is now at an age where your absence could affect his development. Socially, emotionally, the way he perceives and forms relationships, every way."

This was the first time she'd ever said anything like that to him, and it made him irate. It also made his blood run cold.

"Mitch?"

He swiveled his head around. John was beckoning him from the door of his office. Mitch pointed to his phone and held up his index finger, asking to be given a minute.

"Mary, I have to go, but we're not done talking about this. Not by a long shot."

"Mitch," she sighed. "I know you love Andrew."

He wasn't about to gush confirmations of that. To do so would sound either defensive or penitent. "I want to visit the school and talk to the teacher myself."

"Of course. I'll set it up."

"Mitch?"

John again. Mitch cupped his hand over the mouthpiece. "Be right there. I'm signing off." Back to Mary, he asked if there was tuition to be paid.

"I had to put up half in order to enroll him."

"Text me what I owe you."

"You don't have to worry about—"

Enunciating each word, he said, "Text me how much I owe the school for Andrew's tuition."

"All right. Take care."

"Hold on. I'm not finished." He took a stabilizing breath. "Unless it's a medical emergency, don't you ever make another major decision regarding my son without consulting me."

"Mitch!"

"*Coming*," he shouted to John over his shoulder. Then into the phone, "Did you get that, Mary? Not *ever.*"

He disconnected without a goodbye, pushed away from his desk, and stalked over to where John was waiting for him, a deep cleft of concern between his eyebrows. "Everything okay?"

"No."

"Want to talk about it?"

"No."

He shouldered past John and went into the office, where he pinched the bridge of his nose and took a moment to compose himself. Mary's comments about his being an absent father hadn't been off-the-cuff. She'd given this a lot of thought, and her underlying message had left him both annoyed and spooked. Like walking into a spider web.

But he felt John scrutinizing him, so, for now, he shelved that issue and focused on his job. He asked, "What's up?"

John motioned him into a chair. "You look upset."

"Mary."

John went around his desk and sat down. "Andrew all right?"

Mitch gave a half smile. "He's great. He met a bunny rabbit today. Make that *w*abbit."

John smiled. "He's overdue a visit with Uncle John and Aunt Beth."

"How's Beth doing?"

"Fine. Getting close."

"Another month?"

"Doctor says maybe sooner."

"Those last few weeks are tough on them."

John nodded. "Beth says she looks like a whale."

"With Angela it was a blimp. I thought she looked beautiful."

"She did."

An awkward silence followed the mention of her name. Mitch turned his head to look out the window. John shifted in his desk chair, making the springs squeak, but eventually he eased into the reason for summoning Mitch into his office.

"Sorry for rushing your call," he said, "but Lear and Nix are on their way in from Bayou Coeur. I needed to talk to you before they get here."

Mitch's spirits lifted. "Darcy asked for our assistance with the investigation?"

"This morning. It didn't take him long to draw a parallel between this double homicide and your former colleague's, Randy Nelson. Almost identical MO. The DEA has nosed in."

"Which comes as no surprise," Mitch said.

John nodded. "But they don't want it advertised that they're involved. Darcy emphasized that, and so did Jim Tucker."

"You talked to Tucker?"

"About you. He called shortly after I'd spoken to Darcy. Tucker thought I should know that you're still sporting a hard-on for Roland Malone."

"Metaphorically speaking, of course," he quipped.

"This is no joking matter, Mitch. Tucker said to tell you that he's got people on 'that element,' and that you are *not* to interfere. He wants to keep Malone clueless of their interest."

"Message delivered and received." Mitch placed his hands on the arms of the chair and was about to stand up to go.

John stopped him. "Stay. As I'm speaking, Nix and Lear are coming this way to break the news to us about the Nelson murder connection to Bayou Coeur. Act surprised, and not a word about Malone. Tucker was adamant about that."

Mitch turned his head just as Nix thrust open the office door and strode in, Lear trailing her with less vigor. Mitch turned back to John. "Darcy asked for our help, and you assigned them?"

"That's right."

"John—"

"If you have a problem with that, we'll discuss it later."

"You bet your ass we will."

After a moment of palpable tension, John offered Nix the extra chair, but she remained standing. Lear propped his butt on the window sill, causing the blinds to rattle, which momentarily reminded Mitch of Dylan's office window.

Nix had either anointed herself spokesperson, or she and Lear had agreed ahead of time that she would take the lead. In any case, she did.

"Darcy finally got an ID on the girl." She referred to an iPad she'd brought in with her. "Mandy Adams. Seventeen years old, came from a small town in central Mississippi. Several months ago, she ran away. She'd been expelled from school for drug usage on campus, and not for the first time.

"Two notable ironies. Her mother is on the faculty of the high school that expelled her, and her dad is the town pharmacist. Both of them are well-respected pillars of the community. This girl was a disaster waiting to happen."

Mitch, who'd been focused on a nick in the wood on the edge of John's desk, didn't raise his head, but lifted his gaze to Nix and said, "That would be a catchy epitaph for her." The statement was laden with anger and sarcasm.

"Mitch," John said in a chastening tone.

Mitch looked at John, then at Nix, and said, "Mandy Adams might have been trouble, but I don't think she was waiting for a disaster like almost being decapitated. Some mean fuck did that to her."

A strained silence lasted until Lear bravely cleared his throat and contributed to the discussion for the first time. "I was with Darcy when he questioned her parents. They hadn't heard from her since she ran away. They didn't know where she was or how she was surviving. No idea who Paul Adler was, or how she'd come to be with him. They're devastated. Her body will be released to them tomorrow."

Nix gave the devastated parents five seconds of respectful silence before resuming. "One big development today. The DEA is now in on the investigation. One of their agents was killed in a similar manner a few years ago. Darcy told us you knew him," she said to Mitch.

"Yeah. He and I worked closely together for a while. He was killed six, seven months after I left the agency. When he was reported missing, John and I were tipped by a junkie we had in jail here in Auclair. He was trying to swing a plea deal and wanted to barter information.

"He told us that the last time he'd been in New Orleans, he'd heard scuttlebutt on the street that an undercover fed had been dumped in Bayou Coeur. John and I had fished in that channel, so we were familiar with it. We assembled a search and recovery team. Took us two days, but we found Nelson's body tangled up in the root system of a cypress grove."

John picked up there. "We leaned on the snitch to tell us where Nelson had been killed and by whom. He was a weasel. If he'd have known, he would have given it up. He didn't."

"You never had a suspect?"

Mitch looked at John, who sat in granite-jawed silence, his eyes sending a silent warning for him not to go against Jim Tucker's stern instruction that Roland Malone's name was not to be breathed. "No," Mitch replied in a clipped tone. "Nary a suspect."

Nix asked, "Do you think the same person killed these two?"

"It's not my case," Mitch said, "but if I were a betting man..." He raised his hands, letting them fill in what should be the logical conclusion.

"Any leads at all?" John asked.

"The entire area has been searched for footprints and tire tracks," Nix said. "None found so far."

"Whoever disposed of the bodies would have conveyed them by boat," John said. "As Mitch knows, that bayou meanders for miles, doubling back on itself, has dozens of tributaries that branch off and either dead end or feed into other channels. They could have put in anywhere. I'm sure Darcy will keep searching for that spot, but I'm not optimistic he'll find it."

Nix consulted her device again, then lowered it to her side. "That's all for now, I think."

Lear stood up. "Darcy's also got deputies searching for the weapon, but—"

"They won't find it anywhere near where the bodies were dumped," Mitch said. "They weren't killed there."

"What I meant," Lear said patiently, "is that he's got people looking for where one goes to buy a garrote like that."

"It would have been custom made," Mitch said, "and I'm betting—maybe I am a betting man—that it wasn't made anywhere around here."

John summed up the meeting by asking the two detectives to keep him apprised of developments. Even Nix looked dispirited as she and Lear left.

"Unless you need me for anything," Mitch said as he stood up.

"Stay a minute. Close the door."

Mitch did, asking, "Do I need to sit back down?"

"I'll make it brief. I spoke with Dr. Reede yesterday. She said she'd seen you that morning."

Mitch chuckled. "I went to tell her to expect a call from you about Monday night."

"I sensed that she was more miffed at me for being worried you might take your anger out on her, and less miffed at you for showing up at her office after hours."

"She indicated that to me, too."

John arched his eyebrow. "Monday morning's appointment. Again Monday night. Then yesterday morning. That's three visits within twenty-four hours."

"Let's see, two on Monday, plus one. Yep, that's three." Mitch raised his shoulders in an innocent gesture, like he didn't understand what John was getting at, although he knew exactly what he was getting at.

"And you'll see her again tomorrow?" John said.

"Ten o'clock. And, lest I piss you off, I don't dare be late."

John lowered his voice. "Just be sure to stay focused on the purpose of seeing her."

Mitch narrowed his eyes and shook his index finger at John. "You know what this reminds me of? About two and a half years ago. Remember? Sure you remember. Your life wasn't worth shit."

John squirmed in his chair causing it to squeak again.

"Then this woman unexpectedly enters it," Mitch continued. "Her name is Beth. She's a looker. She's also a suspected loony tune because she thinks there's a serial killer on the loose who's going to strike again on the night of the impending blood moon. Like you didn't already have enough crap to deal with, you got all hepped up about her hypothesis.

"And I remember—now correct me if I'm wrong—that you enlisted my help, which I was glad to provide. But I also remember pulling you aside and asking if you were getting all excited about cracking the Mellin cold case based on Beth's wacky, way-out-there theory, or if it was Beth her own self who had you as randy as a billy goat."

"And I remember telling you to fuck off."

Mitch laughed. "In so many words."

"Is that what you're telling me to do now?" John asked.

"In so many words."

They held stares. Mitch didn't know what John was thinking, but he was thinking that they were on familiar ground here, and he missed it. He missed the guy talk you could only swap with a best friend with whom you shared so many memories, good and bad.

But he wouldn't, *couldn't* crack. All he said was, "See ya," and went over to the door.

"Mitch."

Heaving a sigh, he turned back.

"Don't forget what Tucker said about Malone."

"There's nothing wrong with my memory."

"It's not your memory I worry about. It's your judgment. Don't do anything rash."

He gave John a mock salute, then yanked the door open and soundly pulled it shut. Ignoring the curious observation of his colleagues, he returned to his desk, where he'd left his phone. He picked it up and saw that he'd received a text from Mary.

> Tomorrow morning 10 a.m. The teacher will meet you at the school to escort you around. I've told Andrew you're coming. He can't wait to show you the bunny.

Mitch dropped his phone back onto his desk. Fabulous. She'd scheduled him on the one day and time that he had to be somewhere else.

Chapter 14

Dylan left her office shortly after seven o'clock following her last patient's session. As she turned onto her street, she saw a black vehicle parked at the curb in front of her townhouse. The darkly tinted windows, oversized tires, brush guard, light bar, and winch made it look more like a monster truck.

Incongruously, it had a child seat.

Mitch Haskell got out of it as she pulled into her driveway.

She slammed her car door and marched across her lawn to where he stood waiting. She wasted no time on niceties. "My office door was unlocked yesterday morning. Did you break in before I got there? Did you pick the lock again?"

"Guilty."

She was astonished. "You admit it?"

"Why deny it?"

"How dare you? What were you doing inside my office?"

"Looking to see if you were there."

"Did you try knocking?"

"Twice."

"When I didn't answer, didn't that signify that I wasn't there?"

"It signified that you could have been in your inner office, or in the waiting room, or using the ladies'. I poked my head in and called your name. About that time, I heard the elevator on its way up."

His explanation had been so casually and guiltlessly given, it was either the truth or a facile lie. She suspected the latter. "I shouldn't have let you get away with breaking in on Monday night. But don't ever do it again. If you do, I'll report it to John Bowie."

"I didn't see the harm, but I won't do it again."

She glanced beyond him toward his SUV. "How did you know where I live?"

"I'm a cop."

"Don't be cute."

"Fine. Full transparency. I followed you home Monday night."

A second admission, no less surprising.

"In my defense," he continued, "you shouldn't have been leaving alone. Downtown is practically deserted at that time of night except for predators on the hunt for easy pickin's like you. Were you armed?"

"You mean with a gun?"

"A gun, pepper spray, brass knuckles, slingshot, pea shooter, anything?"

"I wasn't armed."

"What I thought. Walking to your car in the dark like that—"

"There's a light in the parking lot."

"One. With a forty-watt bulb that flickers. It only makes it easier for a bad guy to spot you."

"Or *stalk* me."

That stopped his banter cold. He placed his hands on his hips, lowered his head, and stared down at the ground, then gave the street a slow visual sweep before coming back to her. "Pretty cul de sac."

"Thank you. What are you doing on it?"

"I'm not being cute, Dylan," he said with a sigh. "I need to talk to you. For real. No bullshit, no joking."

He seemed serious. He looked downcast. For all her misgivings where he was concerned, she found herself believing him. "You have an appointment tomorrow morning."

"I can't make it. That's why I'm here."

"You could have called."

"And gone through that endless menu I've memorized by now? It took less time to drive here."

"How did you know that I would be at home?"

"I took a chance. It's that important. Can we talk? You can add the time to John's tab. Double your normal rate." He flashed a half grin. Still, she hesitated, and he picked up on it. "Look, we don't have to go inside. We can sit in my truck, or in your car."

Those confines would feel even more intimate and inappropriate. She shook her head.

"Okay, what if we went someplace public?"

"You want to talk about something 'that important' with other people around?"

"I'd rather not, but if you make that a condition, I will."

"Like where?"

"There's that café at the highway turnoff. The one with the blue neon crawfish on the sign. Never have understood why it's blue and not red, but how about there?"

To give herself time either to talk herself out of this or to rationalize agreeing to it, she looked at her wristwatch. But she already knew she was going to agree to it. "I'll meet you there in fifteen minutes."

"You promise? You're not just saying that to get me to leave so you can lock yourself inside your house? I can pick locks, you know."

Tightly, she repeated, "I'll meet you there in fifteen minutes."

He gave her a thumbs-up, jogged back to his truck, and drove away.

Telling herself that she must be crazy, that she was the one in desperate need of therapy, she retrieved her briefcase from her car, let herself inside the house, and went straight upstairs to her bedroom. She changed from work clothes and heels into a pair of jeans, a white tee, and a black linen jacket. Black flats for shoes. All very tailored. Definitely not date clothes.

She brushed out her ponytail, but made a fresh one even tighter than the original. She applied lip gloss. Looking at herself in the mirror, she said, "That will do." But on her way out, she changed her mind, and went back to whisk her cheeks with blush and her lashes with mascara.

When she got to the café, she pulled in beside Mitch where he'd parked at the side of the building. They didn't verbally greet each other, although she was aware of him looking her over.

As they entered the café, a waitress trundled past them carrying a large tray loaded with platters of food. "What'll y'all be wantin' to drink?" They ordered iced teas. She nodded. "Sit wherever. I'll find you."

Mitch gestured toward an unoccupied booth in a less busy section. It was only large enough for a party of two. When they slid in across from each other, their knees bumped.

"Sorry," he said. "I'll go right, you go left." She was aware of him stretching his legs out, taking up most of the empty space under the table.

When they were situated, he said, "Are you sure you wouldn't rather have a glass of wine? A beer?"

"No thank you. Would *you* rather?"

"God, yes," he said with a groan. "But I'm abstaining. Have you been here before? Food's good."

"This isn't a social occasion, Mitch."

He bobbed his chin. "Right."

The waitress delivered two tall glasses of iced tea and laid a pair of laminated menus on the table. "When y'all are ready."

Once she was out of earshot, Dylan asked, "What's keeping you from tomorrow's appointment?"

"Straight to the point, then?"

"You're on the clock."

"Got it." He sat back and drew a breath. "My mother-in-law." He took a sip of tea, then cupped his fingers around the glass and moved them up and down, collecting condensation.

Dylan had noticed his hands before. The backs of them were ropy with plump veins, his fingers slender and strong-looking. They were the hands of a soldier, but one who would admit to shedding tears while watching his son sleep.

She tried not to think about how much she liked that combination, and instead to concentrate on why he'd sought her out. If it was about his mother-in-law, it must relate to his son, which would qualify it as being "that important."

"I've already told you that I don't know what I would have done without my in-laws," he said. "But Mary and I butt heads every now and then, and today was one of those times."

He told her what Mary had done. "I'm all for Andrew going

to preschool," he said. "What pisses me off is that she took the liberty to get him enrolled before I even knew about it."

"You have every right to be angry, Mitch. She assumed a parental privilege and authority, which rightfully belonged to you. Did you ever grant her permission to make decisions such as this before consulting you?"

"No." He looked down at the menu and traced the outline of the blue crawfish with his fingertip. Then he said with chagrin, "Or maybe I did. Not outrightly, nothing said, nothing written down. But I might have conceded the right to her through neglect."

"Neglect?" She frowned. "I very much doubt you've been neglectful of Andrew."

"Not intentionally. But, to be perfectly square with you, I never thought about preschool. It never occurred to me." He leaned forward and braced his forearms on the table. "It should have, though. Why didn't it?"

"Not out of neglect."

"What would you call it?"

She thought, then said, "Wiring."

Taken aback, he said, "Of all the words I thought might come out of your mouth, that wasn't one of them."

She smiled. "Then allow me to elaborate. Based on what you've told me, you had a traditional marriage and a traditional family dynamic. Consequently, the division of labor would also have been traditional."

"I changed plenty of diapers."

"I'm sure you did. Willingly. But who put diapers on the grocery list?" She could tell by his expression that he got where she was going with this. "Checking into preschool enrollment wasn't on your to-do list, any more than getting an oil change and tire rotation would have been on Angela's."

"She would have been on top of it, but I would definitely have been interested and involved."

"I'm certain of that, Mitch. So let yourself off the hook for letting it slip your mind."

"It didn't slip my mind. It didn't *enter* my mind. I'm as mad at myself for this oversight as I am at Mary for overstepping."

"Well, to prevent something like this from happening again, I advise you to set boundaries with her."

"Believe me, I did. I came down pretty hard on her, but I guess I should have been thanking her for seeing to it." He frowned. "On the other hand..."

When he paused, she said, "Don't stop there. On the other hand, what?"

"It was a rite of passage for Andrew. She denied me the experience. It wasn't me holding his hand when he walked in. I didn't get to see his first reaction to the bunny."

He turned his head and gazed out the window. The sun had fully set, but there was still a rim of gold on the western horizon. That last sliver of sunlight picked up the lighter streaks in his brown hair, turning them to filaments of copper. It made his eyes so blue they appeared to be electric.

But there was no mischief in them now. His expression was introspective and forlorn. She didn't interrupt whatever he was reflecting on. Finally he turned back to her and stated, "I don't know how to be a mother."

She wanted badly to reach across the table and place her hand over his, but feared that touching him, even in consolation, could be hazardous. To her, if not to him.

"You weren't programmed to be," she said softly.

"Not wired that way."

"Precisely. How you *are* wired and what you are to Andrew is going to be sufficient."

He looked at her as though he wanted desperately to believe that. "I'm going to Lafayette tomorrow, tour the school, meet the teacher. At ten a.m. I'm sorry to skip out on you, but I can't reschedule because Mary already told Andrew that I'm coming. He's excited to show me the rabbit. I can't disappoint him."

"See? You're more than sufficient."

Under the table, he restlessly drew his knees up, then stretched out again. "Well, Mary is questioning my sufficiency. This afternoon she called me an 'absent parent' and cited some negative effects my absenteeism could have on Andrew's development."

"Oh," Dylan said with sudden insight. Sensing what was coming, she now understood his urgency to talk to her.

"Yeah. She delivered me a gut punch, because there was an underlying suggestion that it might be better for Andrew if the present living arrangement was made permanent."

"That she and Hank get guardianship?"

"She didn't come right out and say that, but I sensed it's occurred to her to try."

"Have either of them ever broached that with you?"

"Never. Which is why it jarred me. I may not be programmed to be a mother, but I'm Andrew's father. I'd go to hell and back before giving him up." He chuffed a bitter laugh. "I have gone to hell and back."

He hunched his shoulders, propped his elbows on the table, and with praying hands rubbed the center of his forehead. In her peripheral vision Dylan saw the waitress approaching. She gave a small shake of her head. The waitress took in Mitch's body language and retreated.

Half a minute lapsed before he lowered his hands. "I'm not very good company tonight. Not a single joke or wisecrack springs to mind. Sorry."

"No apology necessary. I'm getting to see another side of you."

"Is it an improvement over the other?"

She smiled, but didn't respond to the question, afraid he would misinterpret if she told him she liked both sides of him. Instead, she asked, "When you said you'd been to hell and back, were you referring to your deployments?"

"They were hell, for sure. I was lucky to come through them with only a few dings." Then he shot her one of his grins. "And a couple of tats, but you'll never see them unless we get better acquainted. *Much* better acquainted."

She felt her blush, and he must have noticed, because he gave a short laugh before becoming serious again. "No, the hell I was referring to was the aftermath of Angela's death. You already know about that. At downward spirals, I'm an Olympian."

"Do you want to talk more about it now? Here?"

"I never want to talk about it, even though you told me that sitting and saying nothing wouldn't be very helpful."

"I stand by that." She didn't want to prod him to the point that he would become sarcastic or shut down completely, but she felt she would be derelict not to prod a little. "You should talk about it, Mitch, because I don't think you'll be the person, or the parent to Andrew, that you want to be until you unleash the anger you're harboring."

"I couldn't agree more, Dr. Reede. I'm on the brink of unleashing it. When I do, it's liable to get bloody."

Chapter 15

His tone and the glint in his eyes were alarming to Dylan. "Mitch, you can't undertake a vigilante retaliation against men who you assume caused Angela's death. Violence is not a problem solver."

"Oh, I think violent retaliation would fix me right up." He leaned back against the booth, his expression unyielding. "Do you know how she died? Did John tell you?"

Dylan glanced around. The café had filled since their arrival. There was a lot of bustle, laughter, and noisy conversation, the clatter of dishes and flatware. Lively zydeco music played through scratchy speakers.

Coming back to Mitch, she asked, "Are you sure you want to talk about this now?"

"By all means," he said, making a grand gesture. "I want to get it over with."

She thought about trying to talk him down, but in his present state she feared causing a scene. Besides, she'd been encouraging him to talk about this. The setting was far from ideal, but he had chosen to continue, so she went with it, afraid that it might be her only opportunity to get to the root of the pain he suffered.

Quietly, she said, "In answer to your question, yes. Bowie told me that you came home one night later than usual because you and he were working on a case. You found Angela inside her car, with the motor running, in a closed garage."

"An obvious asphyxiation suicide."

"Bowie didn't say that. He said the coroner pronounced it death by suicide and that the medical examiner bore that out."

He snorted with bitterness. "They actually believe that Angela committed suicide with Andrew asleep in his crib upstairs."

Dylan didn't respond.

"Did John tell you that she was on medication for postpartum?"

That came as a mild shock. "No, he didn't."

"She was. Which, of course, added fodder to the suicide theory."

"Was her postpartum severe?"

"No, but it was real. She had been a clerk in a law firm, a job she loved. She had worked right up until Andrew was born and was having difficulty adjusting to her new job, which was stay-at-home and around the clock.

"She readily acknowledged that she needed help, and we got it. She was prescribed medication, and had almost weaned herself off it. She was on the upswing."

Dylan hesitated before saying, "Maybe that's what she wanted you to believe."

He leaned forward again, elbows on the table, but instead

of praying hands at his forehead, he clasped his hands tightly and tapped the double fist on the table to emphasize each word. "She did not kill herself."

"Tell me why you don't think so."

"I don't think, I *know* she didn't. How do I know? Because she was so devout in her faith. Suicide is a mortal sin, an unforgivable transgression. For her own salvation, Angela Kathleen Duvall Haskell wouldn't have taken her own life.

"And even if she'd wanted to, she wouldn't have been that selfish. To leave Mary and Hank believing that she'd died unshriven? Never. To leave Andrew motherless? No. *Hell no.* She loved him too much to have..."

He stopped, looked down at his clasped hands, squeezed them tighter, then opened them slowly, seeming to force them to relax. "She never would have abandoned our baby. Never. And with all my heart, I don't believe she would have condemned me to speculating every day for the rest of my life on why, why, *why*? She would not have done that."

Dylan knew he believed with every fiber of his being everything that he'd said. The rawness of his emotion made it impossible for her to remain entirely objective. Her heart was breaking for him. "What do you believe actually happened that night?"

"Thank you for asking. Most people don't, you know? They take that suicide scene at face value. I didn't and never will. I'm certain her murder was staged to look like a suicide, but I have absolutely no evidence to back up that assertion, which is why it was dismissed by everybody. Friends and relatives. The authorities. Everybody. I looked like the raving, grieving widower who couldn't accept that his wife chose death over living with him."

"John Bowie?"

"No, no," he said, giving his head an adamant shake. "John

knew Angela very well. He knew the strength of her faith. Beth, too. They took my part. He helped me in trying to prove she'd been murdered.

"He and I went over our house with a fine-tooth comb, several times, looking for any scrap of evidence that someone else had been there that night. We found nothing. No sign of forced entry. Nothing stolen. No fingerprints, no fibers, nothing.

"The other thing was that Angela didn't have a mark on her. No bruises or blood. No sign that she'd struggled. And Andrew had been left untouched. Which was a miracle, and like all miracles, I couldn't explain it."

He furrowed his brow. "I still can't. All I know is that Angela wouldn't have gotten into the car and started it voluntarily. Somebody compelled her to do it by threatening her that if she didn't, the consequence would be a thousand times worse. Something unspeakable, unthinkable. Anathema."

Dylan thought through all that. Assuming that he was right, and someone had come into the house and forced Angela to do something as heinous as to stage a suicide, why would he, or they, have spared the baby? She put the question to him.

He shrugged. "Maybe he didn't know Andrew was in the house."

"Maybe it was a mercy."

His lips tightened. "If it was, it won't be taken into account when I get my hands on the son of a bitch."

She didn't doubt that at all. Mitch Haskell was fresh out of mercy. "Monday night…" Then she drew herself up with a sudden realization. "That was only two nights ago."

"When I busted in on you? Yeah, night before last."

"Seems so much longer."

It seemed longer because recollections of those few forbidden moments when he'd been holding her wrist hadn't left her alone. Such a seemingly innocent action had created memorable sensations. Remembrances of them had taunted and tantalized her throughout her workday and when she was idle and alone. They were ever-present, there even when she slept, there when she woke up.

And now, despite the surrounding noisiness and commotion, she was reliving those moments when he'd felt her pulse, and his whisper had been a warm breath wafting across her face, and he was looking into her eyes. His had been hot and avid.

Just as they were now. "Seems longer to me, too, Dylan."

That statement, spoken in a rough undertone, made it very difficult for her to force herself back into the present and the serious subject that had to be dealt with delicately. She took a sip of tea before picking up where she'd left off.

"As you were leaving Monday night, you told me that you believe two men were responsible for Angela's death."

He nodded.

"What motive would they have had?"

"To destroy me."

"Why?"

"Retribution."

"Then why didn't they kill *you*?"

"I've thought on that a lot and have come to the conclusion that they considered death too lenient a punishment. Even if they'd tortured me first, death would have been a welcome reprieve. No, they wanted to hurt me in the worst possible way. They wanted my suffering to last for a long time. So far, they've succeeded."

"Why such harsh retribution? What had you done to them?"

He was about to speak, but caught himself. "You can't

disclose anything about your patients, right? Unless you've softened your policy on that."

"I haven't."

"I didn't think so. In the same way, I can't talk about ongoing investigations."

"Is the investigation into Angela's death ongoing?"

"For me it is."

"I understand your desire for answers, Mitch. I do. I only hope your quest for them doesn't cause even greater damage. Please keep that in mind."

"I will."

She gave him a rueful smile. "I doubt it."

He moved his tea glass aside and leaned farther across the table. "Tell me. Am I your most challenging patient to date?"

"You're certainly in the running."

He snickered. "Good. I don't want to be mediocre." He grinned, and she smiled back, but with seriousness, he said, "Thanks for agreeing to seeing me. As hard as it was to talk so openly about all that, I guess I did need to air some things."

"I hope I helped."

"Actually," he said, speaking low, "you've made my situation a lot more complicated."

"In what way?"

He gave her a slow once-over, his gaze lighting on her lips, in the vicinity of her breasts, and, when his eyes reconnected with hers, he said, "I think you know."

She could withstand his laser-blue stare only so long before lowering her head. She wasn't aware that the waitress had returned until she said, "Y'all had time to consider?"

Dylan hastily replied, "Oh, we're not eating."

Just as Mitch said, "What would you like?"

The waitress harrumphed. "Wasn't referring to the menu choices." Looking back and forth between them, she asked, "Which is it, awkward first date or a breakup?"

"Awkward first date," Mitch said.

"It's not a date," Dylan stressed.

Mitch said to the waitress, "We're only here because she didn't want to be alone with me."

"How come?"

"I can't figure it." He made a show of scratching his head. "I'm devilishly handsome. I have a good personality, and I'm a stickler for dental hygiene. I keep myself fit." He patted his abs. "Why do you think?"

The waitress said, "'Cause you're a smart-ass."

He laughed, then the waitress laughed, then Dylan couldn't help herself. She joined in. But she insisted that they were leaving. They settled with the waitress by each of them giving her a ten for renting them the table. As Mitch handed her his share, he asked why the logo crawfish was blue instead of red.

"I've always wondered that myself but never took the trouble to ask." She looked at Dylan and grinned. "He might be worth a second date."

Outside, the air was soft and humid, but there was a breeze light enough to be comfortable, yet strong enough to discourage mosquitoes. A half moon was rising. Venus shone brightly. As they walked side by side toward their cars, Mitch reached for her hand.

She tried to take it back. "What are you doing?"

"Just seems like a time to hold hands."

"You and I can't hold hands."

"Okay." He let go of her hand, then hooked his arm around her waist and pulled her beneath the eaves of the building. "How about this?"

He drew her close and nuzzled her behind the ear, even as he reached back and removed the band from around her ponytail, freeing her hair to fall past her shoulders front and back. His breath fanned her ear, causing her tummy to rise and fall like a bouncing balloon.

"Mitch." She pushed against his chest and had the fleeting thought: *I wonder where his tats are?* The exotic possibilities that came to mind shamed her, but inflamed her imagination. "Please stop this," she said, unsure if she was addressing him or herself.

In any case, he complied. He drew up straight and angled back, but didn't say anything, just looked at her, his eyes roving over her face, across her collarbone, down into the V-neck of her T-shirt. The view it offered made him smile.

"Mitch."

He brought his eyes back up to hers. "Hmm?"

"Listen," she said sternly.

"Listening."

"This is..." She sawed her hand back and forth between them. "What you're doing is a classic psychological phenomenon. Transference. That's what it's called."

"I've never heard it called that. I've heard it called necking, smooching, pitching woo, making whoopee, making out—"

"Will you stop with the joking, please?"

"—mugging, foreplay, kissing, French kissing."

"We weren't kissing."

"Not yet." He cupped her face between his hands and planted his lips firmly against hers. And then less firmly. Then tenderly. And when he slanted them across hers, hers parted.

"Mitch," she sighed.

"Hmm?"

Whatever she had intended to say was never said. He slid

his tongue between her lips. It flirted with hers until she realized she was seeking his, inviting it deeper into her mouth. Without breaking contact, he tilted his head, found a better angle, and each sank into the kiss, which was definitely French.

His hand on her cheek moved to the back of her head, his fingers threading through her hair. His other hand slipped inside her jacket and settled on her waist, urging her closer until they were bumping middles.

Then the bumping stopped, and after one slight adjustment they stayed in place, fitted together so perfectly that he made a growling sound, pressed more firmly into the complementing depression, and lowered his hand from her waist to her bottom.

Although she was lost in the deliciousness of the kiss and the pleasure spreading from where they were snugly joined, the squeeze of his fingers against the seat of her jeans brought her back to reality. She jerked herself away from him and stumbled back a step.

She stared at him in dismay. By reflex, she reached up and touched her lips. They were damp with the taste of him—the marvelous taste of him—verifying how ardent his kiss had been, how fervently she'd kissed him back, and affirming how badly she wanted him to kiss her more, to touch her, to touch her everywhere, every part of her that was feverish and achy and yearning, and not to stop touching.

All that she desired from him in that moment was mistimed, misplaced, and so, so wrong.

She drew a swift but deep breath, then let it out on a whimper, "Oh, God."

He spoke her name as a plea and reached for her.

She backed away from his extended hand, gave a hard shake of her head, turned away from him, and ran to her car.

Chapter 16

Mitch had texted John that he needed to take the morning off to go to Lafayette, but he hadn't said why. As soon as Mitch got to his desk shortly after one o'clock, John came over even before he had sat down.

"What's going on in Lafayette?"

Mitch told him about the preschool enrollment. "Mary had no right. Made me mad as hell."

"I don't blame you. That was low of her."

"Or high-handed. Either way, I missed out on taking Andrew myself, tried to make up for it this morning."

"How'd that go over?"

Mitch had arrived at the Duvalls' house in time for breakfast. In a petty but satisfying gesture of defiance, he'd brought with him a box of Froot Loops. When it had come time to leave for the ten o'clock meeting at the school, Mary had picked up her handbag and started out with Andrew and him.

"I've got this, Mary."

It had taken a moment to register with her that she was being excluded. "But I need to introduce you to Andrew's teacher."

"I'll introduce myself."

"But—"

"I've got this." He hadn't raised his voice, but he'd been emphatic. Then he'd clapped his hands and said to Andrew, "Let's haul, buddy! I want to see that rabbit I've heard so much about."

He didn't go into those details with John but told him that he'd gotten his point across to his mother-in-law.

John asked, "How was the bunny?"

"White fur, pink eyes, you know."

"And Andrew?"

Mitch grinned. "He's a rock star."

Barbara Nix approached them in time to overhear that. "Who is?"

"My boy," Mitch said.

She smiled. "So you've said. About ten million times."

"Anything new on the double murder?" John asked.

"Nil. There was a discussion about dragging the bayou in search of the murder weapon, but it will take time, money, and manpower that Darcy is short on already. He's doing his best, but it's a shit show with no finale. The kill site remains unknown, as does the place where the assumed boat was put in. Cohorts of both victims have been interviewed. Nobody knows nothing about nothing, or so they say. No suspects, ergo no motive."

Before continuing, she paused and looked at Mitch and John in turn. "I'm glad I caught you two together. What I said yesterday about the girl, about Mandy Adams, being a disaster waiting to happen? That was an awful and inexcusable thing to say. I apologize for my insensitivity."

They accepted the apology with as much grace as she'd extended it, then, once she'd moved away, John asked Mitch how the child abuse case was shaping up.

Mitch gave him a rundown of the charges the couple would be indicted for. "The child who was in the hospital has been released. CPS is trying to find a foster family willing to take all three."

"That may take time."

"Yeah." He waited a beat, then said, "You know, John, someone else could be doing the follow-up with the caseworker on this." He looked around the room. "Clarence could do it. What's he doing up here anyway? When I came in, he was lugging a box up the stairs."

"A new coffeemaker. The old one went on the fritz this morning. He volunteered to replace it."

Mitch muttered, "He's doing about as much police work as I am."

The way things had ended with Dylan last night had left him troubled, disappointed, and horny. Add to that the friction between him and Mary and what might come of it. Frustrated to the max and needing to vent, he ran his fingers through his hair.

"John, my time would be much better spent out there assisting Darcy. You know that. I'd be an asset to his investigating team because the MO of that Bayou Coeur crime matches Randy Nelson's execution to a tee."

John sighed. "I explained to you why. You—"

"I know, I heard it," he interrupted curtly. "Forget I mentioned it." He yanked his chair from beneath his desk, dropped into it, and turned on his computer.

"What about Dr. Reede?" John asked.

Mitch noticed that her name captured Clarence's attention. He stopped fiddling with the new machine and turned to better overhear.

Mitch grumbled, "What about her?"

"You had to miss this morning's session."

"I'll reschedule. So long as I get in two a week, right?"

"That was our agreement."

Mitch turned his chair around and looked up at John. "It wasn't an agreement. It was an order with an *or else* attached."

John looked as though he wanted to counter. Or maybe slug him. Instead, he muttered, "I'm going to lunch."

Mitch watched him thread his way through the room full of desks, his long stride conveying anger. Only after John had cleared the exit did he swivel his chair back to face his computer.

The most constructive thing he did that afternoon was to try the first cup of coffee brewed by the unit's new appliance.

El Paso was in his element.

It was nearing ten p.m. Having to kill time over the past few hours had sharpened his eagerness and made him restless. He was primed for action. Bloodthirsty.

In his twenty-two years there hadn't been a single individual he'd held in high esteem. No one in his life had been deserving of it. This deprivation had scarred his soul and left him with an incurably cynical outlook.

But in the short time he'd known Roland Malone, Malone had earned as much of El Paso's respect as he was likely to award anyone. Malone wouldn't win any contests based on his personality, which was that of an undertaker at his own funeral.

That wasn't to say Malone lacked magnetism. Without having to speak a word, his demeanor was sufficient to bend people to his will. Reluctant to admire anyone, El Paso could appreciate that even fat cats bowed and scraped and were afraid to cross Malone.

He also had the ear of Oz when no one else even knew Oz's identity. What other reason did one need to want to impress Malone and win his trust? Tonight he'd been given an opportunity to do just that. All he had to do was scare the riffraff away from the man's restaurant.

It wasn't hardship duty, because there was nothing El Paso liked better than terrorizing someone. And he was good at it. Considering his line of work, one would think his diminutive size was a disadvantage. One would be wrong. Dead wrong. Nobody expected a runt to be vicious. Several men had died in utter shock over the speed and ruthlessness with which he had ended their lives.

As Malone had ordered, he'd spent last night familiarizing himself with the immediate area. He'd marked businesses where he would blend in with the clientele. He'd scouted out places in which to hide in the event he needed to. Like a rat, he could squeeze into almost any space, no matter how small.

While pretending to have neither empathy nor contempt for his homeless soon-to-be victims, he'd moved among them, observing. He wouldn't tangle with those who were aggressive toward anyone who came close to them. He wasn't afraid of them, but he'd been instructed to keep it simple. Low-key.

He wouldn't target any who were obviously stoned, drunk, or otherwise senseless, either. A threat would be wasted on them. He sought out the docile or infirm.

This evening, he'd ventured into the neighborhood at

twilight, but he'd waited, a predator biding his time. But by now, traffic on the boulevard had become lighter. Crowds in the restaurants had thinned. A few of the bars were just now getting lively, but those groups were focused on partying and hooking up.

Deciding that it was time to act, he bought a hot dog from a street vendor, then began following a man he'd pre-picked. He was older, stooped, walked with a limp. One of the weakest of the herd. Easy prey.

The man was slowly making his way into the alley that ran behind Malone's place, no doubt hoping for a handout. El Paso materialized out of the darkness so suddenly and silently, the old man didn't have a chance to react before El Paso pushed him against the exterior brick wall of a building, pried open his mouth, and stuffed the hot dog into a maw of decayed teeth.

"Eat that, you bag of shit."

He continued to cram the food into the man's mouth, causing him to choke. El Paso grabbed him by his shoulders and forced him to the pavement. Coughing and retching, the old man tried to crawl away, but El Paso rolled him onto his back and put a knee to his throat.

He produced his switchblade, flipped it open, and waved it an inch away from the man's terrified eyes. "If you or any of your friends come back into this alley begging for food, I'll stick this in your eye and then slit your throat."

For good measure, he nicked the old man's chin with the tip of the blade before retracting it. He stood and kicked the old guy in the ribs, then turned and strolled out of the alley. The assault had taken no more than thirty seconds, but, gauging by the old man's whimpers and the fear in his rheumy eyes, he'd gotten the message.

El Paso walked half a block to a T-shirt shop, which was packed with rowdy customers picking through the crappy merchandise. He spent the next fifteen minutes chuckling over the crude sayings and graphics on the shirts and baseball caps. During that time, nothing happened out on the street. No hue and cry was raised. No one shouted for help for the old bum. No police cars arrived looking for an assailant with a switchblade.

El Paso reasoned that the homeless man was as reluctant as he was to create a stir.

Not wanting to press his luck, he resisted the temptation to shoplift one of the shirts sporting an especially creative drawing of female genitalia. He slipped out of the store without anyone having acknowledged his presence. Shoulders slouched, stride relaxed, he started down the sidewalk in search of his next victim.

He figured three ought to do it. Word would spread like lice.

Dylan looked at her watch, then signaled the waiter to bring her check. As though he'd been assigned to wait on her exclusively, he'd been hovering near her table throughout her dinner at Ristorante Italiano. He glided over now and asked if she would like a refill of coffee.

"No thank you. Just my check please."

He gave her an unctuous smile. "You're Mr. Malone's guest."

"A paying guest," she said.

"I wouldn't hear of it," said Roland in his gruff voice as he came toward them. He dismissed the waiter with a negligent hand motion and sat down across from Dylan at the table for two. "How was your meal?"

"Delicious. My compliments to your chef. But I really can't let you treat me."

"Nonsense."

"It's compromising, Roland."

"Compromising? Who makes these rules? Who's checking to see if they're obeyed? Say thank you, and let that be the end of it."

Against her better judgment, she thanked him and left it at that.

He'd been her patient for a while, but this was the first time she'd come to his restaurant. He'd often issued her off-handed invitations. "You need to eat at my place," or "What's your favorite Italian dish? I'll have it made up special for you."

But yesterday when he'd called her after weeks without hearing from him, he'd been surprisingly insistent that she accept his invitation. "You've done a lot for me. Let me repay you. How about tomorrow night?"

"Tomorrow? That's short notice. You're probably already booked to capacity."

"I own the place. You'll have the best table."

He'd continued to press. She'd run out of excuses, and, when she finally agreed, he'd said, "I'll send a car for you. Be ready at six-thirty."

"I'll drive myself, thank you."

"Unnecessary. I have a car and driver on standby. Most of the time I'm paying him to twiddle his thumbs."

"I'll come on my own, Roland, or not at all."

"Jeez, you're stubborn. What time should I expect you?"

"I'll be there by eight."

Tonight when she arrived, she'd been escorted to one of the more secluded tables in a corner. On it were a white damask tablecloth, a leather-bound menu with a silk tassel, a flickering candle, and a crystal decanter of red wine. But only one place setting.

She'd been vastly relieved that her client wouldn't be joining her for the meal. Last evening she'd shared a table with Mitch Haskell. There'd been no tablecloth, candlelight, or wine. On the menu was a stenciled blue crawfish instead of a tassel.

And look where that had led.

"Glad I talked you into coming?" Roland asked now.

"I am. Very. Your timing was good. I needed a change of scenery."

"Oh? Why's that?"

He'd asked the question casually, but he leaned back against the tufted velvet chair as though to scrutinize her more fully. He also began turning his pinkie ring, a habit she'd noticed during their first session. She'd once asked him what significance the ring held for him.

"It was my old man's. He's dead."

He hadn't elaborated, but she'd thought it telling that while he often referenced his mother, he never again had mentioned his father. Whenever she had subtly tried to steer him toward revealing more about their relationship, he had just as subtly switched topics.

In answer to his question, she said, "I thought a night out would do me good, that's all. No specific reason."

Which was a bald lie. The reason was her longing to have sex with her patient, Mitch Haskell. With very little guile or persuasion on his part, she'd crossed lines with him that couldn't be uncrossed. If her misconduct were found out, her professional reputation would be irreparably damaged.

And, on a personal level, she had spent years carefully

establishing barriers against romantic involvement. To continue chipping away at those self-imposed restrictions could ultimately result in a broken heart. She'd had one. She didn't want another.

After leaving Mitch last night, she had resolved that she must stay away from him. Not a parting, a severance. Which meant dropping him as a patient.

She just hadn't worked up the gumption to notify him of it yet.

"You work too hard," Roland was saying. "Hell, it would get anybody down to listen all day, every day, to people bellyaching about their plight in life."

"I don't think of what I do as *work*. It's more like a calling."

"You sound like a nun."

Thinking of the way she'd moved against Mitch's hard body in an effort to get closer, gain more ground, she said, "Believe me, I'm not a nun. But it is gratifying whenever I help patients through a rough patch or enable them to see themselves from a different and emotionally healthier perspective." Softly, she added, "Such as yourself, Roland."

"Yeah, you helped me look at some things different." He guffawed. "Talk about hard work."

She laughed.

Then he said, "Maybe you should cut back."

"Cut back?"

"On your number of patients. Get rid of a few and don't take on any new ones."

At first she thought he was still speaking in jest. Then realized he wasn't. "I have no intention of cutting back or turning away anyone who comes to me seeking help."

"It would go against your nature? You're a bleeding heart? A sucker for a sob story?"

She frowned. "No. Because I empathize with people who are struggling to recover from a problem or traumatizing experience that seems insurmountable."

He must have sensed that she'd been put off by what he'd said. "Look, I meant no offense. But, you know, I'm used to chewing ass." He waved his hand to indicate the busy restaurant. "I'm tough on anyone who screws up so they'll be sure not to again."

She could envision that, and was glad she was his therapist and not his employee. "This has been lovely. Thank you again. But I need to get on my way." She picked up her purse and pushed back her chair. He came around to hold it for her.

"I have a car and chauffeur waiting to drive you home."

"So do I, Roland," she said with a light laugh. "I wanted to indulge in a martini *and* wine, so I changed my mind about driving myself." As they made their way to the door, she said, "You haven't made another appointment for a session."

"I'll give you a call."

She looked at him askance. "It's been six weeks."

"I've been busy."

"I sensed an urgency when you called yesterday. Is there something specific you need to talk about? I would make time for you."

"You would?"

"Of course."

They had reached the door, but rather than opening it, he turned to face her. "Do all your patients get special treatment like that?"

"When I feel it's called for."

"Huh. Are any of them as interesting as me?"

Am I your most challenging patient to date? You're in the running.

She gave another soft laugh, but it was over that tidbit with Mitch, not over Roland's question. In answer to him, she replied, "None come close."

"Come on," he drawled in his Bronx accent. "I bet you've got some really messed-up characters coming to you." He leaned in and spoke in a confidential tone. "You don't have to name names. Just give me a hint of what ails them."

"Even that would violate privilege, Roland. You know I won't do that."

His eyes held steady on hers. He didn't even blink. "Good to know. Real good." He held the stare for seconds longer, then pushed the door open, held it for her, and followed her out.

"That's my car." She waved to a black sedan parked at the curb some distance away. To signal that he'd seen her, the driver blinked the headlights.

Then her attention was drawn to the median of the wide boulevard where two men appeared to be in a scuffle, pushing and shoving, swapping insults.

When her hired car pulled up to the curb and blocked her view of what was happening, she went up on tiptoe in order to see over the roof of the car. By now the scuffle had escalated into a full-fledged fight. The two were going at each other with intent.

A young woman, who'd been walking across the median hand-in-hand with a small boy, screamed.

Beside Dylan, Roland began luridly cursing under his breath.

The woman's child was now wailing with fright. She pulled the boy to the ground, protected him with her body, and yelled at the two fighters to stop. Her shouts and the child's hysteria seemed to bring the fighters to their senses.

They broke apart suddenly, falling back from each other. But their stances remained combatant, and there was a moment when one of them seemed on the verge of attacking again.

But he must have reconsidered. He shoved past the other and streaked down the middle of the median until he saw a break in traffic and crossed the street in a dead run. When he reached the other side, he disappeared into the narrow, dark space between two buildings.

The other, who'd run in the opposite direction, leaped from the median directly into oncoming traffic. He narrowly missed being struck by a delivery truck. Horn blaring, it swerved into the median and crashed into a tree. That didn't slow the runner down. He made it across the street far down the block from Roland's restaurant and disappeared from Dylan's view.

The woman had stopped screaming, although her little boy continued to cry hysterically. Concerned witnesses ran to the median to see if they needed aid.

The driver of the delivery truck, apparently uninjured, had jumped from his cab and was attracting a growing audience of curiosity-seekers by gesturing wildly at the smashed grill of his truck while giving his account of the incident.

Roland, who'd been taking in all the action, turned to Dylan. "I'm sorry about this. It's the fuckin' homeless. We're being overrun. They—" The high-pitched wail of a siren interrupted his tirade. "Jesus," he hissed. "All we need."

A police car rounded the corner, lights flashing. It screeched to a halt parallel to the median. Two officers charged out of the car and plunged into the thick of the increasing chaos.

Roland swore. "This is bad for my business."

People who'd been having dinner in his restaurant were

pushing through the door and spilling out onto the sidewalk. She and Roland were soon encircled by people who were either frightened or merely curious and demanding to know what was going on. Wild speculations about bombs and shooters were creating even more confusion.

Roland spotted his maître d' and pulled him aside. "There was a skirmish in the median. It's over. Calm everyone down and get them back inside. I'm gonna go talk to the cops, smooth things over."

The tuxedoed man responded without question and did his best to circulate and spread the word that there was nothing more to see. But not everyone was as willing to return to the dining room as others.

In the shuffling crowd, Dylan got separated from Roland, who was halfway across the boulevard by now, oblivious to motorists who were honking at him. When he reached the median, he plowed his way through the throng that had formed.

Dylan was jostled by Roland's customers, who were either heeding the maître d's suggestion that they return to the dining room or moving in the opposite direction in an attempt to get a better view of the happenings.

She'd lost sight of her hired car because she'd been moved back so far from the curb and there were dozens of people now between her and it. As undignified as it would be, she'd have to push her way through.

Murmuring, "Excuse me," she was attempting to step around a rather large man when her elbow was hooked from behind.

"This way."

Before she was fully aware of what was happening, she was wheeled around and propelled forward. She immediately dug her heels in and tried to wrest her elbow free. "Let go of me."

"It's me, it's me. Keep walking."

She jerked her head up and looked into the face of a homeless man who had Mitch Haskell's brilliant, unmistakable eyes. "Wha...What are you doing? What's that on your face? Why are you dressed like that? Is that *blood*?"

"Yeah. The little fucker stuck me."

"You were..." She braked again and motioned back toward the median. "You were...The fight...?"

"Wasn't a fair fight. He had a blade."

Suddenly she realized that his breathing was rapid and hot. Beads of sweat rolled out from under a stocking cap down his forehead and into his eyes. His right hand still had a grip on her elbow. His left was pressed against his left side. Blood was seeping through his fingers.

"My God, Mitch. You're hurt. We've got to get you help."

He shook his head. "We've got to get the hell out of here."

"You need a doctor."

"I've got one, *Dr.* Reede."

Chapter 17

"I'll call 911."

Mitch caught Dylan opening her small evening bag one-handedly and taking out her phone. He snatched it from her before she could tap the SOS. "No 911 call, no nothing. Except I could use that thing draping your neck."

Without asking permission, he pulled off her pashmina wrap and stuffed it between his side and his left hand. "Damn, that hurts."

"Mitch, what are you doing?"

"Don't want to leave a blood trail, and my clothes were getting soaked. I'll buy you another thing."

"I mean, *what are you doing?* You've been assaulted with a knife. You're leaving the scene of a crime."

"Where an undercover cop can't be exposed as such."

Her footsteps faltered. "Oh."

"Did you think this getup was for Halloween?" He took a swift glance over his shoulder to see if anyone was in pursuit.

Pedestrians and motorists alike were gawking at the ongoing action taking place in the median. Best he could tell, no one was paying attention to the ragged homeless man escorting a babe wearing high heels with sparkly stuff on the toes.

But he didn't take for granted that no one had noticed them. It was vital that they get out of sight. He secured Dylan's elbow more firmly and hustled her along. "Here's a cut-through." As he squeezed them into a dark, narrow alleyway between two walled courtyards, he felt her hesitation. "Keep up, Dylan."

"You know your way around here," she remarked.

"Yep, and we've got blocks to make."

"To where?"

"Anywhere but here. Like right now."

"You're covered in blood, Mitch."

"It's a scratch."

"You need immediate medical attention."

"Negative. Hurts like a mother, and I'd like to kill the little shit that cut me, but it's not that bad."

They came out of the alley and took a right turn down a buckled sidewalk shadowed by the widespread branches of venerable live oaks that sheltered condemned houses. After another few blocks, they reached the parking lot where he had left his piece-of-shit pickup.

Digging into the deep pocket of the baggy, dirty trousers, he found his key and ushered her around to the passenger side. She said, "This isn't your truck."

"It's one of them," he said, swinging open the door. "Get in." He attempted to boost her up, but she resisted.

"You get in, I'll drive."

"You think I'm stupid?"

"Yes!" she said. "Incredibly stupid. You've been knifed!"

"Um-huh. And if I let you drive, you would head straight for the nearest ER." Somewhere from back the way they'd come, a siren wailed. "There's no time to argue, Dylan. *Get in!*"

She huffed something under her breath, but climbed up into the passenger seat, made difficult because of her stilettos and skinny skirt. He went around the battered hood and hauled himself up into the driver's seat, where he whipped off the cap with the fake, mangy hair, and tossed it into the floorboard. Reaching behind him with his right hand, he took his pistol from its holster at the small of his back and tucked it between his thighs.

With alarm, Dylan said, "Who are you going to shoot at?"

"I don't know yet."

He started the truck's reliable engine and left the parking lot in a hurry. As he drove through a maze of side streets, he kept one eye on the road, the other on the rearview mirror. He didn't detect anyone coming after them and began to breathe a little easier. But only a very little.

He could feel Dylan's baleful stare on his profile. Holding on tight as he took turns sharply, she didn't distract him by talking until they were a couple of miles away from their starting point. "You realize that the doctor in front of my name doesn't designate me as a physician of medicine."

"Of course I know that, Dr. Reede."

"God knows what was on that knife, Mitch. You need to go to an emergency care center."

"No can do."

"You're trying to be tough? A hero?"

"If I wanted to be a hero, I'd be back there hunting down that son of a bitch with the switchblade."

"Surely we're far enough away by now that—"

"I'm not going to an emergency center with a knife wound. The facility would be obligated to report it to the police."

"You're the police."

"Right, so what would be the point? Please just drop it. It takes too much energy to argue."

She stopped arguing, but, still obviously frustrated, turned her head away. Then, "There! There's a drugstore."

It would be impossible to miss. The familiar chain store was lit up brighter than the Las Vegas strip.

She said, "Pull over. I'll go in and—"

"Try again." He blew past the store.

"I could get some bandages, antiseptic, pain relievers. I could—"

"You could call any-damn-body."

"I won't. I'll leave my phone with you."

"You could borrow one."

"I wouldn't. I swear."

He glanced at her but didn't let up on the accelerator. "On security cameras you'd be seen buying first aid stuff for somebody who just might have a fresh knife wound."

"Nobody is looking for *me*."

He gnawed the inside of his cheek to keep from commenting on that. There was plenty to talk about on that subject, but later.

She said, "Isn't it a little late for you to be concerned about security cameras? This vehicle has probably been picked up by dozens of them by now."

"It has a blurred license plate, and there aren't any cameras at that defunct business where I left it, which is one of the reasons why I chose that spot."

Having had that argument shot down, she resorted to pleading, "Mitch, please. You're bleeding."

"It looks worse than it is."

"How do you know?"

"Because my guts aren't spilling out."

"The cut should at least be cleaned."

"It'll keep for a while."

"Damn you! Stop somewhere and let me see to it."

Her impassioned shout was so unexpected, his neck popped when he turned his head toward her.

Her chest was rising and falling with agitation. "I had an injured man who ignored me. He insisted that he was fine, that he would be all right, that it wasn't that bad, and he died. He *died*. I would prefer not to experience that again."

Her voice had cracked. Her body was rigid, her expression stark. The appeal in her eyes was desperate.

Cursing under his breath, Mitch dragged his attention back to the roadway. He moved into the right-hand lane in time to turn into the parking lot of another super drugstore. As they rolled to a stop in the darkest area available, he said, "Got any money? Cash, not a credit card."

Having collected herself, she gave a curt nod and took a small wallet from her handbag. She was about to open the car door when he said, "Hold on." He reached into the narrow space between the seats and the cab's window and pulled out a wadded-up windbreaker. "I don't use this for undercover. It's not pretty, but it's clean. Put it on and pull the hood up."

"Is this really necessary?"

"If I say it is, it is." He placed his right arm on her seat back. "Dylan, here and now, in these circumstances, I'm the experienced professional, so what I say goes. Understand? Besides, it's starting to sprinkle."

She looked none too happy, but after a moment of mutinous

glaring, she put on the windbreaker and pulled the hood over her head. Without saying another word, she got out and shut the door harder than necessary. He waited until she was inside the store, then took his cell phone from the pocket of his dirty, threadbare "homeless" jacket.

He had Jim Tucker's number on speed dial. He thumbed it, and his former DEA colleague answered immediately, stating only his name by way of greeting.

Cheerfully, Mitch said, "Guess who."

Tucker groaned. "What do you want? I'm busy."

"Not as busy as you're gonna be. I have a tip for you."

"Let's hear it."

"Tonight, a homeless man was assaulted with a deadly weapon."

"Gee, that's too bad."

"The assailant was a short, spry male in his early twenties."

"And you're calling me with this *why?*"

"The incident occurred in the median of Esplanade, directly in front of a locally owned restaurant with a loyal clientele. We know it well."

Tucker sighed a handful of swear words. Mitch could picture him removing his eyeglasses and rubbing his tired eyes. "Any ID on the homeless man?"

Mitch said nothing, figuring that Tucker would read between the lines of his silence. That was confirmed when the agent added more words to his foul litany. "Was there bloodshed?"

"Some."

"Which of the two?"

"I can say with absolute certainty that one of them was wounded."

"Gunshot?"

"Knifing."

"Jesus. How bad?"

"He'll live."

"Did the other one bleed?"

"No."

"How'd it start?"

"The runty bastard pounced on the homeless man. No provocation whatsoever."

"I find that hard to believe."

"I'm telling you. None whatsoever."

"Okay. Could he have recognized the homeless man?"

"Not under all the matted hair, dirt, grubby clothes, et cetera."

"Did the homeless man recognize his assailant?"

"No."

"You sure about that?"

"Positive," Mitch said. "With no provocation, and being unknown to each other, why did the punk attack?"

"Just meanness, I guess," Tucker replied.

"Maybe."

"You think there was more to it?"

"I think the 'more to it' isn't so much about why it happened, as *where*."

"Ah. The heart of the matter."

"I have it on good authority that the owner of the restaurant doesn't have a warm fuzzy for the homeless."

"On whose good authority?"

"An eyewitness. Two nights ago."

Tucker got the message because he cussed some more. "How'd the incident tonight pan out?"

In short-speak, Mitch explained about the mother and child. "The screaming spooked them both. They split. The whole thing lasted ninety seconds max."

"Police presence?"

"They were quick to arrive, but, as far as I know, the assailant got away."

"What about the homeless guy?"

"He got the hell out of there."

"Undetected?"

"Unapprehended."

Tucker snorted. "He's one lucky son of a bitch. Batshit crazy, but lucky."

Mitch couldn't think of anything to say to that.

Tucker said, "The short and spry guy may have nothing to do with that restaurant or its operation."

"Or he may."

"It's a stretch."

"It is, but I'd like to know, wouldn't you?"

Tucker cursed. "Goddammit, it's like this every friggin' time you contact me."

"Like what?"

"Like I wish you hadn't. But I'll look into it. Right now, though, I'm busy with something else."

Mitch recognized that particular tone. His antenna went up. "Involving what? Who?"

"Can't say."

"Don't know? Or can't say?"

"*Won't* say. Bye-bye."

"Wait. There's more."

Tucker blew out a gusty breath. "There always is."

"A new item appeared on the restaurant's menu tonight."

It took a moment for Tucker to interpret that. "Appetizer or main dish?"

Dessert, Mitch thought, but he said, "I don't know yet. It needs to marinate."

"What's it called?"

"Can't say."

"Don't know? Or can't say?"

"*Won't* say."

"So, you're familiar with the dish, but this is the first time you've seen it on the menu?"

Mitch didn't answer, which made Tucker testy. "You realize that this batshit-crazy homeless man had *no business* being anywhere near there."

"He thinks otherwise."

"He's been *instructed* not to hang out around there."

"Yeah, well..."

"If he's caught... Christ. Does the homeless man's friend JB know anything about any of this, about his nocturnal pastime?"

Through the plate glass storefront, he saw Dylan approaching the checkout with a basket of goods. "We'll address that later. This phone might be compromised. Next time I call you, it'll be from a burner, so answer your phone even if it doesn't ID the caller."

"Roger that, but—"

"Gotta split." He clicked off and deftly removed the battery from his phone. He palmed Dylan's, considered taking its battery out as well, but she was pushing through the exit.

He slid his phone back into his pocket just as she reached for the passenger door handle.

Chapter 18

He drove around to the back of the store where the pickup couldn't be seen from the road. First, he pulled away the wrap he'd taken from Dylan, which had stanched the blood flow by absorbing a lot of it. Looking at her apologetically, he tossed it onto the floorboard.

Next, he awkwardly took off the jacket and another two layers of garments he used for his homeless disguise. Under them he'd worn one of his own T-shirts. The left side of it was solid red now, but the blood was already drying and sticking the cloth to his skin.

"Well, doc, you'll be glad to know that I'm not gonna bleed out on you. It's congealing."

After gingerly peeling away the T-shirt, he pulled it over his head and assessed the wound more closely. The cut was deepest just beneath the left side of his rib cage, tapering off as it arced across his abdomen toward his navel.

With more relief than he would ever admit to, he said, "It is only a scratch."

"A big, bad, deep one." Dylan was giving the wound a lingering appraisal, and when he caught her at it, she, in an annoyed manner, began taking items out of the shopping bag.

"What all did you get?"

"Alcohol, gauze pads, antiseptic salve, self-adhesive bandages of various sizes, butterfly closures, Motrin, and a bottle of water to wash down the capsules. None of which is sufficient. That gash needs stitching."

"Naw."

With resignation, she handed him one of the gauze pads she'd already saturated with alcohol. He took a deep breath and applied it to the cut. He hissed, cursed, and gasped as he dabbed at the gaping wound. When that one was blood-soaked, she had another ready. They worked methodically until he felt he had sanitized the entire wound.

"Burns like bloody hell," he said.

"It's supposed to."

"You could help by blowing on it."

He flashed her a cheeky grin, which she responded to with a drop-dead look as she extended him the tube of antiseptic cream. He shook his head. "Just one of those bandages, please."

"You need the salve first. Then use the clips to pull the skin together."

"All I need for now is a bandage." He reached across the console, grabbed the box of bandages, opened it, and shook the contents into her lap. He selected the largest, ripped it open with his teeth, and placed it over the deepest segment of the cut, then applied two smaller ones where it wasn't as bad. He made sure the adhesive was sticking, then looked across at her. "Nothing to it. All patched up."

But she wasn't looking at the bandage on his abdomen. She

was looking at the tattoo on his right deltoid. "That's one," he said. "If you're curious about the other, I'll have to get more comfortable."

Rather than reacting to his innuendo, she looked up from the tattoo to meet his eyes. In her professional/therapist tone, she asked, "What does that represent to you?"

He was on the brink of spontaneously telling her, but caught himself and said instead, "A drunken impulse. That's all."

"I don't believe you."

That cool voice and the knowing look she'd fixed on him made him feel more exposed than being shirtless. "Can I have my windbreaker back?"

She retrieved it from her footwell where she'd dropped it after taking it off. He pulled it on and zipped it up, restarted the truck, and drove them back to the road.

Dylan replaced the first aid supplies in the shopping bag, shook two of the pain relievers into her palm, and passed them to him. He asked for a third and swallowed them with a long drink from the water bottle before placing it in the cup holder.

She said, "You could use what's left of the water to sponge that stuff off your face."

"It can wait. I'm used to looking dirty. Part of the disguise."

"You're no longer with the DEA," she said, "but you were working undercover in New Orleans, which isn't even your jurisdiction. Why there? Did Bowie send you?"

"That's classified."

"And that's avoidance," she snapped. "Who cut you, Mitch? Who was he?"

"I don't know, but I'm going to find out."

"Did he recognize you as a law officer?"

"He wouldn't have. Couldn't have. I think he took me for a homeless person."

"Then what provoked him?"

"I'd like to know that myself. I didn't do anything. Didn't even look him in the eye. He strutted up to me. Cool like. Arrogant. With attitude."

"You would recognize those traits."

He nodded. "Many a time, I've played that type."

"You are that type."

He cast her a sideways glance but didn't argue with her, because she was right. "Anyway, next thing I know, he's all over me. Kicking, punching, cursing, and calling me names. I believe he expected me as a down-and-outer to take the abuse. And I would have so as not to give myself away. But then he flipped that blade. I counterattacked. He didn't expect that, and it startled him. That and the lady's screaming. He was already on the run when he swiped me."

"It was vicious enough to cut through all those layers of clothing."

"Vicious and expert. If he hadn't been in such a hurry to get away, I very well could have been gutted."

Innate reflexes, plus military training, had prompted him to defend himself without pausing to consider the risk. But in retrospect, it sobered him to think that he'd been in mortal danger. The little thug could have fatally stabbed him, even accidentally. Andrew would have been left without either parent. The thought made him slightly nauseated.

During his contemplation, Dylan had sat silently by, nervously twisting the button on the cuff of her blouse, which was the color and texture of heavy cream. He'd have to be a blind eunuch not to have noticed that it delineated her breasts as though it had been poured over them.

Sounding hesitant, she quietly asked, "Why were you so frantic to get away from the scene?"

"I told you. If I'd hung around, been questioned by first responders, my cover would have been blown." He waited, then added with what nonchalance he could muster, "Plus, just about the time I was attacked, I spotted you coming out of the restaurant."

Ever since he'd taken her elbow and hustled her away, they'd been waltzing around that elephant. He felt it was time to address it, and he didn't want to do it while driving.

By now, the city was miles behind them. To avoid being ensnared in a major freeway interchange, he whipped into the right lane, took the next exit ramp, and drove half a mile before finding a road with little commerce and negligible traffic. He pulled onto the shoulder of it, turned off the headlights, and cut the engine.

He turned in his seat to face her. She hadn't asked about the sudden rerouting maneuver, but she was regarding him warily. She'd pressed herself against the passenger door as though trying to force it open.

She said, "Did you follow me there tonight, Mitch?"

"No. But I came back for you. I could have made a clean getaway and you never would have known I'd been one of the men fighting in that median. Instead, I circled back around."

"For me."

"That's right."

She assimilated that, then asked, "If you didn't follow me, how did you know I would be there?"

"I didn't. Shocked the hell out of me to see you there. I'd

been in the median for a little over an hour when you came out. I hadn't seen you arrive." Watching closely for her reaction, he asked, "Did you enter through a private door?"

"Private door?" If her mystified look was faked, she faked it well. "I went in the same way I came out."

"What time did you get there?"

She frowned. "A better question would be why that's any of your business."

"Because it is, Dylan. Literally speaking, it *is* my business." Across the short distance separating them, he could feel her apprehension growing.

She said, "If you weren't spying on me, it's awfully coincidental that your 'undercover work' was in a large city where neither of us live, and that you were in direct line of sight of the restaurant where I was having dinner."

"Do you go there often?" He asked that in a quasi-friendly way, as though they were at a cocktail party getting acquainted.

Under that creamy, dreamy blouse, her breasts were rising and falling with agitation. And agitated was exactly what he wanted her to be. He didn't want her calm, cool, professional, detached, and discreet. So he pressed by asking the same question but phrased it differently. "Are you a regular there?"

"Tonight was my first time."

"Huh."

"You don't believe me?"

"You just up and chose tonight of all nights to hire a car—I saw you had one waiting on you—and come to New Orleans to have dinner in a restaurant you'd never tried before? I find *that* very coincidental."

"Why would I lie about it?"

"You tell me, Dylan. Why would you lie?"

She sat up straighter, more defensively. "I've never been there before tonight. And I'd like to know what difference it makes to you where I ate dinner?"

"It makes a difference because it was that particular restaurant, and because you were in the company of and looking chummy with its owner, Roland Malone."

Her eyes widened. Her lips parted. "You know Roland?"

"I haven't had the pleasure," he said, deadpan. "But you know him, don't you? Pretty good, too, from the looks of it."

He waited, but she remained silent.

Though it pained his injury, he leaned forward across the console, moving closer to her. "I'll save you the trouble of answering from behind the shield of professional privilege with a lie, or a half-truth, or an evasion.

"I don't know what else Roland Malone is to you. Bosom buddy. Dutch uncle. Money lender. Sugar daddy," he said tightly. "But I know that he's your patient. He's sat on that comfy sofa with all the throw pillows and has shared with you his deepest, darkest secrets."

He reached into a self-fashioned pocket he'd added to the inside of the baggy trousers. From it, he took his badge, palmed it, and held it up close to her face. "And, Dr. Reede, what I want to know from you is what Roland Malone has confided."

Chapter 19

The first two police officers on the scene of the altercation in the median were joined by two more.

Roland told them that what he'd witnessed had amounted to nothing more than a shouting match and a little pushing and shoving, and that the woman had screamed only because she was concerned for her child's safety.

"Who started it?" one of the officers asked.

"Beats me. By the time I realized something was going on, it was over. One went one way, one the other."

"Can you give us descriptions?"

He shook his head. "One ran in that direction," he said, pointing to the far side of the street. "Lost sight of him right away. The homeless guy nearly got run over crossing the street."

"Could you describe him?"

He shrugged. "Homeless. They all look alike."

The young cop smiled wryly. "Thank you, Mr. Malone. I hope the rest of your evening is uneventful."

Roland had then returned to his restaurant, where he'd assured his clientele that the incident had been blown out of proportion and had turned out to be nothing more serious than a squabble. He apologized for the interruption of their meal and offered everyone a drink on the house.

He'd ordered his staff to carry on as though nothing had happened. "Don't talk about it among yourselves or with customers. I don't want something made of nothing, understand?"

He'd then taken up his traditional place at the entrance in order to bid goodbye to diners as they left. From that vantage point, he could monitor the police activity in the median and on both sides of the boulevard.

He also had trusted and well-paid informants in the neighborhood and within the NOPD who'd kept him updated on progress, or the lack thereof.

He'd been told that the homeless man involved had disappeared. Few had seen him well enough to provide a description, and those were conflicting. Not even his age and ethnicity had been established. The truck driver who'd almost struck him identified him only as a "fuckin' moron."

The last report that Roland had received was that the homeless man was yet to be found and probably never would be because he didn't want to be.

Likewise, the fleet-footed second party had also vanished before anyone had gotten a good look at him. One man told police he looked like a teenager. "Thirteen, fourteen, maybe. Hassled the homeless guy for the hell of it is my guess."

The officers must have come to the same conclusion. No real harm had been done. The damaged truck didn't belong to the driver, but to the company he worked for, and it was insured. The woman and her little boy had had a fright, but were fine.

After an hour and a half, the officers drove off in their squad cars. A police report would be filed, and that would be the end of it.

At least as far as the NOPD was concerned. But not for Roland Malone.

After overseeing the restaurant's closing, he had retreated to his office, and, because the events of the night required something stronger than red wine, he poured three fingers of scotch.

He thought about saying the rosary, but decided to wait until all the employees had gone. He didn't want to be interrupted, at least not until after he'd said the Fatima prayer.

When he'd returned from his talk with the police, he'd noticed that Dylan's hired car was gone. He called her now, got no answer, and left an apology for abandoning her on the sidewalk. "A big to-do was made over nothing. I'll call you tomorrow."

His conversation with her tonight had dispelled any reservations he had about her trustworthiness. She was solid. She was committed to her profession. Hell, she thought of it as a calling. Therefore, it was highly unlikely she would ever break her vow of confidentiality to a washed-up cop. On that score, he had nothing to worry about.

Oz was another matter. He had to be told about tonight's incident, and he wouldn't be happy. Not when he was focused on those three trucks with a huge stolen payload having to cross Texas and Louisiana without incident.

Roland decided to hold off on that conversation until after he'd finished his drink and had time to mull over exactly what he was going to say. He'd have to grovel a bit, because it was he who'd recommended using El Paso.

And speaking of, he would have to track El Paso down.

When he found him, he would make him an example of what happened to someone within the organization who disobeyed a direct order.

He was relishing that thought when his cell dinged. It was his chef. "That new kid just came in through the kitchen door. Asked if you were still on the premises. Are you?"

Roland was stunned. He hadn't expected El Paso ever to show his face again. Should he let the little shit sweat, unsure of how he was going to react and what his punishment might be? Maybe.

But Roland was curious to hear what he had to say, how he would account for his screwup. Besides, his coming here would save Roland the trouble of having to track him down.

"Send him back." He set his highball glass aside and settled into his chair. When the awaited knock came, he said, "Get in here."

As insolent as ever, El Paso sauntered in and had the gall to head straight for the chair facing Roland's desk and flop down into it.

Without a blink or any other indication that he was about to erupt with rage, Roland stared at him for half a minute before speaking. "If you want to keep your balls attached, you will vacate that chair."

With an attitude that needed drastic realignment, the kid gave an eye roll, placed his hands on the armrests, and pulled himself up.

Roland said, "You call that spectacle tonight low-key?"

El Paso bristled. "I don't even get to tell my side?"

Roland envisioned wrapping his garrote around the kid's neck. It was so scrawny, it wouldn't take much pressure to kill him. But rather than act on the impulse, he turned his ring several times, then negligently motioned for El Paso to continue.

"I didn't expect him to fight back. Ahead of time, I'd picked out the ones I was gonna mess with, the ones who'd likely be afraid of me and wouldn't cause a scene."

"Obviously you're a bad judge of character."

"Not the first two. I got nothing but sobs and pleading for me to leave them alone. I couldn't find the third one I'd settled on, but I saw this guy in the median and watched him for almost an hour. In all that time he didn't move. He wasn't panhandling. Hadn't talked to anybody. I thought he was asleep and would be easy. He was at first.

"But when I opened my knife, he sprang up and came at me fighting. That woman started screaming loud enough to wake the dead. I got in one swipe at him, then I got outta there."

Roland stared at him, unmoved.

"I don't know what you're upset about," the kid mumbled. "I didn't get caught, did I?"

Roland stared harder. The prick was challenging him and his authority. "First of all," Roland said without inflection, "you don't get a 'side.' I tell you to do something, you do as you're told. What I told you to do was scare a few of the homeless and keep it *low-key*. Oz wanted it kept *simple*."

He motioned to his cell phone lying on his desk. "Now I gotta call him, tell him how we had police in the neighborhood, interviewing witnesses, talking to people. Are you seeing the problem now, genius? It drew attention. And this guy who came up fighting? We've got no idea who he was, where he went, or what he might do."

"Do?" El Paso scoffed. "A bum like that? What's he gonna do?"

"As we speak, he may be talking to the cops, giving them a description of you, which would make you a blip on the PD's radar. DEA, FBI, who knows?" Roland didn't believe that, but he wanted to watch El Paso squirm.

"You put Oz's entire operation in jeopardy tonight. People who fuck up that bad are usually found dead the next morning in a swamp, if they're ever found at all. Remember the guy you replaced? He's history because he thought he was smarter than Oz and me."

That reminder made El Paso jittery. He shifted from one foot to another. "That tramp's not gonna do nothin'. He might even be dead. I stuck him good."

Roland figured he was lying to make himself look better. "Is that right? I saw the guy myself running like hell."

"I tell you, if he ain't dead, he ain't feeling so good."

Roland wanted to stand up, reach across his desk, and wipe off El Paso's smirk with his fist. He said, "I talked to the cops. Not one mention of blood. If there had been blood in the median, they would've found it."

"I drew blood, all right." As quickly as a striking snake, El Paso produced a switchblade and flicked it open. "See this?" He thrust the knife toward Roland. "Blood on the blade. I don't miss."

Roland hadn't flinched. He didn't think the kid would stick him, but his sass made Roland want to kill him. On the other hand, the kid had balls that Roland grudgingly admired. El Paso reminded him of his younger self.

Keeping his expression blank, revealing none of what was going through his mind, he said, "Put that away and don't ever pull a knife on me again." El Paso closed the knife and slid it back inside his clothing.

"That blood on your blade you're bragging about is probably the old man's. The one you jumped at the end of the alley.

Cops found him, questioned him. You scared the bejesus out of him. He swore that he couldn't describe you, but they didn't think he would have even if he could've."

"I only nicked him on his chin. The other wasn't a nick."

"If that's true, you had better hope the bugger *is* dead. He saw you, up close and personal like. So I don't think anything short of the police finding his stiff corpse will satisfy Oz. He hates loose ends. He hates them more than anything." He waved his hand toward the door. "Now, get out of here. I've got a call to make."

"To him? Oz?"

Roland picked up his phone and extended it. "Unless you want to tell him your side."

El Paso shook his head.

"I didn't think so."

"What do you want me to do?" he asked sulkily.

"Do? To make amends, you mean? Don't do a goddamn thing until I give you the go-ahead. Lay low, keep out of sight. Until I tell you otherwise, that's what you can do. Are you listening?"

"I got it, I got it."

Roland hitched his chin toward the door.

El Paso stood there for a few seconds, then turned and left, not looking nearly as contrite as he should.

Roland shot the last of his scotch, then called Oz.

Allen pushed his sleep mask up to his forehead and grabbed his phone. "What?"

"A news flash that can't wait."

"The trucks from Chihuahua got intercepted at the border?"

"It's not quite that bad."

Allen sat up, reached for his can of Mountain Dew on the nightstand, and took a swallow. "I sense it's not that good, either."

"I told you about our homeless problem."

"You said that new kid was going to take care of it."

"It got a little out of hand."

Allen listened as Roland related the events of the night. "Jesus Christ," he said when Roland finished. "Was anyone in the restaurant tonight who wouldn't want to be seen?"

Roland named a player for the New Orleans Saints. "He was having dinner with his girlfriend. He wouldn't want his wife to find out. I escorted them out through the kitchen. I went around to everybody we do business with and personally assured them that the police presence had nothing to do with either the restaurant or our enterprise."

"Do any of them know this kid, El Paso?"

"No."

"Or that he was acting on your behalf?"

"No."

"What about the restaurant staff?"

"They've seen him but don't know what he was doing for me tonight, and they don't ask questions about anyone I take into my office."

Allen removed the sleep mask and got out of bed. Carrying his can of soda with him, he padded over to a cheval glass and checked himself from several angles as he thought over everything Roland had told him.

"The kid said the homeless man hadn't moved for an hour and then came up fighting?"

"'Sprang up.'"

"When he saw the knife."

"Right. Until then, he'd just sat there hunched over and took the abuse."

"Seems strange that he was so passive, then suddenly got aggressive."

"Survival instinct, I guess," Roland said. "Although I don't entirely trust El Paso's story."

"You don't believe he actually cut the guy?"

"He might've stretched the truth to impress me, get back in my good graces. Yeah, there was blood on his knife, but I've explained that. And if El Paso did injure the other guy, it couldn't have been as bad as he made out, or else the man wouldn't have been able to run away like he did."

"Hmm."

"Lucky for us, El Paso got away, too. Both were motivated to clear out quick."

"No idea where the homeless man went?"

"None. The delivery truck missed him by a hair. Would have been better for us if it had killed him."

Allen couldn't agree more. "At least then we would know he wasn't a threat."

"We don't have to worry about that. I let on to El Paso that we did, but I don't actually think it. I laid it on pretty thick, told him he'd put the operation in jeopardy, but I said that only to knock him down several notches."

"Did it work?"

"No." Roland paused. "He's arrogant as hell. I've told you as much. I thought he'd be a handy guy to have around, you know? Lots of guts. Zero fear. I like that about him. Still do. But he's gotten way above himself, way too fast. I told him to scare a few people, not to create the friggin' circus he did."

"He didn't do as told," Allen said. "He seized the initiative and overstepped."

"Yeah, and if things had ended different, it could've been bad for us. So, what do you think? Kiss him goodbye before he becomes more of a liability than an asset?"

Allen took a sip of his soda, wandered back over to the bed, and sat down on the edge. Looking down at his bare feet, he realized he needed to call his pedicurist in the morning. "You need to ask?"

"Figured," Roland said.

"When will you handle it?"

"As early as tomorrow."

"I'm getting a pedicure tomorrow. Wait until the day after. I'd like to be there to personally bid El Paso farewell."

After several seconds of dead silence, Roland said, "Excuse me?"

"The way you describe him, he was defiant. Uncaring about the potential damage he could have caused. He's more audacious than that skimmer, Adler. In this operation, being too audacious is as dangerous as being too stupid. I want to watch the comeuppance of El Paso."

"I get that, but—"

"Don't worry. I'll stay out of sight and just observe." He chuckled. "Besides, it's not like he's going to live to tell about it."

Roland snorted. "No. So, day after tomorrow. Late. After I close the restaurant."

"How will you get him there?"

"That's the easy part. But I'll have to dump him somewhere other than Bayou Coeur. I heard from Auclair today. As of now, the sheriff's office is still investigating."

"I thought they would have given up by now."

"Just as well if they had. I was told that Darcy's got nothing. I was also told that Haskell was champing at the bit to get in on it, but Bowie is keeping him at his desk."

"Why would Haskell be so eager to get in on it?"

"He's an adrenaline junkie."

"Hmm." Allen set down his soda. "Night after next." He clicked off without further discussion.

He stretched out on the bed but didn't put his mask back on. His mind was churning too fast to go to sleep. Several aspects of the account he'd been given were troubling. Roland seemed to think there wouldn't be any repercussions from tonight's incident. But Oz wasn't comfortable discounting the possibility of blowback of some kind, no matter how minor.

Of course El Paso could be lying or exaggerating as Roland suspected.

But Allen couldn't help but wonder about a homeless man who had sprung up fighting, had possibly sustained a knife wound, yet had possessed the speed, agility, and derring-do to play chicken with a delivery truck, and then have enough wiliness to vanish.

What were the chances?

Slim to none.

Chapter 20

Mitch lowered his badge from directly in front of Dylan's face but held her stare of patent disbelief as she asked, "What did you say?"

"Roland Malone is your patient. I want to know what he's confessed to you."

Her breathing was rapid, shallow, and seemingly insufficient. She wet her lips. "That's what I thought you said, but I hoped I was wrong. You know I can't divulge—"

"Don't give me that privilege crap, Dylan. You can divulge it."

She made several attempts to speak but seemed incapable of forming words. He should feel good about that. He'd gotten her right where he'd wanted her—distressed and dismayed.

But it didn't feel good. Not at all. Not like he had imagined it would. When they had come face-to-face for the first time in her office waiting room and she had extended her hand to him, he'd wanted to bust through that barrier of cool composure. He'd wanted to see her rattled and rendered speechless.

But he knew now that her aloofness was an affectation, one she armed herself with in the name of professionalism. When they'd kissed last night, her safeguards hadn't stood a chance against the fire they'd stoked. And they hadn't even turned on the furnace full blast.

No, he didn't want to take a victory lap over the bewilderment with which she was looking at him now. But he steeled himself against letting the softer emotions he'd developed for Dylan, the woman, become a deterrent to cracking Dr. Reede, Roland Malone's counselor.

"What has Malone confided to you, Dylan?"

"All of this, your undercover work tonight, everything, has been about Roland?"

"Yes."

"Is he the reason you came to me as a patient?"

"John mandated it."

He could practically hear the gears grinding in her brain. "Yes," she said, nodding slowly, "John Bowie mandated it. But you made certain that he would."

He admitted to that with a half shrug. "For a long time, he had been after me to get help. So, yeah, ding ding," he said, tapping his forehead. "If I pushed him into making it compulsory, I could get to you."

"Why not just make an appointment to see me on your own?"

"Malone would have smelled a rat."

"I don't understand. How does he even know you?"

"We'll get to that. Anyway, I protested loudly and obscenely to John's insistence, then made it look like I gave in under duress."

"So you devised this elaborate scheme. You faked the drunken rampage."

He nodded. "Counting on John's response to it. I figured he would make therapy mandatory."

"What if I hadn't been on his list of psychologists?"

"I would have kept rejecting them for one reason or another until your name came around. But when he gave me his list, there you were. Actually, I wasn't all that surprised. John would have shopped top of the line for me. The shrink the department typically uses works on the cheap, and his track record for turning somebody around sucks, while you have a four-and-a-half-star rating."

He paused, frowning thoughtfully. "You could probably bump it up to five stars if you upgraded the candy in the waiting room to Snickers instead of those hard things."

She had gone from dismay to distrust to outright anger. He'd watched the evolution. That last remark set her off. "Don't you dare be cute with me." Fury-generated tears filled her eyes. "Do you not see that what you've done is despicable, or do you just not care?"

Mitch pretended to be unmoved by her increasing anger.

When he made no attempt to defend himself, she placed her fingertips vertically against her forehead and rubbed it, as though to erase all the negative connotations of what he was telling her. "Ellie told me that while you waited in the lobby, you seemed nervous, that you were stunned when you learned I was a woman. That was all an act?"

"Putting on acts is a crucial part of my job."

"You're very good at it," she said with emotional huskiness.

The disillusionment in her eyes hurt him to his core.

"How did you find out that Roland was my patient? And if you say that it's classified, I'll scream."

Jim Tucker had told him. He hadn't asked Tucker how he'd come by the information, because Tucker wouldn't have told him. But as soon as Tucker had shared it with him, he'd begun devising this plan.

He said, "I was tipped by a colleague who knew I would be interested to learn that Malone was routinely coming to Auclair for sessions with a Dr. Dylan Reede."

"Why would that interest you?"

Rather than answer, he asked, "Why did Malone pick you? Or is that one of the confidences you're sworn to protect?"

"I have several patients who come to me from out of town, usually because of one privacy issue or another."

"Okay. He's known because of his popular restaurant, so, for the moment, I'll accept the privacy factor."

"Like your hush-hush, out-of-town AA meetings."

"Yeah, like that," he said, frowning at her. "Anyhow, after I was given your name, I looked you up and admit to being surprised that you weren't male as your name had led me to assume.

"In your waiting room that morning, I pretended to be out of my depth when, in fact, I knew exactly what I was wading into." He hesitated, then added, "However, I was prepared to meet Roland Malone's Dr. Reede. I wasn't prepared for *you*."

"Oh, how sweet." Her tone was sugary; her eyes were throwing daggers. "And I suppose you expect me to believe that when you kissed me that morning, it was spontaneous."

"It was.

"Of course."

"I swear."

She chuffed and turned her head aside.

"Think about it, Dylan. If you had ratted me out to John, told him you couldn't continue with me, the jig would have been up. My scheme, as you call it, would have been screwed. So, yeah, that kiss was spontaneous, and it surprised the hell out of me, too."

He waited her out until finally she looked back at him, then he said, "Why didn't you tattle on me? You've never given me a straight answer to that, only some psychological stuff about transference and manipulation. Was that the real reason you didn't tell John? The only reason? Or was it because you felt the earth move the same as I did?"

Whispering, "Damn you," she raised both hands to cover her face and screamed behind them. Her body shook with the effort it took to contain the emotional outburst. This Dylan was the polar opposite of the one with the tight ponytail, her face a mask, sitting primly on the edge of her sofa while jotting down notes about her truculent new patient.

This wasn't the way he had wanted to watch her fall apart.

By a force of will, he kept himself from touching her while she struggled to temper her outrage. Ultimately she did, but even when she lowered her hands and looked at him, her eyes were glossed with tears borne of fury, her aspect hard and accusatory.

"All the trickery? What was it for? Besides making a fool of me, and continuing to, why did you do it?"

"Not to make a fool of you."

"Then why?"

"I told you why. Roland Malone."

"Then you've wasted your time and hoodwinking talents. I will not disclose anything about a patient. For which you should be very grateful, because I would have plenty to say about you. Like you breaking into my office on Tuesday morning. Were you after information on Roland? What were you looking for?"

"You. Remember? I told you I thought you might be in another room."

"Which is a damn lie that insults my intelligence." She looked ready to throttle him. "Go play your cop games, Mitch, but leave me out of them."

She turned in her seat and reached for the door handle, but before she could open it, Mitch placed his hand on her shoulder. "Listen to me, *listen to me*."

She stopped her struggle to open the door and turned her head, making a point of focusing on his restraining hand. He removed it immediately.

She said, "I'm done listening. You lie. You connive. I would never trust another word out of your mouth. Nothing. Not ever again."

"There are things you should know about Malone, if you don't know them already."

She was fumbling with the door handle, her efforts to unlatch it becoming more frantic. "Do you have a child lock on this?"

"No, it's an old truck. The handle is contrary." She stubbornly continued to yank on it. "Dylan, stop it, for god's sake. Look around us. You can't get out of the truck here."

"Watch me."

"How far do you think you'll get in those shoes?"

"I'll call Uber."

"No telling how long that would take, if one would come at all. It's dark out here. There's nobody around. It's beginning to rain in earnest. And—"

"What? And what?"

"And I have your phone." Since taking it from her when she went into the drugstore, he'd had it tucked between his thighs along with his nine-millimeter.

"Give it to me!"

"I know you're angry, but—"

"*Angry?*" She laughed with an edge of hysteria. "That doesn't come close. I'm infuriated. Give. Me. My. Phone."

"Shit!" he said under his breath. Then, "Listen. Just… please listen. I admit to everything you've accused me of. The playacting, conniving, all of it. Hoodwinking?" He leaned in and said with emphasis, "You're damn right I use trickery, because many a time my life has depended on fooling people. If I weren't good at it, I'd be dead several times over."

"Your life didn't depend on it this time."

"That remains to be seen."

She laughed. "What possible threat do I pose?"

"Malone."

She took a breath to speak, but didn't. She closed her mouth and visibly brought her rising temper under control again. She settled back but continued to regard him with suspicion. If he were to guess, he would think that in spite of herself, she was curious to know why he was interested in Malone.

He moderated his tone. "Give me a chance to explain why I tricked you. Please. Then if you still want to get out here in the middle of nowhere, I won't stop you."

"Why should I believe that?"

He thought for a moment, then replied in all sincerity, "If I were you, I wouldn't."

Her eyes searched his. After a time, she let go of the door handle and folded her arms across her middle. He didn't need a degree in psychology to read that body language.

She said, "I'll listen. Say what you will, but at the conclusion of your explanation, I still will not talk to you about one of my patients."

"It's not just any patient, Dylan. It's Roland Malone. How much do you know about him beyond him sneaking into Auclair to visit you? It's inconvenient and time-consuming, an hour and a half drive both ways. But he's not going to do sessions virtually, because heaven forbid that you record them.

"How does he pay you? No, let me guess. It's with a credit card for some obscure limited liability company that nobody's ever heard of. Blink if I'm getting warm."

She didn't blink. She didn't do anything. She kept her expression impassive and said nothing.

"All right, if you won't tell me anything about him, I'll tell you." He paused to segue. "For starters, he works for a big-time drug dealer who peddles product out of South and Central America through Mexico."

Finally: involuntary reactions. Her lips parted, her eyes opened wider.

He went on. "I'm not talking weed. I'm talking hard stuff, drugs that are either sold straight-up or laced into others. Buyer-beware-or-turn-up-dead kind of drugs. And this organization supplies them in such huge quantities they're readily available, even to kids. But that's the least of Malone's offenses."

He lifted the console cover and took from the compartment underneath a sheet of paper folded three times like a business letter. He unfolded it and reached up to switch on the map light above the rearview mirror.

"I had a DEA colleague, Randy Nelson. Thirty-four years old. Single, but engaged to be married. Good agent. Likable guy. Not movie star handsome but passably so. This is how he looked when John and I fished him out of Bayou Coeur."

He held the sheet out toward her. Reluctantly, she took it, looked down at the medium closeup photo of the late agent. A police photographer had taken it minutes after Nelson's body had been recovered.

Dylan raised a hand to her lips and looked up at Mitch in horror.

"Malone's handiwork. He doesn't hawk Oxy pills on street corners, Dylan. This," he said, tapping the picture with his index finger, "is his specialty. That picture of Nelson is over two years old. This week, Malone did the same thing to a seventeen-year-old female runaway and a dealer she'd been living with. Like Nelson, they were killed somewhere else and their bodies dumped in the bayou. You probably heard about that gruesome discovery on the news."

He took the paper from her listless hand, refolded it, replaced it in the console, and shut the lid. He turned off the light. A picture being worth a thousand words, he gave Dylan time to absorb what she'd seen and let her be the one to end the thick silence that ensued.

She gave a slight shake of her head. "You must be wrong. He owns a restaurant."

"A classy one," Mitch said. "Profitable. Which makes for an excellent front."

"He's owned it for years. It's his life work."

"That's true. And I've observed—"

"From your position in the median, disguised as a homeless man?"

He didn't acknowledge the question. "In the restaurant, Malone is hands-on. He greets his customers at the door and escorts them out. But how many restaurateurs do you know who have a chauffeur on call twenty-four seven? A chauffeur who packs heat, and not a popgun pistol, either. Serious weaponry.

"Malone put the guy in that position the day he got paroled after serving ten years for a long list of felonies, all drug trade related. Most of Ristorante Italiano's staff have comparable résumés."

While she processed what he'd told her, she turned her head and stared through the windshield, which was now streaked with rivulets of rain. Coming back to him, she asked, "If Roland is guilty of what you allege, why isn't he in prison?"

"Lack of evidence, and that's all I can say about it."

"Oh, I see. You can't divulge any information, but you expect me to be a fountain of it."

"I'm the one with the badge."

"And I'm the one with the doctorate," she fired back. "Which prohibits a breach of confidentiality."

They could pivot around that argument all night, and, regardless of what he'd told Dylan about his truck not being easily detectable, he could be wrong and was anxious to get it off the road.

Speaking more urgently, he said, "Malone has friends in high places. Compromised, corrupt friends in high places. New Orleans is a city well known for favors being swapped. I don't want to make a move on him until I have something an honest and by-the-book prosecutor can and will sink his teeth into."

"That's where I come in, I suppose. That's why you orchestrated this charade."

He just looked at her, not having to verbally verify that she was correct.

She shook her head again, this time with more decisiveness.

"I've listened, Mitch. But you've gone to a lot of trouble for nothing. I would never share what a patient has confided to me." She extended her hand. "My phone, please." He withheld it for several seconds before reluctantly laying it in her palm. "Thank you." She tried the door again. When it didn't open, she sighed. "Please unlock the door."

"Let me ask you one question."

"Unlock—"

"It's pouring out there." He motioned at their surroundings made virtually invisible by darkness and heavy rain. "Even I'm not sure where this road goes. Do you know?"

"I'll figure it out."

"One question."

She folded her arms again.

"Thanks."

"Just ask the question."

"Were you telling me the truth when you said that tonight was the first time you'd been to Malone's restaurant?"

"Easy answer. Yes. My first time. Why is that important?"

"What prompted you to go tonight?"

"I didn't agree to answering a second question."

He raised his eyebrows. "This one is harder to answer?"

She stewed on that for a moment, then said, "Roland invited me."

"Is that a first, too?"

"No. I had an open invitation."

"Any particular reason why you decided tonight was an ideal time to take him up on it?"

"No. Well, yes."

"Huh. Conflicting answers to one simple question. In police

parlance, we call that hedging. Which means not exactly lying, but—"

"I know what hedging means."

He snapped his fingers. "Right. You have a doctorate."

Obviously irritated by that, she said, "Roland extended the open invitation many times. But he made the invitation for tonight more specific."

"Emphatic?"

"*Specific.*"

"Why specific? Special occasion? Your birthday, maybe?"

"No special occasion."

He propped his elbow on the steering wheel and stroked his lower lip with his thumb, not breaking their eye contact. When she began to become impatient, he said in a drawl, "Want to know why I think he made tonight specific? I think he heard about the new patient you acquired this week."

"Who would have told him?"

He chuckled. "A career criminal like him has far-reaching tentacles. Any number of paid snitches could have alerted him to my first visit to your office."

"A lot of law enforcement officers get therapy."

"Yeah, but to Malone, I'm not just any cop. He doesn't know that I keep tabs on him, but I know he keeps tabs on me. And now I'm seeing his therapist? Ooooh, trust me, that would have shaken him. So he invited you to dinner. Did he do a little fishing about your practice?"

"He asked some general questions. Nothing about you. Why would you be 'not just any cop' to him?"

"Number one, because of my undercover work with the DEA. That's how he knows me. After I was out, he learned who

I was. Number two, I've maintained that my wife's death was staged to look like a suicide, when in fact she was murdered in retaliation for my work.

"Number three, as of this Monday, after two years of bereavement and alcohol dependency, I began opening up my heart about Angela's tragic death to a therapist. Who also happens to be *his* therapist."

He recognized the instant it dawned on her what he was getting at. "Are you saying that Roland killed Angela?"

"Yeah. That's what I'm saying."

Chapter 21

Dylan sat for a while, staring through the windshield. Rain was beating on the roof of the pickup, but at least it relieved the silence between them. Mitch had laid a lot on her and respected her need to think it through.

Eventually she said, "You told me that two people were responsible for Angela's death."

"I can't get to the second one until I have Malone."

"You don't even know that he was involved."

"Yes, I do."

"How do you know?"

"I *know*."

"I, I, I. You always talk about this in first person. Whose authority are you working under?"

When he didn't respond, she huffed a sound of disbelief. "No one's? No agency? This is a personal crusade?" She laughed softly but without mirth. "Considering your actions tonight, why should that amaze me?"

"I'm not working in a vacuum. I have some help."

"But this is your fight."

"It's my *war*. These are evil men. I'm going to put them out of commission."

She frowned with apparent concern. "What if you're caught doing something illegal and sent to prison? What if you're caught in a crossfire and injured more seriously than you were tonight? Or killed? Think about what that would mean to Andrew."

"I've got that covered."

"With your in-laws?"

"I've got it covered, all right?" he said testily. "That's all I'm going to say about it."

"Because I obviously struck a nerve."

"No, because the less you know, the better. For your own protection."

"From what?"

"From Malone, Dylan. From Malone."

"Why would I need protection from him?"

"Think about it. Why else would he have urged you to come to his restaurant, first time ever and on short notice, except that he found out I was seeing you, and that bothered him."

She bit her lower lip. "I'm not conceding the point, but I can see why you might jump to that conclusion. As a detective, it's your job to look for possible motives. That doesn't mean you're always right."

"True, but let's say that this time I'm spot on. He must be at least a little nervous that you, being an upstanding citizen, might relax your professional code of confidentiality, and, in the name of justice, share with me at least some of what he's unloaded to you."

"I wouldn't. I *won't*. I've told you that. I've told him that."

"Yeah, but guys like Malone live with a chronic case of paranoia. What I think, Dr. Reede? Your patient is shitting bricks right about now." He motioned toward her phone. "Open it and check for texts. Several came in while you were in the drugstore."

"And you're just now telling me?"

"There hasn't been time. You're the one who insisted on rendering first aid." Ignoring her censorious look, he said, "I'm betting that you have at least one from Malone."

Looking resentful, she tapped in her passcode. "There are three from the driver who was picking me up. I'm sure he's wondering what happened to me."

"Cancel."

"I will, but only because he's probably already headed back to Auclair." She glanced toward his midsection. "And because you're bleeding. Also because you're deranged, a danger to yourself and others, and shouldn't be left unsupervised. I'm licensed to make that determination, you know."

"Unlicensed people have determined that, too."

"Don't you dare joke," she admonished crossly.

"Wasn't joking."

She quickly sent the text canceling the car and using Venmo to pay. Then she cast a cautious glance toward Mitch. "There is a text from Roland."

He leaned over and looked at the screen. "No name ID, but you obviously recognized the number. How often do you two correspond?"

She didn't reply to that but opened the text and scanned it. "He apologized for abandoning me, asked if I am all right." Looking at Mitch, she said, "I left during the dust-up in the median without an explanation or a goodbye. Doesn't it stand to reason that he would be concerned enough to text me?"

"It does stand to reason, so text him back. Tell him you made it home without incident and that you're looking forward to a quiet, relaxing weekend. Thank him for the dinner. Sign off."

"I would do that without you instructing me to."

"Exactly. He would expect it. So, not to arouse his ingrained paranoia, make nice."

"I'm not acknowledging that he's paranoid," she said as she typed the text.

Before she sent it, he said, "May I see?"

He took the phone from her, read the text, said, "Very good," and sent it. But when she reached out to retrieve her phone, he held on to it, deftly took the back off, and removed the battery.

"What are you doing?" she cried.

He dropped both her phone and the battery into a pocket of the windbreaker. "What does it look like?"

"Like you're rendering my phone useless."

"Good guess. Mine's already disabled. For the rest of the night, we're off the grid."

"Are you insane?"

"Just deranged."

"Mitch!"

"You won't be missed for a day or two."

"Missed for *a day or two*? I have patients."

"Not tomorrow. Your office is closed. Three-day weekend. I know because I called to make an appointment. Ellie told me she had to go out of town to see her sick sister, so you decided to take a long weekend, too, and didn't book any appointments for Friday." He gave her a look that dared her to contradict him.

She didn't, but she was vexed. "You're taking me home, Mitch. Right now!"

"Not tonight. Not until I learn how Malone reacted to the incident in the median."

"He had nothing to do with that."

"We'll see," he said in a doubtful tone. "But until I'm sure of that, you stay within my sight. No more argument. Buckle up."

He started the truck and executed a jerky three-point turn that pulled at the knife wound and caused it to hurt. Securing the steering wheel with his right hand, he pressed his left against his side. His palm came away wet with fresh blood. "Shit."

Having seen the problem, Dylan said, "Mitch, please be sensible. Find the nearest emergency center and get stitches."

"We'll put some of those clips on it when we get there."

"Get where?"

He looked at her and grinned. "You're in for a treat."

An hour and a half later, Dylan wouldn't use the word "treat" to describe the environment in which she found herself.

The large, cluttered room was dominated by the stuffed head of a snarling razorback. The boar shared the faded-wallpaper walls with other hunting and fishing trophies, yellowed and curled Mardi Gras posters from years gone by, and photographs and artifacts representing aspects of the Cajun culture.

If everything collected here had been displayed in glass cases inside a modern building surrounded by civilization, it would qualify as a museum.

But there hadn't been any signs of civilization for the last few miles Mitch had driven in order to get here. There hadn't been a signpost on the narrow state highway to indicate a turnoff, but Mitch had known where it was and had taken it at an indiscriminate speed, plunging them into a forest as eerie as any in a Grimm brothers' fairy tale.

The darkness was unrelieved by any light source save for the pickup's headlights. The beams bounced off low-hanging tree branches draped in Spanish moss, and once caught the shiny, agate eyes of some species of wildlife.

The rutted track they'd taken off the highway led to a building that was barely detectible. Mitch boasted that he and John Bowie had painted it in camouflage themselves. He'd gone through a tedious process to unlock and open an overhead garage door. Inside the structure was a compact car.

He'd steered his pickup in alongside it and helped her to squeeze out. He'd gathered up all the bloody clothing and used gauze pads from the floorboard and bundled everything into the jacket he'd worn to look homeless.

He'd asked her to grab the bag of first aid items, then had reversed the process to secure the garage. To Dylan, its near invisibility made the security measures seem superfluous.

Taking her hand, he'd said, "Don't let go, or you might never be found," and had struck off on foot through the woods.

"Couldn't we use a flashlight?"

"Definitely not. They attract the gators."

She stopped in her tracks. *"What?"*

"Kidding." Tugging on her hand, he'd claimed not to need a light. "I know my way."

Contributing to the creepiness was a thick fog, which had made it impossible for her to see anything clearly, and the falling mist was so fine, it had felt like a sheer veil drifting across her face. She'd tried to keep from tripping over exposed tree roots, or getting bogged down in the spongy ground, or stumbling over the natural debris that littered it.

Mitch's surefooted tread had been soundless.

They hadn't gone all that far before she saw the blurry outline of a structure. It gradually had taken the shape of a house built in the Acadian style with a sloping roof and wide front porch.

When they reached the front steps, Mitch had cautioned her to be careful of the second one. "It rocks, but that's on purpose."

"Why?"

"To alert anyone inside of an unexpected approach."

The explanation had an ominous ring, but she'd let it pass.

Mitch had produced a key from under a porch floorboard, used it to open the door, then had ushered her inside and flipped a wall switch to turn on a bright overhead light.

Noticing that she'd blinked against the sudden glare, he'd gone around the room turning on lamps, then had extinguished the overhead fixture. He'd also switched on a wall-mounted AC unit that coughed and sputtered but produced a stream of cool air that relieved the stuffiness.

Now he was facing her, apparently amused by her stupefaction. "John told me Beth had the same reaction the first time she was here. Kinda dumbfounded."

"I don't quite know what to make of it."

"It's a fishing camp, handed down through generations of John's family, his father's, I think. It now belongs to him by default. Nobody else wanted it."

"Well, it is rather hard to get to."

"Except by water. We're on an island, surrounded by a network of bayous, which you have to know like the back of your hand to find the place. That track we took from the highway to the garage is the only way to drive on and off it."

"It's an inconvenient location."

"Not for moonshiners and bootleggers." He grinned. "But that was a century ago. Now, it's sorta John's secret hideout. Maybe I should've blindfolded you before I got to the turnoff."

"Don't worry. If tortured I couldn't tell anyone where I am. Do you come here often?"

"Yeah. John and I spend a lot of time here. Well, we did," he said and shrugged ruefully. "I'll be right back." He turned away.

Unable to suppress her sudden panic, she said, "Where are you going?"

"To wash the blood off my hands. If you need a bathroom... through there." He pointed to a doorway on the far side of the large room.

He went into a room on the opposite side and closed the door.

She stayed where she was, feeling the glassy eyes of the stuffed animals staring down at her. Eventually she ventured into the kitchen area, set the drugstore bag on the dining table, and washed her hands in the large, utilitarian sink, using liquid soap from a dispenser. As she was drying them with a paper towel, Mitch rejoined her.

He took two bottles of water from the refrigerator and passed one to her. She was too thirsty to refuse it, but after taking a long draught, she said, "Mitch, we can't possibly stay here."

"It's rustic in character, but it's got electricity and a freezer full of good Cajun cooking. After John and Beth married, she insisted on upgrading the bathroom fixtures. A toilet hasn't backed up since, so you're safe on that score."

He looked down at her evening shoes, which the walk from the garage had all but finished off. "I'm sure Beth's got some shoes here that you can swap out for those. You appear to be about the same size."

"It's not the amenities, Mitch. It's—"

"I know what it is. You're afraid you won't be able to resist my animal magnetism. Hey, it happens. Especially in a secret and sultry atmosphere. Tell you what. To avoid temptation, you can bunk in John and Beth's bed. I'll use the guest room, where I sleep when I'm here." He indicated the room he'd gone into to wash his hands. "I have a designated drawer and everything."

She exhaled. "Stop being funny. I'm telling you *seriously* that Roland was busy in the restaurant all evening. From eight o'clock when I arrived until you saw us come out, I can vouch that he was in the dining room.

"When the fight in the median started, he was livid, cursing a blue streak, which isn't the reaction of someone who expected or planned it. He blamed it on the homeless infiltration of the neighborhood.

"He wouldn't have had an inkling that you were the homeless man. He certainly wouldn't draw a connection to me. So I assure you that I'm safe to go home." She scoffed. "You thought my office building was unsafe. This 'hideout' has a rocky porch step as a security system. In any case, I'm not bunking here. I'm not going into hiding."

Following her long monologue, she anticipated he would counter. But really, what was there for him to argue? When he didn't come back with so much as a murmur, she motioned toward his side. "Since you stupidly refuse to go to an ER, I'll tend to your side as best I can, then you will take me home."

"In the morning."

"Tonight."

"After the sun comes up."

"Tonight, Mitch. Otherwise this is kidnapping. You don't want to add that to your other offenses." She stepped around him, went to the dining table, and began removing items from the shopping bag. "Your clothes are filthy. Before we start, you should shower. Use a disinfectant soap if there is any."

He walked to the bedroom he had claimed was his. Before going in, he looked at her over his shoulder and winked. "Three minutes and already you want me naked."

She turned her back on him. He was chuckling as he pulled the door closed.

He emerged fifteen minutes later, clean and shampooed, his face free of the "dirt" makeup, which had begun to itch. The jeans he'd taken from his assigned drawer in the antique bureau were old and worn with stringy hems. He'd slung a T-shirt over his right shoulder, but hadn't seen the point of putting it on only to take it off. He was also barefoot, and, seeing that Dylan noticed, he said, "We go casual around here."

"I gathered."

"You've been busy." He surveyed the dining table, where she had organized the first aid articles. "You could moonlight as a surgical nurse. Here." He handed her a bottle of peroxide he'd discovered in the bathroom medicine cabinet. "I might put it in the wrong place, and I'd hate to mess up the system you've got going."

"This is a good addition," she said, placing the bottle just so. "How's your side?"

"Stung in the shower. I didn't want to stain Beth's white towels, so I scrounged around and was lucky to find this one."

He pulled a gray towel away from his side and peered beneath it. "Still leaking. But not as bad. All the same..."

He looked her over and clicked his tongue against the roof of his mouth. "That blouse is killer. It would be a shame to get a bloodstain on it. Beth wouldn't mind loaning you something to change into."

"I'd only have to change out of it when I leave."

He withheld his comment on that.

She pulled a chair out from under the table. "Sit."

"You sit. I'll stand."

"Why?"

"Because if I'm on my feet and it starts hurting, I can run away."

She laughed softly. "Mitch, I don't think you've ever run away from anything in your life."

"Yes, I have."

"Like what?"

"Idleness. Boredom. Safety."

"That I can believe."

"Uh-oh. You're wishing you had your notepad, aren't you? You'd jot that down."

"Maybe the lure of action and danger is something we should talk about in our next session."

"Maybe not." He motioned down at the chair. "You sit. You'll have a better vantage point, and I don't want you making any mistakes."

She sat down and inspected the gash. "Well, I don't think it's a mortal wound."

"That's a relief."

"Nevertheless," she said, "hold that towel under it while I douse it." She used the peroxide, which he told her didn't burn like the alcohol had. "But you can still blow on it." She rolled her eyes up toward him, and he grinned. "A guy can try."

"Some have to try harder out of necessity."

"Oh, now that hurt, and I'm not talking about whatever that stuff is you're smearing on me now."

"Antiseptic cream."

He flinched a few times, although her touch was light, and he liked looking down on the crown of her head. As she turned it this way and that, her hair slid from one shoulder to the other, all sleek and satiny.

Fantasizing how it would feel sliding over his belly and thighs fell into the category of "impure thoughts," which required extra time in the confessional booth. He tried to sweep them from his mind and picked up on what she'd said a moment ago. "Others have tried?"

Carefully dabbing on the cream, she asked absently, "Hmm?"

"Men."

She raised her head from her task and looked up at him.

"Others have tried?" he repeated. "Did any succeed? Or give up and go away? Are any still trying, lurking about in the desperate hope that you'll change your mind?"

"Are you asking if I've had affairs?"

"I'm on pins and needles."

She returned to applying the salve. "I thought we'd established that I don't talk about my personal life with patients."

"Before we decide whether or not to talk about it, let's establish whether or not you have one. Do you?"

"If I answer that, I'm talking about it."

He smiled, although she was looking at his belly and didn't see it. "I didn't want it to come down to this, Dr. Reede."

At his stern tone of voice, she raised her head again.

"I could play the cop card, you know. Take you to the station for formal questioning."

"About my private life?"

"With a focus on your friendship with Roland Malone."

"He's a patient, not a friend."

"So say you now. But I'd be interested to hear what you have to say after spending countless hours in an uncomfortable interrogation room."

"I would say the same."

"Oh, I wouldn't be too sure of that. When I really start applying the heat, big, burly bad guys crack after only an hour or two. It wouldn't take near that long with you. I think the CAP unit has a pair of thumbscrews in a junk drawer somewhere."

He saw her trying to conceal the smile tugging at the corners of her God-I-want-that-mouth-on-me mouth, but she calmly returned her attention to his wound.

She squeezed a dab of the cream from the tube onto her fingertip and began smoothing it over the thinnest part of the cut, which was just beneath his navel. She applied it in a swirling motion.

Sweet Jesus, if lust could kill you, this would be a mortal wound.

When satisfied that she'd covered the area, she capped the tube of antiseptic and reached for the box of butterfly closures. Taking out several, she lined them up with precision.

"What's it going to be, doc?" he asked. "You talk to me here, or I haul you in."

"Please do," she said. "I could tell John Bowie about your escapade tonight. I would accuse you of kidnapping, you would be severely reprimanded for questioning me without an attorney present, and I would file a lawsuit against the police department for harassment and false arrest." She opened the first closure and held it above the deepest part of the gash. "This may hurt."

Chapter 22

It hurt like the very devil, but Mitch remained stoic while she laid a track of closures along the cut. When she finished with the last one, she assessed her handiwork, then pushed back her chair and went over to the sink to wash her hands.

"They're holding for now," she said, "but I don't recommend you do anything strenuous for the next several days."

As he pulled on his T-shirt, he grimaced. "I promise I won't."

"If it looks like it's getting infected—"

"I've already taken a couple of antibiotic capsules. John keeps a stash here."

"He keeps a stash?"

"The swamp teems with germs and hazards. There are lots of ways to get sick, debilitated, or dead."

"Well, I won't be here long enough to experience any of that." She finished returning all the first aid supplies to the shopping bag and, after tying a loose knot to close it, handed it to him. "Take this with you and keep it handy. Those closures will need replacing. Don't forget to use the salve. As soon as I use the bathroom, we can go."

"Not until I've eaten something. You indulged in Roland Malone's fine cuisine. I didn't have dinner of any sort, and I'm starving."

She looked perturbed and ready to argue, but all she said was, "Excuse me," and went into John and Beth's bedroom.

As soon as the door closed behind her, he went over to a sideboard attached to the wall. The upper half of it had open shelving loaded with mismatched dishes and glassware. The bottom was formed by three deep drawers. One of them contained another of John's stashes: a collection of burner phones that had never been used. They were good to have on hand.

He chose one that was fully charged and sent Jim Tucker a text: **Anything?**

By the time Dylan returned to the kitchen, he was opening a can of soup. "Steak and potato. A whole meal in a can. I'm happy to share," he said as he emptied the contents into a saucepan and turned on the stove.

"No thank you."

"Something to drink?"

"Water's fine." She picked up the bottle she'd left on the table and took a drink. "Isn't that John Bowie in the picture on the nightstand in the bedroom?"

"With the tall, lanky girl? That's John and his daughter from his first marriage. Molly. That picture was taken about eight years ago. Out of high school, she got a scholarship to a ritzy art school in Manhattan. She's up there now."

"Do they have a good relationship?"

He scoffed. "They'd walk through fire for each other. Fortunately, she doesn't mind sharing him with Beth. She and Molly took to each other from the start."

While explaining that, the soup had heated. He took a box of crackers from the pantry, tested one for staleness, and decided they were fresh enough. He ladled soup into a bowl he took from the sideboard, got a spoon from the silverware drawer, and carried everything over to the table. "Sure you don't want anything besides water?"

"I'm sure."

He motioned toward the empty chair across from him. "Have a seat."

"Mitch, I need to get home."

"Are you just going to hover while I eat?"

She sighed and, with exaggerated annoyance, pulled out the chair. He didn't sit until she did, then he ate a couple of spoonfuls of soup and a cracker, reached for a napkin in the holder in the center of the table, and wiped his mouth. "What happened down there in Central America?"

Dylan yanked her gaze from the stuffed alligator mounted on the wall. Her posture, her expression, everything about her went *en garde*.

He said, "You had just as well talk about it, because I already know what happened."

"Of course. You looked me up and pieced bits together to form a history."

"Yeah, but you miss a lot when you're working with bits. You can overlook key pieces. To a detective, that's like having a dull toothache that hangs on until those missing pieces come to light and you get the full picture."

Rather than look at him directly, she stared at the strands of

Mardi Gras beads dangling from a wall sconce a few degrees to the left behind his head and just below the gator.

"Where did you meet George?"

He could tell she considered ignoring him. Then, seemingly resigned, she looked at him directly. "At school."

"Duke University."

"Since you know so much, would you rather tell the story?"

He made an apologetic gesture that invited her to proceed while he methodically ate his soup.

"George was finishing grad school at the same time I got my bachelor's. We married within months."

"Was he also a psych major?"

"Philosophy and sociology."

"That makes sense. All his goodwill work." He scraped the bottom of his bowl and pushed it aside. He ate one last cracker and took a drink from his bottle of water, waiting to see if she would continue without prodding. She didn't.

He said, "I know the basics, Dylan. What can it hurt to share a few details? I'm not even asking about you, per se."

"You told me you weren't sure what that expression meant."

"I was lying."

"I know."

He waited a beat. "It's George I want to know about."

"Why?"

"Curiosity. In all the media about what happened, he comes across as being so noble. Was that an acquired trait, or was he born that way?"

"He wouldn't have seen himself as being noble."

"That's what made him noble."

"God! There's no arguing with you."

He gave her a contrite smile. "That's what Angela always

said." He folded his arms on the table and leaned on them. "Tell me about George."

She stared at the gaudy beads again, either trying to figure out how much she was going to relate or puzzling over why the beads were hanging on the light fixture, which was something he'd always wondered himself.

Eventually she began. "When I met him, he had already spent a lot of time in Central America. Through high school and college, he'd spent every summer volunteering with one welfare organization or another. He'd visited just about every country numerous times, was fluent in Spanish, and had a working knowledge of many regional dialects. He was keen to write a book."

"About his experiences?"

"Not so much about himself, but an exposé on the political corruption, the squalid living conditions of thousands, the lack of modern medicine and basic education."

"Violent insurgencies."

"Yes," she said softly.

It was a bad idea to cast aspersions on a knight in shining armor, especially a deceased one. He figured the best tactic was to ease into it. He stalled by taking another drink of water and finally said, "Despite the volatile political climate and poor living conditions, George volunteered to go back down there and take you with him."

"Yes. He signed on with a welfare program and committed us to a year."

"A year. You agreed to that and went willingly?"

She gave a soft laugh. "I was a newlywed."

"Starry-eyed."

She conceded that with a nod. "In love with a man who

passionately wanted to help people in oppressed areas where each day presented a challenge to their very survival."

"He was an idealist."

"You can call him that if you like, but he wasn't quixotic. He was also a realist. He saw a desperate need and genuinely wanted to fill it. That's why I fell in love with him."

"You never entertained second thoughts about committing yourself to spending a year in a potentially hostile environment?"

"Not really."

It was a qualified denial, and Mitch didn't believe it anyway.

She must have sensed his skepticism, because she came back defensively. "We were sent to a very remote village in a region where there hadn't been any political unrest. We were warmly welcomed by the villagers. Their homes were hovels. The school was a hut on the brink of collapse. Our mission was to build a proper one. We worked diligently. The school was almost finished." She stopped and her expression turned bleak.

"And then?"

She took a deep breath. "There was a coup in the capital city. The president was executed in a public square. Sides formed. Rebels, contra rebels, vigilante gangs who were completely lawless and indiscriminately preyed on all factions.

"George tried to remain neutral, but it was inevitable that being a norteamericano he would come under suspicion, as would the villagers who'd come to idolize him. One night, one of the most infamous gangs raided the village. Two of the young men who were helping George build the school were murdered. Brutally, in front of their families.

"During the exchange of gunfire, George was shot in the thigh. One of the gang members was also killed. The attackers retreated into the jungle but not before vowing reprisal for the death of their compatriot.

"George insisted that I return to the United States immediately. Not without him, I said. But he refused to leave until the school was finished. He had promised the villagers, and himself, that he wouldn't abandon the project until it was completed.

"He insisted that his leg wound wasn't that serious. No severed artery, no broken bone. We had a limited supply of penicillin he could inject into himself to stave off infection. He could walk with the help of a walking stick stout enough to use on mountain trails. He would be fine, he said. It was barely a scratch. And so forth."

She gave him a meaningful look before continuing. "He would be right behind me, he said. Another week, two at the most, the school would be finished. I pleaded with him to come with me then, but..." She reached for her water bottle, uncapped it, and took a drink.

"The following day tension was high. Everyone was fearful the vigilantes would return. When darkness fell, one of the brave young men of the village drove me through the jungle to a landing strip still operated by the country's military, which by then was ragtag at best.

"The welfare organization had sent a small plane to fly George and me out. The pilot was shocked to learn that he wasn't with me. He warned me that he might not be able to return for George and gave me only minutes to decide whether to stay or go."

She raised her hands in a helpless gesture. "Obviously, I boarded the plane. I was flown to San José, Costa Rica. From there, I took a commercial flight to Dallas."

After taking another sip of water, she continued. "When we

landed, the captain came on over the speaker and instructed everyone to remain seated while a passenger was escorted off. I was led by a flight attendant to the jetway where I was met by emissaries from the US state department.

"They escorted me to a room. Of course I knew then that George was dead, but they made it official. He'd been killed by 'hostiles.' The unfinished school had been set on fire. George and roughly half of the villagers were either shot or hacked to death with machetes."

The silence that followed was interrupted by the drip-drip of the faucet. Mitch waited a full minute before saying anything. "Dylan, you can't blame yourself for leaving when you did."

She raised her head from the study of her hands tightly clasped on the tabletop. "I don't. I made the only choice I could. I was pregnant."

Mitch's stomach dropped.

"I'd been back in the States for only a week when I miscarried," she said. "I gather from your stunned reaction that that was one of the missing pieces you didn't know."

He ran his fingers through his hair. "No, I didn't know. Did George?"

Smiling ruefully, she shook her head. "I knew if I told him, it would only strengthen his insistence that I leave. But... but if I had told him, if he had known that he was going to be a father, maybe he would have left with me. I'm haunted by my decision not to tell him."

It was that decision that kept her inside the bell jar. And Mitch understood her need for that self-defense mechanism all too well.

He got up, cleared the table, and rinsed out everything he'd used before turning back to her. "I told you that the night I lost

Angela, John and I were working late. Tough case, and we were getting nowhere. We decided to shut down and pick up in the morning. As we left headquarters together, I suggested we stop and get a beer. I'd already told Angela I was going to be late. What were a few more minutes?"

Dylan covered her mouth with her hand. She knew what was coming.

"When I found her, her body wasn't even cold," he said, his voice cracking. "I'm haunted by those extra twenty minutes I took to drink a beer."

They were looking into each other's eyes with such complete understanding and compassion that they both jumped when the burner in Mitch's pocket rang.

Only one person knew to call it.

Chapter 23

"I've gotta get this." With no more explanation than that, Mitch left Dylan sitting at the table, went swiftly into the guest bedroom, and clicked on the phone as he pulled the door shut. "Jim. Find out anything?"

"El Paso."

"What?"

"Short and spry goes by the name El Paso. Even Malone refers to him that way. No one knows his real name."

"So he *is* one of Malone's men."

"A kid. Early twenties at most. And he's only been around for a week or so, coinciding with Adler's departure."

"Where'd you get this information?"

"A paid informant."

"Reliable?"

"He has been as of tonight, and nobody's wise to him."

"You know this how?"

"He's still breathing."

"Okay, why'd this kid jump me?"

"You weren't the only one he jumped, just the last one." Tucker told him about two previous incidents involving homeless people that had occurred within blocks of Malone's restaurant. "Malone has zero tolerance. Our snitch thinks he dispatched El Paso to spook a few so all of them would move to greener pastures."

"I was a random pick, then."

"I hope."

"Had to be, Jim. No way he could have known I was a cop."

"I hope. But we don't know that for sure, do we? He might've been stabbing homeless people, believing them to be you, doing exactly what you've been doing, which is unauthorized spying on his boss."

"Not a chance he knew me. I'd never laid eyes on him."

"Somebody could've pointed you out to him," Tucker argued. "Malone himself, maybe."

"Then why would he attack the other two?"

"To make you seem random."

Shit. That made sense. Uncomfortably so. Mitch moved on. "Does your informant know where El Paso went after he attacked me?"

"When I asked him that, he dried up."

"Bullshit."

"I swear."

"You're holding out on me."

"No. He got antsy and amnesia at the same time. He's scared of Malone. *And* of El Paso. Says he has evil eyes."

"What else about him?"

"Nothing else."

"That's it? He's a twenty-year-old with evil eyes? That describes my nephew. I need more than that."

"Well, that's all I've got. Look, I'm busy here, juggling with one hand. I need to go."

"Wait." Mitch rapidly strung together everything Tucker had told him and added it to the agent's sudden haste to conclude. "When a snitch dries up, he or she is replaced. Pronto."

Tucker said nothing.

"Jim? I'd bet my left nut that one of your undercovers got a sudden hankering for Ristorante Italiano's pasta."

Nothing.

Mitch persisted. "Your new person spotted El Paso. He recognized him from the description your first snitch and I provided, right?" He waited, then said, "Your stone silence confirms I'm right. So tell me where the knife-wielding little bastard went after our fight."

Tucker swore lavishly. "Mitch, I can't."

"You *can*. Please."

After more obscenities, the agent sighed. "It was too late to order dinner. My person had tiramisu and coffee."

"Was Malone still in residence?"

"Yes. After closing, my person hung around and spied El Paso slinking in through the kitchen door in back. About fifteen minutes later, he left by the same door and headed down the alley. My person followed, but lost him in the dark."

"So you don't know where El Paso lays his head?"

"No."

"Swear?"

"Swear."

Mitch believed him, but only because the agent sounded

frustrated, too. "Okay. Keep me posted. If I change phones, you'll get a text. Otherwise, use this number to reach me."

"Hold on," Tucker said. "I have a question for *you*."

"No, the cut across my gut wasn't fatal, but thanks for asking."

"Not that. Tell me about the restaurant's new menu item."

Mitch's heart thumped. He glanced toward the closed bedroom door separating him from the main room. "What about it?"

"Buzz is that it was quite a dish. A *hot* dish."

"Who gave you that?"

"The paid snitch. Before he dried up, he was very animated on that particular topic. Told me that for the better part of the evening Malone himself oversaw that it was served just right. Sat at the table where it was being served for maybe ten minutes. Gave personal attention to it."

Mitch realized he was grinding his teeth. "Did your snitch get its name?"

"'Mr. Malone's guest.' That's it."

"Huh."

"So what's its name?" Tucker asked.

"Can't say."

"Can't or won't?"

"Won't. The tenderizing marinade is taking longer than I thought."

"That's cute, Mitch, but this is serious shit. Your meddling could screw the pooch for us—us being the agency and me—in an already combustible week."

"Why combustible?"

"Meddling could also get you killed."

"Why combustible?"

"Or both."

Mitch relented. Tucker had told him all he was going to about the combustibility of this week. "At least get me some intel on El Paso, please."

"Did you hear what I said?"

"I'm being careful, Jim."

He gave a bitter laugh. "And I'm farting Chanel Number Five." With that, he disconnected.

Mitch sat on the bed for a time, reviewing what he'd been told and thinking over what he should do with it. Reaching a decision, he called Auclair PD dispatch. When the duty officer answered, he identified himself.

"Hey, Mitch. Couldn't tell it was you. ID says caller unknown."

"My cell's out of juice. I'm using a spare."

"I thought it might be a whack job calling in."

"Well, some in the department would think so."

"I didn't mean nothing by that," the officer said quickly. "I wasn't referring to you having to see the shrink and all."

"No offense taken. Is Clarence on patrol tonight?"

"Let's see." After a moment, "No, he's got the morning shift. Goes on at seven."

Mitch checked his watch. It was two-forty. "Well, he owes me a favor. Do you have his cell number handy?"

When he went back into the main room, Dylan was pacing, eyes to the floor, tapping her fist against her chin. Immediately she stopped and turned to him looking inquisitive and anxious. "Who was that?"

"Tell me about El Paso."

She gazed at him blankly. "The city?"

"The person."

She bowed her head and pressed her temples with the heels of her hands. "Mitch, I can't keep up. I have no idea what you're talking about."

He didn't think her bafflement was faked. But there was too much at stake not to persist. "You created a buzz at the restaurant tonight."

She scoffed. "Hardly."

"Oh, you did. Mr. Malone himself personally oversaw the service you received."

"I was his guest."

"That was noted, too."

"By whom? Who called you? Despite denying it, were you having me spied on?"

"This is my interrogation, not yours. Do you know any of Malone's associates?"

She rolled her lips inward, sealing them. Then, "Take me home now. Right now."

"Answer the question," he said, raising his voice.

"I don't have to," she shouted back.

"You do if you want a ride home."

That astounded her. She flung her arms wide to encompass the room. "What is this, house arrest? Before you start interrogating me, shouldn't you flash your badge or read me my rights? Can I expect thumbscrews? An ankle bracelet?"

"It's a simple yes-or-no question, Dylan. Do you know any of Malone's—"

"*No!* Until tonight he and I have never even met outside my office."

"Who was at the table with you?"

"I ate alone. That also should have been noted," she said snidely. "There was no buzz. I didn't even talk to anyone except for the maître d', the waiter, and Roland. We chatted for a few minutes before I left."

"Where?"

"He sat down at the table with me."

"Just the two of you?" He crossed his arms over his chest, widened his stance, and cocked his head to one side. "What did you and Row-land talk about?"

His mocking tone pissed her off. If he'd been in her shoes, it would have pissed him off, too. She stretched up to her full height and narrowed her eyes. "Nothing that concerns you."

"Don't count on it."

Her story coincided with what he'd been told about her evening. If she had been in someone's company during dinner, Tucker's informant would have told him. Although it turned his stomach to think of her in private conversation with Malone, how much significance should he give it? A host making certain his guest had been satisfied? Fine. But he didn't like it, and his viewpoint wasn't entirely objective.

She was still miffed. "Is that it? Did I pass? Are we done now?"

"No."

He walked over to a three-legged end table that separated a pair of matching easy chairs. He picked up a baseball, which, for some unknown reason, was sitting in an ashtray from Pat O'Brien's.

Casually bouncing the ball in his hand, he said, "You weren't introduced to El Paso? He was around tonight."

"So we're back to that?" She looked helpless and bewildered. "Is that a trick question? Are you trying to lay a trap for me, or is that really someone's name?"

He lifted the hem of his T-shirt. "He's the guy who did this. He works for Malone."

Taken aback by this new piece of information, her breath hitched, her indignant posture relaxed, and she turned her head aside as though needing time to process.

He continued bouncing the baseball in his palm. "After the scuffle, after the restaurant closed, after you and I were long gone, El Paso was seen clandestinely entering the restaurant through the kitchen door."

"But if he works there—"

"He doesn't wash dishes or sweep up, Dylan. He knifes people. There were two other assaults on homeless people tonight. While you were enjoying your dinner, that kid with the swagger and the switchblade was out doing your patient Roland's dirty work. And El Paso, or someone of his ilk, may not be finished for the night. Which is why you're staying here."

"Mitch—"

"Arguing about it won't change my mind, so save your breath. You texted Malone that you'd made it home without incident. I'm ninety-nine percent certain that he will check to make sure you're there."

"Why would he do that?"

"To test your honesty. That's what tonight's spontaneous dinner was about. He was feeling you out because of—"

"Your sessions with me."

"Well, good! You're finally getting it."

He dropped the baseball back into the ashtray and sat down in one of the chairs. Its seat cushion had been worn thin by Bowie family posteriors.

And Mitch's own butt had contributed to the indentation in the cushion's center. He couldn't count the hours that John and he had sat side by side in this pair of chintz eyesores and talked over cases, or planned their next fishing excursion, or laughed over escapades they'd shared that got more exaggerated with each retelling.

He missed his friend. He missed Andrew. He missed having a life beyond anything except this fucking quest for revenge. It might eat him alive before he achieved it.

But he couldn't give up now. He'd made Angela a vow. He wouldn't let her down a second time.

Dylan hadn't moved from where she stood, arms crossed and hugging her waist, watching him with uncertainty, which, he realized now, was justified.

He said, "You can charge your after-hours rate, but let's make this an unscheduled session so that what I'm going to tell you is confidential. Deal?"

She nodded.

"Okay. Earlier tonight, you asked me how I know that Roland Malone killed Angela." She nodded again.

"Fair question. Deserves an answer."

He rested his head on the back of the chair and stared at the stamped-tin ceiling. "One of the factors that convinced everyone Angela had committed suicide, in addition to the postpartum depression, was that she had taken off her wedding ring."

Without moving his head, he cut his eyes toward Dylan, believing that she would understand the implication of that. Gauging by her sorrowful expression, she did.

"I couldn't fathom why she would do that," he said. "To my knowledge she hadn't removed it since I'd slid it onto her finger at the altar. To everyone else, it seemed like a clear sign that she hadn't been in her right mind, that she had harbored more resentment toward me and the baby than I was aware of. So on.

"I shot down those suppositions because they were too painful for me to contemplate. But I couldn't come up with an alternative explanation for why she would have taken off her ring.

"So doubts have stalked me, bedeviled me, made me question Angela's mental state, our marriage, her love for me and Andrew, my failure to recognize or acknowledge the depth of her depression.

"Gin helped to keep the doubts at bay, but I couldn't drink enough to wash them down. They stayed with me, always there at the back of my mind, jeering at me."

He lifted his head from the cushion and looked directly into Dylan's eyes. "Until this Monday night."

She'd been listening raptly, without moving. Now she blinked, she swallowed. "What happened Monday night?"

"I got the explanation for why Angela had switched her wedding band from her left ring finger to the pinky finger of her right hand."

She assimilated that, and, when understanding dawned, she actually shuddered.

"Um-huh," he said. "The last thing she did while she was still conscious was clue me to who had made her get into that car and start the motor."

Chapter 24

Dylan walked over and sat down in the chair separated from Mitch's by the table. She leaned over the chair's stuffed arm in silent encouragement for him to tell her more.

"I'd been surveilling Malone and his customers for months." He told her how he'd come to be at Malone's kitchen door on Monday night. "I only wanted to look inside the place, but, suddenly, there he was, practically filling up the doorway.

"I've dealt with plenty of tough customers, but I don't think I've ever looked into a pair of eyes as empty as Malone's. Soulless. You never noticed? Or is he different with you?"

She didn't answer.

"Can't even comment on that?" he asked, hitching up an eyebrow. "Well, anyway, when I saw that ring, it took more self-control than I knew I had not to shoot him right then and there. Right between those vacant eyes. I wanted to be looking into them when he died, to see if they would register a smidgen of humanity even then."

"Thank God you didn't act on that impulse," Dylan murmured.

"Reason prevailed, but my bloodlust put up one hell of a fight."

He stopped there, having said as much as he intended to. If she was going to respond at all, now was the time. He looked at her expectantly, hoping she would feel compelled to give him something.

She said, "Granted, Roland's size and stolid demeanor can be intimidating."

"Has he ever intimidated you?"

"No."

"Warned you against telling tales about him?"

"Mitch, I can't and won't reveal anything that Roland has discussed with me. But I *will* tell you what he *hasn't*. He hasn't told me anything about his business affairs other than to complain about the day-to-day headaches of managing a successful restaurant.

"He's never mentioned any associates, by name or otherwise. Never." She paused before adding, "He hasn't confessed to a crime, certainly nothing like the ones you've attributed to him."

"Then what do y'all talk about for fifty minutes, the weather?"

She shot to her feet. He reached for her hand and held on. "Bad joke, bad timing."

"It was," she said and pulled away.

He raked his hair back and kept his hands cupped around his head. Jesus, he was tired. He closed his eyes and tried to remember when he'd last slept. He lowered his hands and wearily looked up at Dylan.

"I've made my position plain. You've done the same. I don't know what more either of us could say." He tipped his head toward the main bedroom. "Go to bed. I hope John changed the sheets before he left the last time he was here."

"What about you?"

"Oh, I always change the sheets for company."

She laughed, then said softly and with concern, "Will you sleep? You look exhausted. Does it hurt?" She motioned toward his middle.

"Twinges, pulls a little, but it's not bad. I'll hit the hay after shooting a text to Mary to show to Andrew as soon as he wakes up. I send him silly GIFs. He likes those." He nodded toward the bedroom again. "Off you go."

"Good night."

"Don't let the bedbugs bite."

"Ugh! Don't even joke about that."

"Wasn't joking."

But she knew he was. She smiled a small smile, the kind where your lips don't separate and it never quite makes it to your eyes. Then she turned and took a few steps before coming back around.

"Mitch, if Malone had confessed to doing something like you've alleged, I'd be wrestling with a moral dilemma that would test my professionalism and code of ethics to the extreme. Please believe that."

Saying nothing further, she went into the bedroom. Within minutes after she closed the door, the light underneath it went out. Mitch stayed as he was and pondered the ambiguity of her exit line.

She hadn't said that if Malone had confessed, she would heave professional privilege out the nearest window. She'd said only that her code would be *tested*. But she'd referred to him as

Malone for the first time, not Roland as she always had before. He hoped that signaled that she was looking at him through a different lens.

He went into the guest room and fished his phone and its battery from the pocket of the windbreaker. He replaced the battery only long enough to find a GIF he thought Andrew would like. He sent it, ending the text with, **Tell Andrew that he's my rock star and that I love him.**

Roland was sitting on the edge of his bed, anxiously awaiting a phone call. Following his conversation with Oz about getting rid of El Paso, he'd gone up to the luxurious residence he'd created for himself above the restaurant and gotten into bed. But his brain had refused to shut down and let him sleep.

He'd tried to pinpoint the cause of his insomnia. Then, in his mind, the events of the past few days had begun to overlap, forming a troubling convergence. There had been a series of seemingly unrelated disruptions of routine, slight indications of a shake-up beneath the surface of normalcy. His mother had referred to them as niggles.

"Never a good sign, niggles," she had declared while shaking her bony index finger at him. "Could mean a quiver or a quake. You never know. So pay attention to them."

Roland liked things kept smooth. No wrinkles in the tablecloths. No lumps in the chocolate mousse. No out-of-joint occurrences that were seemingly random.

There was that word again. *Seemingly*. It was an untrustworthy qualifier. You could die within a week after discovering a seemingly benign tumor.

Several strange events had taken place this evening alone:

El Paso's disobedience and defiance; a homeless man who hadn't moved for over an hour leaping up in self-defense; Dylan leaving the restaurant unobserved.

When he'd returned to it after dealing with the ruckus in the median, he'd asked staff if they'd seen "his guest" leaving, but no one had, not even the maître d', who'd been outside on the sidewalk shooing diners back into the dining room.

The security cameras around his place were kept permanently disabled for the protection of his clientele, so they were of no help to him now when he needed them.

He'd assumed that she had simply gotten tired of waiting for him to come back and had left. He'd texted her an apology for leaving her stranded. She had replied with a polite thank you and assurance that she'd arrived safely home. He'd taken her at her word.

But, in retrospect, perhaps he shouldn't have. Since his initial, favorable opinion of El Paso had proved faulty, perhaps he'd also been misled by Dr. Dylan Reede. Maybe he'd been naive to trust her confidentiality.

Like maggots on rotten meat, he'd felt the niggles crawling all over him.

On impulse, and despite the late hour, he'd called her cell phone, but had gotten her voice mail. Three times. It was unlike her to ignore repetitive calls from him. Because of his atypical work hours, she'd given him her personal number and had invited him to call her when convenient for him. She'd never failed to answer, not even in the wee hours or over a weekend, so why wasn't she picking up tonight?

Adding that discrepancy to the growing chain of niggles, he'd determined that preemptive action was called for. He contacted his mole in the Auclair PD.

"Two things. I want you to go to Dr. Dylan Reede's house."

"Haskell's therapist?"

"Yeah. Right now. I want to know if she's at home. You don't need to know why."

"All right."

"While on your way to her place, call this car company." He'd provided the name. "Identify yourself as a concerned friend. She'd told you she should be home from New Orleans around eleven-thirty. She hasn't shown up and you've been unable to reach her. You'd like to know where she was dropped so you can make sure she's all right."

"They may not tell me anything unless I play the cop card."

"Only if you have to."

"Yes, sir."

Ten minutes later, his mole had reported disturbing information: "Dr. Reede never got in the car."

"Say again?"

"She was at the curb when the driver pulled up."

"I know that already. Go on."

"Well, she didn't get in, and then he lost sight of her in the gathering crowd. He didn't specify what crowd."

"I know what crowd. Go *on*."

"The driver told his dispatcher that there was some kind of disturbance in the median that was holding up traffic in every direction. He circled the block several times, texting Dr. Reede, asking where she was. He was about to give up and leave without her when *she* texted *him* and canceled. She apologized for not notifying him sooner and tipped him an extra fifty for the inconvenience."

"Are you at her house yet?"

"No, but—"

"Get there!"

And now he was waiting for that report. He was holding his phone in his hand when it beeped. "Talk to me."

"I'm here, but I don't think she is."

Roland's blood pressure rocketed. "What about a car?"

"None out front. Hers could be in the garage, but the door is down, so I can't be sure. The house is completely dark."

"At this time of night, wouldn't it be?"

"Yes, but there's mail in the box, plus a UPS package on her front porch. Wouldn't she have taken that inside if she were here?"

She hadn't gone home. She'd never even gotten into the fucking car! She had lied to him.

"Sir? Do you want me to keep watching the house? It's on a cul de sac. I'm afraid staying might arouse the suspicion of neighbors, and it's only a few hours before I have to be at work. What do you want me to do?"

Roland thought for a moment, then gave the mole another assignment with explicit instructions. "Can you do that?"

"It won't be easy."

"I didn't say it would be easy," he growled. "I asked if you could manage it."

"Yes, sir."

"Good. Then report for your shift. This didn't happen. Understood?"

"Yes, sir."

"You breathe Dylan Reede's name in connection to mine, I'll cut out your tongue. Focus on Haskell. Anything regarding him, I want to hear about immediately. Got it?"

"Ten four."

Roland disconnected but remained sitting on the edge of

the bed, rotating his signet ring, literally gnashing his teeth as he ruminated over this unexpected turn.

Tonight, his confidante and a homeless man had vanished at approximately the same time from outside his restaurant. The homeless man had the aggressiveness, agility, and speed of a cagey ex-fed who had, just this week, begun seeing Dylan for therapy. What are the chances?

That was a niggle with the magnitude of a quake that his mother had warned him about.

Roland opened his nightstand drawer and took out his spare rosary.

Chapter 25

Mitch didn't think he could sleep, but he must have. When the burner phone rang, it woke him up from a bad dream. Andrew was lost, he could hear him crying, "Daddy, Daddy," but couldn't find him.

He was lying on his back, holding the phone on his chest so he wouldn't miss a call from either Tucker or Clarence. He answered on the second ring. "Here."

"Hi, Mitch, it's me."

Clarence. Earlier, he'd called in a favor of the young cop. Clarence had been happy to oblige when Mitch had asked him to stake out a house. "It'll give you a chance to brush up on your surveillance skills."

"Sure. When?"

"As soon as you can get there, and I'd like you to stay until sunrise."

"Oh. Okay."

"I'll pay your overtime rate, but out of my own pocket, so

don't turn in the hours. And take your own car, not a squad car."

"Okay."

He'd given him Dylan's house address. "It's a cul de sac. If there's a vehicle on it that doesn't look like it belongs, or if you see anything hinky, get out of there and call me. If not, stay and keep an eye on that house, then notify me if anyone does show up."

He knew the young, green officer would be way out of his league if he tangled with anyone on Malone's payroll, so he'd emphasized that Clarence wasn't to approach or engage if he saw someone.

"Call for backup and notify me immediately. You're only there to watch, not to follow or chase. Understand? Don't let them know you're there. Got it?"

"Got it."

He'd issued those instructions a couple of hours ago. If Clarence was calling now, still a few hours before dawn, he had something to report. "What's up?"

"When I got there, nothing was out of the ordinary," Clarence said. "But a little while ago, a car pulled onto the street and parked in front of that house."

"Why are you whispering?" Mitch asked. "Is the car still there? Can you be overheard?"

"No, it left. This just feels, you know, secretive."

"It is secretive. That's sorta the point of surveillance." There followed a dead silence. "Clarence? You all right?"

"Yeah, I'm fine."

But Mitch sensed he wasn't entirely fine. "What's the matter? Did something happen?"

"No, but, uh...uh...I...I..."

Mitch heard him swallow hard. *Shit!* "What went wrong?"

"Nothing, nothing. But I looked up whose house that is. It's your shrink, right?"

His knowing that could prove to be inconvenient, but not necessarily catastrophic. He decided to respond lightheartedly. "Uh-oh, busted. Second time you've done that to me this week."

"I'm sorry, Mitch, but—"

"No sweat. If I'd been you, I would've looked up who lived there, too. In fact, I'm impressed you did the research. Shows your potential as a detective. But let's go back to the car. It's gone, right?"

"Yes."

"And nothing happened?"

"No."

"What kind of car?"

"Dark sedan. No markings."

"How far away were you?"

"Near the end of the cul de sac. I parked in the driveway of a house for sale. It was vacant, but I thought it would look like the owner still lived there."

"Good thinking. Could you see the driver?"

"Too dark."

"Did the driver ever get out, go up to the house?"

"No."

"Did you get the license plate number?"

"I used the zoom on my phone and took a picture."

"Text it to me. How long did it stay?"

"Around five minutes. I wrote down the times if you—"

"No, that's okay." Was five minutes long enough for someone to determine whether or not Dylan was inside the house?

"Did you see anyone jogging, somebody walking their dog, watering the flower bed, anything like that?"

"At this time of night?"

"Exactly. It would be out of the ordinary."

"Nothing like that. But there was a package on Dr. Reede's porch. I noticed it as I drove past."

"A delivery?"

"Yes."

"Huh." Based on that, Mitch himself would've reasoned that Dylan hadn't been at home that evening. Whoever Malone had sent to check on her likely would have drawn the same conclusion.

He wondered if Malone knew yet that he'd been snookered by Dylan's text about arriving home. He hoped so. He hoped the bastard was writhing in an agony of anxiety.

"Mitch?"

"Yeah, sorry. Still here. Just thinking all this through. Listen, for the time being, let's keep this between us, okay?"

"Even from Bowie?"

"For now."

"Uh, okay."

"Discretion is part of your surveillance training," Mitch said.

"All right. But can I ask why you sent me to her house in particular?"

Great! Clarence was getting brighter and growing a pair at the worst possible time. "It's nothing bad. It's just..." *Think, Mitch!* "Kinda embarrassing," he said.

"Embarrassing? Why?"

"Come on, Clarence. You know. Guy to guy? She's smokin' hot and...Like that."

"Oh," Clarence chuckled, sounding relieved. "I get it. You wanted to know if she had company."

"Now you see why I didn't want it talked about? Guys in the unit would give me shit and never let up."

"I won't say anything."

"My man! Thanks. Go on home, try to get some rest before your shift."

They signed off, and Mitch took a long, deep breath.

He ran the license plate of the car. As expected, it was registered to an LLC that had a name comprised of capital letters that didn't spell anything and probably stood for nothing, either.

He did a Google search of the address on the registration. It was a vacant lot for sale and had been on the market for more than seven hundred days. He called the phone number on the real estate listing, and a recording informed him that the number was no longer in service. "Shocker," he muttered.

He shut down his laptop and turned out all the lights in the main room save for one small lamp. It didn't shed much light, but enough to assist him in opening John's bedroom door with as little noise as possible. Which wasn't easy to do while holding a pistol in one hand. He made his way across the room to the bed, where he set the pistol on the nightstand and then lay down with as little jostling as possible.

In spite of his precautions, Dylan turned from her side facing away from him onto her back.

"I tried not to wake you."

"I was only dozing. What are you doing?"

"Keeping watch over you."

"I don't need watching over."

"Yes you do, Dylan," he said somberly. "You do."

"I'm still not convinced that Roland poses a threat to me. But even if that is so, no one in the world could find me here."

Back to *Roland,* he thought with irritation. "That's why I brought you here. No one can find you. But say someone did, that big room out there is too much distance between us."

She glanced at the nightstand. "Is the gun necessary?"

"I hope not. But no sudden moves, please. I chambered a bullet."

"Why all these safety measures? What's happened?"

"My hunch was right. Someone went to check your house."

"How do you know?"

"I'm a cop." Her huff of annoyance annoyed him. "Just trust me on this, all right? I'm here, and I'm staying."

"For how long?"

"Till daylight."

"Then what?"

"Then...I don't know. I'm thinking. Go back to sleep."

She lay still for a time before turning onto her side toward him. "Don't take this as surrender. I just don't know what choice I have."

"None."

"With you injured and in a weakened state, I might manage to overpower you and escape. But I doubt I'd get very far in a swamp teeming with life-threatening hazards."

Hearing the irony in her tone, he turned his head on the pillow and pretended to consider her chances of success. "You're fit. You might make it as far as the camo garage."

"If by some miracle I found it, I wouldn't know how to get into it."

He nodded thoughtfully. "Those locking mechanisms are

intricate. But you've got a doctorate, don't forget. You might figure them out. However," he said, holding up his index finger, "even if you did get into the garage, I've hidden the keys to both vehicles."

"And confiscated my phone."

"There's that," he said. "So..."

"So I'm pretty much stuck."

"Pretty much."

They exchanged smiles, then he turned serious. "I'm sorry I badgered you into talking about your husband. I wanted to know why you're inside that bell jar, why you keep a grip on self-control like you're afraid that if you loosened it even a fraction, you would fly apart. Now I know why." He looked at her with regret. "I hadn't counted on it being that bad."

Pensively, she stared at a spot beyond his shoulder before meeting his gaze again. "I think I needed to talk about it. I hadn't really done so in years, not since I went into practice."

"How'd that come about?"

"Once I got George's remains returned to the US, I held a memorial. One of my psychology professors attended. A week or so after, she invited me to lunch, where she urged me to resume my studies.

"I did, and, after earning my doctorate, that same advisor encouraged me to make a clean break. Too many people in my circle had known George and our story. She called the specter of it stagnating, and challenged me to relocate and make a new life for myself.

"She had a colleague here in Auclair who wished to retire but wanted to leave his patients in good hands. She recommended me. Now, four years later, here I am."

"With a thriving practice."

"I've been fortunate."

This is one messed-up situation, he thought. He was a cop after information that she had refused to give up. She could be the oracle that would provide him with what he needed to get Malone. Instead, she stubbornly remained an obstacle.

Yet none of that mattered right now. She lay with her hands pressed together beneath her cheek, looking warm and tender, approachable, touchable, sexy as hell, and he wanted her.

"You relocated to a new place," he said, "but have you made a new life?"

"Are you circling back to the forbidden subject of my personal life?"

"Well, we didn't finish that earlier conversation about it."

"Yes we did. I told you that I don't discuss it."

"Not with patients, I know. Not normally. But think of all that's happened with me that's never happened to you with another patient."

"None has ever broken into my office or come to my house. None has ever kidnapped me."

"See? Transformative experiences. You saved my life tonight," he said, gingerly patting his middle. "In some cultures, saving someone's life binds you to them forever."

She laughed softly. "What cultures?"

"I forget, but I know it's a thing." He turned onto his side to face her. "Don't panic, I'm just getting a crick in my neck."

He made a production of resettling, which brought them closer together. "Ah, much better. Where was I? Oh, I know. Given the life-changing experiences we've been through together, I believe I'm entitled to know a little about your life outside the bell jar."

"Like what?"

"Like if you've had any torrid affairs."

She gave him a look.

"Oh. *Not* torrid? Hmm, that's too bad." He feigned regret. "Well then, how about boyfriends? How many? More than one, less than, say, twenty?" He made a spiraling motion with his hand. "Ballpark."

Another look.

"Okay. Is there a current boyfriend?"

She lowered her eyelids halfway. Her facial features went into repose. He recognized the signs of withdrawal intended to conceal her susceptibility, when actually it did the opposite; it announced it.

"No?" Then, suggestively, he whispered, "Want one?"

Her eyes opened and looked deeply into his with yearning. It was *yearning*, dammit. He knew it. But what she said was, "You can't be a boyfriend to me, Mitch. I'm your therapist."

He slid his hand up under her hair and conformed it to her nape. "Dr. Reede?"

"What?"

"You're fired."

Chapter 26

He covered her mouth with his, possessively and urgently, and, God, she wanted him to. It was a mystery to her how she'd held out for this long without throwing herself against him and clinging. Tending his wound had been sheer torture from having proximity to his body but no intimacy with it, allowing herself only to touch but not caress.

His torso was sculpted with muscles tightly encased in skin nicked with scars, each one of which she'd yearned to kiss. She'd wanted her cheeks and lips and breasts to know the feel of the hair that dusted his upper chest. It was different in texture from the sleek, narrow band that started below his navel and disappeared into the loose waistband of his jeans. She'd imagined it fanning out over the flat plain between his hipbones.

Twice, as she'd applied antiseptic, he'd teased her about blowing on him to ease the burn. When her face was close enough to feel the heat he emanated, had he sensed how tempted she'd been to do just that, to blow gently and then press a kiss on a tender spot?

And now, as his tongue went in search of hers, she realized that her rigid self-control hadn't contributed one whit of happiness to her life. Her guardedness against having too much emotional involvement with someone hadn't alleviated the pain of her tragedy at all; it had only kept her cemented to it.

So, heedless of consequences, she looped her arm around his neck and drew him down even as her back arched up to bring her breasts in contact with his chest, a move that seemed to surprise and delight him.

She didn't see his smile so much as felt it against her lips. Through smoochy kisses, he mumbled, "My animal magnetism got the better of you, didn't it?"

That was such a Mitch thing for him to say, a bubble of joy expanded inside her chest. She nipped at his teasing lips with her teeth until, with a growl of arousal, he seized her mouth again.

He kissed with passion and heat and longing, one kiss melding into another in an evocative continuum until they were starved for breath. Their lips parted, each of them gasping, then he kissed her one more time, deeply and dearly, before breaking it.

He cupped her face between his hands. His eyes roved over her features, pausing on each one, studying it as though adoring it, memorizing it. He spoke her name on a sigh. "I want to keep going with this more than I want to keep breathing. But not if you're going to beat yourself up over it afterward."

"I won't. I've already crossed the line."

"When we kissed outside the café?"

She shook her head to the extent that his cradling hands

would allow. "When I walked into the waiting room and saw you standing there."

He exhaled a sound of disbelief and looked at her as though waiting for her to qualify the statement in some way, then, realizing that she wasn't going to, he gathered her to him and hugged her tightly.

"Careful," she said, "you'll open your wound."

"That won't kill me. But I'm going to die if we don't finish what we've started here."

He lowered his head and burrowed his face between her breasts. She was still wearing the creamy blouse that had made him drunk on dirty thoughts, but he didn't know until he rubbed his face against her breast that she'd removed her bra before going to bed.

Under the silky fabric, her nipple was already hard. He opened his mouth over it and sucked, while his hand sought her other breast, squeezing, reshaping, gently pinching the tip.

Her legs were shifting against his, and he realized she was pushing off the covers that he'd lain on top of when he'd joined her. Once the covers were bunched at the foot of the bed, he took in those long ballerina legs from the red toenails all the way up to an insubstantial pair of panties.

At the sight, his breathing turned harsh. When he hooked his thumbs into the scrap of stretchy lace and pulled it down to the middle of her thigh, he stopped breathing altogether.

But only for the length of a single heartbeat. Then he moved like quicksilver, clawing at the back of his T-shirt and pulling it off over his head, ripping the rivets out of the worn buttonholes of his jeans, shoving them down past his butt, then stretching out on top of her.

Panties now banished, hips and limbs made adjustments. Hers invited him to press up and into the spreading space between her thighs, which he did, until the head of his cock was just *there*.

Then, with one thrust, he was inside her. Deep, but not deep enough. It wasn't deep enough until he was fully imbedded and he could grind against that part of her that was rubbing up against him in supplication.

He levered himself up, hands planted on either side of her head, trying to get the angle perfect and knowing he'd achieved it when her breath caught and she reached up to link her fingers around the back of his neck.

Then he began to move in a primordial rhythm, in concert with her, until their mutual intensity created a friction that sparked a swift climax. She cried out first, and then his entire body went taut, straining with intent, withholding nothing.

When at last it ended, they held as they were, his head bowed over her, she staring up into his eyes with wonder, both of them close to disbelieving the passion that had erupted and overpowered them.

Gradually, her fingers relaxed, her hands slid off his shoulders, and then her arms dropped listlessly to her sides. He lowered himself onto her. He kissed her eyelids, her cheekbones, her lips, which were curved into a satiated smile. He rested his forehead against hers and exhaled a long breath through his mouth.

"God, I've missed fucking."

Against his stomach, he felt hers tighten and vibrate with a small laugh. "So have I."

He raised his head to better see her. "So you haven't...?"

"No."

"Nobody?"

"No."

"Me neither. I think we made up for at least a day of abstinence."

"At the very least."

He frowned with self-deprecation. "I had all the finesse of a caveman. Actually, less than a caveman."

She raised her hands above her head and stretched. "If you'd wasted one second on finesse, I would have combusted."

"I didn't have a second to waste."

"I noticed."

After a lingering kiss, he moved off her, lay on his back, and worked off his jeans. She propped herself up on her elbow and leaned over him to inspect the cut. "Three of the closures came off."

He raised his head and looked down the length of his torso. "I don't see any major damage."

She continued her survey. "So this is where you hide it." Hesitantly she used the tip of her finger to trace the tattoo that began just under his left hip bone and extended down the top of his thigh almost to his knee. "It's Excalibur, isn't it? King Arthur's sword."

"Very good."

"Why that?"

"My dad has one like it on his forearm. He was a veteran of Vietnam. Had to engage in some bad shit over there. When I was old enough to ask about the tat, he told me the legend. He said the sword represented the moral and honorable attributes that a king, or warrior, or any man should aspire to. The tat would be a constant reminder of those virtues."

"Why here and not on your forearm?"

"Well, that's about where a sword would hang, isn't it? Plus, a man should aspire to be as hard as steel. I thought the juxtaposition—"

"I get it," she said, laughing. "Very phallic. I studied Freud, remember?"

Then she lay down on her side, and he turned onto his so they were facing. In a move that already seemed natural and familiar, he placed his hand on her hip. Their legs entwined.

"What about this one?" She stroked the pair of angel wings tattooed on his right deltoid which she'd asked about earlier. Meeting his gaze, she said softly, "Angela?"

"No. I'd had it for a few years before I even met her."

She didn't say anything, leaving it up to him whether he wanted to pursue the subject. It was a therapy technique he'd come to recognize, and this time he gave in to it.

"It's in honor of a buddy of mine. We served together in Afghanistan. He was the Catholic chaplain. He was captured by the Taliban. Him being a priest…" He shrugged. "Didn't sit well with his captors. They wouldn't even let us collect the pieces of him to ship home."

She didn't say anything, just placed her hand on his chest.

He gave a solemn nod, then ran his hand over her ass, squeezing it gently. "Enough of that. Tell me stuff about you."

"Stuff?"

"What's your birthday, favorite food, favorite song and movie, chocolate or vanilla? You know, first date stuff."

"This is hardly a date. You didn't even buy me dinner."

He looked down at the patch of paradise between her thighs. "I didn't have to."

She swatted his butt. Laughing, he leaned over and kissed her. She put up token resistance, but then placed her hand against the back of his head and, after a few ravenous kisses that established their hunger for each other again, he turned the mouth-to-mouth foreplay more languid.

He kissed her throat and moved lower as he went to the top button of her blouse and nimbly undid it. "I've wanted to unbutton you since I laid eyes on you."

Although, with a mind of its own, his cock wished to speed things along, he took his time. Button by button, he revealed lovely breasts. He paused to peck kisses on the upper slopes, to play his tongue over first one nipple then the other, then swept it along the under curve beneath the half-moon fullness.

He eased the blouse off her shoulders and assisted her in pulling her arms from the sleeves, then dropped it to the side of the bed. "I almost hate to toss that. It's my favorite piece of clothing ever stitched. But...you. You're something else."

He lifted her breast and took her nipple into his mouth. His other hand coasted down her body until he could cup her sex in his palm and curl his fingers up into her. The heel of his hand pressed and retreated in a tempting massage.

"Mitch," she groaned. "Just...just."

"Just what?" He raised his head from her breasts. Her eyes were closed, her neck arched, her head digging into the pillow. Keeping up the torment, he whispered, "Dylan?"

"Hmm?"

He withdrew his middle finger from her and wetly caressed slow spirals where she most wanted to be touched. "Just what?" he asked again in a wicked whisper.

"Just...Just don't stop."

Her beautiful body bowed as the orgasm streamed through her. Her hands clutched at the sheet. She gasped his name, her voice cracking on a sob. Tears leaked from the corners of her closed eyelids and rolled into her hair.

She fell apart.

It was a beautiful thing to watch.

He let it subside before removing his hand and sliding into her. The tumult had passed but, lucky him, he got to experience the sweet compressions of the aftermath.

When she opened her eyes, she blinked away the tears and whispered, "That's the first time I've ever cried."

He grinned. "My pleasure, ma'am."

She sniffed, and another tear slid down her temple, but she was also smiling. "How can you make me laugh and cry at the same time?"

"I'm good at multi-tasking."

Smiling even wider, she squirmed beneath him. "It feels so good. You're so full."

"Getting fuller," he groaned. "If you move like that again, I'll get desperate."

"You promise?" She did a bump and grind. He responded with a slow withdrawal followed by one unhurried glide that grafted them again. "Kiss me," she said.

"Gladly." He captured her hands and placed them at the sides of her head. Then palm to palm and mouth to mouth, he made love to her.

Chapter 27

Mitch sat bolt upright and automatically reached for his pistol on the nightstand.

The burner phone rang twice more before he realized that's what had awakened him, not the rocky front porch step, which he'd been subconsciously listening for while he slept.

He grabbed the phone and swiped to answer. "Tucker?"

"Nooo, John Bowie."

"Oh. Oh? Hey, bro. Wait. How'd you get this phone number?"

"Officer Clarence."

"You gotta be shittin' me."

"No. He's here with me now. He was waiting for me when I got here and asked if he and I could talk privately in my office. About you. It's turning out to be an interesting conversation. I'd like for you to be in on it."

"Hate to disappoint. I'm a little tied up."

"Where are you?"

"Isn't it a little early to be calling, hammering me with all these questions? It's not even eight o'clock, and I'm not usually due in until nine."

"Don't use that pissed-off voice with me," John said. "You're up to something. I want to know what."

"Hasn't Clarence filled you in?"

From the background, the cop warbled, "I'm sorry, Mitch."

"Save it. And why are we on speaker?"

"Because you're tied up," John said.

Mitch cursed under his breath.

"I didn't want to rat on you," Clarence said. "I didn't want to get you in trouble, but—"

John interrupted him. "He didn't want to betray your trust, but felt duty-bound to report what he did for you in the wee hours of this morning. You placed this officer in an impossible situation."

"That officer could've talked to me about the impossibility of his situation before going to you."

"I tried, Mitch," Clarence said. "I went to your apartment on my way to work, hoping to talk to you in person, but you weren't there. I thought I might be able to persuade you to stop stalking Dr. Reede."

Dylan had been lying still, but Mitch had been aware that she was awake and listening. At the mention of her name, he saw out of the corner of his eye that she came up on her elbows.

Into the phone he said, "I'm not stalking Dr. Reede." *Fucking her till my balls are blue, but not stalking her.*

"What would you call it?" John said. "Sending Clarence over to her house to see if she had company? That's the definition of stalking. You've arrested men for less."

"Has Dr. Reede herself accused me?"

John said, "After Clarence told me about this, I called her."

"Oh? And?"

"Her service tried to reach her on her cell phone, but got her voice mail."

"Hmm, interesting. Typically she returns calls in a timely fashion," Mitch said.

"I'm not buying your innocent and dumb act, Mitch. I know you too well. You're not at home. You're not here. Where are you?"

"Uh." He was sitting naked on John's side of John and Beth's bed. Dylan was reclined naked on Beth's side of John and Beth's bed. He said, "All good here, John."

"I didn't ask how you are. I asked where you are."

"Okay," he said, sounding put out. "You wanna know what I'm up to? I'll tell you. I got stuck last night."

"Stuck where?"

"In the gut."

"In the... You mean stabbed?"

"Incised. I've got a red line running left to right across my belly like a thin smile."

"Jesus. Clarence, did you know about this?"

"No, sir. Now I feel really terrible."

Mitch muttered, "You should."

"Mitch, how bad is it?" John asked.

"It's all right. I got it taken care of." He looked at Dylan and winked.

"How'd it happen? Where? Who did it?"

Mitch debated with himself about how much he should disclose, then said, "I was following a lead on the Bayou Coeur murders. I know you told me to stay off that case, but I had a notion that just wouldn't let go. So I went to New Orleans to take a look around. Ran into some trouble." He paused before adding, "Here's where you chew my ass."

John grumbled something indistinct, exhaled heavily, then said, "I'm glad you're all right. What provoked it?"

"I guess the guy just didn't like my looks. He jumped me, whipped out a switchblade, sliced me, ran like hell."

"Did you go after him?"

"No. Even I had better sense. Wasn't my turf, it was his. I didn't want to get trapped there by either his buddies or local police, so I split."

"Give me a description of him. I'll alert NOPD."

"Negative."

"Only to put this guy on their radar," John said.

"Nope."

"Then you can add obstruction of justice to stalking a prominent psychologist."

"Damn," Mitch sighed. "All right, but better all around if you don't ID me as your source."

"Understood."

"Okay. He's a little guy. Early twenties. Swagger. Out to prove he's a badass. Even before he attacked, I had him pegged for a street-smart, scary dude."

"Not much of a description."

"It'll have to do."

John said, "Hold on. Lear and Nix are coming this way. Head them off, will you, Clarence? Tell them I'll be with them in a minute."

"Mitch, I'm really sorry," Clarence said.

"Yeah, yeah. Have a nice day."

There was shuffling and a door closing, then John said in a low voice, "You were hanging around Malone's, weren't you?"

"Are we off speaker?"

"Yes."

"Then, yes. Guilty."

"Mitch—"

"Not now. Later, you can have at me, but right now, listen up. The asshole with the switchblade works for Malone. Goes by the name of El Paso. A recent addition to the corps, and I doubt Malone hired him full-time to hassle the homeless population, which is what he was doing when he jumped me. He'd attacked two others before me. He's dangerous."

"Where'd you get all this information?"

"A reliable source."

"Tucker?"

"A reliable source."

John knew that was a yes. "Then are you sure your attacker didn't recognize you from your previous line of work?"

"I don't think so."

"*But?*"

"*But*, if he did, Malone will learn that I was lurking just outside his place. He won't like it a bit. So I'm going to lay low and wait to see how he reacts. That'll determine what I do next."

"Don't make a move without my knowledge."

Mitch said nothing.

"Mitch, I mean it."

"I heard you. Not without your knowledge."

John hissed with irritation. "Where are you laying low?"

"It's not on anyone's radar. Prohibition-defying Cajuns saw to that." He need say no more.

He could envision the dent between John's eyebrows getting deeper, which it tended to do when he was concentrating.

At last, he said, "Playing a hunch here. It occurs to me that Dr. Reede isn't at home and can't be reached on her cell phone. And neither can you."

"You're a genius."

"She's with you," John said. Elaborate cussing followed.

"I know what it looks like, but—"

"Looks like you're holed up with your therapist."

"See? As I said, genius. Do you want to hear *why* we're holed up, or not?" After a pause, he continued. "If Malone learns that the knifed homeless man was in fact an ex-narc, and he wants to know what's going on inside said ex-narc's head, who better to ask than the ex-narc's therapist? That's why I enlisted Clarence the Tell-all Tattletale to watch her house last night."

"That sounds like one of your convoluted rationalizations for pulling a stunt."

"Sounds like that, but isn't. Did Clarence tell you about the car outside her house?"

"Yes."

"Trying to find out who owns that car will take you down a rabbit hole that goes all the way to China, but I'd bank on it belonging to Malone. Who else would take a sudden interest in Dylan Reede to the extent of watching her house?"

"*You*," John said. Then he sighed. "But I get what you're saying. So your plan is to keep her under lock and key—my lock and key, by the way. How does she feel about it?"

Mitch looked at her and raised his eyebrows; she gave him a bashful smile. "She came around," he said. "Like Beth did when you stashed her here."

"That was different."

"Damn right it was," Mitch said. "You didn't know who your bogeyman was. I know who mine is. And yet I can't—"

"Hold on, my desk phone is ringing. Could be Darcy with something new on Bayou Coeur."

Mitch stood by while John answered the incoming call. He reached over to stroke Dylan's arm. With a rueful smile, he said, "Some morning after, huh?"

Before she could reply, John was back. "Mitch, it's Mary."

"Calling you?"

"Because she couldn't reach you. She's upset. They're in the ER."

Chapter 28

Three hundred sixty-five days a year, Allen Busby put himself through a punishing hour-long workout in his home's sleek, high-tech gymnasium. He did aerobics, lifted weights, and kept flexible by finishing with yoga stretches. He was determined to stave off a middle-age belly and jowls.

Roland Malone knew all this. He also knew it was an unforgivable offense for that hour to be interrupted for any reason short of the mansion catching fire or a SWAT team closing in.

But this morning's developments compelled Roland to break the rule. He called Oz shortly after eight o'clock when he would be roughly ten minutes into his workout.

His first two calls went unanswered. Oz answered the third, huffing and puffing, "Don't tell me the trucks have been intercepted."

"Not to my knowledge," Roland said, unable to keep the edge out of his voice. He was still sour over Oz's not telling him about the heist he'd pulled on the Caballeros until it was done.

Of course, as evidenced by what he'd said when he answered the phone, the booty wasn't yet in his possession and he was anxious over it.

Still huffing and puffing, Oz asked, "Then why did you interrupt my workout?"

"We should take care of El Paso tonight." Roland heard the treadmill winding down. He had Oz's attention.

"Why?"

He wasn't going to use the word "niggles" with Oz, so, prior to making the call, he'd composed a spiel that would explain the necessity for El Paso's removal sooner rather than later. It was the truth, slightly restructured.

He began, "I had a call from my mole in Auclair this morning. Haskell's in deep dutch with Bowie. He's doing some stuff that even Bowie thinks is freaky."

"Like what?"

"Like stalking his therapist. This Dylan Reede, who turned out to be a woman. Remember, I told you?"

"I remember. You said it could be a good thing."

"I may have been wrong about that. Haskell's keeping close tabs on her. Claims it's a guy thing, like he has the hots for her, and he might. But I think there may be more to it. The coincidence is just too convenient."

"Stop beating around the fucking bush. What's going on?"

"She had dinner here last night."

"The therapist?"

Here came the restructured part. "I didn't know it was her. At the time, I was sucking up to a Saints player and his mistress, but I see this good-looking gal come in. I mean a real stunner. She's by herself. Maître d' practically waltzes her to a table reserved for one. I assigned our best waiter to her and told him to treat her like royalty. I mean, here's this babe, eating alone. I wanted to impress, you know?"

He paused for breath. So far, so good. Oz was listening, not interrupting. "She had a vodka martini, a glass of red, three courses. When her coffee was served, I went over, introduced myself as the owner of the place, and asked if I could join her. She smiled and motioned me into the chair. Five, ten minutes, we made small talk.

"I covered her check. She protested, but I insisted. It was her first time, yada yada, I wanted her to come back. I walked her out and offered my chauffeur to take her home. I mean, you never know. I could've got laid.

"Anyhow, she'd hired a car. We're standing there waiting for it to pull up so she can get in, when El Paso jumps the guy in the median. You know the rest about that."

"I thought I did. I thought *you* did."

"Right," Roland said. "So imagine my shock when I got a call this morning from my mole telling me that Haskell and his therapist have gone underground together. Bowie was beside himself when he learned that Haskell had sent a cop to her house last night to check out things."

"Why did he do that? If Haskell was with her, he wouldn't be sending someone to spy on her."

"Exactly. Doesn't fit. I asked myself: Who was Haskell expecting to show up at his therapist's house in the middle of the night? That's when I started piecing it together."

"Piecing what together? You're still talking in riddles."

"Think about it," Roland said. "It's this doll's first time to the restaurant. She comes alone in a hired car. There's a ruckus involving a homeless man who El Paso had been eyeing for over an hour. Said the guy hadn't moved a muscle in all the time he'd been sitting in the grass right across the street from the front door of my restaurant."

"Jesus Christ. You think the man El Paso attacked was Haskell?"

"I know it was him," Roland said dourly. "The mole says Haskell and Bowie had a heated telephone conversation, during which Haskell tells his boss that he'd been in New Orleans last night. Ran into some trouble, got cut with a switchblade, and—here's the worst part—he gave Bowie a description of El Paso. A sketchy one, but still."

"Did he mention the restaurant?"

"No. But Bowie is going to phone in El Paso's description to NOPD. They may put it together with the attacks on the other homeless. Which is why we need to make El Paso disappear, so his connection to me can never be proved. He won't exist. Nobody even knows his real name."

Oz thought on it for a time, then said, "I had an intuition. There was something off about that homeless man. It worried me all night. You think he sent his therapist to the restaurant to act as his scout?"

Roland said, "That's why I interrupted your workout. There was a lot of bad mojo in the air last night. Soon as I signed off with my mole, I put on my bathrobe, went downstairs to the maître d's stand, and looked at last night's reservations.

"Eight o'clock. 'Mr. Malone's guest.' No name. She must've called in the reservation, made out like I had invited her, and I played right into her soft, dainty hands. Great legs, too."

"Forget her legs. Have you confirmed that this babe *was* Dr. Reede?"

"I have. I went through the car company. I called and told them their fare had left a pricey scarf in the restaurant, told them I needed her name and contact info so I could make arrangements to get it back to her. Dylan Reede. I got her home address and cell number.

"I've called it several times. I was going to admit to calling the car company to get her name. Act like I was smitten, you know. But I didn't have to put on an act because she's not answering. Phone goes straight to voice mail. So I guess she and Haskell are making cozy somewhere. I wish El Paso had gutted the bastard like he bragged of doing."

He sighed with self-deprecation. "I thought she was an expensive call girl, or some gal with an itch and looking for action. But Mitch Haskell's shrink? Fuckin' unbelievable.

"One good thing, though," he continued in a more upbeat tone. "She didn't do anything suspicious while she was in the restaurant. I got the waiter in here, grilled him good. Had she used her phone? Taken pictures, anything like that? He swears not, and I believe him because she was his only table and he'd been told to be at her beck and call. He said she didn't even go to the powder room." He paused before concluding. "So, that's where we are."

Oz went into one of his think-tank cycles. Roland turned his ring 'round and 'round and said several rapid-fire Hail Marys.

"Haskell was supposed to be a drunken burnout," Oz said at last. "Turns out he's still clever as a fox. Why would he be watching you?"

"The mole says he had a notion about Bayou Coeur."

"Nothing about his wife?"

"No. No way he could know about that." There was a stretch of silence, then Roland said, "All we gotta do is make El Paso disappear. Then what's Haskell got? Nothing. I'll take care of that cocky kid tonight. No reason for you to be there. Which

I thought was a bad idea anyway. The more distance you keep, the better."

"I agree. I didn't want any wrinkles this week."

"When do you expect the haul from Mexico? You said end of the week. This is Friday."

"Last report, the trucks were somewhere in East Texas."

"All good?"

"All good."

Roland chuckled. "That's good mojo."

Oz must not have seen the humor. He was mapping out his day. "I'll finish up here, get my pedi, then put in an appearance at the office and congratulate the rank and file on the excellent work they're doing.

"Tonight, while you're handling the screwup, I'll have a quiet dinner at home…while I plot how we're going to get rid of Haskell. I'd like there to be as little muss and fuss as possible."

"I've been giving it some thought."

"Think about the shrink, too. No telling what Haskell's told her. She should go."

"Yes." Roland wanted to stand and cheer. He was mentally giving himself a fist bump. Dylan had made a fool of him. She knew how much he feared the fires of hell. She'd be screaming in terror of them by the time he got through with her.

"Any idea where they could be hiding?"

Oz's question drew him out of his gruesome fantasy. "No, but I told my mole to make it a priority to find out. ASAP."

"Is this plant reliable?"

"Very. Her name's Barbara Nix. Want to hear something funny? Bowie assigned her to help Darcy investigate the Bayou Coeur case."

Chapter 29

Mitch had instructed John to tell Mary that he would call her immediately. "Tell her she won't recognize the number." He disconnected from John and fumbled the phone in his haste to call his mother-in-law.

Dylan laid a hand on his shoulder in a silent gesture of support.

She could hear his mother-in-law's phone ringing. After the second ring, he growled, "She's gotta have the damn thing in her hand. Why doesn't she answer it? Come on, come—"

Then Dylan heard the woman say, "Mitch? Finally."

"Is Andrew hurt? Is he sick?"

"It's Hank. He's had a heart attack."

Mitch reached for Dylan's hand and squeezed. *It's not Andrew,* he mouthed with visible relief. But he automatically switched to concern for his father-in-law. "How bad is it?"

"We don't know yet. They're running tests."

"What happened?"

"He got up, had coffee. I was making breakfast. Everything was normal, then he just…" Her voice began to hitch. "He dropped to the floor. He was gasping, like choking, grabbing at his chest. I called 911. Seemed like forever, but it wasn't long before they got here. They started an IV and carried him to the ambulance. By the time I got to the hospital—"

"How long ago was that?"

"A little over an hour. I've been trying to reach you."

"I'm sorry. My phone is…Never mind all that. How's Hank? Is he conscious?"

"Yes. He's stable now."

She told Mitch they'd done an EKG and had been told to expect further tests. The typical maddening hurry-up-and-wait of the ER.

"Sounds like they're on it, Mary. That's good." He was looking at Dylan anxiously as he asked, "What about Andrew while this is happening? Did he see Hank in crisis, all that?"

"No, thank heaven. I hadn't gotten him up yet. After the ambulance left, I scurried around and left Andrew with my neighbor."

"Mrs. Gibbons? Next door?"

"I couldn't bring him with me, Mitch," she said.

To Dylan, her tone sounded defensive, which explained the panicked look Mitch flashed her at the mention of the neighbor. "No, no, I get it. I'll be on my way in five minutes. In three minutes."

"Mitch?"

"What?"

"I'm afraid." Her voice broke altogether. "I can't lose Hank. Not after Angela. How much more am I supposed to give up?"

Dylan had been watching Mitch and reading his swiftly changing expressions: the relief to learn that it wasn't Andrew's emergency, instantly replaced by worry over his father-in-law's condition, then the guilt of not being reachable when he was most needed. Now, he seemed moved that Mary had exposed her vulnerability to him when their relationship had often been adversarial.

"I know the feeling," he said softly. "Believe me, I do. Tell Hank I'm on my way and will be there as soon as I can. In the meantime, if you have to call me, use this number."

After exchanging rapid goodbyes, they disconnected. Mitch took a moment to absorb it all, cupping his hand over his mouth and chin, squeezing his eyes shut. Perhaps he prayed to the God he claimed to have denounced.

But the moment was fleeting. He shot to his feet, bent down, and scooped his jeans and T-shirt off the floor where they'd been flung the night before. "Mrs. *Gibbons*? She's a *hundred and ten years old!* Andrew will be scared. Hell, *I'd* be scared."

Dylan scrambled off the bed, took him by both shoulders, and held on tightly. "Andrew will be fine. But if he's upset when you arrive, then you need to calm down. The worst you could do is to charge in there like a wild man. He'll take his cues from you."

He inhaled a series of deep breaths. "You're right. Of course you're right. What are you, a shrink or something?" He gave her a quick smack on the lips, then reached around her and took his pistol from the nightstand. With his clothing tucked under his arm, he headed out of the bedroom, affording her a view of his tight, bare butt. "Meet me at the front door in three minutes."

"On your way through town, you can drop me off at my office. I'll find a way home."

"Oh, no," he said over his shoulder. "You're coming. I'm not leaving you at the mercy of Malone and gang."

She halted in the process of stepping into her panties. "I don't have any clothes."

"Wear last night's. Or hit Beth's closet and chest of drawers. She won't mind. Three minutes."

Following the second time they'd made love, she had thought she was replete, that she only wished to lie there forever, feeling sublimely boneless and drowsy. But then he'd issued her an invitation to join him in the shower, and she couldn't resist his naughty grin.

Naked, he was simply magnificent. Although she'd been careful of his wound, she couldn't keep her hands or mouth off him. His Excalibur—and its adjacent sword—got extra attention that eventually had brought him to his knees. He'd warned her that he intended to explore every inch of her, not exclusively by hand, and he'd stayed true to his word.

Being all wet and soapy had made the foreplay incredibly erotic and had led, inevitably, to them joining, moving against each other, her clinging, him clutching, until the shower stall walls had echoed their climactic cries.

After drying, she'd replaced the closures on his abdomen that had been sacrificed to sex, then, exhausted, they'd crawled onto the bed and instantly had fallen asleep.

Now she was relieved that she was at least clean, because she had time to do nothing more than rinse her mouth out with toothpaste, secure her hair into a ponytail, and dress.

She put on her skirt from the night before, but raided Beth Bowie's closet in search of a top that was more suitable for daytime than her silk blouse. She also found a pair of sneakers to replace her ravaged evening pumps.

When she joined Mitch in the main room, he gave her an approving once-over and picked up a child car seat where it sat near the front door. "I keep a spare here."

His expression was intent, his manner all business. He made

quick work of locking the door and replacing the key beneath the porch floor plank, then plowed into the swampy forest, which to Dylan didn't look any less menacing in daylight than it had the night before. Mitch navigated it with the ease of a wraith. The borrowed sneakers made the going easier for her.

After opening the garage, he installed the child seat in a drab, gray two-door car. "It's not pretty, and the blanket in the back seat smells like wet dog. His name's Mutt."

"Yours?"

"John and Beth's."

He secured the garage with his disreputable-looking pickup inside, then they jounced along the rutted track that led to the highway. He turned west onto it and drove aggressively, speeding up to pass any vehicle not going fast enough to suit him.

He was wearing his game face, the one he'd displayed last night when he'd taken her elbow and hustled her away from the commotion outside the restaurant. A man on a mission. The focused, special ops soldier face except without the makeup.

Quietly, she said, "You really should drop me in town, Mitch."

He didn't even take his eyes off the road. "There's a Quick Stop a mile up ahead. I'll get us some coffee."

"Did you hear what I said?"

"The breakfast burritos aren't bad."

"It would be for the best."

"Forget it, Dylan."

"I've already imposed on John and Beth to an embarrassing degree." She looked down at the pull-on top she'd pilfered, and thinking about the bed she'd had to leave unmade made her cheeks hot. "Dealing with your family situation is going to be difficult enough. You don't know what to expect, and matters could change in an instant. I shouldn't intrude."

"You're not intruding. I'm giving you no choice."

"Which will require an explanation."

"I've got ninety miles to think of something."

He steered into the parking lot of the convenience store, put the car in park, but kept the engine running. He cupped the back of her neck and pulled her toward him. "I'm not going anywhere without keeping you in sight." He kissed her, and this time it was more than a smack. It wasn't a lingering kiss, but the kind that counted all the same. And when it broke, to underscore his intention, he said, "That's settled."

He pulled into the driveway of the Duvalls' house, saying to Dylan, "The old lady lives next door." He got out and jogged across the connecting lawns, counting on Dylan to follow him, which she did also at a jog.

He rang the doorbell, and, for extra measure, knocked and called out, "Mrs. Gibbons. It's Mitch Haskell."

A few seconds later, from within the house he heard Andrew exclaim, "Daddy!" followed by pounding, running steps on a hardwood floor.

"I'm coming, I'm coming," Mrs. Gibbons called out.

She apparently had more door locks than the Auclair jail, and each one seemed to challenge her dexterity. Mitch muttered out the side of his mouth, "If the house were to catch fire..."

"Shh," Dylan said just as the door was pulled open.

Andrew pushed against the screen door just as Mitch pulled on the outside handle, so that his son literally tumbled into his waiting arms almost before he could crouch down to catch him. Never mind that his exuberant welcome probably dislodged a few of the closures.

Mitch hugged him tightly, rocking to and fro. "Glad to see me?" Andrew nodded against his neck.

Looking on, Mrs. Gibbons said, "Mary called and told me to expect you. Andrew's asked me about every sixty seconds how many more minutes before you'd get here."

"Well, now I'm here, you can stop asking," Mitch said to Andrew as he covered his face with kisses.

The boy giggled over his affection, then angled his head back and said solemnly, "Grandpa's sick."

"I know. But the doctors are going to get him well."

That concern dealt with and dismissed, Andrew asked, "Can we play cars?"

"For sure. But later. We've got stuff to do first."

It was then that Andrew noticed Dylan. He looked at her curiously. Mitch said, "This is my friend, Dylan. Dylan, this is my rock star, Andrew."

"Hello, Andrew."

He just stared at her until Mitch gave him a squeeze. "What do you say?"

Andrew said hello, then shyly buried his face in Mitch's neck. He introduced Dylan to Mrs. Gibbons, then said to her, "I'm sure Mary has already thanked you, but I want to also. I appreciate you looking after him."

"He's welcome to stay for as long as need be."

"That's very generous and kind of you, but I'm taking him off your hands now."

"Oh." Mrs. Gibbons turned to Dylan as though looking for confirmation of that startling announcement. Going back to Mitch, she said with uncertainty, "Mary said nothing about that to me."

"She and I haven't had a chance to talk about it yet. Soon

as I gather up some things for Andrew, I'm going to the hospital straight from here."

"Oh," she said again, nervously reaching for the top button of her blouse and twisting it. "Mary packed a bag for him before she left for the hospital."

"Great. I'll just take that."

"Well, all right, I guess. Come in. I'll fetch it from the back room."

"We'll wait here, thanks."

Looking disapproving, she turned and headed down a hallway. "It smells like oldness in there," Mitch mumbled.

Dylan gave him a chastising look. "She's not a hundred and ten."

"My mistake," he whispered. "She's a hundred and *twelve*. And how hot is it in there? Andrew's hair is damp with sweat. It smells like Mutt's blanket."

"I want to go," Andrew said.

Mitch patted his back. "Don't worry, buddy. We're going."

"Here we are." Mrs. Gibbons reappeared pulling Andrew's small suitcase.

"Thank you so much," Mitch said. He felt resistance when he tried to take the handle from her.

"Mr. Haskell, I'm not sure Mary—"

"We all owe you for looking after Andrew until I could get here. Thanks, Mrs. Gibbons." Still holding Andrew against his chest, he turned to Dylan and tipped his head toward the Duvalls' house. "We'll make a pit stop, then be on our way."

Chapter 30

He spent only a few minutes gathering up more clothing, books, and toys for Andrew's indefinite stay with him. As he moved around the room, Andrew stayed on his heels, as though afraid Mitch would disappear. His boy appeared to be all right, but it had been a sideways morning. He had to be feeling some insecurity.

To reassure him, he knelt down and clasped Andrew to him and tried to devise a way to tell him how much he loved him, how essential he, his well-being, his happiness, were to him, but Andrew wouldn't understand the concepts. Dylan's concepts, he realized.

So he set Andrew away from him and whispered conspiratorially, "Hey, want to see my boo-boo?"

Andrew nodded.

"Are you sure you're ready for it? It's a doozy."

Andrew nodded even more enthusiastically. Mitch raised his shirt, being careful not to lift the back of it to expose his holstered pistol.

As expected, Andrew was awed and impressed by the incision. "These are bandages, see?" Mitch said. "They're holding my skin together. You can touch one, but be easy." Andrew barely made contact with the closure.

"What I need," Mitch said gravely, "is for you to help me get it healed up. Remember when you cut your finger, and I had to keep medicine and Band-Aids on it?" Andrew held up the formerly injured finger. "Right. See? It got well. Now it's your turn to help me get my tummy well.

"And while you're helping, it's Froot Loops every day for breakfast. Do we have a deal?" Mitch raised his hand, and Andrew high-fived it. "Good. Now, grab that bucket of cars, and I'll get the suitcase, and let's go find Dylan."

They found her in the living room, standing in front of the fireplace, looking at pictures lined up on the mantel: Angela as a baby, as an adolescent in a soccer uniform, kneeling with him at the wedding altar, and beside him at the baptismal font holding Andrew in her arms.

Andrew, distracted with retrieving all the cars that had fallen out of the overloaded plastic bucket, didn't see Dylan's poignant expression as she turned to Mitch and said gruffly, "What a beautiful woman. What a beautiful family."

He walked over and looked at the pictures, although he had spent hours staring at them while steeped in sorrow and pledging revenge. "They robbed her of our family, stole her from us, ended her life. Can you understand now why I want to see them suffer and die?"

"I've always understood the why of it, Mitch." She glanced over at Andrew, who was in conversation with one of the semi trucks in his collection. Coming back to him, she said, "But are you willing to pay what getting vengeance may cost you?"

He held her troubled gaze until Andrew announced that he had to pee-pee.

Mary was sitting in a chair by Hank's bedside in the cardiac ICU when Mitch walked in. Hank was asleep. His right hand was crisscrossed with tape to hold in the IV shunt. Mary held it in her palm while, with her other hand, she was stroking his arm.

Sensing Mitch's presence, she turned her head. "They let you in? It's only supposed to be one visitor at a time."

"I talked my way."

She gave a weak smile. "I'm sure. Thank you for coming."

"As if I wouldn't." He walked over, she turned up her cheek to him, and he kissed it. As he straightened up, he kept his hand on her shoulder. "It had to have been scary for you."

"Oh, Mitch," she sighed. "I thought he was going to die right there on the kitchen floor."

He pressed her shoulder. "But he didn't. Give me the skinny on his condition."

She gave him a rundown of the standard tests. "The cardiologist suspects several arterial blockages. If he's right, and since Hank has already had an 'episode,' the doctor recommends that they be corrected as soon as possible."

"Surgery?"

"The procedures haven't been fully explained to us yet." She looked up and behind him. "Please turn that down. It's so irritating."

She'd referred to the TV mounted on the wall, where the King of Cash was sermonizing on the merits of his law firm. "You can't escape that jerk," Mitch said as he reached for the remote control lying on the bed tray and muted the TV.

To his surprise, Hank said, "I was watching that ball game." He opened his eyes and smiled up at Mitch. "But it's a replay of last night's game, and the Astros lost by five, so it's just as well."

Mitch pretended to be stunned and affronted. "All the drama you caused, I thought you'd be a lot sicker."

"He is sicker," Mary said.

"I didn't even stop for breakfast," Mitch said. "Busted my ass to get here."

His performance got a smile out of Hank, who said, "You put Mrs. Gibbons in a right tizzy."

Mitch looked at Mary, who said, "She called, said you took Andrew without so much as a how-dee-do."

"I didn't owe her a how-dee-do. I owed her my thanks, which I extended more than once. But I wanted to get Andrew out of there and make sure he was okay. He had to have been confused, possibly even frightened, by all that was going on and the suddenness of the two of you not being around."

Mary sighed. "I tried not to show how frantic I was. But I'm sure he picked up on it. I did my best, Mitch."

"I'm confident of that. But Andrew needs me now."

"Betty Gibbons is very capable."

"I'm sure she's capable of getting on and off the commode without assistance, but I doubt she's capable of chasing an energetic little boy around that greenhouse she lives in."

Hank said, "Please, don't you two start. And, Mary, you know he's right about Betty's house. If only her disposition was that warm," he added under his breath.

Mitch said, "Forgive my remark about the commode. Last thing y'all need is me spouting off. I wasn't questioning your judgment, Mary. You did what you had to do in an emergency situation, and it was kind of your neighbor to take on responsibility for Andrew."

Mary acknowledged his apology with a nod. "She told me you had someone with you."

He hadn't seen that coming, and it threw off his timing. "Uh, yeah. Her name is Dylan Reede. She's a psychologist." Usually so glib, he could think of nothing to say unless they wanted to hear about Dylan's last orgasm in the shower. "I... I didn't know what all Andrew had witnessed or how traumatizing it might have been, so I thought Dr. Reede could be helpful."

"She's a child psychologist?" Mary asked.

"Uh, no. Just regular. But real smart." He hitched his thumb over his shoulder. "She's looking after Andrew downstairs in the lobby. When I left them, he was acquainting her with his new Nikes."

"You're taking him to Auclair."

"Yes, Mary, I am."

"How will you handle having him underfoot?"

"How will you? You can't while being here with Hank around the clock as I know you want to be."

"But your work—"

"I'll figure it out. I'm sure Beth will volunteer to help. I'm taking him," he said with finality.

Looking resigned, Mary stood up. "I want to tell him goodbye, and I had better do it now before they come to take Hank for the angiogram."

Mitch shook his finger at Hank. "Cooperate. Do what they tell you. Don't be a pain in the ass. Honey always attracts more flies. And pretty nurses." He winked, and his father-in-law winked back. "Anything I can do for you before I go?"

Giving Mitch a meaningful look, he said, "Stay for a minute longer."

Mary, who had already walked toward the door, turned back and hesitated. Mitch said, "I'll be right down. Andrew pitched camp there by the aquarium."

She nodded and said to her husband, "Have the nurse text me if they come for you." Hank gave her a thumbs-up. She left them.

Mitch sat down in the chair she'd occupied and asked bluntly, "Okay, gloves off. How are you doing?"

"I feel like shit."

"Well, you scared the shit out of us." Then, "Hey, all this…" He gestured to include the cannula, the IV pole, the blinking, bleeping monitors, "…is nerve-wracking to us. But these ICU people do this every day. So what intimidates the hell out of us is routine for them. Do you trust your cardiologist?"

"Seems okay. He might be old enough to shave."

Mitch smiled. "Better that than some old fart." Mitch clamped him on the shoulder. "If you have to undergo some corrective procedures, this scare will have been worth it. You'll feel a lot better. The episode this morning will have been a blessing."

"I thought you didn't believe in blessings anymore."

"For you, I'm hedging my bets."

Hank smiled before turning serious again. "Listen, son, Mary puts up a strong front, especially around you. But she's a lot more fragile than she lets on. Losing Angela…" Tears filled the older man's eyes, and Mitch took pity on him.

"You don't have to say anything more, Hank. If something happens to you, be it tomorrow or twenty years from now, I'll be there for Mary. You don't have to ask me."

He paused to consider how he was going to say what he felt needed to be said. "Also, just so you know, I'm never going to give over guardianship of Andrew. As recently as this week, Mary led me to believe she'd been thinking along those lines. It's not gonna happen. For as long as I'm alive, Andrew is one hundred percent mine."

"She gets crosswise and may throw out hints to that effect, but she would never go through with it. She knows, just as I do, that Angela would want him with you."

"I'm certain of that, too." Mitch held out his fist, and Hank bumped it with his. "Hang in there. Mary will keep me updated, and I'll be checking in. See you soon."

As he was stepping out of the elevator on the ground floor, he met Mary about to board. They moved aside and gave up the elevator to others who were waiting. Mary looked weepy. "I hated saying goodbye."

"I'll try to keep Andrew so busy he won't miss you too much." He looked beyond her to where Andrew and Dylan were methodically picking up the cars he'd been playing with and replacing them in the bucket. Andrew held one up for Dylan's inspection; she smiled approvingly and pointed to one of the model's features and asked him a question.

"Mrs. Gibbons told me she was pretty."

He shifted his gaze back to Mary and dropped his smile when he realized how sappy it must look. "Pardon?"

"Is it serious?"

He glanced at Dylan, then came back to Mary. "What? Her and me? No. Hell, no. We really just met a few days ago."

Mary gave him that look that a woman gives a man when

she knows he's being less than honest. He said, "You need to get back to Hank."

She nodded. "Give me a hug." As they hugged, she said, "We love you, Mitch."

"I love you, too."

"We worry about you."

"I worry about me, too," he said, then cracked a smile.

She sighed and flapped her hand at him. The elevator door opened, and she stepped inside. Then, as though suddenly remembering, she said, "Andrew said something about a boo-boo?"

"My neck." He touched the red mark left by the cut from the broken gin bottle. "You saw it on Sunday. It's almost gone now."

As the elevator door slid closed, she gave him another one of those looks.

Chapter 31

Roland was having a bad day.

Mitch Haskell's antics continued to gnaw at him. First his encounter with El Paso last night, and now the overnight disappearing act he'd pulled with Dylan.

On top of that worry, half an hour ago, Oz had called him with the alarming news that the three-truck convoy carrying the Caballeros' stolen cargo had gone incommunicado. No one had been able to reach either the drivers or those guarding the payload.

"Somewhere in East Texas they stopped checking in on schedule, and they're not replying to calls or texts. If you hear anything, let me know immediately."

Oz had been just that brief and then had hung up before Roland could say I told you so.

"What a fuck-up," Roland now muttered to himself. On top of everything else, this was all they needed.

But what really worried him was that Oz might forget that

this audacious but reckless plan had been his, not Roland's. When even the slightest hiccup occurred within the operation, it was never Oz's fault. Blame was laid on someone else. A ghosting convoy trundling through East Texas was more than a hiccup.

Roland shook two antacid tablets into his mouth, then took his rosary beads from the drawer. He'd just finished the Fatima prayer when his chef came to his office bringing what amounted to a grocery list for Roland's approval. He scanned the categorized list hurriedly.

"Looks okay. But tonight I'll go to the meat locker myself and check on the inventory of veal and beef. I'll let you know tomorrow how much to order."

Just as the door was closing behind the rotund man, one of Roland's phones dinged. It was Barbara Nix. "Tell me something good."

Speaking sotto voce, she said, "Haskell's father-in-law in Lafayette had a heart attack this morning. Wasn't fatal. He's in the hospital."

"How'd you get this?"

"Same way. Clarence, village idiot and the CAP unit's grapevine. He delivered a cup of coffee to Bowie in his office. He was on the phone with his wife, telling her about it, said that Mitch may not be in for the next few days." She paused for breath. "He's got to go see his ailing father-in-law, right?"

"How many hospitals are there in Lafayette?"

"I took the liberty of doing some research."

She had called around until she'd isolated the one in which Mr. Henry Duvall had been admitted.

"How'd you know his name?"

"Haskell's personnel file. After his parents, Duvall was listed as next of kin."

She had then dispatched one of their dealers in Lafayette to cruise the hospital's parking lot looking for Haskell's truck, for which she had gotten the make, model, and license plate.

"He drove 'round and 'round. It wasn't there."

"Maybe he missed it."

"He couldn't have. It's obnoxious. I'd also given him the Duvalls' home address and suggested he also look there. But no truck and seemingly no one at home."

"You've been mighty busy," Roland remarked.

"I also drove past Dylan Reede's house again. No sign she's been there. Package is still on the front porch. Her office is closed today."

Roland sat thinking, turning his ring.

After a time, Nix said, "Haskell's son lives with the in-laws. If we wanted to bring Haskell to the surface quickly, we could put the fear of God into—"

"No," Roland declared in a manner that brooked no argument.

The baby in the crib.

He'd debated doing just as Haskell's wife had fearfully conjectured: that regardless of his promise, he would kill the baby after she was dead. He had climbed the stairs with that intention. He'd stood over the sleeping child.

But there he'd paused. What if the baby hadn't been baptized yet? He would be responsible for condemning the boy to hell. That might be an unforgivable sin. No matter how many times he petitioned Fatima to spare him hell's fires, for killing an unsanctified baby, he might burn for eternity.

So, he'd left the kid sleeping, and now, he said to Nix, "Don't act on that. Not yet anyway."

"All right. Get back to me if you change your mind."

Nix was good. She was eager. During the years he'd had her inside the Auclair PD to keep an eye on Haskell, she'd had little to do because Haskell had been such a washout. It had hardly seemed worthwhile to keep a spy of her caliber in that backwater. But with the unwelcome surprises coming in rapid succession over the past few days, she'd been invaluable.

However, it occurred to Roland now that she might be too clever for comfort. If she ever put two and two together and figured out that he and Haskell shared Dr. Reede...

Perish the thought. He had successfully gotten around that hurdle with Oz by giving him that embroidered account of last night's events. But the energetic Nix could unwittingly—or possibly not—discover his secret. If she did, what would she do with it?

Trying not to sound as troubled as he felt, he said, "Haskell has to poke his head out sometime. Keep your eyes and ears open."

"Always," she said, sounding a bit let down that she hadn't been given a more adventurous assignment.

Just as he ended that call, another came in from Oz. He answered, and Oz said, "Disaster averted. The drivers got wind of two speed traps on I-10. Texas DPS. Didn't want to risk it. They separated and each took a different back road, and, as an extra precaution, turned off their phones till they were well past the traps."

"Good news," Roland said, meaning it.

Oz clicked off before saying anything more. That was that. Things were looking up.

Soon after they disconnected, someone knocked on his office door. "Come in."

El Paso strolled in looking surly. "Some asshole woke me up, said you wanted to see me, drove me over here."

He'd sent his chauffeur to the flop house where El Paso had gotten lodging. Roland looked him over. "You're stoned."

"Duh." El Paso shut the door hard and raised his shoulders in an insolent shrug. "You told me to lay low, I was laying low."

"Get sober by closing time tonight. Meet me at the kitchen door ten minutes after closing. You're running an errand with me."

His red-rimmed eyes brightened a bit. "Cool. I guess I'm forgiven?"

"Pending."

He scoffed. "Pending." Then said, "See you ten minutes after closing, boss," and slunk out.

Roland went over to the door and locked it, then returned to his desk and opened the lower drawer. He took out a new garrote and gave it a few test tugs. Perfect. His cousin never failed him. His stock was getting low. Tomorrow, he would need to place an order for a couple more.

With that in mind, he picked up the phone he used to communicate with Dylan and read again her sweet but lying text. On a whim, he called her number, just out of curiosity for how she would sound and what she would say. It went to voice mail.

That was all right. It gave him more time to savor the thought of killing her.

Chapter 32

As soon as Mitch returned with Dylan and Andrew to the fishing camp, he called John to update him on Hank's condition, Mary's state of mind, and Andrew's transfer of watch care from the neighbor to him. "Poor kid was so glad to see us."

"'Us?'"

"Dylan."

"She went along to Lafayette?"

"I wasn't going to take her home or leave her out here alone."

"Nobody knows about the camp."

"I'm not taking any chances with this bunch, John. When we came out of the hospital, I noticed a car in the parking lot slowly making laps up one row and down another."

"Looking for an empty space."

"He passed them up. He wasn't looking to park his car. Now call me paranoid, or maybe it was just my ops training working overtime, but I was glad we were in a car that wouldn't be recognized."

"How would Malone and company have known you were going to a hospital in Lafayette?"

"Come on, John."

"Walls with ears?"

"Right-o. And these sons of bitches are smart and bold. If they pick up even a tidbit, they're gonna act on it."

"I don't need convincing."

Hearing the dejection in John's voice, Mitch asked, "What now?"

"You know Lear. Dogged. Meticulous. He's been poring over maps of Bayou Coeur, including one that was hand-drawn."

"By who?"

"A relative of his who fishes it. Anyway, he found a tiny inlet that wasn't on any of the other maps. Darcy sent a team to check it out. Sure enough, the investigators found fresh scrapes on a clump of cypress knees, like the kind a hull would make if a boat was dragged across them into the channel."

"That's great! That's a starting point."

"It's a dead end. The area had been swept clean."

"What?"

"Darcy had personnel combing it on foot and shoulder-to-shoulder. What soon became obvious was that it was too clean. Hardly even sticks on the ground. The culprits had cleared the area from the waterline all the way back to the road."

"They covered their tracks."

"They *eliminated* them."

"Which is why I brought Dylan here and why I'm keeping her."

"Till Malone makes a move."

"Then we'll see."

"Okay. There's gumbo in the freezer. I think some steaks. Help yourselves to whatever you can scrounge."

"Thanks. I'm also taking a new burner out of the drawer. This one's probably outlived its healthy life span."

"Text me the number."

"Roger that."

"Mitch?"

"Yeah?"

He was sitting cross-legged on the floor. Beside him was a makeshift ramp he'd constructed out of books. Andrew was rolling his cars down it, delighting when they crashed at the bottom.

Dylan braced herself for an argument. "I need to call my answering service." When she saw that Mitch was about to protest, she raised her hand to stop him. "A patient may be quickly unraveling to a dangerous level."

"Do you have patients that whacked out?"

"'Whacked out' isn't a clinical term, but I do have several with severe depression. I need to check to see if anyone is in crisis."

"Sure." He reached into the front pocket of his jeans and extended a phone up to her. It was one that he'd only recently taken from the drawer in the sideboard.

"My service may not answer an unidentified caller. Please put the battery in my phone."

She could tell he didn't like it, but he came to his feet, told Andrew that he would be right back, and went into the guest bedroom, returning with her phone. "The battery is low, but you should have enough juice."

"Thank you."

She typed in her passcode and checked her texts. She had

two, but neither was of any consequence. She also had one missed call. From Roland.

First, she called her answering service. Other than John Bowie's attempt to reach her early that morning, no one had called for her. Which came as a great relief.

Mitch had rejoined Andrew on the floor. Each had a car now, and they were racing them. Smiling over Andrew's tire-screeching noises, Mitch looked up at her and must have noted the tension in her expression.

He got Andrew interested in a fire truck, then stood up. "What?"

"No calls to my service except for John Bowie's early this morning."

"That's good. No one is in trouble."

"But Roland called my cell."

"When?"

"Shortly after one o'clock this afternoon."

"He leave a message?"

"No."

Andrew was running the fire truck up and down Mitch's thigh. He ruffled Andrew's hair but never took his eyes off her. "What do you usually do when a patient calls and doesn't leave a message?"

"Call back to see if everything is all right."

"So call him."

She nodded and turned away, but he hooked her elbow. "But I listen in."

"You will not."

"If I have to play the cop card, I will."

She pulled her arm from his grasp. "On what grounds?"

"Malone's employee took a switchblade to three people last night, including me."

"He may not have even known about it. I told you he reacted as though he didn't. That El Paso may have been up to meanness that had nothing to do with Roland."

"So it's *Roland* again? I can't believe—" he began in a raised voice. He looked over his shoulder at Andrew, who was now involved with guiding his fire truck along the armrest of the sofa. Mitch came back to her and continued in a moderated but no less truculent tone. "I can't believe you're defending him."

"It's not about defending him. You have responsibilities and you take them seriously." She flattened her hand against her chest. "Well, I also have a responsibility to every patient, which I take seriously. That includes Roland Malone, even if he is a criminal.

"Besides, Detective Haskell, think about it. If I don't follow up, it will make him wonder why. Especially if he knows I lied to him about arriving safely home last night. If you don't want him suspicious of me, *more* suspicious of me, you should let me call."

In frustration, he placed his hands on his hips, but she could tell that her reasoning had made sense to him. "Make the fucking call," he said, mouthing the eff word.

She moved to the other side of the room for privacy, but it wasn't needed. Her call wasn't answered. After numerous rings, a recording told her there was no mailbox set up for that number. The tightness in her chest eased. Despite her adamant argument, she had hoped she wouldn't be forced to talk to Roland and tell more lies.

She went back to Mitch and ungraciously returned her phone to him. "He didn't answer. There was no voice mailbox, so I couldn't leave a message." She waited a beat before adding, "And don't you ever pull that cop card crap with me again." She stood there, meeting his eyes, daring him to challenge her.

He didn't, but asked, "Was this our first fight?"

She turned her back on him, walked to the front door, opened it, and stepped out onto the porch. As she closed the door behind herself, she heard him say, "Guess so."

Chapter 33

In the alley behind the restaurant, El Paso got in on the passenger side of a rattletrap panel truck. Roland was already in the driver's seat with the motor running. "You're late."

"Only by two lousy minutes." He looked around the plain and slightly odorous interior of the truck. "Where's your fancy car with the chauffeur?"

"His night off."

"No bodyguard, either?"

As Roland steered out of the end of the alley, he said, "You're acting as my bodyguard tonight. You up to it?"

The kid saluted him. "Do I get a gun?"

"Not till I say."

Roland had looked closely at him when he'd gotten into the truck. This morning's glassy eyes had cleared. If he was still high, it was only barely. In fact, it might go easier if the little asshole was a bit mellow.

"Where are we going, anyway?" he asked.

"You'll see when we get there."

"How far is it?"

"Not far."

"Can we have some music?" he asked, reaching for the radio dial.

"No. This isn't a joyride. You're supposed to be keeping your eyes on the side mirror to watch for anyone tailing us."

"Got it."

Roland tried not to let his anticipation show. The day had gotten off to a rough start, but it was ending on a much better note. Dylan and Haskell were still no-shows, but they would be sniffed out, then snuffed out, sooner or later.

The restaurant had been crowded and busy tonight, but he'd taken a call from Barbara Nix, who had reported that Darcy and his team had found the inlet on the bayou where the boat carrying the bodies of Adler and the girl had put in, only to discover that the cleanup crew had done an excellent job of ridding the area of evidence. Even if a scrap had been found, by now it would have been so compromised by the elements that a prosecutor would consider it useless.

Just before securing his office and heading for the back door, Roland had made a call to Oz to pass along that good news. "Nix organized the team herself. She's been one step ahead of Darcy and his bunch the whole time."

The young woman really was remarkable, but Roland had resolved to keep a tight leash on her. Go-getters often got ahead of themselves, ahead of their bosses. And he wouldn't let that happen.

He went on to inform Oz that he and El Paso were scheduled to leave for the meat locker within minutes.

Oz had signed off with, "Call me when it's done."

Now, having reached his destination, Roland pulled the truck right up to the garage door at the back of an unpromising edifice. He looked across at the smart-ass who was sitting forward, gazing through the windshield at the brick building looming just beyond the blunt hood of the truck.

For over a century, the unsightly structure had been at the mercy of hurricanes and other erosives. It had withstood them, but their damaging effects were visible. Several of its windows were cracked despite the chicken wire in them. Mortar that was crumbling or missing altogether had left wide gaps between its faded and chipped red bricks.

El Paso said, "I got all dressed up for this?"

Ignoring the kid's droll remark, Roland got out. El Paso, who'd gotten out on his own, took a look around at the area, which, in days past, had been a thriving industrial hub. Most of the factories and warehouses were now derelict and unoccupied except for squatters.

Anyone giving a casual glance to the building Roland approached with El Paso would think it was deserted and decaying like its neighbors. There wasn't a sign designating either its owner or that it was Ristorante Italiano's private meat locker.

He used a remote to open the garage door. It creaked and clattered as it rolled up, and at halfway an alarm began chirping. Roland stepped into the dark maw and punched in the code on the control box just inside. As soon as he and El Paso cleared the door, he used the remote to begin its noisy descent.

Roland flipped a switch, but the only lights to come on hung from the ceiling in a single file down the center of the cavernous space. The smell of fresh meat was redolent.

"Jesus, it's cold in here," El Paso said, hugging himself and running his hands up and down his arms.

"Of course it is. It's a meat locker." Roland gestured to his right where, hanging by hooks, were sides of beef.

El Paso looked at them with interest. "Did you see that old movie *Rocky*, where he beat the shit out of that cow carcass?"

"Yeah, I saw it."

He turned to Roland and smirked. "Is this where you practice your boxing?"

"This where I butcher meat."

"No shit. You cut it up yourself?"

"Sometimes. Sometimes I need an assistant." He poked his ringed pinky finger against El Paso's shoulder. "That's why I brought you. Business is about to pick up. I want you to start assisting me."

"I don't know anything about cutting up cows."

"Not cows. People. You know a lot about that, don't you, David Rodriguez?"

Looking a bit thrown off, El Paso took a step back.

Roland didn't move a muscle as the kid sized him up. He continued in his monotone style. "Butchering meat can get messy. So can cutting someone's throat. I have a hose back there bigger than a stallion's dick. It's connected to a tank of water that's kept almost to the boiling point. Like sterilizing, you know. Washes everything down a drain that's as wide as you are tall. I let the bodies practically drain dry, then...relocate them."

El Paso's initial caution had been replaced by interest. "That guy whose place I took? Adler? That's how he bought it, right?" He made a slicing motion across his throat.

Roland took a step toward him. He thought of the lectures he'd received from his mother, always shaking her finger at him. But he kept his hands at his sides and used his cold gaze to get his point across.

"The first thing you gotta learn if you're going to do this for Oz's operation. Never talk about it. Don't boast about a hit, not if it's a two-bit dealer like Adler, or a politician who won't play along, or a strung-out celebrity with a loose tongue. Even if you kill a narc who thinks he's smarter and tougher than us, you don't take credit. You keep your mouth shut. You say nothing. Not ever. Got it?"

"Yeah, man, I got it. How much money are we talking?"

"For your first, five grand."

"That's chicken shit!"

"That's the offer. You do well, maybe I can persuade Oz into being more generous. He wasn't convinced you were ready for this. Especially after that stunt you pulled last night. I had to twist his arm into letting you in on this."

He took a step closer and then another. "But hear me good. From now on, you don't call the shots. You don't even get an opinion. You don't ask questions. *You do as you're told.*"

By now he was right in El Paso's face. He waited several seconds, then stepped back and shot his cuffs. "Don't fuck up again, kid. Impress me, impress Oz, we'll renegotiate your pay."

El Paso relaxed, gave a little shiver as though to shake himself out of a trance, then shrugged. "I'm in."

"Okay. Let's get started. There's a lot you gotta learn."

Roland motioned him forward. The kid went ahead of him. Like a sheep to slaughter, Roland thought as he reached into his jacket pocket for the garrote.

They'd taken only two steps before a voice boomed out of the darkness behind them.

"This has been an interesting conversation."

Startled, Roland turned. "Oz?"

"*Oz?*" El Paso repeated, sounding both awed and terrified.

Roland was almost as shocked as the kid. He had impressed upon Oz how risky it would be for him to show up to witness El Paso's departure. But Oz was staying out of sight as he'd said he would. He was completely undetectable within the blackness beyond the narrow field of light shed by the row of overheads.

"So this is the famous El Paso," he said. "Or, should I say, infamous?"

El Paso said nothing.

"This is him," Roland said. "The one who caused such a ruckus last night by slicing open a cop."

"*What?*" El Paso squeaked.

Roland turned back around to face him. "Oh, yeah. Working undercover. A guy named Haskell who's always been a pain in the ass to our organization, and you just made him a bigger one." He hadn't raised his voice, but he had frozen El Paso where he stood.

The kid's lupine eyes were shifting to and fro as though looking for an escape. Not surprisingly, he whipped out his switchblade and opened it. Roland didn't react, didn't even blink. He'd been expecting it.

"You fuckin' fat man," El Paso sneered. "What's up with this?"

"Easy, El Paso."

Behind Roland, Oz's voice floated out of the darkness soothingly, as though he were trying to calm an excitable animal. Which, Roland thought, wasn't far off the mark.

El Paso watched in horrified realization as Roland withdrew the garrote from his pocket, gripping the handholds and testing the tautness.

"You didn't do as you were told last night, did you, El Paso?" Oz asked.

"How could I know that bum was heat, that he would fight back? What would you expect me to do?"

"I would expect you to obey orders," Oz said. "Roland told you to keep it low-key, and, because you didn't, there have been a series of consequences you're unaware of. That should teach you a valuable lesson. You don't always know why you're given an order. It's not your place to know. It's mine."

El Paso looked at the garrote that Roland was relaxing and then snapping taut. Roland was watching the switchblade, which the kid was now waving unsteadily, nervously. And yet, he maintained his swagger.

"Come on, man," he said, appealing to the void of darkness outside the light. "Give me another chance. I won't do nothing like that again."

"You'll do as you're told?" Oz asked.

"Yeah, yeah." Then, "Yes, sir."

"Without hesitation or question?"

"Without question. I swear it."

Oz said silkily, "It's a little late in coming, but I'm very pleased to hear that."

Chapter 34

Andrew's bashfulness and sweet countenance had endeared Dylan to him from the get-go. He also had Mitch's eyes, which might have had something to do with the little boy's appeal.

But she also found herself observing Andrew from the standpoint of a psychological analyst. It was an occupational hazard.

While waiting with him in the hospital lobby, he self-pacified by playing with his cars, delighted in the tropical fish in the aquarium, and watched other people with open curiosity but no perceivable fear of strangers.

He also seemed right at home in the unique wonderland of the fishing camp. She'd remarked to Mitch that she was surprised he wasn't frightened of the hunting trophies, especially the razorback.

"The one time he showed some fear of it, Molly told him that he shouldn't be afraid because Roger the Razorback was a friend of hers. That was that. He thinks Molly hung the moon, so anything she says is scripture."

By the end of the day, Dylan had concluded that being shuttled between Mitch and his grandparents seemed not to have had a negative effect on the child. He was well adjusted and well behaved, usually minding after being told only once either to do something or to stop.

Now, however, as they were having dinner, his good behavior began to deteriorate to that of an obstinate two-year-old-going-on-three.

She and Mitch were eating "John's famous" gumbo. Andrew was having a single portion of microwaveable mac and cheese, which Mitch had bought in a convenience store on their way back from Lafayette. He'd also bought a box of Froot Loops, which he'd hidden in the pantry so Andrew wouldn't want the cereal for dinner.

After having eaten only half of his macaroni, Andrew was making a smeary mess of it on his plate. His hand was covered in orange goo. Mitch, losing patience, wiped his hand clean and pushed a spoon into it. "Use your spoon."

Andrew dropped it onto the table, where it landed with a clatter. "I want to get down. I want to play cars."

"Not until you use your manners and finish your dinner. Eat your apple slices."

Andrew picked up one and threw it to the floor.

Mitch pointed his index finger at him. "*Enough*, Andrew!"

Andrew's lower lip began to tremble, then his whole face crumpled. He opened his mouth as wide as it would go and released a wail. Fat tears puddled in his sapphire eyes.

"Meltdown." Mitch sighed. He pushed back his chair and stood. He lifted Andrew off the makeshift booster seat, a stack of old telephone directories, and hoisted him onto his hip.

Andrew, wriggling in an effort to get down, burbled, "I want to play cars."

"No way. No way, José. You didn't act nice at the dinner table. It's off to bed for you, buddy." As he carried his squalling son toward the guest room, he said over his shoulder to Dylan, "Catch you later," and shut the door behind them.

She cleared the table and put the dishes in the dishwasher. She was just finishing up when Mitch came out of the bedroom, closing the door quietly behind him.

"He's down for the count." Noticing that she'd cleaned up, he said, "You didn't have to do that."

"It was nothing."

Her dismissal had come out sounding curt, and he caught it. He tilted his head. "Are you still mad at me?"

"No."

He didn't say anything immediately, then gave a small nod. "I heard from Mary. Hank had four arterial blockages. Tomorrow, he'll undergo angioplasty to insert stents. After that, a week, ten days of taking it easy. Prognosis, good."

"A relief to Mary, I'm sure." She carefully folded a dish towel and draped it over the edge of the sink.

He said, "I think you're still mad."

"I'm not."

Again, he studied her for a moment before continuing. "Sorry about Andrew's tantrum. They're rare, but he can pitch a good one."

"You handled it very well." He arched his eyebrow skeptically. "No, I mean it. He challenged your authority, and you didn't give in. His bad behavior wasn't rewarded. You showed him that bad choices have consequences."

"I made him tell me he was sorry, then read him a story, hugged him, told him how much I love him, and lay there with him until he went to sleep."

"All good. Actually, I didn't even hear him crying after you took him into the bedroom."

"Well, the deal was that if he didn't get over the fit that instant, he wouldn't get to shower."

"Shower?"

"At his grandparents' house, he takes baths. When he's at my house, I take him into the shower with me." He walked slowly toward her. "And you know how much fun that can be."

Her femaleness betrayed her by instantly responding to the rumbling tone of a man aroused. Her sensory receptors sizzled with memories of the night before. And damn him! Fresh from the shower, he smelled so good. He came close enough for her to feel his body heat, and yet he wasn't nearly close enough. She wanted him pressing against her. Into her.

But when he leaned in and attempted to kiss her, she turned her head aside and took a step back. "I've been behaving badly and making consequential choices myself, Mitch. Topping the list is sleeping with a patient."

"I'm no longer your patient." He closed the distance between them again. "One of the best choices I've made in a long, long, long time was to fire you last night."

"Only John Bowie can fire me, and your therapy is mandatory, so you remain a patient. Besides..."

"What?"

"I am mad at you."

"Yeah, I got that."

"You were high-handed. You pulled rank. I didn't like it."

"I didn't like it, either. I was an ass. You should've decked me."

In spite of herself she blurted a soft laugh, then said with irritation, "Don't joke."

"Wasn't joking. Are you still mad?"

"A little, yes."

"Good."

"Why good?"

He leaned in again and brushed his lips across the smile tugging at the corner of hers. "Because make-up sex is my favorite thing."

Then he pulled her against him and kissed her for real. Desire spread through her like a potent liqueur, leaving her body weakened and willing, and her saner self in jeopardy. She broke the kiss. "Mitch, we can't keep doing this."

"Then stop enticing me."

"I *don't*."

"You *do*. You don't play fair. If you want me to leave you alone, stop wearing this face, this hair." He threaded his fingers through it. "Stop looking at me through those eyes and, for god's sake, do something about those legs that I mistakenly thought went on forever. They don't," he purred. "Last night, I discovered where they led, and... oh my, it was good."

She made a whimpering sound and went along when he took her hand and led her over to one of the ugly chintz armchairs. He sat down, gathered up her slim skirt until it was bunched around her waist, and pulled her astride his lap. Several drugging kisses later, he reached for the hem of her borrowed top and began pulling it up.

"No," she said, glancing toward the bedroom door. "What if Andrew wakes up?"

"He won't. He's out. Besides, if he caught us, he wouldn't know what we're doing."

"*I* would know."

"Okay, leave the top on. That almost makes it dirtier, and dirty sex is my second favorite thing." He reached beneath the borrowed top and unhooked her bra. Sliding his hands back to her front, he cupped her breasts and tweaked her nipples between his fingers.

Then he ducked his head beneath the top and took her nipple into his mouth. Each tug caused a reaction down low where she was open to him. He felt it, too, and soon they were breathing swiftly and rubbing against each other lustily.

He brought his head out from under her top, hastily unbuttoned his jeans, and worked them down. When the waistband got past the hilt of Excalibur, her breath hitched at the sight of his erection.

He grinned and said, "Up," as he helped her to stand on her knees. It wasn't graceful, but, working together, they managed to get her panties off.

Before her knees folded, he kept her upright and nuzzled her, breathing her in, and exhaling in soft, humid puffs that caused flutters of sensation on her skin as well as within. His tongue flicked against her cleft, then went deeper, seeking the ultimate pleasure point and finding it.

He didn't stop until she came, and the instant he felt it, he bracketed her hips between his strong hands and lowered her onto him. He held her secure there, one with him, and kissed her mouth with uncontested passion and possessiveness.

He released her hips only long enough to remove her top and bra after all. "No way are you going to ride me and me not get to watch."

He rubbed his face against her breasts, his scruff delightfully scratchy, his mouth damp and ardent. His hands returned to her bottom and initiated a rocking motion, their give-and-take movements in perfect sync. Her sensitized flesh drew on his until she felt another climax about to claim her. She bore down even as he pushed up.

And what happened simultaneously between them then wasn't a culmination. It was an awakening.

As the ecstasy of it ebbed, they sagged against each other and held fast. After his breathing returned to near normal, he eased her away so he could pull off his T-shirt. Craving to be skin to skin with him, she helped.

Then he placed his arms around her, splayed his hands over the middle of her back, and drew her to him. He settled his bowed head on her breasts. She felt her heartbeat beneath his rough cheek.

Still inside her, his breath hot on her skin, he whispered, "Dylan, you are the last thing I expected."

She folded her arms around his head, and buried her face in his mussed hair. "I didn't expect you, either."

Chapter 35

Mitch's Friday had begun very early and had ended late, and all the events during the day had been physically exhausting and emotionally draining.

Nevertheless, he hadn't slept well or long and now lay staring at the ceiling and thinking that the timing couldn't be worse for Andrew to be with him indefinitely.

Today, as he played with Andrew, listened to his chatter and laughter, even during his tantrum, he'd begun nursing a heart-stopping fear that his son might somehow get on Roland Malone's radar.

Malone would remember the infant he'd left alive on the night he'd killed Angela, a decision he might regret and wish to rectify. It made Mitch ill even to think of it.

So now, in addition to Dylan's safety, he had Andrew's to worry about.

Regarding her, he couldn't continue keeping twenty-four/seven vigil. Even if it was feasible, she wouldn't stand for it. She could argue that Malone had dispatched someone to check on her house simply because he'd been concerned for her safe return from the city. Mitch didn't believe that, but it also wasn't as though Malone had issued her a death threat. She still didn't accept what a danger he posed.

She also wasn't going to abandon her patients. Come Monday, when her office reopened, she would insist on being there to resume her appointment schedule. And her receptionist, Ellie, wasn't exactly bodyguard material.

Whenever Dylan returned to her normal life, where would that leave them? After two years of celibacy and indifference toward the opposite sex, he was smitten, moonstruck, randy, and ravenous.

As evidenced last night in that ugly chair, he couldn't get enough of her. Engaging in a liaison that was compromising to them both had been darkly and deliciously erotic.

At least it had been with her. Despite the scene in *When Harry Met Sally*, which had given pause to every man in the human race, Dylan hadn't faked it. He hadn't anticipated that a woman who maintained such self-control in every other circumstance would be that uninhibited sexually.

God, it had been a-*maz*-ing.

But this was the kicker: In the mellow but still simmering aftermath of their armchair consorting, when he'd told her she had been unexpected, he hadn't been referring to carnality, but to the magnetic pull he felt toward her emotionally.

He hadn't counted on that. Not at all. And he didn't know what he was going to do with, or about, it.

Giving up on trying to sleep, he looked over at Andrew and smiled at the air bubble that had formed between his lips. He kissed him on the forehead, then eased out of the bed.

After a quick trip to the bathroom, he dressed and left the bedroom.

It wasn't quite daylight, but he could tell that it was going to be a gloomy day. He went into the kitchen and started a pot of coffee in a Mr. Coffee that should have been junked four decades ago. Except that it turned out damned good brew.

The machine had been in that spot on the counter when John had first brought him out here for a weekend of fishing. They hadn't known each other for long, but, over those two days, their friendship had been forged.

They'd spent the days in John's boat, fishing unambitiously while sipping cold ones iced down in an Igloo. In the evenings, they talked. Got maudlin over John's dissolving first marriage and Mitch's wartime buddies who'd died bloody. They'd also laughed their asses off.

Now, before nostalgia elbowed its way into his already troubled and overcrowded brain, he carried his mug out onto the front porch. As expected, the air was thick with moisture. Every leaf on every tree was weighed down by the humidity. The Spanish moss looked even droopier than usual.

He lowered himself into the least rusty '50s-era metal lawn chair, blew on his hot coffee, took a few sips, then swiped on his most recent burner phone.

Jim Tucker's cell number rang several times before he answered, but he didn't speak a word. Mitch said, "It's me."

"I was afraid of that."

"Too early for you?"

"No, it's not the hour that bothers me."

Tucker wasn't obligated to communicate with him. In fact, it would be his ass if he was caught doing so. Nevertheless, Mitch couldn't help but be a tad resentful. "You were gonna keep me updated on El Paso."

"You changed phones."

"Felt I needed to."

"Doesn't matter. I didn't call you."

"Why?"

"Because I'm not supposed to be talking to you, Homeless. Is the Dish still with you?"

"You want to swap intel? You go first. Tell me what you've learned about El Paso."

"I don't have anything."

"Bull. Shit. If you didn't have anything, you would have said so immediately and told me that you would call when you did. Instead, you said that you weren't supposed to be talking to me. Which makes me think that you *do* have something, but you're reluctant to share it."

Silence.

Mitch said, "Thought so." He glanced over his shoulder to make sure that neither Andrew nor Dylan had woken up. In a softer but even more imperative tone, he said, "Don't you want to nail these fuckers?"

"Stupid question. It doesn't deserve a response."

"All right then. So help me help you. Tell me what you've got. If we can arrest him—"

Tucker interrupted. "There is no *we*."

"Hell there's not. That little shit cut me. He could've hurt me a lot worse. If we find him, I can bring him in and slap a felony assault charge on him."

"Bad idea. *Bad* idea," Tucker repeated with emphasis. "El Paso's arrest would shake, rattle, and roll Malone. We should just as well post on social media that we're surveilling him.

Malone would tip Oz to it. Both would go underground and the agency would be screwed. And how would Bowie feel about your butting into a federal case?"

"He knows. I told him about El Paso myself yesterday morning." He took a breath. "Back to what I was saying. If I can get El Paso in custody, I'll scare the bejesus out of him. It may take a while to grind him down, but if I hammer him hard enough, he'll eventually break.

"And maybe, just maybe, when he's saying he's sorry and crying for his mama, he'll give me something on Malone that's substantial enough to turn over to a prosecutor who's got the balls to run it through the express lane of jurisprudence."

"You think so?"

"Yes. Underneath all the attitude, he's a snot-nosed kid."

"He's a member of the Caballeros."

That knocked the wind out of Mitch. He didn't need it explained to him who the Caballeros were, or what it said about the young man who was a member. They were merciless. Feral.

Tucker gave Mitch a few seconds to absorb the shock before continuing. "He's going by the name of David Rodriguez, but the cartel set up a false identity for him in case Malone checked him out before welcoming him into Oz's fold."

"What's his real name?"

"To you, that's irrelevant."

Mitch let that snide remark pass. "The Caballeros sent him here to infiltrate Oz's operation."

"Yes. Because, under pain of death, one of Oz's dealers in Juarez told them that Oz planned to steal a shitload of their product from a warehouse somewhere out in the desert. It was to be trucked here to New Orleans, then shipped up the Mighty

Mississipp' to St. Louis, where a customer is eagerly awaiting to buy it from Oz. At an inflated price, of course."

By now, Mitch had set his coffee mug on the floor beside the chair and was sitting with his elbows on his knees, head lowered, his fingers dug deep into his hair. "Was the theft successful?"

Silence.

"The warehouse in the desert had to have been heavily guarded. Body count?"

Silence.

"Is the product on its way?"

Silence.

"Is it already in New Orleans? Will El Paso—"

"El Paso, the snot-nosed kid?" Tucker chuffed, interrupting Mitch's chain of questions. "Be glad you've still got your guts. Before being accepted into the Caballeros, the kid had to earn his spurs. He's credited with a dozen kills that we know of. He was never indicted, but his first suspected victim was his own mama, whom he killed for fucking a member of a rival cartel.

"We think his most recent victim, besides you, was Oz's turncoat dealer in Juarez who tipped the Caballeros to the planned theft. He was found lying on his bed, bound and spread-eagled, sliced open from scrotum to Adam's apple."

He stopped there and, after a moment, said, "The point is, Homeless Man, this isn't just a punk with an attitude who can be ground down. He sure as hell won't be crying for his mama. He won't break. He can't be broken. Not by anybody, not by *you*."

Following Tucker's abrupt disconnect, Mitch sat on the porch until it began to rain. The cloud cover was low and bulging with precipitation yet to fall. The dismal weather seemed befitting.

He retrieved his coffee mug and went indoors. Dylan was in the kitchen, pouring herself a coffee. He joined her, held up his mug, and she poured him a refill. He gave her a soft kiss before saying, "I didn't know you were up."

"I heard you talking."

"Sorry. I tried to keep my voice down."

"Nothing bad about Hank, I hope."

"No. Mary promised to call me after the angioplasty."

"Did you and Andrew sleep well?"

"One of us did," he said wryly. "You? Nice PJs, by the way."

"I found them in a drawer. I doubt they're Beth's. They'd be too large. And too ugly."

The pajamas she was wearing were old and ugly as sin, but soft-looking, and baggy, and she looked adorable in them. He curved his arm around her waist and drew her to him. "I think they're hot."

He kissed her deeply while slipping his hand into the waistband of the pajama bottoms and squeezing her bare bottom. She hummed in pleasure and returned his kiss, but, before he was ready to release her, she laid her hand against his chest and pushed back. "Don't start something."

"Too late. It's already started." He bumped her middle so she could feel his arousal.

She made a little sound of pleasure, then said, "Andrew could wake up at any second and want his Fwoot Roops."

He smooched on her ear. "He's not a bad bed partner, but I missed sleeping with you."

"We've only slept together for a few hours the night before last."

"What can I say? You're habit-forming. I'll go into withdrawal when we leave here."

"Which we must," she said softly.

"Yeah. About that." With a regretful sigh and a *down, boy* to his hopeful dick, he released her, then hesitated, watching her closely to gauge her reaction to what he was about to propose.

"I want to ask you for a favor, but I'm afraid it'll piss you off if I even ask. After last night's incredible lap dance, and the urge to lift you onto the counter and have my wicked way with you here and now, I'd rather us not be on the outs."

Her cheeks blossomed rosily, but she responded with pragmatism. "You won't know my reaction until you ask."

"Come over here."

He led her to a card table where he'd left his laptop to charge overnight. He dragged one of the other chairs over beside his, so that they both were facing the monitor, but he turned in his seat to address her.

"Consider me still your patient and keep this confidential."

"You still are my patient. Confidentiality is guaranteed."

"Okay. You know that for a while I've been surveilling Malone's restaurant."

At the mention of Malone's name, she uneasily shifted her position, but nodded.

"I've also been observing the people who come and go. I've been taking pictures of them and have compiled quite a file. If by some miracle, Malone was indicted, and if by an even bigger miracle his boss's identity was discovered, it would take nothing short of an act of God to get what I have on this computer admissible in court. As it stands, this file has little value."

"I'm following you, Mitch, but I don't know where you're leading."

"Will you look through them?"

"The pictures?"

"If you recognize someone whose name Malone might possibly have dropped during one of your sessions, you could indicate—"

"I won't do that."

"You don't have to tell me what he said about the individual, just...just...if anybody in that file rings a bell, you could—"

"No, I couldn't. I wouldn't. Besides, he never talked about his associates, his friends, or enemies. If he has any, I don't know who they are. I thought I had made that clear to you. I won't know anyone," she said, gesturing to the monitor. "I don't know anything."

"You might know something and just not know that you know it. The smallest remark, a key word, facial reaction—"

"Roland doesn't react facially."

"See? That's what I'm talking about. That's *something*."

"But how does it help you?"

"Maybe it won't, but it could. Please, Dylan. Before Andrew wakes up. It's too early to do anything else, anyway."

"I was going to ask for my phone so I could call my service."

"Fine, but give me fifteen minutes first. I'll zip through them like a slide show. If you say no, no, no, no, it'll take less than fifteen. I've already deleted obvious tourists and locals who I've determined only go there to eat. There's also a lot of repetition among his regulars, so once you've said no to someone, we can skip them the next time they pop up."

Considering it, she pulled her lower lip through her teeth.

He took her hands in his. "You've repeatedly made clear how you feel about this. I respect your stand on it. I do. I wouldn't ask you to violate your ironclad code of ethics except that I learned this morning some information that made my blood run cold.

"El Paso is a much worse character even than I took him to be. Trust me, Dylan, these people are ruthless criminals who do not screw around." He paused and added as though underscoring it, "And I can't screw up a chance to bring them down. I'm not asking for much. A tiny bend in your rule, that's all. It's not black-and-white, it's gray territory. Please."

She looked down at their clasped hands for a time before lifting her gaze back to his. "I have a question."

"Fire away."

"Is this why you've had sex with me?"

The question rendered him speechless. He stared at her for several seconds before he was able to speak. "You can't possibly think that."

"Can't I? Since the first morning you came to my office, you've probed into my private life. With digs, innuendos, jokes. Charm." She spoke that last word emotionally. She swallowed. "And it worked. I've told you about my heartaches. I told you about my lack of a love life. Did you see that as an opportunity to probe... *me*... in order to get what you've been after all along, which is insider information on Roland Malone that you wouldn't otherwise have access to?"

Although his ears had begun to buzz with anger, and his jaw was clenched so tightly it ached, he let go of her hands, calmly pushed back his chair, got up, and sneaked into the guest room where Andrew was still sleeping soundly.

He reinstalled the battery of her phone, then, returning to the main room, delivered it to her. "Call your service."

"Mitch—"

He held up both hands palms out. "Don't. Just don't."

He sat down and scooted his chair under the table. Out of the corner of his eye, he saw her get up. She went around him and into the bedroom where she'd slept and closed the door.

With the rigid control that a person can only achieve when completely losing their shit is the alternative, he began scrolling through the photographs he had looked at dozens of times. Hundreds of times.

The mayor, city councilmen, judges, other elected officials, all but kissing Malone's ring. Were they drug dealers, or merely paying homage to a successful businessman in their fair city?

Fuck if he knew.

A Catholic priest and a bishop who came to dine together the first Monday of each month. They probably profited richly off their faithful flock. But peddling drugs as a sideline? Mitch couldn't see it.

The obnoxious personal injury lawyer on TV showed up occasionally, sometimes alone, sometimes with a female companion. Mitch wondered if the guy ever shut up long enough to eat.

A prominent socialite was a regular. She'd had as many facelifts as husbands, and had come away from each marriage millions richer than she'd been at the altar. Malone didn't exactly fawn over her. He wasn't a fawner. But he always greeted her with a stilted bow.

Could Oz be a woman? That had never occurred to Mitch, although it should have. But he didn't think the socialite was the head of a cartel. She was too prominent.

Mitch paid special attention to Malone's clientele who were more discreet. They wore sunglasses after dark. Malone conferred with them privately when they arrived and held their handshakes longer as he bade them goodbye.

He finished scrolling through his file without having been struck with insight or clarity that had previously escaped him.

Discouraged and depressed, upset over Dylan's insulting suggestion about his intimacy with her, he pushed back his chair and wandered into the kitchen. He tossed his cold coffee into the sink and reached for the carafe of the Mr. Coffee, but changed his mind before lifting it off the hotplate.

"Fuck it." He opened the pantry and reached for the bottle of whiskey he knew John kept on the top shelf.

Chapter 36

Mitch had just poured a shot of the whiskey when Dylan emerged from the bedroom carrying a bundle of bedsheets, towels, plus the articles of clothing she had borrowed. Except for Beth's sneakers, she was dressed in her own clothing, including the fantasy-making, memory-stirring silky blouse.

Seeing the liquor bottle on the table, she stopped in her tracks. When she looked at him, he raised his chin a half inch, as though daring her to challenge him. He picked up the glass he'd poured and extended it toward her. "Join me for a drink?"

She gave him a withering look. "Is there a washing machine?"

He pointed. "Outside that door, hook a right. Washing machine and dryer are in the enclosure on the back gallery."

She headed that way, but before reaching the door, she dumped the laundry onto the floor and turned to face him. "What are you doing, Mitch?"

"What's it look like?"

"Like you're being an idiot."

She was right, and he knew she was right, and that made him furious. He slammed the glass down onto the table and pressed the heels of his hands into his eye sockets.

She said, "What's wrong?"

"What's *wrong*? Hell, I could alphabetize all that's wrong."

"Specifically, in this moment, what's the wrongest of all that's wrong?"

"Why can't I get to Malone? Who is Oz? I'm smarter than this, dammit. I'm spinning my wheels, getting nowhere." He lowered his hands from his eyes and looked at her with frustration. "Why the devil can't I figure this out?"

"For one thing, you're exhausted. Did you sleep at all?"

"Cat naps between trying to figure out what I'm missing and worrying about how I'm going to protect Andrew and you from Malone."

"Andrew?"

"He let him live once. If he finds out my son is under my roof again, he may rethink that."

He sat down in one of the dining chairs and pushed aside both the whiskey bottle and the glass he'd poured but hadn't even tasted. He propped his elbows on the table and massaged his temples.

"I feel like there's something I know, but it's gotten lost up here somewhere." He pressed his skull between his hands. "Two dots floating around inside my brain that I can't connect no matter how hard I try. Something important that I'm supposed to remember."

"Like what?"

He unlocked his elbows, and his forearms and fists dropped onto the table with a thud. "If I could remember what it was, I wouldn't be pouring a neat Jack Daniel's before the sun comes up, would I?"

Even he was offended by his rebuke. Turning his head away, he looked out the front windows. A ponderous rain was falling. Without gutters, it streamed off the sloping tin roof in sheets, obscuring everything beyond the overhang of the porch. "Not that the sun will shine today."

When he turned back, he was surprised to see that Dylan had left the laundry where it had landed and had sat down at the table directly opposite him. He said, "I'm being a jerk. Sorry."

"You're angry with me."

"Yes. No. I'm more angry at myself, but taking it out on you."

"Maybe I can help."

"I asked for your help, Dylan. You said no."

"Not that way," she said, gesturing toward the card table and his laptop. She was searching his eyes, no longer with censure but with the concern and empathy of a clinician. "You're striving to remember something, but the pressure you're applying may actually be working against you."

"So, what do I do? Stop striving?"

"In essence, yes. You know how when someone's name, or a movie title, any fact that you know you know, but it's escaped you. And when you strain to call it up, it's not there. Later, when you're not thinking about it at all—"

"It hits you."

"Exactly."

"I get what you're saying. But the thing is, I don't have time to wait for *it*, whatever it is, to hit me. We're on borrowed time, because—and you can count on this—Malone will learn that you and I are in cahoots."

"I wouldn't put it that way."

"No, but he will. And he's not going to stand for it, because he doesn't know that you're sticking to patient privilege. I think he'll strike, and he'll strike like Thor's hammer. I don't want that to happen while I'm sitting idle, waiting for a cerebral cloud to part."

"Then let me help you reconstruct."

"What's that mean?"

"We try to reconstruct the scene where that something that is escaping you caused a visceral reaction at the time. Something seen, said, or done either by you or someone you were with. It might not have seemed very important at the time, but, for whatever reason, your mind latched on to it, and it's still there," she said, pointing to his forehead. "Let's see if we can take you back to that time and place and allow it to reveal itself."

"Dylan, I—"

"Close your eyes."

"This is a thing?"

"Yes."

"John will pay for it?"

"I'll charge him double. Now close your eyes."

He sighed to let her know he thought this was hooey and a waste of time, but he closed his eyes anyway.

"Good," she said. "Now relax your shoulders." He did. "Now free your mind. Let it drift. Retrace the places you've been."

"The birth canal." He opened one eye, and, sure enough, she was rolling hers.

"Won't you at least try this?"

"Aren't you supposed to be swinging a pocket watch while I count down from ten?"

"This isn't hypnotism. If you're not going to cooperate, I'll do the laundry."

He gave another sigh and closed his eyes.

She started again, speaking in a low, velvety voice that, in other circumstances, he could make love to for hours.

"More recently than your birth," she said, "where did you experience a strong emotion? Like anxiety or fear. Not necessarily fear of being harmed, but of being rejected or misunderstood. Did something raise your hackles recently? A conflict or—"

He opened his eyes. "That would be everywhere. Starting with the barroom brawl last Saturday night and jail on Sunday morning. Every place I've been since then, I've been in a conflict of one kind or another."

She gestured for him to close his eyes again. He did. "Then let's narrow it down to the places you've been this week. My office? Was it during our initial encounter?"

"No, my reaction to you was a little bit south of *visceral*."

He heard her sniff of disapproval.

He couldn't help but grin. "Just sayin'. But no, it wasn't—" He stopped.

"Wasn't what?"

"I don't know, but it wasn't about you. It was work." His eyes popped open. "John and me. I was in his office."

"Keep your eyes closed and mentally reconstruct the scene." She waited until he complied. "Were the two of you sitting or standing? Were you having a pleasant conversation or quarreling? What were you feeling, Mitch? Resentment and anger toward him or—"

"Futility."

"Futility?"

"That's what I was feeling. I remember now," he said, opening his eyes. "It was during that meeting."

"Meeting. So there were other people in the room. Who?"

"John, me, and the officers on the task force."

"Task force for what? The Bayou Coeur case?"

"No. John put me in charge of a task force that's training school guards on how to handle active shooter incidents."

"Your feelings of futility stemmed from the fear of that happening in Auclair?"

"Yes, but that's not... not quite it."

"Take a moment."

He squeezed his eyes shut. "I remember thinking that these are nice, genial, well-meaning people who are committed to protecting schoolchildren. And... and... fearing that no matter how well we trained them, and despite their earnestness, they still wouldn't be prepared, because they wouldn't see past..."

He got up from his chair, rounded it, and braced himself on its ladderback. He lowered his head and looked down at the floor, but what he was envisioning was himself in John's office. John and the other officers appearing to be confident that they were making strides with the program, while he was feeling doubt and futility.

Remembering how he'd been reluctant to speak his mind, he said to Dylan, "I didn't express my pessimism because I didn't want to end the meeting on a downer. John, especially, wanted to give the superintendent a positive progress report.

"The others left, but John knew something was bothering me. He made me stay and told me to spit out whatever was on my mind. So I did. I told him I didn't believe that our instinct could be *instilled*. That he and I had been born with it, that you either had it or you didn't."

"Your instinct for what, Mitch?"

"For... for..." He was now rocking the chair back and forth on its back legs.

Dylan said, "Visualize John's expression. How did he react to what you were saying? Did he disagree?"

"No, no he understood exactly what I was talking about."

"He knew exactly what you were talking about when you said..."

"When I said... when I said that he and I had an instinct for looking past the obvious and spotting what *isn't*."

As he spoke the words aloud, he got chill bumps. He raised his head and looked straight into Dylan's calm, clear, incredibly beautiful and intelligent eyes. "That's it," he said gruffly. "That's *it*. That's what I've been trying to remember."

She scooted forward in her seat. "Why was it significant in that moment and worth remembering now?"

"Because the school guards were picking the stereotypical hardened criminals from the pictures I'd showed them and missing the ones who looked least likely to shoot up a school, but who actually had. Dylan, this is the *it*. Who's the least likely person you would expect to be the head of a drug cartel?"

He began snapping his fingers in rhythm with his rapidly tumbling thoughts. "Yesterday in the hospital, Mary said, 'Turn that off. He's obnoxious.' And I said, 'You can't escape that jerk.' And in EATS, the diner across from your office, Dodi—the waitress. Been there a million years. She commented on him, said he was a loudmouth."

His thoughts were coming so fast, he was panting as though running full-tilt. "I've been looking at the people Malone whispers to conspiratorially when they leave the restaurant. The ones whose handshakes are hand-*clasps*.

"But this guy, no. He always breezes past Malone, never giving him a second glance before ducking into his chauffeur-driven car. He flaunts his wealth, he boasts about it, so nobody even thinks to question how he comes by it. And what better place to hide your identity than behind the face that every-fucking-body recognizes?" He laughed. "That clever son of a bitch."

He stopped, suddenly realizing that he'd been speaking his thoughts out loud and Dylan was listening. "You're a genius." He made it around the table in two strides, pulled her up out of the chair, and kissed her hard.

Then the loose porch step knocked against its bearings.

In a mercurial motion that was virtually second nature, he pushed Dylan to the floor, while, with the other hand, he reached for his pistol where he'd placed it on top of the sideboard out of Andrew's reach, and, dropping into a crouch, swung it toward the front door.

"Coming in! Don't shoot us!"

The door flew open. John and Beth rushed in, propelled by a gust of rainy wind. John slammed the door shut.

Then the four of them froze, forming a bizarre tableau where the only thing moving was the rainwater dripping off the police-issue slickers John and Beth were wearing.

Eventually Mitch released his captured breath, lowered his pistol, and stood upright as he assisted Dylan to her feet. Crossly, he said, "You could have given me a second or two of advance warning. And, anyway, what the hell are you doing here?"

John made a show of taking a look around the room before coming back to him. "This is my house."

Mitch noticed that Beth gave her husband a subtle nudge

in the ribs. Unlike John, who stood there glowering, she smiled. "Good morning." She pushed back the hood of her slicker and unsnapped it, revealing her very pregnant belly. "I apologize for barging in. I know it's early, but John—"

"Aunt Bet!" Andrew came charging out of the guest room and tackled her around the knees. John reacted quickly to stabilize her. "Hey, partner. Careful there or you'll shake the baby out."

As soon as Beth had begun to show, she, John, and Mitch had sat him down and explained about the baby growing inside Aunt Beth's tummy. She'd used her Doppler kit to let him listen to the heartbeat. It was still an abstraction to him, but when John cautioned him now, he patted Beth's stomach. Then he turned and pointed to Dylan. "That's Dwon. She's daddy's friend."

"I gathered." Beth removed her slicker and passed it to John, who hung it along with his on the coat tree, then together they walked over to where Mitch and Dylan still stood close to each other near the dining table.

Disregarding Dylan's deer-in-the-headlights expression, Mitch made the introductions. "Dylan, Lieutenant Bowie. John, Dr. Reede. Y'all have talked on the phone. About me."

She extended her hand. As they shook, John shot Mitch a look and said, "I think we can move past the formalities. Nice to meet you in person, Dylan."

"Likewise."

"This is my wife, Beth."

"Hello, Dylan."

The two women shook hands, but Dylan's embarrassment was obvious. She said, "I'm sorry for imposing on your hospitality." Addressing John specifically, she said, "The gumbo was delicious." Then to Beth, "I was about to wash the things I used." She gestured at the pile of laundry on the floor. "And I'll replace your sneakers. The shoes I was wearing—"

Beth reached out and touched her arm to stop the flow. "I understand perfectly. I was involuntarily sequestered here once."

"At least I bought you some clothes," John muttered.

"No, you didn't, I did," Mitch said. "Remember, Beth?"

She looked at John and raised a shoulder. "He did. He took me shopping at Target."

Mitch gave John a beatific smile. But the satisfying moment was ruined when Andrew announced, "I need to pee-pee." He was looking frantic and pinching his bits. "Excuse us." Mitch took his son's hand. "Potty training is recent. He's doing well, but sometimes his aim is off."

"Which unfortunately will never improve," Beth remarked in an undertone.

As Mitch led Andrew into the guest room, he heard John ask if there was any coffee left, and Dylan offered to brew a fresh pot. Mitch oversaw Andrew using the toilet then took off his pajamas and dressed him.

When they came back into the main room, the women were seated at the table, laughing as they compared their initial reactions to the fishing camp. John had propped himself against the counter, but he didn't appear to be tuned in to their chitchat. Mitch recognized his familiar scowl of heavy-duty concentration.

Andrew spotted the box of Froot Loops and carton of milk already on the table and ran toward it. Dylan got up and hoisted him onto the stack of phone books in the other chair, saying as she handed him a spoon, "Show Aunt Beth how you use your manners."

As Mitch was making his way over, John set down his mug of coffee and intercepted him. "I need to talk to you."

"I need to talk to you, too. Your room or mine?" Mitch asked.

"Outside."

"It's raining."

"All the better." They went out onto the porch but stayed well under the overhang. "Any word on Hank?"

"Mary is supposed to call me after the angioplasty." Mitch consulted his wristwatch. "Couple of hours yet. What's up?"

"How's your cut?"

Mitch raised the hem of his T-shirt to show him. "It's closing."

"Did Dr. Reede help you with placing the sticky things just so?" When Mitch failed to reply, John added, "It's none of my business, except that—"

"Right. Not your business. I'm not accountable to you about my—my that."

"No, but, Mitch, the timing—"

"Sucks. Yes. Thank you. I'm aware. It's damned inconvenient, especially in light of what I need to tell you."

"Okay, but first I need to tell you that—"

"No, I get to go first. I think I know who Oz is."

John looked like he'd been hit between the eyes with a two-by-four. "Since when?"

"Since seconds before you barged in and I nearly made Beth a widow."

"Who?"

"The King of Cash."

John just looked at him, then sputtered. "That guy on TV? He's an asshole. A clown."

"That's exactly what he wants everybody to think."

"Is this one of your jokes?"

Solemnly, Mitch shook his head.

John held his gaze, and when he saw how dead serious he was, he said, "Give me a minute." He walked the width of the porch and back again while stroking the dent between his eyebrows. "What's his real name?"

"Allen Busby. I've seen it at the bottom of my TV screen so many times, it's like it's stenciled on my brain."

John looked at him and shook his head. "Mitch, it's ludicrous."

"Which is why it works."

"How did you come to the conclusion that it could be him?"

Mitch told him. "Dylan called it reconstructing. It's hard to explain, but it's a therapy technique that worked. But it doesn't matter how I got to it. What matters is that I *did*. I've been looking at the stereotypes, like Malone is, and completely skipping over Busby."

John was still skeptical. "I'm not doubting Dylan's ability, and I see where you're coming from, but without even an iota of evidence—"

"I know, I know." He took a step closer to John as though that would help convince him. He told him about Busby's frequent visits to Malone's restaurant. "Busby is the only regular he virtually ignores. I think that in itself is a giveaway, because he makes a big deal over sports stars, socialites, and such. Then to practically ignore a TV personality like the King of Cash? Un-huh."

John's expression remained a study in skepticism.

"Okay, okay. Say I'm crazy. In any case, John, it's imperative that we get Malone. He's key. He's the only one who can expose Oz, no matter who the hell he is. Malone knows his identity, the scope of his narcotics empire, and where the bodies are buried. Literally."

"Mitch—"

"Wait, there's more." He gave John the bullet points of what Jim Tucker had told him about the payload Oz had stolen from the Mexican cartel. "And, hello! El Paso is a Caballero plant. I'm guessing he was sent to find out where the stolen product will be delivered and to stage an ambush to recover it."

John took that in. "Makes sense."

"To me, too."

"How long have you had this information?"

"An hour, maybe."

"Tucker?"

Mitch didn't say, but he gave an affirmative indication. "It was like pulling jaw teeth with a pair of eyebrow tweezers. He didn't tell me everything, of course. For instance, whether or not the goods are still in transit or already in New Orleans. But I have a sneaking suspicion that they've arrived or will be here soon. My friend was wound up tight. The way you get right before a raid."

"He's always wound up tight."

"Granted. But he knows, as I do, that there's bound to be a reckoning when Malone realizes that El Paso is an infiltrator, and that the last thing El Paso is likely to feel is Malone's garrote around his neck.

"If El Paso winds up facedown in Bayou Coeur, we lose the opportunity to get Malone. If we lose Malone, we lose Oz. We've got to act. We've got to act *soon*. We may have to get creative on the charge, but we've got to get Malone in custody for something."

John took out his cell phone and began swiping and tapping. Mitch huffed. "Have you heard a goddamn word I've said?"

"Yes. Shut up a minute and listen."

"*What?*"

"This morning, a package addressed to *you* was delivered to headquarters by a courier service. Clarence called me at home, said maybe I should come in early, take a look."

"Why?"

"It was leaking."

"*Leaking?* The package?"

"When I got there, I took the liberty of opening your gift. I brought you a picture."

John turned his phone around so that Mitch could see it. It was a closeup of a heap of standard, brown wrapping paper. It was obviously soggy with fresh blood that had drained from a severed pinkie finger lying in its midst, signet ring still attached.

The ruby stone had caught the flash of John's phone camera.

Disbelieving what he was seeing, Mitch lowered himself onto the seat of the lawn chair and stared at the gruesome image, then raised his head and looked up at John, who said, "The rest of Roland Malone was found hanging from a hook in an old factory turned meat locker."

Chapter 37

Dylan and Beth sat across from each other at the dining table, conversing over cups of coffee. Having finished his breakfast, Andrew was at their feet, making motor noises as he scooted his cars across the floor.

Dylan had warmed to Beth immediately. She was charming and sweet, and seamlessly guided their conversation from one topic to another. But Dylan got the impression that Beth was keeping her occupied and distracted from whatever the menfolk were talking about out on the porch.

Was Beth that incurious herself? No, Dylan thought. It was more likely she already knew what they were discussing. Their surprise arrival had seemed urgent, not social.

Dylan didn't have long to wonder about it. When the two men came back inside, it took only seeing Mitch's expression for her to ask, "What's happened? What's the matter?"

Neither he nor John answered her. Even Andrew seemed to pick up on the tension the two had brought inside with them, because he stopped making engine noises and said in a tentative voice, "Daddy?"

Mitch hunkered down beside his son and patted him on the head. "That's some semi you've got there, buddy. What do you figure it's hauling, huh?"

"Milk."

"Oh, I see now."

John went directly to Beth, leaned down, and splayed his hand over her distended belly. "You're sure you're okay to stay here with Andrew?"

"I'll enjoy having a day with him."

"Call me if you have the slightest twinge," he said to her. "Promise."

"I promise."

"Don't even think about taking the boat out."

"Do you think I'm crazy?"

"No, but you're stubborn."

"I wouldn't dream of taking the boat. I'd tip it over."

"The sedan will be in the garage in case of an emergency." Beth nodded. "And you know where the g-u-n-s are and how to use them."

"Don't hesitate," Beth said, apparently repeating previous instructions.

"That one would get anyone's attention, and it's loaded."

Dylan looked in the direction John had indicated with a tilt of his head and saw a double-barrel shotgun resting in a rack attached to the wall about seven feet off the floor.

Beth smiled up at her husband and covered his hand still covering her abdomen. "We'll be fine. Promise baby and me that you'll be careful."

He promised, they kissed, and then looked at each other

with such transparent love and adoration, it made Dylan feel like a voyeur. As John straightened up, he gave her a nod but said nothing except her name, then turned to Mitch. "See you at headquarters."

Mitch said, "Coming right behind you."

At the door, John put on his slicker and flipped up the hood. As he left, a whoosh of rain-laden wind blew in behind him.

Dylan scraped back her chair and stood up. "What is going on?" she demanded of Mitch, who had left Andrew to his toy truck.

Now wearing his intense, expressionless game face, he said, "In here." He motioned her toward the guest bedroom. She balked at the curt order and looked for support from Beth, who gave her a solemn nod.

Feeling resentful for being treated with no more deference than Andrew, she followed Mitch into the bedroom. The instant he closed the door, she rounded on him. "Are you going to pat me on the head and spell out g-u-n-s to me, too? What is going on that only the grownups know?"

"Roland Malone is dead."

She fell back a step and, dumbfounded, looked at him with stark disbelief.

"Sometime last night, he was murdered." He gestured her toward the bed. Gripped by shock, she backed up and dropped down onto the edge of it. Mitch said, "Before dawn, a bulletin went out to regional law enforcement departments that Malone's body had been discovered. Apparent homicide."

Dylan's throat worked. "Discovered where? By whom?"

"A patrol officer cruising around a derelict industrial district noticed the garage door of an old factory had been left open. Went to check it out, wandered inside, discovered the building had been converted into a meat locker. Sides of beef. You know. Later, it was verified that the building belonged to one of Malone's numerous LLCs and was used by his restaurant exclusively."

With foreboding, Dylan waited while he paused to take a deep breath.

"Malone was hanging from a meat hook. He'd been eviscerated. The NOPD detective told John he'd been 'field dressed.' His innards lay in a heap on the concrete floor. His blood had been washed down a large drain." Mitch thought for a moment, then mused aloud, "That's probably where Malone has been killing his victims before ditching them."

Dylan was no longer looking at him, but staring vacantly straight ahead, trying to assimilate everything he was telling her. "Who would have done such a thing?"

"Someone handy with a knife."

"El Paso?"

"He would top my list, but I don't think he took it upon himself. I'll get to why I think that is in a sec. But first…" He stopped for a beat before continuing. "Look, Dylan, I'd spare you the coarse language and gory details, but I need to impress upon you that these perpetrators have no limits. None. I know that from my experience of pretending to be one of them. They get off on making grand gestures like disemboweling Malone. It's a terror tactic.

"I'm also sensitive to the fact that until two days ago you had known Roland Malone only as a patient, and you have a fierce loyalty to your patients. I respect it. I realize that your emotions must be in chaos right now, not knowing how to feel about this. I wish I could give you more time to sort it out, but I can't. I've got to play the cop card."

At that, she looked up at him, but simultaneously, he squatted down to bring them on eye level. His eyes, which she'd seen alight with passion, were now dark with purpose.

"Malone wasn't gutted while hanging from a meat hook because a customer got pissed off when his order came out cold. Malone was a central player in a criminal organization where people die all too frequently. They kill their enemies, or those perceived to be. They kill traitors or suspected ones.

"They kill mercilessly. Insidious deaths like Angela's staged suicide. Or bloody, vicious deaths like Randy Nelson's and those two people we found this week in Bayou Coeur. When it came to eliminating Malone, his longevity counted for nothing. He'd worn out his welcome. He was the death du jour. I'm trying to prevent the next one."

"The next one?"

He took a phone from his pocket and swiped it on. "I was sent a heads-up." He palmed the phone and held it so she could see it.

She gave a soft cry, covered her mouth with one hand, crossed her arm over her stomach, and turned her head aside.

Mitch set the phone on the bed. "Early this morning, the severed finger was delivered by courier to our department and addressed to *me*. Whoever killed Malone was sending me a warning. John recognized it as such. That's why he and Beth beat it out here."

He placed his knuckle beneath her chin and turned her back to face him. "I don't think El Paso sent that thing. He probably had Malone's blood and guts on his hands, but he's not a thinker, he's a cobra. He acts on animal instinct. Strikes quick. A much more sophisticated mind would have thought up doing that," he said, indicating the phone.

"That picture is a threat of *imminent violence,* Dylan. And what really scares me is that it probably includes you and Andrew in addition to me. You can't violate the trust of a dead man, so whatever information you have on Roland Malone you need to share. Right now."

She groaned. "I understand, Mitch, but I've told you time and again that if he had any deep, dark secrets he never confided them to me."

"He *had* to have had secrets. Something was eating at him, or why did he start coming to you for therapy?"

"It took me a while to determine that myself. In general, I think—and this will sound out of character. I think it was for religious reasons."

"Religious?"

"He feared dying unforgiven. He didn't want to go to hell."

Mitch gave a scornful laugh. "Good luck with that, Roland." He ignored her look of mild reproach and asked, "What makes you think that was his hangup?"

"I speculate that he did something in his youth that he felt was unforgivable. I don't know what, but he remarked once or twice in jest about having an imaginary evil twin that he had to keep in line."

"Like having an angel on one shoulder and a devil on the other?"

"Yes. And he feared that devil's influence would invoke God's wrath and condemnation. I'm paraphrasing, but that was a recurring theme of our sessions."

"Sounds to me like you served as a stand-in priest."

"Of sorts, I suppose. But he never confessed to committing a blood-curdling crime."

"He chalked up a lot of them, but he wasn't the mastermind."

He paused, his eyes narrowing on her. "Did Malone ever drop the name Allen Busby?"

She frowned. "That's vaguely familiar, but I don't know why."

"He's on TV all the time. Gaudy neckties, shellacked hair, white teeth."

"The lawyer who does all the commercials?"

"The King of Cash. That was my epiphany earlier."

"When you looked past the stereotype?"

"Um-huh. Busby looks like a clown, not a criminal. But behind that flashy persona on TV, he's the mastermind, the drug kingpin. Malone did his bidding, including killing Angela."

"How do you know this?"

"Well, that's the hitch. I feel it in my gut, but I can't prove it. I can't even officially allege it until I have more than a strong hunch. I was hoping to get to him through Malone. That opportunity is lost to me. So I need to know if Malone ever dropped his name to you. Did he ever indicate that he knew the King of Cash, or even boast that he was a regular at the restaurant?"

She was shaking her head no, and no, and no. "That's not something I would likely forget. In fact, I probably would have noted it as something to pick up on later. But perhaps somewhere in Roland's file—"

"Going through all your notes on his sessions would take time. I need something now. *Imminent* harm, Dylan. Please try to remember. From your first session to the last, in any context, did Malone ever mention him?"

She pressed her fingers to her temples, trying desperately to remember but already knowing there wasn't a memory to recall. "I'm sorry, Mitch." She leaned forward and placed her hands on his shoulders. "If Roland had confessed to committing a crime or had talked about anyone who had, I would tell you now. I *swear*."

He nodded, then his head dropped forward until his chin almost touched his chest. He said wryly, "I believe you. Malone would never have confessed, would he? No matter how much he feared burning in hell, he'd have been too cautious, too paranoid to admit a mortal sin out loud. He wouldn't have told even a priest in a confessional."

Quietly, she said, "I would hope you believe me because I've won your trust."

Then, raising his head and meeting her eyes again, he reached up and ran his hands over her hair and drew her face closer to his. "That, too."

"Thank you."

"You're welcome."

After exchanging a tender kiss, he said, "I've got to go. You're staying here with Beth."

She opened her mouth to protest, but he held his index finger vertically against her lips. "No argument, please. John wanted to ask you, but thought that the request should come from me. Beth looks ready to pop, and Andrew is a handful. If she got down on the floor to play with him, she might not be able to get back up."

"That's not the real reason you want me to stay here."

"That's John's reason." He cupped her head more firmly. "Mine is that Malone's finger was sent to me as a harsh reminder that I've been living on borrowed time."

She clutched handfuls of his shirt. "You're frightening me."

"The good news is that catching bad guys is my job." He grinned his grin and winked. "And I'm good at it."

His grin didn't work this time to alleviate her disquiet, but when he kissed her, it was deep and meaningful, and she kissed him back in kind.

When it ended, he pecked a light kiss on her lips and said, "Save my place, but I've gotta run. You and Andrew will be safe here. No one except us knows this place exists. Malone's out of the picture, and Oz wouldn't know—" He broke off when he read her stunned expression. "What?"

In a thin voice, she said, "Oz?"

"The drug kingpin's street name."

"Also Roland's evil twin."

Chapter 38

Mitch's departure was rushed but emotional.

Only half teasing, he told Beth that now wouldn't be a good time to hatch her chick.

He picked up Andrew and hugged him fiercely. "Who's my rock star?"

"Me."

"You betcha. Be a good boy for Daddy."

Andrew gave him a sullen okay.

Mitch held him close and whispered in his ear, "Your mommy loved you so much. Now I get to love you twice as much. Once for her, once for me. Have I told you that?"

Andrew nodded. Mitch hugged him tightly and kissed his face several times before setting him down. But Andrew, along with Dylan, trailed him to the door, where he pulled on the slicker Beth had worn.

When he looked into Dylan's watery, anguished eyes, he

said, "I told you early on about the vow I'd made to Angela. I've got to finish this."

"How?"

"To be determined. I'll try to keep you updated, but I forecast a busy day. I'll be back as soon as I can."

He realized then how empty that assurance must sound to her. Her late husband would have made a similar pledge when he sent her away, telling her that he would be rejoining her soon. It was an unfulfilled promise that continued to haunt her. He looked deeply into her eyes. "I will be back, Dylan. You can bank on it."

Then he gave her a quick kiss, reached down and ruffled Andrew's hair, and left. As he crossed the threshold, he almost yielded to the temptation to go back inside for one last round of hugs. But as soon as he soundly pulled the door shut behind himself, it was as though a switch was flipped. A burst of energy surged through him. He was one step closer to nailing Oz.

He plunged into the torrent and jogged all the way to the camo garage, where he retrieved his beat-up pickup, which he was glad to have. It was good cover.

Once he was on the highway and headed for Auclair, he called John's cell to tell him about Dylan's revelation. He got John's voice mail, but he didn't want to leave a message. John would return his call.

He then called Jim Tucker, who answered with, "I don't have time for you."

"It's pissing rain, and I'm driving in it. You'll have to speak up."

"I said, I don't have—"

"I heard that part. What do you know about Malone?"

"He's dead as a doornail."

"That much I know."

"How'd you hear?"

"Via special delivery." He told Tucker about receiving the severed finger.

"Jesus," Tucker said. "I hadn't heard about the missing finger, only that the crime scene was barf-worthy."

"Yeah. Makes me wonder what meat is in the restaurant's Bolognese."

Tucker said, "NOPD served a search warrant. Lots of incriminating goodies were found in Malone's office there."

"What about El Paso?"

"No sign of him, but the search is underway. After the restaurant closed last night, he and Malone left together. Just the two of them."

"Huh." Mitch wasn't surprised. "That young man has a lot to answer for. Has a BOLO been issued for him?"

"Yes, but the PD didn't consult us before putting it out there."

Mitch instantly picked up on Tucker's disgruntlement. "You wish they hadn't issued it?" When Tucker didn't answer, Mitch pressed. "Why do you wish they'd waited on the BOLO?"

Nothing.

Mitch figured that something was about to go down, and Tucker would rather El Paso be there when it did, instead of in police custody already lawyering up. "Are you about to ruin our knife-wielding friend's day?"

Silence.

"Come on, Jim. A simple yes or no."

He didn't say either, which meant yes.

"Where and when?" Mitch asked.

"No can tell. I'm relying on my pension."

"Can you at least—"

"No. *Nada*. I gotta go."

Nada. The Spanish word was a clue. El Paso had a foot in both cartel camps, the Mexican Caballeros and Oz's. His capture would be a shiny trophy for the DEA.

Mitch guessed that Tucker hoped to catch him preventing Oz's people from receiving the haul they had stolen from the Caballeros. Or perhaps El Paso had seen that the grass was greener on Oz's side and would be there to take delivery of the payload on behalf of him.

Either way, that handover would make for some party, and the timing for federal agents to crash it would have to be perfect. Even if they went in at precisely the right time, there were still about a million ways that a raid of that magnitude could go FUBAR.

Mitch understood why Tucker was wound up and close-mouthed. He felt for him, but this might be their last opportunity to talk for a while. "I know you're in a hurry, Jim, but one more thing."

"I gotta go."

"One sec. Months back, you told me you had a snitch tucked away. A felon who'd bartered lesser charges in exchange for testifying against Malone if you ever got enough on Malone to indict."

"Marvin Davis. Given that Malone is dead, he's no good to us now."

"He might be. Is he still under lock and key?"

"Guest of the US Marshals service."

"Give me a phone number."

"What for?"

"I need to know if this guy ever heard Malone talking about Allen Busby."

"That jerk-off lawyer on TV?"

"He's Oz." He could tell that had knocked Tucker for a loop. His silence now was one of shock. Mitch envisioned him processing this new information at ninety miles a minute. Ultimately, he said, "That's crazy."

"I know."

"Where the hell did you come by—"

"From the Dish. It's a bedtime story I'll tell you later. In the meantime, you've got a raid to organize, and I've got a call to make to a US marshal who's guarding a felonious star witness. Now give me a fucking phone number!" He took a breath. "Please."

By the time Tucker came back on the phone, Mitch feared he'd decided he needed to be institutionalized and had cut him off. But Tucker rattled off a phone number, which Mitch memorized. "Thanks, Jim."

"Go fuck yourself."

"If I'm right, you'll be thanking me later."

"*Big* if."

"Do some digging on Busby. And tell your agents to leave El Paso alive if they can. If he's captured, I want a crack at that runty piece of shit."

"For cutting you?"

"For killing Malone. He robbed me of the pleasure."

"Hear ya." Tucker then disconnected.

Two hours ago, Barbara Nix had arrived at work as usual. But the sight that had greeted her was anything but normal. Almost everyone in the CAP unit had been clustered around Mitch Haskell's desk.

"What's going on?" she'd asked Clarence, who'd been standing off to the side, looking fidgety and green around the gills.

"You might not want to look."

That had only enticed her to see what had everyone's attention. She'd elbowed her way through those congregated and moved up beside Bowie, who'd shot her a warning glance before she looked down at the desktop.

She'd recoiled, not so much in horror at the severed finger itself as in knowing whose finger it was. Trying to sound like her strident self, she'd asked, "Besides formerly being attached to a right hand, where'd that come from?"

"It was delivered by a courier service based in Houma," Bowie had told her. "We questioned the lady who drove it over here. She said the package had been left on their doorstep before they opened for business. Since the destination was our PD and it was addressed to Mitch Haskell, she figured it was important and rushed it over."

"Lucky us." That from Lear, who had moved up behind Nix and was peering over her shoulder at the gory sight.

Coolly, she'd asked, "Has the previous owner been identified?"

Although she'd known the answer, of course, she hadn't been entirely braced for Bowie's reply. "The late Roland Malone."

The *late* Roland Malone? Malone was *dead*? Her knees had gone weak.

"Obvious homicide," Bowie said. "He owned a restaurant but was reputed to have some shady business dealings, including illegal drug trafficking. Too slippery ever to be indicted."

He'd then gone on to describe the crime scene, which had

made her both physically ill and deeply disturbed. Someone had wanted Malone not merely dead, but dead in a way that sent a warning. *What did this portend for her future?*

Having heard the juicy details, everyone else besides her and Lear began dispersing. Still playing dumb, she'd asked Bowie why anyone would send Mitch Haskell a restaurant owner's pinkie finger, ring and all.

"I intend to put that question to Mitch myself. That is, as soon as I can locate him," he'd said, his annoyance plain. "All I know is that Mitch has had Malone in his sights for a while."

"For what?"

"He attributed Randy Nelson's execution to Malone."

"Ahh," Lear had said. "So Mitch thinks it was Malone who killed the two found in Bayou Coeur this week?"

"Yes, but keep that under your hat. DEA is trying to connect Malone to a local drug cartel. They're after a bigger fish than Malone."

"Has Darcy been told about this?" Lear had asked.

"Yes. I've filled him in."

Bowie had then taken a picture of the grisly package with his cell phone, assigned one of their crime scene techs to preserve it for evidence to be turned over to the New Orleans PD, then had announced that he would be gone for a while but wanted to be kept informed of any developments.

He'd left, Nix assumed to search for the elusive Mitch Haskell.

For the past two hours, she had tried to look busy at her desk, behaving as though Malone's ghastly murder had been of no importance to her. In reality, she was in turmoil. Her only line to Oz's cartel had been cut, leaving her adrift in turbulent waters.

Now, while reviewing open cases that didn't require her review, her cell phone rang. She didn't recognize the number, but from the day that Malone had placed her in this position as his mole, she had grown accustomed to seeing "Unknown Caller" in her phone's readout. But who would be calling her now?

She was unsure it was even safe to answer. The call could be a trap. Did the police have Malone's cell phone? Had they found her number in it?

Don't borrow trouble until you have to. Tamping down her misgivings, she answered with her customary brusqueness. "This is Nix."

"Barbara, isn't it?"

The smooth male voice sent chills down her spine. Out of caution, she didn't respond, but she didn't disconnect, either.

He said, "Ah, you're being circumspect, which indicates to me that you've learned about the demise of a famous restaurateur we both knew well."

"Yes." That single word was all her tight throat could muster, but it was a neutral reply that conveyed neither joy, sorrow, nor panic over Malone's death.

"Our acquaintance spoke highly of you," he said. "You've been in place for a while and did a good job for him. It really is remarkable that you've been able to deceive your police department cohorts so thoroughly and well."

While the praise was gratifying, she didn't say anything.

"By now you've probably guessed who this is, and your reluctance to speak suggests that you're at risk of being overheard, so I'll get right to the point. You've proven yourself to be discreet and capable. Because of our friend's sudden demise, I have a vacancy to fill, and time is of the essence. Are you prepared to work for me directly, without an intermediary?"

Her heart leaped. "Yes," she said on an expulsion of pent-up breath. "Absolutely."

"Wonderful. You can begin immediately by telling me if Mitch Haskell received a parcel this morning."

"It was delivered, but he wasn't here. John Bowie took a picture of it and has gone in search of Haskell."

"He hasn't resurfaced? Before our mutual acquaintance… died… he mentioned that Haskell was out of pocket. It's assumed he's with his therapist."

"Yes. Our mutual friend was unhappy about that."

"I picked up on that, too. Do you know why?"

"No, sir. I'll try to find out."

"I like your initiative. I'm also curious to know how Haskell reacts when he learns about the death of our acquaintance. Watch and listen. Keep me apprised. For the time being, use this number."

Without further ado, he disconnected.

After his conversation with Tucker, Mitch called John again, and this time he answered. Mitch asked, "Are you at headquarters yet?"

"I stopped to grab a sandwich from Dodi. Just now wheeling into the parking lot."

"Don't go inside. I'm five minutes out."

By the time Mitch pulled into the lot, John had scarfed down his sandwich. They alighted from their vehicles simultaneously and ran toward the employee entrance, where they huddled under the narrow overhang to keep out of the rain.

Mitch pushed back the hood of the slicker. "Malone's phobia was a fear of going to hell." He briefly summarized what

Dylan had told him. "He talked to her about an imaginary evil twin he had to keep in line. Guess what he called him. Oz." He'd said all that in one breath. "Oz," he repeated. "That links them, John."

The cleft between John's eyebrows deepened. "It links Malone to Oz, maybe, but we still haven't confirmed who Oz is." Before Mitch could object, John said, "Let's get out of this rain."

They went inside and started down the corridor toward the elevator bank. Other staff were coming and going in and out of offices, so Mitch didn't continue about Oz, and, instead, gave John an update on Hank's condition.

"Mary called as I was driving in. The procedure was routine. He's gonna stay a couple of days in the hospital, but everything looks good."

Upon hearing the report, he had expressed his genuine relief, asked Mary to tell Hank that he would drive over soon to make sure he was behaving himself, and had reassured her that Andrew was doing splendidly.

Though all the while he'd been talking to her, he'd felt like a hunting dog who had picked up a scent but was leashed to a post. He hadn't drawn out the conversation with his mother-in-law for longer than was courteous, and she'd been anxious to get back to Hank anyway.

Now, as John approached the elevator and punched the button, he said, "Next time you talk to them, extend Beth's and my well wishes."

"Sure."

The elevator arrived. Blessedly, they had it to themselves. As soon as the door closed on them, Mitch said, "I talked to Tucker." He gave John a rapid rundown of their conversation.

"I sensed that shit is going down today. What, when, and where, he wouldn't say, but it was clear to me that Tucker wanted El Paso free to be captured."

"That's an oxymoron. Or something."

"But you know what I mean." John nodded and Mitch continued. "Tucker also told me that NOPD served a search warrant at Malone's restaurant, where they found incriminating goodies."

John said, "I talked to a NOPD detective who was in on the search. It yielded a shitload of cash, a spare garrote, an arsenal of handguns, an AK-47 in a closet, and a rosary in a drawer. Beads were rubbed smooth, the detective said."

"Which supports what Dylan told me about Malone's fear of hell." Seeing that they were about to reach the third floor, Mitch punched a red button that brought the elevator to a jarring halt. "What about Allen Busby? Did they find anything in Malone's stuff relating to him?"

"Nothing."

"Did you ask the detective specifically?"

"No, Mitch, but he didn't even mention Busby's name. He would have if they'd discovered a *voilà* about him, especially since he's a celebrity."

"No, exactly the opposite, John. They'd want to keep that hush-hush. Keep the media from getting wind of it. They'd want to bust Busby before he became aware or had a chance to flee."

John gnawed on that. "Has Jim Tucker ever mentioned Busby?"

"No."

"Doesn't that tell you something?"

"Tells me the son of a bitch has been scrupulously careful to keep his identity unknown. If this raid Tucker is orchestrating puts a dent in his operation, he just might clean out his safe and take off for Timbuktu. We've got to jump before he can cover his tracks."

John set the elevator in motion again.

"Listen a damn minute," Mitch said. "You risked everything, your whole career, to catch that blood moon creep, when nobody—*nobody*—was even looking at him. I put my ass on the line to help you because I trusted your gut. I would expect the same from you now. Go with my gut, John. Busby is Oz. I know it."

Before John could respond, the elevator door slid open, emptying them into the CAP unit. Every head turned in their direction. John stepped out first. Looking over his shoulder, he gave Mitch a meaningful look and said, "We'll pick this up in my office in five."

Chapter 39

El Paso couldn't get over the rain. In his life, he'd never experienced this kind of rain, the gray, noisy, *wet* monotony of it. How did people live in a climate like this? Give him a blistering sun, hot air, and the dry, dusty desert any day of the week.

He hunched deeper into the high collar of his sweatshirt, but it had absorbed a lot of moisture and felt clammy. The least Oz could have done was give him a raincoat before sending him on this assignment.

Last night seemed like a weird dream. He'd been in that spooky warehouse watching Malone tightening the garrote destined for his throat. He'd been pleading for his life and promising to obey any future orders without hesitation or question.

That's when Oz had said, "I'm very pleased to hear that." Then, "Kill Roland."

Without thinking twice, he had plunged his blade deep into Malone's gut, thrust it upward beneath his rib cage and through layers of dense tissue, and the deed was done. Before Oz's command had fully registered with Malone, he was already dying.

He'd fallen backward onto the concrete floor. He'd pawed at the gaping wound that had ripped open his torso, but he hadn't had a chance of living, and he'd known it. El Paso had watched dispassionately as he'd drowned in his own blood.

Later, El Paso would admit to himself that he had feared what Oz then had in mind for him. There'd been no cause for worry, though. Oz hadn't revealed himself, but a calm, disembodied voice had come to him from out of the concealing darkness. "Well done, El Paso."

Then Oz had told him to put on the gear hanging from pegs in the wall. Rubber boots, a long rubber apron, a clear visor that covered his entire face, gloves that came up to his elbows. He thought he must look like Darth Vader.

Oz had proceeded to issue instructions on how to do this, how to do that, where to find certain implements to use on Malone until he was dangling from a meat hook, his entrails scooped onto the floor.

"Cut off his right pinkie finger below the ring."

By then, feeling more confident, he'd had the gall to ask if he could keep the ring as a souvenir.

"You cannot," Oz said. "Wrap it in some of that butcher paper and then toss it to me."

He'd done as told and pitched the bundle into the darkness. He hadn't heard it hit the floor, so he'd said, "Good catch. I guess *you* wanted the souvenir."

Oz didn't seem to appreciate his attempt to lighten the mood a little. He said, "Now, get Roland's phone and the keys to the panel truck. Toss me the phone, hang on to the keys."

He'd found them in Malone's coat pocket and pitched the phone. It hadn't landed on the floor, either. Oz thanked him.

Then, he'd said, "I know you're a Caballero spy."

And he'd almost shit his pants.

"You *were* a Caballero spy," Oz continued, smooth like. Like he hadn't just dropped a bombshell.

"You have a choice to make. With a phone call, I can see to it that you're arrested, charged, tried, convicted, and executed for killing Roland Malone. Or you can start working for me."

"I'll work for you."

"Not so fast. We must come to an understanding first."

"What understanding?"

"You're obviously skilled and extraordinarily efficient. But your smug and arrogant attitude won't do. Get rid of it. As of now, it's history. Have I made myself clear?"

"Yeah. Clear." For good measure, he'd added, "Sir."

Oz had left him standing there shivering in the refrigerated cavern for what seemed like forever before he spoke again. "The contraband I stole from the Caballeros arrives tomorrow, as I'm sure you know. You were sent to intercept it, kill as many of my people as you could, then oversee the return of the product to Mexico, yes or no?"

"Yes."

"Well, that's not how your Saturday is going to play out. You won't be there for the fireworks."

He'd then gone on to give him detailed instructions on where to go and what to do to whom.

"Can you remember all that, the names and addresses?"

"Yes."

"You're certain?"

He tapped his temple. "All up here. But can I ask you a question?"

"Why?"

"Because I don't want to piss you off and end up like him," he said, glancing at Malone's carcass, which by then had almost bled dry.

"All right, ask."

"I thought you two were thick. Why'd you want him dead?"

"Roland was doing something behind my back. He was unaware that I knew. It was something that could have compromised him, me, the entire operation. But I tolerated it because I needed him. I was biding my time until someone came along who was as dispassionate about killing as he."

"Me?"

"You have the job if, when I tell you to do something, you get it done quickly without getting caught. If you do get caught, you're on your own. It can't come back to me because you don't know who I am."

"Malone knew."

"Yes, and you see how vulnerable that made him."

He'd looked over at the corpse again. "Yeah, I get it. I'm better off not knowing."

"Exactly. Now, listen and do everything I say. Use that hose to wash the blood down the drain. That barrel behind you is full of bleach. Put all the gear into it and replace the lid. Then, wearing a fresh pair of gloves, drive away in the truck, but ditch it soon, preferably in an area where it's certain to be stolen and taken to a chop shop within half an hour. There's a phone for you under the driver's seat. Don't forget to take it. For the time being, that's what I'll use to communicate with you."

"What about the garage door, the alarm?"

"Never mind. Just walk out and get into the truck."

And that had been the conclusion of his bizarre job interview. He didn't know how Oz had gotten into the building. Even Malone had been surprised by his unexpected appearance. He hadn't heard him leave, and that was unnerving. He'd stood there for a time, wondering if it was safe to leave. But then, when nothing else happened, he'd gotten busy. Fearing Oz might still be observing him, he'd followed his directives to the letter.

He'd gotten away clean, no hassle.

It had been so easy, he'd even given some thought to playing double agent by calling the Caballeros and telling them that Oz was wise to them. But he'd decided that his prospects for advancement were more favorable with Oz.

So here he was, and here he'd been for hours, following Oz's specific orders.

And it sucked.

He was huddled behind a dumpster beneath the corrugated tin covering of a used car dealership's parking lot. He was stiff from staying in the same position for so long. His sneakers were wet, his clothes were damp.

His stomach was growling, and his mouth was watering because the nearby diner was giving off the aroma of hamburgers cooked on a griddle. But he'd noticed that many of the customers were cops and, in any event, he didn't dare be seen so near the place where he was about to kill somebody.

He'd thought that becoming Malone's replacement would entitle him to more benefits, that he'd have more prestige. Being sent to squat behind a dumpster was anything but glamorous. Where was his chauffeur-driven car?

Malone had bragged about how brilliant Oz was, but he might have exaggerated. Or just been wrong. This could be a fool's mission. Or maybe Oz was using this shitty detail to test his loyalty and endurance. In any case...

His mother had been a filthy two-dollar whore, but she hadn't raised him stupid.

"Enough of this shit."

He had a better idea.

Chapter 40

Dylan turned away from staring out the window at the unrelenting rain and said, "I must get Malone's file."

Beth was on the sofa with Andrew, supervising his artistic endeavors in a coloring book. Startled by Dylan's sudden announcement, she looked up. "Pardon?"

"Adhering to patient privilege was the ethical and right thing to do. But it wasn't the good thing to do for Mitch. Now his reputation, his career, his *life*, depend on him being right about who ordered Angela's murder.

"He's about to make allegations based on nothing except Roland Malone's references to his evil twin, whose pet name *I*," she stressed, "never gave a second thought."

Beth said, "I'm sorry. I'm not following."

"I realize how rambling this all sounds to you." She took a breath. "Basically, I have pages of notes and analyses of Roland Malone's therapy sessions. I've denied Mitch access to Malone's patient file, but he needs it now more than ever."

"So offer it to him."

"I did. He said it would take too long to go through it all. But there could be a vital *something* in there that I've forgotten or dismissed as insignificant. Before Mitch does something rash, I've got to scan through it at least. I might find some ammunition he could use."

"Where's the file?"

"On my office computer."

"Can you use Mitch's laptop to access it?"

Dylan glanced toward the card table. "I don't know his password, do you?" Beth shook her head. "I must go to my office."

Beth left Andrew to his vigorous coloring with a red crayon and heaved herself up from the sofa and onto her feet, cradling her bulk in her arms. "I don't think Mitch would approve of your leaving here."

"Wouldn't approve? He'd have a conniption. But I need to do this for him."

"Dylan, it's clear that you two have grown... close. I see you feel that you've let him down, but—"

She interrupted. "With all due respect, Beth, you don't see it. Not from a clinical standpoint. I've had patients who were so intent on getting revenge that it consumed them to the point that therapy didn't help. The obsession continued to feed on itself until their life took a tragic turn. Loss of job, marriage, and family, sometimes loss of life.

"I don't want to see that happen to Mitch. To..." She nodded down at Andrew. "I'm afraid that Mitch's better judgment won't stand up against his commitment to getting vengeance. But whether he succeeds or fails, the attempt itself could cost him dearly. If it's possible that I can help him, I've got to try."

When she moved to go around Beth, Beth placed herself in front of her. "There must be a way to retrieve this file without you physically having to do it. We'll call Mitch and get his laptop's password. Then he or someone could access the file and email—"

"No. Even my assistant doesn't have the password to my computer. I wouldn't give anyone access to my patient files. They're inviolate. But that rule no longer applies to Roland Malone."

"Can't you wait until Mitch or John—"

"No. Mitch said he's on borrowed time. Didn't you sense how eager he was to get out of here?"

"That was only Mitch being Mitch."

"Exactly. Mitch was being his starting-gate self. You just made my point."

Beth winced. "I did, didn't I? But whatever he's planning to do, he's doing it believing you're safe. It would be reckless and dangerous for you to go chasing off—"

"'Go chasing off' like you went chasing after the blood moon psychopath?"

Beth was about to counter, but closed her mouth. Opened it again. Closed it.

Dylan said, "Mitch has told me all about that day. How courageous you were. What compelled you to take such a risk?"

"I was in pursuit of a serial criminal."

"And?"

Beth gave a wry smile. "I was worried about John and the risk he was taking. Wild horses couldn't have held me back."

Knowing she'd won, Dylan squeezed Beth's shoulders. "Thank you. I knew that you of all people would understand. If you'll close up the house, I'll gather Andrew's things, and then we'll get on our way."

"Andrew and I don't need to go. We'll stay here."

"Abandon you here without any means of transportation?" Dylan shook her head. "Your husband would kill me."

"He'll kill me if I don't tell him what we're doing."

"So…?"

"So I won't tell him till it's done."

The package with the severed finger had been removed from Mitch's desk. A custodian had cleaned and sanitized all the surfaces, but to Mitch it still smelled like a fresh meat market. He used that as an excuse to move to the far side of the CAP unit where there was a vacant desk and a lot more privacy.

John had given him five minutes before they reconvened. He hoped that by then, he would have something substantive to report. He called the number of the US marshal that Tucker had given him.

A scratchy smoker's voice answered. "Greer."

"My name is Mitch Haskell." He hastily identified his police department and rank. "I'm calling about your charge—What's his name? Something Davis?"

"Marvin."

"Right. I don't know if you've been notified yet, but Roland Malone is dead. Gutted. Gone. Marvin Davis no longer has to fear reprisal, so I'd like to talk to him, see if he'll cough up something about Malone, his associates, the operation, and Oz, the leader of their band."

After several beats, "Who did you say you are, again?"

Mitch's head dropped forward. He shot a look over his

shoulder and saw Nix marching through the unit toward John's office, Lear trailing her. He wasn't surprised that John had invited them to join their meeting.

He went back to the marshal and repeated his name. "Jim Tucker gave me your number because any information Davis gives over could help us apprehend someone who we suspect is Oz. Will you let me talk to Davis, see if I can shake something loose?"

"Hmm. This came from Tucker?"

"Directly. He and I worked together at the DEA."

"Okay, I'll see what I can do. Might take some time to set it up."

"Sorry. I don't have time. It's gotta be today. Say within half an hour."

"Half an hour? We just ordered lunch. It's on the way."

Mitch glanced at John's office again. The three were conversing. He wondered what they were talking about without him. "Have your lunch, then give me access to Davis. Please."

"Why didn't Tucker call me himself?"

"He's got his hands full today."

"But he knows about this?"

"How else would I have gotten your cell phone number?"

He gave it some thought, then said grudgingly, "All right. I'll bounce it off Marvin. He'll probably want to wait on his lawyer, though."

"That could take forever. I need to talk to Davis *now*."

"Who're you after?"

"I'm not at liberty to say. You know how Tucker is about leaks." Tucker sure as hell wouldn't want the King of Cash's name bounced around.

"Must be somebody big," Greer said.

"He is."

"Marvin's no genius, but he's bright enough to figure that now that Malone is dead, he's lost his bargaining chip. No quid pro quo. He's going to prison for a long time whether he talks to you or not. He'll want to know what's in it for him."

"Tell him I'm promising a reduced sentence, a room with a view, better food, cigarettes, dirty magazines, conjugal visits once a week."

"That'll never happen."

"I know that, but he doesn't."

"That's coercion."

"I'll beg forgiveness later."

"Whoever you're after, you want him bad."

"I do. And so does Tucker. And so should you. Davis may seem like a nobody, but he may know something that could be key to nailing a fat prize, and I shit you not. Federal, state, and local would all love a piece of this guy."

While Greer was mulling it over, Mitch looked toward the other side of the room. John was at the door of his office, craning his neck, watching him, saw him looking, waved him in. Mitch held up his index finger.

"Look, I've got to run," he said. "Talk to Davis over lunch. If he hem-haws, bump it up to conjugal visits twice a week. Call me right away to let me know what he says."

"This number?"

"This number. And, Marshal Greer?"

"Yeah?"

"Thanks for not hanging up on me."

Having delivered Beth and Andrew to the Bowies' house and seeing them safely inside, Dylan drove straight to the medical building. The parking lot was empty, so she parked close in and used the employee door to enter, ducking her head against the rain.

Without anyone occupying the building, the wet rubber soles of Beth's borrowed sneakers sounded abnormally loud against the terrazzo floors, as did the rear elevator's grinding gears as it made its slow ascent up to the sixth floor.

She let herself into her office through the private exit and was about to pull that door closed behind her when she hesitated. She was often here after hours when the building had emptied. Mitch had admonished her for leaving after dark alone, but she'd shrugged off his overprotectiveness. It came naturally to him; he was a cop.

But the dreariness of this rainy day had created a false dusk inside the empty building. In light of recent events, being alone felt eerie enough that she decided to leave that door ajar for no longer than she would be here.

She flipped on the light and was about to walk into the sessions room when she noticed an empty water bottle standing on the round table near the window. The janitors who came early each morning to clean the building's offices must have overlooked it.

But as she surveyed the room, she also noticed that the cushions on the sofa that patients used had been sloppily misplaced. Mitch had shoved them aside when he'd been here, but that had been days ago, and they'd been righted several times since then. She didn't think that rearrangement could be attributed to the janitorial crew.

Giving in to uneasiness, she went into the lobby. A low light shone down from the top of Ellie's computer monitor, but it was left on permanently to serve as a nightlight. Her desk was as orderly as ever. She had been the last one here, so Dylan went over to the main door to make certain that she had secured the office when she left for the long weekend.

Of course she had. The door was solidly closed and locked. But a sheet of paper was lying on the floor. Apparently, it had been pushed in under the threshold.

It was a notice that the cleaning service personnel had had an outbreak of Covid and that, out of an abundance of caution, they wouldn't return until Monday. They apologized for the inconvenience.

Chiding herself for wasting time on a case of the jitters, she returned to the patient room, straightened the pillows, tossed the empty water bottle into the wastebasket, then walked into her inner office and reached around the doorjamb to turn on the light.

Chapter 41

After thanking the US marshal for not hanging up on him, Mitch immediately disconnected and practically jogged across the CAP unit, almost running smack dab into Clarence, who placed himself directly in his path.

"Uh, Mitch, I—"

"Not now, Clarence," he said, edging around him. "They're waiting on me. Catch you later."

He opened John's office door and barged in even as he apologized for being late. "I was following up with the lady who delivered Malone's finger," he lied. "She had the gift of gab."

John asked, "Anything new there?"

Before Mitch could reply, Nix chimed in. "I talked to her earlier."

Mitch was relieved to yield the floor to her, which she readily seized. "Houma PD is checking security cameras in the area of the strip center where the courier business is located. No vehicle has been isolated yet. So far all they've got is an unrecognizable individual in a hoodie arriving on foot, dropping the package on the doormat, and then taking off at a sprint."

Lear deadpanned, "That narrows it down."

Nix turned to Mitch. "Somebody wanted you to receive that package awfully bad."

"Go figure. It's not even my birthday."

"Any idea who sent it?"

"Yes."

That goosed a surprised reaction from her, and even from Lear, but John was quick to say, "Mitch and I have been following some leads, but so far they're unsupported."

"*Unsupported?*" Mitch said with incredulity. "Like hell."

John gave him a quelling look, but didn't address the outburst or the anger behind it. He began passing along to Nix and Lear information that Mitch already knew about Roland Malone. He only half listened, his mind on what arm-twisting and bartering tactics Marshal Greer was using on Davis.

He tuned back in when John asked the two detectives if they'd seen the BOLO for a person of interest on the Malone homicide.

"David Rodriguez," Nix said with her know-it-all briskness. "Goes by El Paso."

John said, "That's where he's from and where he's well known to authorities in Texas and Mexico. He's a member of the Caballeros. If he was their emissary to New Orleans to negotiate a deal with Malone, who it's generally believed was active in our regional drug trade, the meeting must've gone south."

Lear asked, "Was Malone affiliated with Oz?"

"As yet unproven but suspected," John replied.

Nix said, "Maybe Malone *was* Oz."

Mitch, seated with his elbow propped on the chair's armrest and his hand cupped over his mouth, said, "He wasn't."

Nix didn't relent. "The cartel might have sent El Paso here to eliminate the competition. If Malone was Oz, mission accomplished."

"But Malone wasn't Oz."

Mitch's second mumbled contradiction caused her to bristle. "How do you know?"

He lowered his hands and answered quietly but clearly. "Malone was an assassin who did Oz's killing for him. But it has occurred to me that possibly Oz himself was behind Malone's murder. Maybe he was looking to replace Malone as his chief hit man, and killing Malone was El Paso's audition."

Nix scoffed. "What reason would Oz have to replace his chief hit man?"

"I guess he fell out of favor."

"*Guess* being the operative word," she said.

Mitch barely restrained himself from giving her the finger.

Lear was expressing his own skepticism. "If El Paso went over to Oz, Caballeros would consider him a traitor. He'd be signing his own death warrant."

"Just a theory," Mitch said.

"Based on what?" Nix asked.

Mitch had no time to answer because his phone vibrated. It was sitting on his thigh. He glanced down at it, grabbed it, and shot out of his chair. "I've got to take this."

"An emergency with Hank? Andrew?" John asked.

"No, but it's important."

John stood up. "This meeting is pretty damn important, too, Mitch."

"And this is pertinent to it," he said in a raised voice. "I'm taking the call." He flung open the door, stepped out, and brought the phone up to his ear. "It's me. What?"

Jim Tucker said, "Raid was a success. Three truckloads of product seized. A much larger haul than we even estimated."

"Casualties?"

"Not a single nick on our side, but three of Oz's men and two of the Caballeros are in body bags."

"El Paso?"

"A no-show."

"*What?*"

"Two of his compadres escaped capture, but the rest are in custody and being interrogated. They're playing deaf, dumb, and ignorant, but one spat when the agent asked about David Rodriguez aka El Paso. Apparently he was expected on the battle front, but went AWOL. Anyway, he's still unaccounted for."

"*Fuck!*"

"Right. Gotta go. Later."

When the overhead light came on in Dylan's inner office, the young man sitting behind her desk with his muddy sneakers propped on a corner of it smiled with insolence. "Hi."

She turned and ran, but he was on her before she got halfway through the sessions room, grabbing her around the waist, pulling her back against him, and placing the blade of a knife— she knew it to be a switchblade—against the top of her neck directly beneath her chin.

He said, "He told me you'd come here today, and hell if he wasn't right."

"Who told you that?"

"What he didn't tell me is that you're a looker." He blew hot breath into her ear, then laughed when she shuddered. "Don't like that? I can always think of something else to do." Then his tone changed as he asked, "Is the detective with you?"

"I'm alone. Can't you tell that?"

"A looker full of sass. I like it." He squeezed her waist. "There must be an elevator back there, right? I heard it coming up. Only one set of footsteps between it and the door you unlocked to let yourself in. So it's just you and me."

His insinuating tone made her shiver on the inside, but, as though she had the upper hand, she asked, "How did you get into my office?"

"Came through your lobby. Very nice. Magazines, water cooler. I helped myself to several pieces of candy. Hope you don't mind."

"That door was locked."

"Oh, I know. I had to pick it. Locked it back up after I came in."

Mitch could pick locks. She thought of him with yearning and desperation. Thought of his last kiss and his adamant promise to come back. She thought of how forlorn Andrew had looked when she'd dropped him and Beth at the Bowies' house.

"Where's my daddy?" he'd asked in a whine. "When's he coming?"

"As soon as he and your uncle John get finished with their work."

"Will you?"

"Come back, you mean?" And when he nodded, she'd said, "If you want me to."

He'd thrown his arms around her neck and hadn't let go until Beth told him how glad Mutt was going to be to see him.

All that went through Dylan's mind now at fast-forward speed while El Paso had been saying, "I was ordered to kill you quick, and I'm not supposed to question orders. But since I don't know that much about computers, I'm gonna hold off and let you do the computer work for me."

Still holding her face-out against his chest, he swung her around and propelled her back into her inner office and over to the desk, where he pushed her into the chair he'd recently been lounging in. "Boot it up."

Mitch walked back to the enclosed office but remained standing in the open doorway and addressed John directly. "DEA just pulled off a whopper of a raid in New Orleans. Oz lost men, so did the Caballeros. Our agents came through unscathed, thank God, but El Paso wasn't at the scene and is still at large."

John grimaced and said to Nix and Lear, "This is an all-points bulletin. To get back to his home turf, he has to go through Louisiana. Circulate this new info. Make sure everyone is up to speed."

Before they could act on the directive, Mitch said, "Hold on a sec. This raid was no small potatoes. It's gonna have impact. Oz was expecting a bonanza but got a bust. This, coming so fast on the heels of Malone's murder, might send him running for cover."

"What are you saying?" John asked.

"Don't you think we need to be a bit more proactive? If we have any leads, however 'unsupported,' we ought to act on them before Oz has time to get out of Dodge."

"I would agree with you if we knew who Oz was," John said.

"We know who we suspect."

"Who *you* suspect, Mitch."

"I know I'm right." He looked at Nix and Lear and John

in turn, then stayed on John. "I lied about who I was talking to before I joined you. It wasn't the courier lady. It was a US marshal who, for months, has had a guy in protective custody. He used to work for Malone."

He recounted his conversation with Greer. "He's laying it out to this guy as we speak. With a little persuasion, he may give us something confirming that my suspect is Oz."

"He's not a suspect," John said with fading patience.

"Okay, let's call him a person of interest. Who, by the way, owns a private jet. It's gassed up and ready to take off later today."

John asked, "How do you know that?"

"After I heard about Malone's murder and the pending raid—"

Nix pounced on that. "Who told you about the raid?"

Mitch ignored her interruption and continued addressing John. "Knowing what was coming, I played a hunch, called the FBO where my suspect keeps his jet, pretended to be a caterer for his flight today.

"If he hadn't scheduled one, I would've said, 'Sorry to have bothered you, somebody must've got the date wrong.' But guess what. He *does* have a flight scheduled. Wheels up at six o'clock this evening." He let that settle, then said, "John, if we don't make a move, he'll fly the coop."

"If we make a move without more than you've got to go on, this department could get sued for harassing a prominent citizen who could turn out to be law abiding and innocent of any crime."

"You're more worried about a lawsuit than catching Oz, who you know masterminded Angela's murder?"

"I *don't* know that, and neither do you. It's pure speculation on your part, and this department—"

"Department," Mitch sneered. "When did you start being a goddamn bureaucrat instead of a cop?"

"And when did you let your thirst for revenge over Angela override everything else in your life? Mitch, you've lost all reason and perspective. You're on the brink of making a mistake that could cost you your career, cost you your *son*."

"Don't bring my family into this!"

"I didn't. *You* did. You did when you made that vow of vengeance over Angela's grave."

John's shout reverberated. He drew himself up, as though just now becoming aware that Nix and Lear and most everyone in the unit stood frozen in place and attentive. "Give us some privacy," he grumbled to Nix and Lear. "Close the door as you leave."

"Don't bother," Mitch said. "I'm outta here. I'll do this by myself."

"Mitch!" John shouted, "We're not done. Come back in here."

Mitch didn't acknowledge John's angry shout, or close the office door behind himself, or slow down as he headed for the exit.

And *goddammit*, there stood Clarence blocking his path again. "What, Clarence?"

"Are you mad at me for telling—"

"No, forget it." Mitch tried to go around him, but he wouldn't move. "Look, we're cool, okay?"

"Okay," Clarence said, "but, uh, I was having lunch at EATS?"

"Yeah. And?"

"Dodi says hi."

"Thanks for telling me. Now, I'm in a hurry," he said, finally getting around him.

"Are you on your way to check on Dr. Reede?"

Mitch stopped and turned halfway around. "Check on her? What are you talking about?"

"Well, she's in there all alone and—"

"In where?"

"Her office."

"No. She's not there today. It's Saturday. The building is closed."

"Yeah, I know. She let herself in through the employee entrance in back."

Mitch came fully around. "Clarence, whoever you saw, it wasn't Dr. Reede."

"I'm positive it was her. She's hard to mistake."

Mitch's breath was beginning to hitch unevenly. His heart began to thud the ominous and dreadful way it had on the night he'd entered his house half an hour late, calling Angela's name and being greeted only by the low hum of the car's motor inside the garage.

He began walking backward toward the exit. "When was this?"

"As I left the diner," Clarence said, coming toward him to maintain the short distance between them. "I drove around the corner and passed the parking lot. Caught her just as she went inside."

"Was she by herself?"

"Except for the repairman. That's what kinda bothered me. Her being—"

"What repairman?"

"I watched him from the booth at EATS. He was working on a window on the third floor."

"On the fire escape?"

"Yeah. How'd you know?"

Because he'd broken that window last Monday night.

"He must've got it fixed. He managed to squeeze through."

Mitch spun around and knocked aside chairs, trash cans, personnel, anything that got in his way as he bolted toward the exit. He lunged down the stairs, jumping over several at a time.

He couldn't be late. He pled with the God he no longer believed in not to let him be too late. Not this time, not *again*.

Her hands were trembling, but she did as told. When it came to typing in her password, she hesitated. He poked the tip of the switchblade through her hair and up against her brain stem. "Do it." She typed in her password, then he asked, "What do all those letters stand for?"

"What difference does it make?"

"Not a fuck. But it had better work."

She hit enter, and Microsoft opened up.

"Good girl," he said. "Go to the records you keep on patients."

"Any patient in particular?"

He nudged the back of her chair with his knee and said playfully, "Guess."

"Roland Malone."

"Got it on the first try."

"It wasn't so hard. Oz must've told you."

"Malone was stupid enough to think Oz didn't know about him, and you, and your talks. When he came to see you, did he lie down on the sofa? That must've been a sight. He was an ox. How are you coming on those files?"

"I've got all these firewalls in place. Did you kill Roland, El Paso?"

"Oh, so you've heard of me," he said, sounding pleased and proud. "I did some of my best work on him."

"I don't think that cutting off a pinkie finger requires that much talent."

"It wouldn't, except that he wanted to keep the ring."

"'He'? You mean Oz?"

"Yeah. The mystery man. Hides in the dark."

"He won't be able to hide for long. They're looking for him."

"Who?" he asked.

"Who isn't?"

He chuckled. "Waaay ahead of you. The ex-narc, right? Haskell?"

Then from behind them, Mitch said, "Waaay ahead of you."

Chapter 42

Dylan responded to Mitch's voice by ducking forward over the keyboard just as he clouted El Paso on the back of his head with his pistol.

He'd taken El Paso completely off guard, but, despite the blow, he reacted instantly by whipping around and taking a swipe at Mitch's throat that missed his Adam's apple by a hair's breadth.

As El Paso made a second pass, Mitch caught him by the wrist, stretched his arm up as high as it would reach, backed him against the desk, and pinned him there with his body to render his legs useless. But he was a fighter. His free arm reached around to pound that fist against Mitch's kidney.

Dylan grabbed that hand, opened the top drawer of her desk, and slammed it hard on his fingers, then held the drawer closed with her hip.

El Paso howled in pain, but he still had the knife and kept trying to make downward thrusting motions against Mitch's resistance. Mitch aimed the bore of his pistol at El Paso's fist. "Let go of the blade or I'll shoot it out."

El Paso scoffed. "Fuck if you will."

"Right. Why bother with your hand when my objective is to kill you?" He poked the pistol into El Paso's eye socket.

El Paso snorted. "You're bluffing. You're a cop."

"A man first. A man whose wife was murdered by Malone. He was mine to kill."

"Aww, too bad."

"For you, definitely."

"You won't shoot me."

"Say adiós, El Paso."

"Go to hell, mother—"

Mitch pulled the trigger. El Paso shrieked. The switchblade fell from his opened fist and clattered to the floor.

"Dylan, let him go."

She stepped away from the drawer immediately, which allowed Mitch to turn El Paso around. He bent his arm behind his back and shoved his empty knife hand up between his shoulder blades, then pushed him cheek down onto the edge of Dylan's desk where his sneakers had left muddy smears.

John, Nix, and Lear rushed in, guns drawn. Nix didn't even break stride as she continued toward them. Mitch yelled, "No, no, no! Don't shoot. Under control, and he's too valuable."

She braked, and Mitch heard John order her to stand down.

Then, leaning over El Paso, who was struggling, he whispered into his ear, "I missed on purpose, you know. I really wanted to rob you of your knife hand."

"Go fuck yourself."

"Yeah, yeah," Mitch chuckled. "I've heard that before."

Count on Lear to produce the handcuffs. He gave them to Mitch, who secured El Paso's hands behind his back.

John told Nix to get officers over there to cordon off the building. He instructed Lear to notify NOPD that El Paso was in custody and to alert whoever owned the building that it was now a crime scene and had a bullet fired from Mitch's nine-millimeter in the ceiling of Dr. Reede's office.

The two detectives rushed from the room to do his bidding.

John helped Mitch haul El Paso into the lobby, where they made him sit on the floor, then used another pair of cuffs to secure him to a radiator.

"Thanks for the backup," Mitch said.

"When I saw you bolting down the stairs, I cornered Clarence and he explained. We were right behind you. Now go see to Dylan."

During all the activity of the last sixty seconds, she had stayed out of their way and was now standing in the doorway between the lobby and her sessions room, wringing her hands.

Mitch left John to Mirandize El Paso, while he went over to her and backed her into the parlor, as he always thought of it. "First of all, are you all right?"

She nodded. "Shaky."

"Me, too. I'm all aquiver."

"Don't joke."

"Wasn't joking." He placed his hands on her shoulders. "Secondly, what the hell are you doing here? If I wasn't so relieved to see that you're okay, I'd tell you how mad I am at you for leaving the camp."

"I came for Malone's patient file. To help you."

"Thanks, but, Jesus, Dylan. When I realized you were here—"

"How did you know? Beth wasn't supposed to tell until after I got the file."

"She didn't." He told her about Clarence's stammering warning. "I was scared I'd be too late." He pulled her to him, a little clumsily and roughly. They clung fast to each other but only for moments before he set her away and asked about Andrew and Beth.

"They're at her house. He was a little clingy, wanting you. He's bound to have sensed tension from all of us. But once he sees you, he'll be fine."

From the lobby, they could hear John asking El Paso routine questions that were answered not at all or with an obscenity. After a particularly loud profanity, Mitch glanced back at them, then asked Dylan if she thought there might be something useful in Malone's file.

"I won't know until I get into it."

Mitch said, "Get to it. I've gotta deal with this."

He gave her a quick squeeze, then she headed for her inner office. He rejoined El Paso and John, who said under his breath, "The honor is all yours."

"Looking forward to it." Mitch squatted down in front of the hostile young man and flashed a grin. "How you doin' there, hotshot? Your drawers aired out yet?"

El Paso glared at him with malice. "You Haskell?"

"Good guess."

"Figured you might be."

"Who told you about me?"

"I forget."

Mitch smiled. "Well, I haven't forgotten you. You cut me the other night in front of Malone's restaurant."

For the first time, he displayed some wariness. "That was you?"

Mitch raised his eyebrows.

El Paso looked up at John, who said, "Nasty cut. He's still pissed about it."

To Mitch, El Paso mumbled, "You looked like a bum. How was I to know you were a cop?"

"Well, I am. I'm the cop you cut, and the one who is about to cut short your life span."

He chuffed. "That's a bluff. You could've shot me in there," he said, chinning toward the other room. "You didn't. And you won't, 'cause of your badge."

"No, I won't. But I am putting you in jail, where I don't think you're gonna live too long."

Despite his circumstance, the kid could still smirk. "You think I'm scared of this shit-bird town's jail?"

"Oh, I don't think you're scared of that at all. No." Mitch scooted a few inches closer. "But, see, that's not where you're going. You killed Malone in Orleans Parish. So you'll be incarcerated there...along with your Caballero amigos who you turned your back on today."

El Paso's smirk collapsed. Mitch's grin got wider. "You're gettin' my drift, aren't you? Since you abandoned your cartel cronies and went over to Oz's side, I don't think it's going to be a very warm reunion when y'all get together in the jail yard.

"And don't delude yourself into thinking that anyone over there in the Big Easy's jail is going to protect your skinny ass, because half the police force, sheriff's office, and higher-ups in the justice system were getting generous monthly graft from Malone to turn a blind eye to his lucrative drug dealing. You gutted their candy man. They're not gonna take kindly to you, son."

The young man's foxy eyes had begun to dart about as

though looking for a means of escape. But he still put up an arrogant front. "I know how to take care of myself."

"Well, that'll be an interesting matchup to watch. I want a front row seat. What do I think? I think one of the Caballeros is gonna get creative on how to end you."

He squirmed. He wet his lips. His eyes had become furtive and fearful. "What if I were to...you know."

"Betray somebody to save your hide?" Mitch chuckled. "Good try, but I'm making no deals with you."

"I could give you something good. Lots of good stuff."

"I said no deal."

"Really good."

Squinting, Mitch pretended to think on it. He looked up at John. "What do you think?"

John shrugged as though bored with the conversation. "I don't know. Maybe. Depends on how good it is."

Mitch went back to El Paso. "Maybe I could help you out."

"Okay, okay."

"But only if you give me Oz. You have thirty seconds to tell me who he is."

El Paso gaped. "That's what you want from me? Look, man, I don't know."

"You don't know?" Mitch laughed. "Do you think Lieutenant Bowie and I are stupid? Of course you know."

"I'm telling you, I don't even know what he looks like. I never saw him. I only heard his voice."

"Where, when?"

"Last night. In that meat locker."

"Where you slaughtered Malone?"

More eye darting. "I want a lawyer."

"Fine, I'll get you one. And, anyway, your time's up." Mitch made to stand, but El Paso cried, "Wait!" Mitch stayed as he was. "Who is he?"

"I don't know."

"Malone never told you Oz's true identity? Ten seconds."

"No, no never."

"Come on, David. Is that your real name? Never mind. I don't give a shit. I just want Oz's real name. Five seconds."

"I don't know!" he shouted. "That's the truth! I swear I don't. I swear on the soul of my mother."

Mitch laughed again. "You swear on your mother's soul?"

"Yes, yes."

Mitch abruptly stopped laughing. His eyes went cold. "One last chance. In one second, tell me who Oz is."

"I don't know."

The thing was, Mitch believed him. He looked up at John, who, with a subtle nod of his head, conveyed that he believed him, too.

Mitch turned back to David Rodriguez. "Then we can't help each other."

He patted El Paso on the knee as he stood up and turned him over to Lear, who had returned with two patrol officers. As they escorted him out, he resumed his chorus of obscenities.

Dylan came into the lobby, waving a sheaf of papers, her face alight. "I may have something." He and John gave her their immediate attention. "I ran a word search through the entirety of Malone's file and printed out every place that he referred to his evil twin or Oz."

"Did he ever mention Busby by name?"

"No," she said, her expression sharing his disappointment. "And he never confessed to a crime. But the psychological interpretation of things he told me could be significant. During our sessions, I was thinking in conceptual terms, that Malone was subject to negative impulses that were in conflict with his conscience."

"Doesn't everybody struggle with their conscience?"

"Most everybody, of course," she said. "But I believe now that Malone's evil twin and Oz weren't just right versus wrong concepts. They were literal." She pointed to a sentence on the top sheet.

"Look. After our very first session, I wrote in my notes, 'Patient has religious ambiguities. Referred to an evil twin (an alter ego) whom he described as handsome and charismatic, a "showman," while Roland perceives himself to be ugly and off-putting.' And here—"

Mitch interrupted her. "Hold the thought. My phone's buzzing." He removed it from his pocket, saw the readout, and his heart bumped. He looked at John. "This may be what we've been waiting for. Fingers crossed."

Officer Clarence had been one of the first to respond to Nix's call for backup. As soon as he'd arrived, he began boasting to any of the curious onlookers who'd been attracted to the police activity around the medical building that it was he who'd "cracked the case."

Nix had thought he would never shut up.

However, by now the hubbub had died down, the gawkers had dispersed, and unnecessary first responders had left. Left without an audience, Clarence motioned toward EATS and said, "I'm going to get a piece of pie and a cup of coffee. Want to come?"

"No, I'll stand sentry in case Bowie needs one of us."

After she declined his offer to bring her back something, he started across the street, and she hoped the service in the diner was slow. The meeting in Bowie's office prior to El Paso's capture had yielded a lot of information that Oz needed to know, and this was her first opportunity to report it.

The rain had slackened to a drizzle, but she pulled the hood of her slicker over her head before making the call. He answered; she identified herself. "I have a lot to tell you, and I don't know how long I'll be alone. If I hang up suddenly—"

"I'll understand. Start talking."

"El Paso was captured about half an hour ago."

"Where?"

"In Dr. Reede's office. Haskell and Bowie are interrogating him now."

"Haskell," he said with distaste. "And the therapist's condition?"

"Saved in the nick of time by Haskell. He fired a shot to subdue El Paso, but no one was injured."

He said nothing for a moment, then, "Well, no real harm done. El Paso doesn't know my identity."

"There's more. Right before all this, we had a meeting in Bowie's office. Haskell reported that a big drug bust took place today. Drugs were seized. You and the Caballeros lost men."

"Old news, Nix. The men I lost were more expendable than the product."

"I'm sorry, sir. What's worrisome is that Haskell knew about it ahead of time."

"It was a DEA raid. How did he know?"

"I asked. He wouldn't say."

"He must have a friend inside that agency. I'd like to know who."

"I'll try to ferret that out. There's also a snitch in the protective custody of the marshal's service." She gave him the skinny on that. "Haskell didn't name him, either, but he wants to squeeze him for information on Malone, and, by extension, you."

"He can try. But, again, it will be futile. Whoever that individual is, he doesn't know who I am. Now that Malone has been silenced, no one does."

"Haskell believes he knows."

He took a sharp breath, but didn't say anything.

She went on. "He claims he has a suspect, someone who is scheduled to fly out tonight in his private jet. Wheels up at six o'clock."

She waited in anticipation of how he would respond. When he said nothing at all, she continued. "Haskell and Bowie had a shouting match over it. Haskell wanted to go after this suspect aggressively. Bowie was afraid of jumping the gun and being wrong. They went at each other."

"Still having their tiff?"

"It's expanded into more than a tiff. What gets me," she said, "is that Bowie still tolerates Haskell, who, in my opinion, is becoming more erratic each day. Even Bowie said to his face that he'd lost his perspective and all reason."

"If only that were the case."

"Granted. Haskell is clever and motivated by his wife's death. He's also gutsy and unpredictable. He's a problem Malone should have handled for you."

There was another weighty silence, then a sinister chuckle. "It sounds as though you're hoping to assume some of Roland's responsibilities."

"Give me the go-ahead, and I could take care of Haskell, and do it in a way that no one would suspect me."

"I'll think about it."

"I've proven myself to be a valuable asset, sir."

"You have indeed. A valuable asset to the wrong side."

Suddenly she realized that the smooth voice coming to her through the phone was also coming from directly behind her. She turned to discover Bowie and Haskell standing a few feet away.

Haskell had a cell phone to his ear. Speaking in the voice he'd used this morning to convince her that she was communicating with Oz, he said, "You have the right to remain silent."

Chapter 43

By the time Clarence returned from the diner, Nix had been Mirandized and cuffed. El Paso had already been taken away. John had summoned another squad car to come for Nix.

Lear, her former partner, stood in the background, watching with remarkable indifference as Mitch questioned her about Oz's identity. "Did Malone ever tell you Oz's real name? Do you know who he is?"

She didn't speak a word.

When the car arrived, Mitch and John escorted her over to it. Before getting in, she faced the pair of them with defiance. "You've got to admit that I was good. You were completely taken in."

"Until we weren't," John said. "We'd suspected you for months, but after Bayou Coeur, we were ninety-nine percent sure. This morning after we found out about Malone, Mitch came up with the idea of pretending to be Oz. You fell for it hook, line, and sinker."

Mitch flashed her a grin. "See, we're good, too. You've been completely taken in."

She frowned. "By what?"

"Our 'going at each other' and him accusing me of 'losing perspective and all reason.' Our tiff has all been an act."

She divided a look of disbelief between them. "Since when?"

"We debuted it with my unruly drunk episode. John showed up at the jail last Sunday morning with his steely-eyed glower well in place." Mitch shivered. "Scared me into thinking it might be for real. But all those arguments we staged, you were taking straight to Malone, and that's what we wanted."

"The therapy with Dr. Reede?"

"Essential," John said. "We'd learned Malone was her patient. Mitch hoped to get Malone's secrets, hopefully admissions, from her."

"We set it up to look like I was going off the rails so John would insist on therapy for me," Mitch said. "Appearing to be on John's shit list gave me the freedom to operate a little more... How would you put it, John?"

"Unregulated."

"Unregulated," Mitch repeated, then stepped back and motioned Nix into the car. "We've kept you too long, and you've got people at the jail waiting on you."

As John assisted her into the back seat, she said, "Suppose I could help you. Provide you with information about Oz's operation. I could name a few names."

"Can you name his?" Mitch asked.

"No."

"Gee, that's too bad." He closed the car door and thumped the roof of the car.

As it pulled away, he and John looked at each other and

began laughing. "We did it, bro," Mitch said, pulling John into a hug. They slapped each other on the back. "We pulled it off. There were times when even I was convinced it was for real and wanted to club you."

"You were a total prick," John said. "Of course, you're always a prick."

Mitch pulled back his fist as though to slug John, and that was when he saw Dylan out of the corner of his eye, standing under the pediment above the entrance to the building. She was looking at him with stark disillusionment.

Realizing what she must have overheard, his stomach dropped.

John said something unintelligible and moved away.

Dylan seemed not to notice. She hadn't taken her eyes off Mitch. "It was all an act?"

"I admitted to you that it was an act."

"You didn't admit all of it, Mitch. You didn't tell me that you and John cooked it up, or that I was an unknowing participant in a... a police operation."

"No, Dylan. Listen." He jogged toward her, but she backed away from him. He stopped where he was, held up both hands, and patted the air. "All right, all right. Just like I told you, I devised it. Laid it out for John. He and I set it up. The whole shebang, the whole pretense. But you know what part of it became real."

"What part was that, Mitch?"

"You know what part. I— Oh dammit!" His phone vibrated in his hand. He glanced at it. Tucker. He looked at her imploringly. "I've got to get this, but this conversation between us is not over. *We* are not over."

The way she folded her arms across her middle indicated otherwise, but he couldn't miss this call. He clicked on. "I'm here."

"Greer called me."

As hard as it was to do while she was looking at him as though ready to kill, he turned his back to her and took several steps away, saying into the phone, "He was supposed to call me."

"Couldn't get you, so he called me. Marvin Davis came through. He was an errand boy for Malone, who had him doing chickenshit jobs like delivering packages periodically to a mansion in the Garden District.

"He never saw anybody, just put the envelopes in a lockbox hidden in some bushes. On one such errand, curiosity got the best of him. He peeled back a corner of the envelope, and it was—"

"Cash."

"No. Better. Reports on intake and outgo of cash and product. The recipient must've noticed that the envelope had been tampered with, because days after his meddling, Davis sensed that Malone was watching him. Like a hawk, he said. Asking questions. Was he happy working for him? Like that. About that time, Davis was arrested for a mail fraud scheme, money laundering, so on and so on.

"But he told Greer today that he was actually relieved when he was taken into custody. He was afraid that Malone was working up to killing him. He made his deal with the federal prosecutor and has been babysat by marshals ever since."

"Who'd the mansion belong to?"

"An LLC."

"But it's Busby's."

"You're batting a thousand, Mitch. It's him."

Mitch exhaled in a gust, looked over at John, and gave him a wide grin and thumbs-up. But it was too early to celebrate any more than that. Busby still wasn't in custody.

He went back to Tucker on his phone. "After the raid today

that cost him plenty, and with his heaviest heavy hanging in a meat locker, and El Paso in the slammer, Busby's got to be feeling the pressure. We've gotta grab him."

Tucker said, "He's got a private jet. He shows it in his commercials. I've dispatched a couple of agents out there to snoop around."

Mitch chewed the inside of his cheek, looked at Dylan, who still appeared hurt and furious in equal measure, then looked at John, who was now talking on his phone.

Mitch said, "I can give you some info on Oz's flight plans, but I want to be invited to the party."

"Can't do it, Mitch."

"I deserve to be there. You know why."

Tucker sighed. "Fuck it. What have you got?"

Mitch told him what he knew.

"How'd you get that?"

"Tell you later. But we gotta move."

"On it," Tucker said and clicked off.

Mitch went back to Dylan and reached for her hands. She didn't give them up easily, but he clasped them and held on. "It's him."

She took a quick breath, and tears came to her eyes. "Congratulations."

"But we don't have him. I've got to go."

"I know. Go."

"I don't want to leave you, having you think—"

"Mitch!" John rushed up to them, breathing hard. "Beth is having contractions. Dylan will have to stay with Andrew. And you've got work to do."

Chapter 44

"A good job as always, sweetheart," Allen Busby said to the makeup artist as he admired his reflection in the lighted makeup mirror. "But a little more spray right here," he said, indicating the top of his hair.

He'd gotten the idea for this unusual Saturday recording session last evening before going to the meat locker. He'd called his new ad man, whom he'd terrorized earlier in the week, and instructed him to reserve the studio and assemble the crew.

"Guarantee them overtime. Two new commercials. It shouldn't take more than an hour. I want to be in and out. I have plans for the evening."

That taken care of, he'd gone to the meat locker to watch the butchering of Malone. Then, standing unseen in the background watching silently, he'd made certain that El Paso did as he'd been instructed. He had, and Oz had left reassured that he'd made a good choice on the matter of Roland Malone. He'd been too old school, too old, period. And it was bad enough that he'd been seeing a therapist secretly, but having her in the restaurant had been the final straw.

He'd lost tens of millions today in that DEA raid. The entirety of the product had been seized. The three men he'd lost had been reliable in the past. But, in hindsight, they couldn't have been all that good or they wouldn't have been ambushed by either the feds or the Caballeros.

He'd had to alert his customer in St. Louis of the fiasco. Naturally, he'd been furious, but he would get over it, because he wanted to remain in Oz's good graces.

Oz himself had learned of the debacle while winding up a gin rummy tournament at his country club. After reading the text from one of the survivors who'd escaped capture, he hadn't let his outrage show. Instead, he'd invited several of the card players to join him for lunch.

Following that convivial meal, he'd gotten a massage, then had gone from the club to a fitting with his tailor. Now he was about to record a couple of new commercials.

Allen Busby had deliberately spread himself thin this rainy Saturday, in places where he'd been seen by many people. What would he know about a drug raid and the grisly murder of a known gangster except for what he'd seen on TV news?

Hair now perfect, he leaned in to the makeup mirror and peeled back his gums to check his teeth for trapped food, then pronounced himself ready. He strode down the hallway and into the studio, where the crew was double-checking camera positions and making last-minute adjustments to the lighting.

"Ready to roll," Busby called up to the control booth, which was on an elevated platform. He gave a jaunty little wave to those behind the tinted glass.

The director's voice boomed through the studio. "Mr. Busby is on set. Sound?"

"Here."

"Ready to mike him?"

"Ready."

Busby, who'd been adjusting his cuffs so that the jeweled cuff links would show, looked up as a man with a thin, stringy Fu Manchu mustache sauntered out of the shadowed perimeter of the studio.

As the man got closer, Busby saw that his eyes were bloodshot. "Who are you?" he demanded. "Where's the regular guy?"

"He's got the trots. Norovirus, I think they said."

"Who said?"

"The agency. They called me at the last minute. I was available to fill in." He ended on a take-it-or-leave-it shrug. "Ready? I'll thread this up under your tie." He was holding a lavalier mike and its battery pack.

Busby gave him a critical once-over, then looked up toward the control booth. "Does he know what he's doing? He looks higher than a kite."

"The agency said he was qualified. And this Saturday session came up so suddenly, we had to take who we could get."

"Look, dude," the mustached guy said, "I get paid just for showing up. If you don't like me, call the agency and they'll send somebody else, but it is Saturday, so..." Another I-don't-give-a-fuck shrug.

Busby ground his molars, first for being addressed as "dude," and second, because he hadn't wanted to appear rattled over anything on this day of all days.

So, rather than make a big deal over this scruffy sound man, who no doubt was a user of the products he peddled, he said, "Get the mike on, please, and let's get started. I've got a schedule to keep, you know."

"You look taller on TV," the man said as he stepped around him. He lifted his suit jacket in order to attach the battery pack to his belt, but then he jerked both Busby's hands behind his back. "Hey! What are you doing?"

A metal bracelet snapped shut around his right wrist, then his left, and he realized with dismay that he'd been handcuffed. "What is *this*?"

From behind him, the man said, "Your schedule just got trashed, Oz."

Upon hearing his moniker, every blood vessel in his body swelled and began thrumming. Was this a rival? Had the Caballeros sent an assassin? How had they learned his identity? El Paso? No, no, he didn't know his identity.

If his flustered reaction was obvious, he hoped it appeared to be from indignation rather than fear. "You've made a big mistake. Do you have any idea who I am?"

"Allen Busby, the King of Cash. Everybody knows you."

"Right. So you had better explain immediately just what the hell you think you're doing." He looked toward the control booth and yelled, "Who is this guy? Who hired him? If this is a prank, it isn't funny."

"Oh, I couldn't agree more," the guy said. "Felonies are no laughing matter."

"Felonies?"

"Yeah, you know. Murder, conspiracy to commit murder, drug trafficking, probably insurance fraud, too, but it's been a long day, and I'm tired. Suffice to say that you're in a world of hurt. In fact..." The scraggly mustache brushed against his ear as the man added in a whisper, "Life as you know it is over."

Busby's heart began to pound. His mouth went dry. "Drug trafficking? Murder? I don't know what you're talking about."

"Yeeessss, you do," he said in a soft sing-song. "Randy Nelson, Paul Adler, Mandy Adams, Roland Malone. All dead because you ordered it. And those are just the ones I know about."

"You're insane. Get these things off me," Busby said through gnashing teeth. Struggling with the cuffs only made them bite into his flesh. He balled his hands into fists and punched the man behind him in the stomach, but, though he gave a soft *whoof*, the blow didn't have much effect.

"Why isn't somebody doing something?" he shouted into the studio. "Call my bodyguard."

When none of the crew came to his rescue, he began to wrestle in earnest. The man stepped around to face him. Busby dipped his shoulder and continued shoving it into the man's chest until he produced a pistol, aimed it at him, and said in a low, calm, voice, "Don't move."

Busby froze. "He's got a gun!" His shrill, panicked voice echoed through the studio, and still no one rushed to help him. "I'm not armed. There are witnesses. Release me now, and whatever your beef is, we'll work it out like gentlemen."

"My beef? You gave the order for Roland Malone to kill my wife. Her name was Angela."

Angela. With dawning realization and mounting fear, he watched the man peel off the mustache and drop it to the floor. He then popped out contact lenses that had made his eyes look bloodshot, leaving him with an unwavering, glacial stare rife with enmity.

"I'm Mitch Haskell. And you're under arrest."

"You're Mitch Haskell?"

"I am. And you're dead meat. However, you do have the right to remain silent." All through the spiel, Busby was shouting questions and demands to the studio crew. When Mitch finished, he asked politely, "Do you understand your rights as I've recited them to you?"

"Of course I understand them. I'm a lawyer, remember. You're going to be sorry for this. Very sorry. I'm going to sue your ass to high heaven. I haven't done anything, certainly not murder. Drug trafficking? Like I have time for that."

Mitch laughed. "See, I knew you weren't really listening to the Miranda. You just said something that could be used against you in a court of law. You lied to police officers and federal agents."

"Federal agents?"

Throughout the studio, crew members began removing their headsets and deserting their cameras and lights and other production equipment. Several came down the metal stairs from the control booth. All converged to form a semicircle around Busby.

Mitch said, "DEA, FBI, New Orleans PD narco unit." As he named the various agencies, men and women in plainclothes raised their hands. To them, Mitch said, "I'll let y'all sort out who's going to lock him up and charge him first. But I get dibs on booking him for my wife's murder. That was in my jurisdiction."

"Hey, Mitch? Tucker asked to talk to you." An agent who'd been up in the director's booth approached and extended a phone to him. Mitch took the phone and said into it, "I told you not to call me at work."

Tucker snorted a laugh. "Congratulations."

"Thanks. Your people were great. They hustled. Everyone was in place by the time he got here. Glad I caught you before you sent them to the FBO."

Once Tucker had agreed to let him be in on the arrest, he told him that Busby had reserved the studio. Tucker had rerouted the agents he'd sent to the airfield and helped alert the other agencies while Mitch was making the mad drive to the city.

Tucker said, "I haven't had time to ask how you knew he would be here."

"I called the twenty-four/seven hotline he brags about, pretended to be a grateful client who wanted to thank him in person. I was told that Mr. Busby was getting ready for a recording session at five o'clock, but that my thanks would be passed along to him. However, to trap a mole in our department who was on Malone's payroll, I did make up some bullshit story about his jet taking off at six this evening."

"Did the ruse work?" Tucker asked.

"She's in our jail."

"Well, I heard you had Busby scared. You put on one hell of a performance."

"Wasn't a performance. Believe me, for a moment there, with that pistol in my hand..."

"But you got him."

"*We* got him. I couldn't have done it without you, Jim. Thanks. For everything."

Never one for sentiment, Tucker said, "Don't call me again for a long, long time. Bye."

"One more thing."

"Fuck. There always is."

"El Paso did break. I broke him. And he cried for his mama."

Mitch clicked off before Tucker could say anything, but he envisioned him smiling.

Mitch handed the phone back to the DEA agent, thanked him, then pulled out his own phone and called John. He answered, sounding stressed. Mitch said, "You have a baby yet?"

"You have Busby?"

"In cuffs."

"Damn, Mitch. That's great."

"What about the baby?"

"Working on it. Beth's cursing me for doing this to her. Says we're never having sex again."

"She'll get over it. Andrew and Dylan still at your house?"

"She offered to stay with him as long as needed."

"Okay. Go hold Beth's hand and stroke her forehead. Tell her how much you love her and how beautiful she is."

"What, and get kicked in the nuts?"

Mitch laughed. "Send up a flag when the prince arrives."

Just as he clicked off, Busby was being led out. He caught Busby glaring at him and stepped directly in front of him. He said, "I'm a little sad over not blowing your fucking head off when I had the chance. But you've got no reason to look so downcast, Oz. You'll still be on TV." He spread his arms to encompass the studio. "We got it all on camera."

The sedan that Dylan had driven from the fishing camp was parked at the curb in front of the Bowies' house. Mitch pulled his old pickup behind it, got out, and went to the front door. Thinking that Andrew might already be down, he knocked rather than ring the bell.

Dylan opened the door. "Hi."

"Hi."

They stood looking at each other across the threshold. She said, "I got your text. You took Oz down."

"Yeah. It's done. Finally."

Instead of calling her as he was leaving New Orleans for the drive back to Auclair, he'd texted that the operation had been a success, Oz was in custody, and he was on his way back. Up till then, he had been moving virtually nonstop since before dawn. He had needed time and solitude to *think*. The drive had given him that opportunity.

His thoughts had taken him back to the night the two of them had fled the city, him bleeding, her frightened by the situation and mistrustful of him. That had been only days ago. Since then so much had happened that had drawn them closer. But they'd ended on a bad note there outside the medical building, and it had created the present awkwardness between them.

He said, "Can I come in?"

"This isn't my house."

"Mine neither, but you've got my kid."

She gave a half smile and moved aside, and he stepped into John and Beth's familiar living room. "Was he any trouble?"

"None. He's in bed in the guest room. He didn't want to go to sleep until you got here, but he conked out while I was reading to him."

"Must not have been a very good book."

She shook her head. "He said I wasn't doing the voices like you do."

"It's an acquired skill. I'll go in to see him, but I need a minute."

He went over to an easy chair and sat down, placing his

forearms on his thighs and dropping his head between his shoulders. He was aware of Dylan taking a seat on the sofa.

She said, "How was it?"

He raised his head. "Catching him?" At her nod, he said, "Not like I thought."

"In what way?"

He cocked an eyebrow. "That sounded like a leading question asked by a therapist."

"It was. But I won't charge you."

He smiled but lowered his head again. "In all truth, it was a little anticlimactic. I haven't quite absorbed that Malone and Oz are now part of my past, not my present or my future."

"You fulfilled your vow."

"No, I vowed to kill them. But when it came down to it, I couldn't, I wouldn't."

"Are you disappointed or relieved?"

He looked up at her again. "So damn relieved, Dylan. I can't tell you how much. That's not what Angela would have wanted. Not that legacy. Not for me, and especially not for Andrew."

"No, I don't believe she would've wanted that at all."

"You told me as much."

"But you weren't ready to hear it."

Their phones dinged at the same time. "The baby!" Dylan exclaimed.

Looking at his phone, Mitch said, "We're on a thread along with Molly." He read aloud, "'John Preston Bowie the second is here! All well. He's amazing! Beth loves me again. She says the baby has my dent... whatever the hell that means. More TC... Proud daddy.'"

As each was texting a brief reply, Andrew appeared. "Daddy?"

"Hey, buddy." Mitch opened his arms. Andrew sleepily walked over to him and climbed into his lap. Mitch kissed the top of his head. "I missed you."

"We had fish sticks."

"You did? With ketchup?"

Andrew nodded as he yawned.

"Is Dylan a good cook? Were they good?" After another nod, he dropped his head onto Mitch's chest. He stood, cradling the sleepy boy. "Let me put him back down. I'll be right back."

He carried Andrew into the guest room, resettled him, then lay down beside him. He stroked his hair and each of the fingers curled against his flushed cheek. Mitch realized that he was coming down from an adrenaline high, but his eyes got cloudy with tears. "I love you, Andrew. Things are gonna change. I promise you. I've—"

He heard a car motor starting outside. He rolled off the bed, peered through the blinds, and saw the sedan pulling away. He ran back into the living room and to the front door, planning to chase Dylan down on foot if he had to.

But there was a note taped at eye level to the inside of the front door.

"You need time with your son... and with Angela."

Epilogue

Mitch waited nine days.

On that ninth afternoon, he gave her enough time to get home from work, then presented himself at her front door and tapped the brass knocker.

When she opened the door and found him there, she reacted with her customary composure. But he detected a warmth and approachability in her eyes that hadn't been there the day they'd met. He took those cracks in the bell jar as a positive sign.

"Hello, Mitch."

"Hi. Sorry I didn't call ahead."

"You never call ahead."

"Too true. And just so everything is out in the open, I asked Ellie to alert me when you left the office today."

"And she complied?" Then she rolled her eyes. "Of course she did. I suppose you turned on the charm."

"Well, I'm here." He grinned, but she didn't say anything or invite him in, so he kept talking. "Beth told me you went to see the new little Bowie."

"I did. He's adorable."

"Yeah, he's definitely a keeper. Beth is a natural. Calm, competent, perfectly lovely. The best I can say about John is that he's obnoxious."

She gave a light laugh. "A bit."

With that, their small talk died. Apparently it was up to him to keep this going. "How have you been?"

"All right. What about you?"

"Rocking along. Busy."

"Concerning Busby's arrest and all that entails?"

"It entails a lot. Up to this point, I'm done with my part. More to come." He paused. "I've also been busy on personal stuff."

"Oh?"

"I'm looking for a new place to live. Something like this," he said, giving her street a quick survey. "Not a lot of upkeep, but with a patch of yard in back. Andrew's got a hankering for a dog." He could tell that sparked her curiosity, so he hurried to continue. "I went to see Mary and Hank last week."

"Is he recovering well?"

"Says he feels like a teenager."

"That's good."

"Um-huh. Anyway, I was supposed to be returning Andrew to them, but the three of us sat down for a heart-to-heart, and I told them I'm moving Andrew here permanently."

She inhaled deeply but didn't say anything.

"My son belongs to me and with me," he said, repeating what he'd told his in-laws. "I've enrolled him in a preschool that provides extracurricular activities in the afternoons. After nap time. He's already picked out his sleep mat and lunch box. I'm also looking for a reliable nanny type to stay with him when work demands."

She smiled. Either it was his hopeful imagination or it was a little tremulous. "You have been busy, Mitch."

"I never touched Angela's life insurance. It's earned some decent interest, so I can use it to afford this. It'll be an adjustment, and I know going in that it won't always be easy. I'll take it one day at a time and do my best."

"I'm sure Andrew's excited."

"He can't wait. I'm gonna teach him to fish."

She smiled. "Where is he now?"

"Molly came down from New York to meet her baby brother. She invited him to stay over with her tonight. He still thinks she hung the moon."

"His first crush."

"I guess." During the following lull, he shifted his stance. "By the way, you look great."

"Thank you."

"And, Dylan, John and I put on that dog and pony show to catch the bad guys. It worked. We got them. You played a minor role in the grand scheme."

"Minor role?" She looked down at the ground for a time before looking back up at him. "It wasn't minor to me, Mitch. I heard every word you two said in that self-congratulatory conversation. You came to me only to manipulate and use me."

"At first, yes. I've admitted it. But you can't think that what happened between us was part of the act."

"Did Beth know?"

"About the hoax? No. John wouldn't tell even her. In order for it to be convincing, nobody could know except him and me."

She appeared somewhat mollified to learn that even Beth had been unaware.

He said, "You know that over the course of that week, things changed. *I* changed. When I met you, I'd been sober for six months, but I was still obsessed with getting revenge. You made me see how dominating and destructive that obsession was."

She was about to speak, but he held up a hand. "Let me finish, please. The other night at John's house, I hated that you left, but you were right to. I did need that time to reflect, and what I eventually arrived at is this: I'll never let go of the memories of Angela, but I have let go of blaming myself for what happened to her.

"I came to the realization that nobody faulted me, except me. She wouldn't want me to be bound by that guilt. It would break her heart. So, I came here to say thank you for helping me to see that. My resolve now is to put all that behind me, not drag it into the future. Andrew's and mine. And I guess our dog's."

To keep from smiling, she rolled her lips inward and held them that way for a moment. "I'm very glad you got closure on that. I appreciate your telling me." She hesitated, then said, "I've been doing some self-analysis."

"Yeah?"

"Yes. A bell jar is see-through. But most people didn't. See through it, that is. But you did, and you made me realize how confining it had become."

He swallowed hard. "Is that your way of saying I'm forgiven for tricking you?"

"Forgiven? Hmm," she said a tad coyly, as though pondering it. "I'm still thinking that over."

"Fair enough, but there's more, and you charge by the

quarter hour, so I need to get this out fast. In spite of my recent enlightenment, I may backslide now and then and need a refresher course from a reputable psychologist."

She arched an eyebrow.

Hastily, he continued. "Not to be a patient. Per se. Because being a bona fide patient comes with strings attached that, frankly, stink. I'd just like to have, you know, someone I could be with, and... and look at... while we talk."

Then they stood and stared at each other, until he said, "For god's sake, Dylan, you're killing me here."

And she said, "Are you crying?"

"Yeah, I do that," he said, blotting his eyes. "I told you."

"So did John."

"John told you I cried? That asshole!"

"It's nothing to be ashamed of."

"It's not studly, either. I'm a badass cop, is what." By now, she was laughing. He assumed a militant stance. "And, ma'am, I'm here to execute a search warrant."

She stopped laughing, but there was mirth in her eyes. "For what?"

"Your body."

"My body isn't missing."

He laughed. "Damn. That was a good comeback, and it completely threw off my timing. I had a good joke."

"There's nothing wrong with your timing." She reached across the threshold for his hand and pulled him inside, then closed the door.

He didn't wait another instant before enwrapping her and clamping his mouth to hers. Her response was as fervent. She pushed her fingers into his hair and held his head as they kissed with pent-up passion, now freed.

When they took a breath, she said, "The bedroom is upstairs."

"Much too far." He started undoing the buttons of her blouse. "Ma'am, every part of you is going to be thoroughly searched." He peeled her blouse off, then pulled her to him and murmured into her ear, "Then frisked."

Between kisses, they shed their clothes as they made their way to the living room sofa, which, of course, had too damn many pillows on it. Together they sent them sailing.

The room looked like a tornado had swept through it. Their lovemaking was even stormier. Each of them selfish, each of them giving. It was graceless but intensely gratifying. At the height of it, before he even had to ask her to fulfill a fantasy that he'd been entertaining ever since the first time he saw her, she wrapped her gorgeous legs around him.

After, they lay unmoving to savor the coupling that neither wanted to separate.

Eventually, Mitch raised his head and looked into her face. "I loved a woman. I loved her with all my heart. But I've fallen in love with another. Something I didn't believe would ever be possible. Congratulations."

"Congratulations?"

"You're her. The lucky winner."

She gave a soft laugh. "Don't joke."

He placed the tenderest of kisses on her lips. "Wasn't joking."

RAISING READERS
Books Build Bright Futures

Thank you for reading this book and for being a reader of books in general. We are so grateful to share being part of a community of readers with you, and we hope you will join us in passing our love of books on to the next generation of readers.

Did you know that reading for enjoyment is the single biggest predictor of a child's future happiness and success?

More than family circumstances, parents' educational background, or income, reading impacts a child's future academic performance, emotional well-being, communication skills, economic security, ambition, and happiness.

Studies show that kids reading for enjoyment in the US is in rapid decline:

- In 2012, 53% of 9-year-olds read almost every day. Just 10 years later, in 2022, the number had fallen to 39%.
- In 2012, 27% of 13-year-olds read for fun daily. By 2023, that number was just 14%.

Together, we can commit to **Raising Readers** and change this trend. How?

- Read to children in your life daily.
- Model reading as a fun activity.
- Reduce screen time.
- Start a family, school, or community book club.
- Visit bookstores and libraries regularly.
- Listen to audiobooks.
- Read the book before you see the movie.
- Encourage your child to read aloud to a pet or stuffed animal.
- Give books as gifts.
- Donate books to families and communities in need.

Books build bright futures, and **Raising Readers** is our shared responsibility.

For more information, visit **JoinRaisingReaders.com**

Sources: National Endowment for the Arts, National Assessment of Educational Progress, WorldBookDay.com, Nielsen BookData's 2023 "Understanding the Children's Book Consumer"